The Winds of Eshra

Forward

Ever since I was little, my family has been into storytelling and the intersection of fantasy and reality. From a young age, if my mom, Cyndi Hughes, wasn't reading to my brother and I from The Chronicles of Narnia, then she was teaching us how to catch story continuity errors in The Care Bears Movie.

So, while writing a fantasy epic wasn't something, she (or any of us) initially planned, it shouldn't have come off as such a shock in hindsight considering her long-standing appreciation for the way the fantasy enables us to see reality in a better light.

Once she started down this journey, she enlisted Trevor and I to act as sounding boards for story beats as well as to check the continuity. We also brought our flair/love of storytelling from playing story driven video games, often comparing scenes we did or did not like to our favorite scenes in Final Fantasy VII.

We also pushed on her that she needed to make the stakes feel real to the reader, with not every incident ending in a happy go lucky way. So, it is at this point I must admit that Trevor and I are why Finch/Two died in the first book. If it's any consolation, she put up 2 weeks of fighting and an entire box of Kleenex in the process.

For the record, we're not wild about raccoon murder either, but we felt it necessary for a story who's whole purpose is to show through fantasy that life may not always be roses and rainbows, but through perseverance and building your family (whether it's people you're actually related to or the family you make through friends in the words of Maya Angelou) you CAN rise above the bad.

So, through this world of talking eagles, prophesied messengers, mystical cranes, traveling vagabonds and pirate-like packs of raccoons, I guess our ultimate hope is this: we hope, in this fantasy story, you found something real.   -Josh Hughes

Some years ago, when our mom asked me to read a single page she had written I was visibly perplexed which became quite obvious by her reaction. She asked what I thought of this character Eleea, and if I thought there was something there? Now till this time I had never known mama to write fiction nor did I realize she had such a capacity, she always seemed so practical not fanciful. Man was I wrong, and even just a single page written from a young woman's' perspective with almost no pre-knowledge of her ideas, I could feel the emotion behind it so clearly and intensely.

Our mom used to sit every summer morning on the back porch waiting for everyone to get up and for the excitement of the day to begin. There she would talk to and watch the little black and white birds known as chickadees. Year after year she watched, as they built homes, lived in them and eventually migrated on for winter. She loved how when she sat still enough, they would talk with her as if to say "good morning." They had such personalities they made her laugh and just brought the day alive. When mom said she had written this single page about a young girl who could speak to a chickadee I thought to myself, "okay, she's lost it. She thinks she can speak to animals now!" But when she explained it was the start to a fictitious account of a girl loosely based on her young life it was clear, this was actually very good. And not only was it good it grabbed me in a way few stories truly do.

Being young with our mom was a blast, she never poo-pooed our ideas or dreams, nor did she ever just hand us the keys to said dreams. She made us work for them, made us knowing that if we wanted something, we had to work for it since nothing came easy in life. But if in fact it was worth having it was worth the work to have it! So of course, when she said she wanted our input and help with her story, we jumped right in without a second thought! We knew it would be a long road and even a tough one seeing as any kind of story telling can be difficult to not only form cohesively, but even harder to get others to see why it's worthwhile.

But we also knew that if, we worked together, we could accomplish any feat, and that mama had never told us our dreams were too great and that meant we wouldn't think of telling Mom hers were unachievable. Even if we weren't sure how it would go, but it went so well although there were pitfalls and some times where we wouldn't talk since, we had been disagreeing on structure or the killing off of a character, haha, she stopped writing for two weeks on that one, but we ultimately always pushed through. Reading to me at night and Josh reading it in morning, all of us brainstorming during the at day. Ultimately, I am so happy with where it's at and how far this story has come, with these characters who have taken on this crazy life of their own! I am truly in love with this story and the world of Eshra, and I know if you come along for the ride, you will too, and hopefully learn something not only about us, our mom Cyndi, and her magnificent characters, but also about yourself and how to cope with negativity and find resolve to carry on!

My name is Trevor Hughes and thank you for reading this forward, and this book. I truly truly hope you enjoy!

From the Author

It sincerely has been my greatest honor to have my sons, Josh and Trev, walk beside me as I wrote our stories. Their insight, humor and encouragement reflect in the pages of Eshra. I have to chuckle at times, as the fight scenes in the book are reminiscent of the countless hours I watched them play video games as they beat the boss in the game. If not for them, this adventure would have been a lot more difficult.

My heart was to write to help others. To teach coping skills and life lessons to overcome those moments of sorrow and hurt. To encourage all of us we will pass from this pain to joy. Life is worth the struggle. And, if I could reach even one soul to see a better tomorrow, well, then I have accomplished my mission.

Writing fantasy was not what I thought I would do with my life. But once I started, I realized it was where my soul rested. The joy of explaining and describing a scene woven through a mystical land of people and animal or a land which I am somewhat familiar with has been life-changing for me. I too learned to cope much better with life's stressors and conflict.

My favorite scenes are ones mixed with humor. Yet, the scenes of intense trauma still come back to my memory while I interact throughout my days. To learn through these characters as they traverse their world has been overwhelmingly rewarding.

I am excited to see where the next adventure goes as we continue to write about Eshra.

A special thanks to Dawn Sievers at DawnLSievers.com. Her beautiful art graces the covers of our books and we are so very proud she has gifted us with her work.

Chapter One

Deborah woke to silence. She waited for her eyes to adjust to the darkness as she looked at Ayden's empty bed.

Tears rolled down her cheeks while horrible despair gripped her heart. She wiped her face with her hands and quickly dressed to exit the room.

She worked her way down the stairs to the back courtyard. Once she reached the kitchen, she entered to see Zetia sitting with Tarhana.

"Zetia, we have to leave now!" Deborah proclaimed.

"Deborah, we cannot leave without a plan. Nor can we leave without the others who need time to heal," Zetia gently explained to her.

"No. no, no!" Deborah yelled. "There is no time to waste! Ayden needs me now!" she declared as she started to pace the room.

Turning to Tarhana, she demanded, "Tarhana, prepare a bag for me with enough supplies for a month. I have to leave now!" Deborah said as her voice cracked with fear.

"Child," Zetia tried to soothingly comfort Deborah as she nodded to Tarhana. "We all will leave as quickly as we can, but not today. Sit and drink some warm tea with me."

Tarhana hurriedly prepared the drink with the sleeping ingredients in it for Deborah. She placed it in front of Zetia who gently guided it to Deborah's hands, encouraging her to drink it.

Deborah pushed the drink away while she wiped tears from her eyes. "Zetia, I know there is sleep inducing herbs in this. I do not want to sleep. Sleep will not get me to Ayden. Please, do not treat me like a child."

"Agreed, Deborah," Zetia stated. "But, if you wish to be treated as an adult, then you also need to accept we have to have a solid plan to move forward."

"It does Ayden no good for us to go off on a crazy tangent with an unruly strategy. I deeply understand your urgency to get to Ayden. I feel it too. Until all who go with us are ready; we stay here and plan," Zetia firmly said.

Deborah felt her shoulders slouch as she realized she would not be able to convince anyone she needed to leave immediately. "Fine, I will be in my room, then." She nodded at both of them and left.

Tears readily rolled down Deborah's face as she sat on the end of her bed. The last battle raced across her mind as she remembered Ayden being swallowed by the great owl, Choran. Her mind drifted to the loss of Two and she began to cry harder. Her body heaved in wrenching silence as she replayed how the raccoon died in her arms.

Vexia lightly knocked on Deborah's door and entered with a tray of food and drink. She placed the platter on Deborah's nightstand.

"Deborah, you cannot let your body go while you wait. It is important for you to be ready when it is time. And eating healthily will help. I promise there are no sleeping herbs in any of this. Just good food to sustain you," Vexia smiled.

Sitting on Ayden's bed, Vexia fixed her eyes on Deborah. "You will need to walk through your sorrow, Deborah. It will not be easy. You are not alone. We are all here for you," she hesitantly stated.

"When you are ready, reach out, Deborah. We are here." Vexia stood, patted the young girl's hand and slowly left the room.

Deborah kept her eyes down while Vexia spoke. She had no desire to talk to anyone; let alone discuss her feelings and pain.

She played with the food on the tray and picked up a piece of bread with butter and methodically bit small pieces to eat. She took a few sips of juice and finally decided to lay down to sleep.

Startled by her own whimpering, Deborah jolted awake and sat up. "This has got to end," she quietly stated.

"Fine! We can't leave yet. Fine, the reality of this whole mess has gotten me anxious and feeling crazy. And, fine, it seems everyone is in agreement with Zetia. It doesn't mean I can't still do my own recognizance. I will act 'normal' and no one will be the wiser I am gathering information to leave when it is right," Deborah silently decided.

Deborah glanced at the tray of food while she consoled herself. Curious, she moved the juice glass. A small square yellow button with two holes in its middle lay on the tray.

She picked it up and thought, "Why would Vexia put a button there? Did it fall off of her shirt? Well, I will just put it in my pocket and ask her next time I see her." While she was pondered the button, she heard a knock on her door.

Jerin stood in the doorway and entered her room. He compassionately smiled at her as he sat down next to her.

"Deborah, I need for you to know what was discussed when we returned from the battle with Choran. What you did not hear when you fell asleep," Jerin stated with determination.

Deborah noticed Jerin had several surface scars on his hands and face when he sat down. She put her hand above his right eye and examined it. The old wound from the first fight with Nahrita in the wilderness had been aggravated and reopened.

Even though her anger swelled in her heart to think about how Nahrita followed the evil Choran and was partially responsible for the loss of her raccoon friend, she needed to stay focused on Jerin.

"What salve have you put on this Jerin," she asked.

"It is nothing, Deborah, it will heal," Jerin replied. "Tarhana is making sure I am keeping it clean and properly dressed. I am letting it air a bit right now."

Jerin took her hand away and stated, "You need to listen to me Deborah. I know you. I know your willpower and I do not want you to feel you have to carry this burden alone. I am here for you. And, we will get Ayden back Deborah. I promise you," he determinedly stated.

"While you were sleeping, the battle with Choran was reviewed. Gethsemane, Joshua and Callie gave insight into Ayden being swallowed by him," Jerin explained as he cautiously watched Deborah's reactions.

Deborah's eyes watered with tears as she listened and tried to hide her fear. She kept her head down to maintain control of her emotions. The vision of the huge owl swallowing Ayden caused her to gulp back the enormous desire to burst out in tears.

"Because Choran spoke about the Great Crane also being in the bowels of Hollow; all believe Ayden is where the Great Crane is. Choran revealed, when he taunted Ayden, the Great Crane's real name of Ehyah. He knew when he swallowed Ayden, she would be with him," Jerin gingerly revealed, making sure Deborah comprehended what he said.

"The prophecy Joshua gave Ayden about having to sing to release the Great Crane is why she had to go there. It would seem Ayden sensed this when she made all of us stand by the door and released her feathers for each of us to be carried back to Zetia's. We all agree Nip is with her since she had the kitten in her sling and Nip is not with us here," Jerin continued to explain.

"Zetia says Ayden has to grow her feathers back before she can take flight and sing. Her feathers will take several weeks to grow," Jerin revealed.

"Plus, we all agree we cannot return to save Ayden in the same manner as we went the first time. Choran will be watching for us and none of us would survive going into the Dark Cell again." He stopped while he carefully watched Deborah's reactions.

"But," he continued, "Kit came forward and told us we have to go and see the peacock spider to find out how to help Ayden. He will take us there when all are ready to travel."

"Deborah, Kit claims it will be a difficult journey to get to the spider," Jerin finished as he looked at her with sadness.

Deborah intently listened to Jerin's explanation as to why they all had to wait. She stood up to leave.

"I have to go speak to Kit, Jerin," Deborah stated as she looked at him.

Jerin grabbed her hand saying, "Deborah, I want to remind you what you said to me when Two died."

"I cannot take it if you blame yourself. Please do not make me feel this pain for you too,' he stated as he looked into her eyes.

"I know this isn't exactly the same, but please do not shut me out while you deal with this pain for your loss. I am here for you, Deborah," he quietly spoke.

Deborah tenderly looked at Jerin as she gently took her hand away and said, "Jerin, I know you are here, but this is something I have to work through on my own."

Deborah left Jerin sitting on her bed as she determinedly walked out to find Kit the peacock.

Chapter Two

Ayden picked up Nip and put her in the sling as she began to assess the space around them. The dim light from her wings, which she noticed were spotty in places from the loss of feathers, helped her see the unlevel ground.

Everywhere she looked were empty pods from Choran's belly. Yet, no smell emitted from them as one would think from the regurgitation process.

Using her foot, she moved the casings to see how hard or easy they would be to rearrange. Small puffs of dust flew from their resting place. Even though they looked rock-like they were light like formed grey Styrofoam.

She decided to design her path to lead towards the huts which were farther away. As she made her course, she took mental notes around her to help remember where she entered in to what she figured was Hollow.

She estimated the huts were about six to seven hundred yards in front of her and dotted the whole horizon and beyond. Dead trees and shrubs intermingled throughout the buildings. Behind her were pods upon pods for what seemed like miles.

"Nip," Ayden began, "our first piece of business is to make sure we have a safe place to rest. We've got to stay focused in order to move forward in this world you and I have been thrust into." The kitten lovingly nudged Ayden's chin as she listened.

Approaching the outer edge of the huts, Ayden cautiously stopped and looked around to see if there was any movement coming from them. Each building looked like an abstract painting depicted on a canvas of a large city with several different sizes of structures dressed in black.

Above her, the atmosphere seemed to change as if a tremendous storm with thundering clouds was ready to burst forth with a torrential downpour. Suddenly, flashes of light traced the sky followed by deep roaring cracks of thunder. Ayden bolted to the first hut to take cover from what she assumed would be the inevitable pouring onslaught.

Entering the small building she noticed a single room with one lone window at the back and only the door at the front. Even though it had four walls to complete its structure, it was void of any semblance of a dwelling place of peace and solitude.

No pictures on the walls, no bed nor any place to eat or prepare food. A room full of emptiness echoed a hollowness which she felt deep in the pit of her stomach. The walls reverberated the sounds coming from the outside, causing Ayden to look out the door where she saw no rain.

"This pit in my stomach, Nip, this is where Hollow gets its name," Ayden surmised. "Total emptiness surrounds us. I mean, look there are zero niceties to make a home a home."

"Yet, there are so many buildings. What does it all mean? Someone had to have lived here before," Ayden continued to question as she took Nip out of the sling and put her on the dirt floor.

"I am not going to live here without something to make me feel welcomed," Ayden stated as she put her hands on her hips.

"Zetia told me my wings have to grow back when I release them. Now, I wish would have asked her how long it takes for them to grow. But, since we have no answers, I am not going to sit around and do nothing."

"Yep, Nip, we are going to make this place a temporary home while we figure out our next move," Ayden stated.

Ayden peeked out the door to look at the gray sky, even though it really looked nothing like the sky from her world. "Here's the deal, Nip," she decided, "even though this Hollow is nothing like we have ever seen before. We have got to use familiar words from our world to bring a kind of normalcy to our daily living."

"For example, the sky," Ayden lifted her hand, sweeping it across the air, "it isn't our sky, but we are going to call it the sky. This way all those words we know from our world will attach here and maybe, just maybe; we won't feel so crazy about all of this unknown land."

Tears formed in Ayden's eyes as she sat cross legged on the floor by the door. With the tears freely flowing, she picked up the kitten and hugged her.

"I didn't want you here, Nip. But I am so thankful I am not alone," she stated as she continued to cry.

"Ayd, Ayd," Nip began as she licked Ayden's tears. "Ayd, I fight, Ayd. Gr-r-r, Ayd."

"I know you fight, Nip," Ayden stated as she kissed Nip and caressed her neck.

Ayden put Nip back in the sling as she stood. "Well, let's go get some of those pods to make some furniture," she determined.

It took several trips back and forth to carry the pods into the hut. Ayden looked at the pile and began to separate each into a section of the room. Bed, table, cooking and shelf areas took shape as she worked.

She found the pods easy to break apart. And yet sturdy enough to create designs which could hold what she desired; as long as it wasn't too tall.

Her emptied backpack's contents, strewn around the floor, helped Ayden determine what she could make. Strung twine with knots at each section wound through each individual plank-looking pod and produced a fairly sturdy shelf.

She hung it near her makeshift cooking area. As she tethered it, she noticed the ceiling was also made of pods. Kind of like adobe mud huts Ayden thought.

The bed proved to be difficult to make since the pods were so misshaped. Ayden tried to place her whole weight on them to flatten them; but they still semi-bounced back into their old form.

Finally, she decided to use them as a frame and to sleep on the floor with no cushion. The only solace she felt about the bed was at least one pod could be used as a pillow.

Ayden rested against the bedframe, allowing her mind to drift. From her time in East Glacier as a young child to the fight with Choran filled her heart with swirling emotions.

"I still feel like a child," she revealed out loud. "Fifteen years of age is still a child. I haven't even had my first kiss," she proclaimed! Nip cocked her head to the side, giving her a curious look.

She laughed as she rustled Nip's fur. "I know you don't understand my little Nip. But, one day you will my precious little soul. But, like Eleea always says, 'it is time to stay in the here and now.' So, how 'bout some dinner."

Ayden took the bowl and utensils from the lower shelf where she had placed them earlier. She dug through her bag to find the dried food prepared by Tarhana, Vexia and Zetia before they left the sanctuary.

"Nip, until we can figure out how to gather, hopefully other types of food, we are going to have to settle with what is in our bags. After we eat, we sleep. Then tomorrow you and I explore. Explore to see how we can get out of here," Ayden explained while they ate.

Soon, the day's activities took their toll on the two friends. Ayden slipped Nip into her sling, laid down and covered both of them with her right wing.

Chapter Three

Deborah searched the outer courtyard thoroughly before she decided to return to the kitchen. She walked over to Zetia who was making notes at the table.

Placing both hands on the table, she defiantly looked into Zetia's eyes, saying, "OK, Zetia, where is Kit hiding?"

Zetia placed her pencil down. Not taking her eyes off of Deborah, she stated, "Deborah, Kit has left the sanctuary."

"What do you mean," Deborah yelled. "How in the," Deborah stopped and pushed her chin out. With a smirk on her face, she began again, "How in the Hollow are we supposed to leave if Kit is our guide and he is already gone," she declared with anger flushing her cheeks.

"Kit has left to gather intel and resources for our journey. Understand, Deborah, his leaving to do this task not only has put him at risk; it is also very compassionate of him. His desire to take on this mission has overridden his fear and we need to respect his sacrifice here," Zetia stated in a slightly authoritative voice.

"Do not, Deborah, be blinded by anger," Zetia continued with her commanding tone. "Your hurt, your confusion and frustration cannot continue."

"Walk through your pain, child. Recognize your true emotions of loss and sorrow; not anger. Because, if you wish to go with us on this mission you will need to get past this destructive behavior. If you stay where you are in anger, it will cripple you." Zetia stood, put her hands onto Deborah's shoulders and determinedly stared into her eyes.

Deborah quickly looked away from Zetia's penetrating gaze. Turning back, her bottom lip quivered as she softly spoke, "I am sorry, Zetia. I know you're right, but I am so angry. I am so terribly angry right now. You could have prevented Two from dying if you only would have killed Dariat when you had the chance," she blurted out.

"Sit, Deborah," Zetia gently stated as she led Deborah to a chair and sat next to her.

"I could easily blame myself for Two's death. Not killing Dariat or Nahrita is my moral code. Just as I told Jerin when it took place. I will not change my stance on this issue."

"When it is a soul's time to leave this world, none of us can change the event. If it wasn't Dariat, then it would have been another who would have taken Two's life," Zetia softly said.

Zetia wiped the tears from her face as she sighed and continued. "To Compromise one's deep root values is to allow evil to take your soul and win."

"The same with anger. It chips away at your core beliefs because of the pain you feel. And, to refuse to walk to the other side of the pain will leave you in constant despair," Zetia pleaded with Deborah.

Zetia placed her hand on top of Deborah's. Deborah put her other hand on top of Zetia's, she looked into Zetia's eyes and burst into tears as she put her head against Zetia's chest. Both of them hugged each other and cried.

Through her tears, Deborah said, "Zetia, I do not want to live with evil in my heart. I know I will get through this. It is so very hard right now. I feel so lost and so alone without Ayden and Two." Once again, Deborah burst into tears as Zetia hugged her tightly.

Jerin quietly stood in the doorway as he listened to the women exchange words. Slowly he stepped in and nodded to Zetia who moved away. Jerin tenderly put his arms around Deborah, giving her refuge to continue to cry.

Zetia left the kitchen and walked to the pool inside the sanctuary. She listened to the water fall down the rock scenery as she sat at the edge and placed her hand in the water.

Heavily sighing, she replayed the conversation with Deborah in her mind. Tears lightly trickled down her cheeks.

"It is not your fault, Zetia," Eleea quietly stated as he flew to the rock nearest her. "You too need to walk past the pain you feel over all that has happened," the chickadee revealed.

"I know, Eleea. I am beyond sad when I think of Two and so very fearful when I think of Ayden," Zetia stated as she tenderly gazed at the bird.

Gethsemane flew from his perch and landed near Eleea saying, "I have asked Tarhana to prepare a meal for us tonight. We, all, must commune together to strengthen each other. I understand each carry a burden of pain, but none of us can afford to lose sight of the ultimate goal. We meet tonight," the eagle stated as he flew away.

Deborah slowly walked down the stairs from her room where her nostrils filled with all of the wonderful smells from the kitchen. She caught her breath as she looked at Ayden's and Two's old seats.

Two's chair was no longer there. Instead, a tall pedestal draped in purple Lupine and white Elkweed flowers intermixed with ferns and ivy led up to the centerpiece where a new bandana wrapped around a beautifully etched copper, silver and brass sculpture of a raccoon peeking out from a hole in a tree. Deborah smiled as tears welled in her eyes. She quickly blinked to refocus as she looked at Ayden's seat.

Gethsemane had earlier asked Deborah to bring her feather to dinner. The one she received from Ayden when they were all sent back to Zetia's. She now knew why.

Ayden's place setting was filled with the feathers she had given each member during the fight. Deborah walked over to Ayden's chair as tears again welled. She caressed her chair and laid her feather with the rest.

Deborah sat down while she looked around the whole table. New settings had been placed for Deiha, Iza and Raxton who had escaped the Dark Cell with them. The Ten who were saved by Zetia years ago were also present.

"I have asked all of you to dinner tonight to share in your sorrow and fear," Gethsemane began when he saw Deborah had finally sat down.

"I also want all of you to share in hope," he purposefully expressed.

"*Sorrow is a great equalizer,*" Gethsemane explained as he watched each face around the table before he continued.

"*The depth of feelings it exposes will bring a soul to their knees in grief over their loss.*

Each, at different times, will have to walk its path during their lifespan. No one is protected from its grasp.

Yet, these walks are not meant to be where you placidly stay. For sorrow is an event.

Where reflection is tenderly set to be a passage you must take while you are led past the pain,"

Gethsemane stopped speaking as he allowed his words to sink into the hearts of his friends.

"*Sorrow humbles a soul,*" Gethsemane continued.

"*It causes one to deeply realize life is precious.*

It reminds us each day, when we walk, life is a gift.

One must, though, come to terms with this emotion or it will suck all of the life out of you.

To live in sorrow and not look beyond to hope will paralyze you with fear and desperation.

Out of the ashes of the powerful pain of sorrow must rise hope," He passionately stated.

"This is why I asked each of you to *bring* your feather tonight," Gethsemane revealed.

"The gift you all received from Ayden is your beacon of hope," he proclaimed.

"She did not randomly ask each of you to stay strong or please rise up when you finally *release and walk through* your pain. Her sacrifice given with these feathers was her silent speech of telling each of you,

Stand and fight!

Remember me!

Know I am with you!

We will fulfill the prophecy, together.'

She is counting on all of you to help her," Gethsemane proudly stated as he stood tall on his perch.

"Set aside your grief and your fear."

"As you move forward to save Ayden, you will each have time to reflect and heal," he beseeched them.

"But, for now, let us all stand united. Helping each other reach the pressing goal of being there for Ayden," Gethsemane emotionally asserted with eyes of compassion for all who were listening to him.

"I have asked Nadab and Baris to design an attachment for each of your feathers so you can carry Ayden with you. In this way, let it be a gentle reminder she is beside you and depending on you. For now, let us enjoy the remainder of the evening together," Gethsemane stated.

Everyone seemed to appreciate the food. But the mood was definitely subdued and difficult to maintain with light-hearted conversation. Quietly, members dispersed and went their separate ways.

Nick excused himself from the table when he saw Nadab stand up to leave. "Uncle, may I join you," he asked.

Nadab placed his hand on Nick's shoulder as they walked, saying, "I would be honored to spend time with you Nickalli."

Chapter Four

Ayden sat with Nip on the floor as they ate their breakfast in silence. She could hear Tarhana's last words spoken to her,

'Ayden, my heart goes with you. Because we have lived there, I know it will be difficult for all of you. It is a soul-sucking environment.

When you are in the depths of despair down there, remember, Ayden.

Remember what brings you joy and what you have to look forward to when you return.

Persevere, Ayden, do not ever give up. No matter how dark it may become never give up.'

"Whew," Ayden thought. "Who would have guessed Tarhana's words would be so prophetic. Well, persevere I will. No matter what, I have got to keep Nip and I positive."

"Come on Nip. Today we explore. I am seriously curious about the other buildings. I want to go through them to see if there is anything we can use. Or, if they look like someone is still living in them," Ayden explained.

Ayden picked Nip up and slung her gently into her sling. She looked outside and felt relieved there was no longer a storm looming over them.

Together, they entered the next building closest to them. It looked like the one they claimed as their home.

With hours of searching, they discovered each entry upon entry of several of the structures were all the same. Empty and void of life. Each home was the same shape and size as theirs.

As she looked around, she realized the reason they looked taller with what she had thought were several stories. The foundations were made of pods. Like mountains, the constructions were high and low due to the pod's underneath them.

Ayden looked out from the latest building they had entered and realized they were a fairly good distance from their home. She turned to the sky and noticed the swirling motion of formations like she saw when she bolted into the first building the day before. She felt uneasy, and yet curious if it would be the same without rain.

"One more before we head back, Nip," Ayden decided.

Nip, who had been climbing, digging and sniffing throughout their search, happily jumped outside for the next one. Suddenly, her legs went stiff. She hissed as she hopped in front of Ayden.

"What do you smell, Nip," Ayden asked as she loosened her knife from her ankle strap and tightly held on to it.

Nip kept hopping and hissing in the direction where piles of pods were resting against an unsearched building. Ayden grabbed Nip and put her in the sling.

Ayden commanded, "Show yourself."

The adrenaline she felt caused her wings to shine brighter. Ayden stood tall and claimed, "I am the Messenger of Eshra. Again, I tell you to show yourself."

The pods slightly moved followed by whimpers and then long howling sounds. With each howl the pods bounced up and down almost like an orchestration of musical high and low notes.

The eerie sounds caused Ayden's hair on her arms to rise. She tried to see what was making the horrible noise, but could only see the pods.

Nip continued her hissing from the sling. Between the nonstop phfft phfft hiss to the moaning howwwwlll, Ayden's fear lessened as she almost started to laugh at the comedy of sounds.

Ayden kneeled down saying, "it's OK, we won't hurt you."

The howling stopped with only whimpers coming from the pods. Nip's phfft's became less frequent as they both waited to see what would rise out of the disheveled mess.

Slowly, a nose poked out near the pods. Sniffling or sniffing, Ayden wasn't sure which, caused the snout to quiver rapidly. After several minutes, a paw peeked out and then the other paw showed.

"It's OK, we mean you no harm," Ayden reassured the animal. She placed her knife back in its sheath and sat on the ground. The whimpers started again as they waited several more minutes.

Ayden decided to try a new tactic. "Nip," she began. "It looks like we have a new friend to join us on our mission. How exciting, we're not alone anymore in Hollow!"

"Hey! I'm getting hungry. How about you and I eat," Ayden slyly stated as she pulled out her bag of food she had packed.

She placed Nip on her lap and gave her food to nibble. Strategically, she threw a morsel towards the animal's mouth. Ayden made sure it was far enough away when she threw it; knowing the animal would have to leave its safety to eat.

Within seconds a pink tongue emerged as it tried to lick the food closer. Large canine teeth could be seen as it repeatedly tried to reposition its mouth to get the snack.

Fear was replaced by desire as the animal slowly emerged. Staying flat, it kept his head down as he tried to get to the food.

Crawling low to the ground, he reached the snack. It was quickly devoured by the scrawny, matted and frail German Shepherd. He sat up and licked his chops as his head nodded like he was asking for more.

Ayden placed several pieces inches away from her feet, saying, "You will have to come over here if you want some more." She picked Nip up in case the animal turned aggressive and put her back in the sling.

Once again, the animal began to whimper while looking at Ayden with longing eyes of please. Drool formed and dropped from the left side of his mouth. Unexpectedly, he let out a loud bark.

Nip hissed and jumped out of the sling as she began running towards the animal. When she reached him, she jumped up and bit down on his upper right lip. She tightly held on as she growled and thrashed her head.

Ayden, startled by the bark and Nip's reaction, ran to the animal and tried to loosen Nip's hold. The animal lifted his paw, placing it under the kitten; hoping to lighten the pull from her dangling body and teeth. His eyes started to water as he whimpered with a deep o-o-o-w-w-w-w-w sound.

"Nip, Nip," Ayden tenderly stated. "Let go Nip." Nip stopped biting with one final phfft before she allowed Ayden to put her in her sling.

Ayden took the dog's face in her hands and examined the lip where tiny blood drops could be seen from each tooth of Nip's bite. She wiped the blood away as she simultaneously caressed the side of the animal's eyes. The dog leaned into Ayden's right hand and softly whimpered.

"I'm so sorry," Ayden stated as she tried to wipe his tears. "What is your name," she asked.

With his nose quivering and sniffing, he choked out, "Greysun."

"Well, Greysun, Nip apologizes," Ayden turned to Nip and lifted her out of her hiding place around Ayden's neck, "for causing you pain. Right Nip?"

Nip jumped from Ayden's arms and continued to hiss and hop. Finally, she plopped down on her butt giving one final phfft.

She took her paw, licked it and proceeded to clean her face. After the first lick and each subsequent time she licked her paw she would spit several times. Almost like she was trying to get the taste of the dog out of her mouth.

Ayden gently nudged Nip as she rubbed her head. Looking at Greysun, she asked, "Would you like to come live with us in our home?"

Nip's eyes became larger than normal; she stood up and hissed again. She gave a look of disdain, turned her back to Ayden and the dog as she deliberately sat down.

Rolling Thunder had increasingly become louder during the whole encounter with Greysun. Ayden and the animals looked towards the sky.

They began to run while Ayden encouraged both of them to follow her. She finally picked Nip up and put her in the cradle of her arm as she explained to Greysun he must stay with them for protection.

They reached the home as loud cracking mixed with flashes of lightening crossed the whole sky. All three of them huddled near the bed and listened to the sounds. Nip on one side and Greysun on the other side of Ayden.

Ayden put an arm around each of them as they waited to see if it would subside. Soon, all three were sound asleep.

Chapter Five

Nick sat on the stool at Nadab's workbench. Placing his elbows on the table, he put his head in his hands.

"Uncle, I am beyond overwhelmed," he expressed with frustration. "So much has happened and so very fast. I am just lost," Nick sighed.

Nadab sat on the other side of him, looking at Nickalli with compassion. He silently waited for the young man to continue.

"I have no more tears left," Nick explained. "I feel. I feel hollow," he stated as he sat back in his chair.

"All I am waiting for is to go and find Ayden. But I should have protected her where I didn't have to go find her. I would have been with her if I would have known what she was going to do!" Nick declared.

"I am so angry she did not let me know her plan," Nick said as he slouched in his chair.

"Then this whole vision thing," Nick began again. "Great I saw myself as a bear through the reflection of the water. But, what about now! It didn't help me save her! What good is the stupid vision now that it is over!" he yelled as he stood up.

Nick began to pace back and forth as he continued to speak. "She is all alone out there. No one but, hopefully Nip to talk to. And, what good is Nip who can't even form a complete sentence. Plus, Nip is no warrior to help protect her! She is alone with danger all around her. And, and none of us truly know how to get to her," Nick continued to say in a raised voice.

"I don't like it, Uncle," Nick stated as he shook his head back and forth.

"I do not like it at all. Ayden is all alone without me to be there for her. I can't even feel her. In my spirit, I mean. I can't feel she is alive or safe. All I feel is empty. It's not right, Uncle," he forlornly stated.

I can't even," Nick hesitated as his bottom lip quivered. "I can't even tell her I love her, or tell her I am sorry I didn't protect her like I said I would," he quietly stated as tears rolled down his face. Nick sat back down and looked to his uncle for answers.

"Nickalli, I feel your pain, son," Nadab began. "None of us were prepared for Ayden's sacrifice. None except maybe Eleea who spoke to Ayden about it before you all left the sanctuary. Ayden told him she knew she had to go alone. At some point she knew she would leave all of you."

"Her and Eleea discussed this very issue. And both of them agreed they had to trust Eshra for it to work," his uncle revealed.

"Great!" Nick expressed with anger. "Great! Eleea knew, but she never told me!"

"Nickalli," Nadab tenderly stated as he continued. "All of us tend to protect the ones we love. And, sometimes this protection is to keep them from the whole truth."

"What would you have done if you knew Ayden's ultimate goal? You would have thrown caution to the wind to keep her from doing it. And, possibly you could have gotten killed. And, what if she took her eyes off of Choran to protect you? Well, she may have died also." Nadab expressed as he stood and put his hand on Nick's shoulder.

"Remember tonight when Gethsemane spoke of sorrow," Nadab asked. "How it can suck the life out of you? When you allow sorrow to stay stuck, it can sometimes turn to anger."

"This destructive anger will mute all of your true emotions and senses. Sucking away all of your deep and true feelings," Nadab explained.

"It is not that you do not feel Ayden. She is there in your spirit. However, anger has consumed your ability to sense her," his uncle tenderly told him.

"Yes, you have to walk through your sorrow; and through the accompanying anger as this is a natural process. The problem lies when you stay in anger and do not accept how life has occurred," he explained to Nick.

"As for your vision," Nadab continued, "do not throw it away so quickly. There is still more it will reveal as time goes on. Your whole life will be tied to it. It was a powerful vision, Nickalli. Not one to take lightly."

"Get past your anger, son. And, you will see and feel your true purpose again," Nadab wisely spoke to him. Nadab felt Nick's body become less rigid as he spoke.

Baris walked through the door as Nadab finished his sage words to Nick. In his arms were all of the feathers.

"Well, boys," Baris asked, "what shall we do with these beautiful displays of love from Ayden?" He, then, respectfully laid each feather, side by side, on the table.

Nick, walked down the table caressing each feather as he went. He stopped at the second to last one, stating, "this is the one she gave me."

He looked up at his uncle as tears welled in his eyes. "How did I know which one was mine," he asked in a perplexed tone.

"Once you allow yourself the freedom to begin to heal, your spirit breaks forth with knowledge," Nadab stated as he smiled at Nick.

Nick looked at Nadab and then rested his eyes on the feather. He lightly let his fingers trace it as he stated, "Baris I would like the feather to rest near my heart. I want it to attach to a button on my shirt."

He again looked at Nadab saying, "Uncle, I think I need new clothes. I am off to Aunt Lydia's workshop to talk with her. And, thank you, Uncle, thank you," he stated as he grasped Nadab's hand while he leaned in to hug him.

Elora flew to the end of Deborah's bed. "Deborah, I have not stayed with you in the room because Father said you needed time alone to process," she explained.

"Process is such a cold word, don't you think," the chickadee asked. "Anyways," Elora continued, "I don't like sleeping out there. I need to be in here with you."

"It's nice, you, know," Elora continued to ramble. "Nice I am so little where I can go almost anywhere and not be seen. I hear a lot of things, Deborah."

Deborah looked at the little chickadee. She knew Elora was bursting with news she wanted to tell her. But she also knew she would have to play it off as no big deal in order to get Elora to tell the whole story.

"Yeah, Elora," Deborah started, "your size is a great asset to all of us. What you do and see is basically called 'intel' or intelligence gathering."

"You see, it is your intelligence in seeing and listening which gives you great knowledge and understanding. I just don't know what any of us would do if we didn't have you with us." Deborah finished as she charmingly smiled at Elora.

"Yep, you are right," Elora proudly stated. "Just like what happened with Nick and Nadab tonight." Elora excitedly gave explicit details to all that was said between the two men.

Elora finished with, "Nick loves Ayden, Deborah. Not love like you and me love. But, lo-o-o-o-o-o-ves Ayden,'" she expressed with glee.

Deborah attentively listened to each word Elora spoke. "Wow! I have been too wrapped in my own self-pity to see what is going on around me," she said to herself. "I am not the only one hurting in this whole mess. What awesomely wise words Nadab gave to Nick," she continued in her thoughts.

Finally, Deborah looked at Elora and stated, "We have got to keep this to ourselves, Elora. We cannot let Nick know we know how he feels. One, it will embarrass him and two, well two it will embarrass him. My heart aches for him, Elora. You and I have to protect him."

"I agree, Deborah," Elora stated matter-of-factly.

"I also agree with you, Elora," Deborah revealed. "I agree you need to be in here with me. It is time for all of us to be there for each other."

"I still have great sorrow over all we have experienced. Living in the ugly pain of sorrow will not help Ayden. We have got to move forward to find out what we need to do to prepare to leave," Deborah decided.

The girls readied themselves for bed where when Deborah laid down, she immediately heard Elora lightly snoring. She looked at her night table as her eyes began to close.

Instantly, she opened her eyes again. Quietly she moved to a sitting position. She picked up a small black, shimmery purple feather.

Underneath the feather lay a small round topped gold key intermixed with dirt and green shaded matter. She recognized the matter as oxidation from being in the ground.

Slowly, Deborah looked around her surroundings. Then, softly she said, "Thank you, friend."

Within seconds a crow whisped near the foot of her bed. His perfect little brown eyes with a circle of black iris glistened against his beautiful black feathers.

"Hi," Deborah said very kindly and quietly. "Thank you for the button and for the feather and key tonight. What is your name?"

"I am Marley," the bird said as he walked the length of the end of her bed. "You are welcome for the gifts, but they did not come from me. Except for the feather of course," he stated.

"OK, then is the button Vexia's," Deborah asked?

"No, the button and the key came from the same source," the crow stated.

Deborah watched him as he picked at the end of her bed sheets with his beak. He hopped around the whole area as if he was looking for his next pretty.

Intrigued by who the source could be and yet, knowing the bird could be skittish and leave. She weighed how she should ask him.

"What a beautiful name Marley is," Deborah said. "It has a very playful sound to it."

"Yes, my friend said you like names. He said you attach meaning to them," the crow nonchalantly stated as he cocked his head at Deborah.

"Who," was all Deborah could say before the crow whisked away.

Deborah stayed perfectly still for several minutes hoping the bird would return. Finally, she took the key and latched it to her belt. It lay next to the copper charm Two had given her of the Great Crane, the Great Fox and the hummingbird embossed in silver on it.

She wondered if the other charm of the silver and brass fox with copper eyes might have come from Marley before they left the sanctuary to fight Choran. "It seems so long ago," she thought.

She looked at Two's charm she had given him when they had first started their journey and met the crazy raccoon bandits known as the Trevins. 'My Friend, My Hero' lay in the palm of her hand.

Tears easily flowed down her face as she tried to look at Two's charm. "I will always remember you, Two. I will always love you, Finch," Deborah softly breathed.

She looked out her window on the other side of her bed and saw a shooting star race across the sky.

Her brow furrowed as she thought about the crow. "No, way Two is his friend," she thought. "No way. It is not possible," she continued to think.

She laid down on her pillow, trying desperately not to fall asleep in case the crow reappeared. Soon, she too was lightly snoring.

Chapter Six

Ayden woke to see Greysun sound asleep and laid out on his back with all four legs in the air. She silently giggled, thinking, "I bet he has never felt so safe down here." Nip had sometime in the night crawled into her sling and she too was fast asleep.

Since she didn't want to wake either one, she sat and thought about life. "I miss Deborah" she softly spoke. "I really miss Nick too?" She surprised herself as she said it. "Well, I miss all of them," she guessed?

Off to her left she saw the familiar swirl as all sound ceased to exist around her. The Great Crane stood in his majestic stance staring at her.

"*Ayden, you must leave this area. If you stay, you will no longer be,*" Ehyah revealed.

"Hold up, Ehyah?" Ayden exclaimed. "My job was to come down here and release you. Now you tell me you are not here and I have to leave the area. What is up with that," she demanded.

"*Ayden, I am here. But you must leave to the highest peak to reach me,*" he stated.

"*Listen, Child. Listen to the stirring.*

Each step you take sing, Child.

Sing in joy, sing in fear.

And, do not forget, deep from the bowels I will rise," he said as he began to disappear.

"No, no, no, NO!" Ayden yelled. "Stop disappearing with stupid riddles," she screamed.

Both Greysun and Nip began to simultaneously howl and hiss from fear of Ayden's loud voice. Ayden quickly took both of them in each arm and reassured them they were safe. As soon as they seemed to be settled, she released them.

"Here's the deal, guys," Ayden began. "I just spoke with Crane and he says we have to leave this area or we will not exist anymore. Whatever the heck that means," she frustratingly said.

"So, we need to gather everything back into my pack and prepare for the journey to the top of the peak way, way, over there," she stated as she swept her hand towards the far-off mountains.

"I'm just going to tell you guys right now," Ayden expressed in an irritated voice while she gathered everything into her bag. "I have just about had enough of Eshra magic."

Ayden changed her voice to a deep sarcastic tone, "let me give you just a short piece of the message. But the rest you will have to figure out on your own. On your own when you are in the damn middle of chaos," she yelled.

With everything packed, Ayden sat back down. Tears rolled down her face. She put a hand on each animal and caressed their fur.

"I guess we should eat before we start," she determined. Ayden wiped her face and then placed food in front of each animal. She used pods to hold water for them.

Greysun chewed some of his food, looked at Nip and used his nose to push his food in front of her. Nip hissed and hid behind Ayden.

"Greysun, do not take it personally," Ayden explained. "The only type of dog Nip has ever known were coyotes and wolves. And, those dogs attacked us. You basically have the same smell, so she is overly fearful of you," she said as she ruffled his head fur. Nip peeked out from behind Ayden as she talked to the dog and gave a small hiss.

"I know why we have to leave," Greysun timidly revealed.

Ayden intently looked at the dog, saying, "What do you know Greysun?"

Greysun's snout began to shake as his eyes filled with tears. "Once there were many of us," he began. "All of us swallowed by Choran lived here. If you could call it living, really."

"Most of us stayed confused to what we were supposed to do down here. We just wandered around as we tried to make sense of it all. I mean, we knew we would never leave this place, so it was like a living tomb," he sniffled.

"Piece by piece the soul left the body so only a shell existed. And, then it too vanished into dust. The loss of any hope, compounded by the continuous faint smell of Choran's bodily functions created a process of decomposition that eventually takes you away," Greysun explained as he loudly sniffed back tears.

"At first, when we entered, there would always be new souls joining us," Greysun continued to explain. "Some were nice and some were mean. Others were his food and ended up in the pods."

"Then all of a sudden, no new souls came. The last one who came said Choran was keeping the pods with him and making them rise again with magic to fight his enemies" Greysun explained.

"Everyone I knew disappeared. I was all alone walking amongst the pods and homes for a very, very, very, long time," Greysun cried as he covered his eyes with his paws and whimpered.

"It was so lonely," Greysun whimpered again. "I had resigned myself to let my soul go too, just like the others."

"Then a man came to me. He lifted my chin into his hand and told me I would live. He kissed me on the head. He had the kindest eyes and touch. He said I would live a long life and I was the key to the Messenger who would come one day. He said he could not stay with me, but I was to stay strong as I had to be here for the Messenger of Eshra," Greysun stated with a sense of hope in his voice.

"When I heard you say you were the Messenger of Eshra, all I could do was howl," Greysun stated as his kind eyes looked into Ayden's eyes.

"I have waited and waited and waited for you, Messenger," Greysun choked out the words.

Ayden excitedly asked, "Greysun, what did the man look like?"

Greysun put his chin on his paw as if he deeply considered how to answer. "Well, he was tall and had long black hair," he stated. "Oh! And he had wings. He flew to the mountains way over there," Greysun said as he pointed towards the distant range.

Once again, the dog began to cry, saying, "I have waited for you for so long."

Nip cautiously walked out from behind Ayden. She walked over to Greysun and put her paw on his leg.

"OK, Gaysin, OK, "she said to him. Greysun cried even more as he took his tongue and gave Nip a sloppy dog kiss.

Ayden welled with tears as she watched the two of them. "Greysun, you will never be alone again," she said.

"And, you do not have to call me Messenger. My name is Ayden and this is Nip." She informed him as she stood up.

"We had better get started," Ayden proclaimed. It is a long way away to the top of those peaks over there. I too, have wings, but they are not strong enough for me to carry us to fly to get there. So, we walk. Walk until we get tired; and then rest and walk again."

Chapter Seven

Phum sat high in the pine tree with his back against the trunk and one leg dangling back and forth off the limb. He stared off into the distance deep in thought, not really noticing anything around him. He took his tail and wiped it across his moist eyes as he sighed.

Trevin startled him when he jumped from an upper branch onto the limb he was perched on. He looked at Phum and put his paw on the squirrel's shoulder.

"Trevin, I did not see you up there," Phum stated as he tried to regain his composure.

"My friend," Trevin began, "come spend time with us at the lake. It is not good for you to be alone all of the time."

Trevin readjusted his bandana on his raccoon head and sat on his haunches, saying, "Phum, we are animals. We see things differently than humans. We understand death to be a necessary part of our existence. No, it is still not easy to watch. But it is something that will inevitably happen."

"Come walk with me to the lake," Trevin encouraged him.

Phum jumped down to the ground with Trevin following right beside him. "I understand what you say, Trevin," Phum stated as the two of them hopped through the brush.

"It is just. I never settled to have a family before," Phum expressed.

"A lone courier had always been my greatest desire; and I did the job quite well," the squirrel proudly explained.

"Being on this mission has changed me," he disclosed. "Actually, it has changed me for the better. I see my world so much more differently. None of us are ever truly alone," Phum specified.

Phum stopped, looked at Trevin and said, "Our memories carry us, Trevin. Memories of the joy, memories of the discovery or even memories of the sorrow we shared with others will always be in our hearts."

"My tears are not just for sorrow, but for the beautiful memories we shared with those who are here and those whom are now gone," Phum explained.

"Yes, I agree we animals see death differently," Phum stated. "For us, it is more fleeting as our main objective is to avoid danger at each turn. Yet, when you add emotions to the mix," Phum stopped to think. "Well, when emotions are added it can become discombobulated," he chuckled at his memory.

"Now, you get it," Trevin expressed with joy as he put his paws on his hips. "Did I not say, no emotion!" He laughed as he took off towards the lake.

Phum shook his head and tenderly smiled at Trevin's philosophy. He quickly took off after the raccoon as he decided clams at the lake sounded too good to pass up.

Jerin found Tybin in the sun room, convalescing. "How goes the shoulder, brother," he asked.

"It is not healing as fast as I would like," Tybin stated as he rubbed his right arm and shoulder.

"You do not realize how hard it is to not have use of a side of your body until it is immobilized," Tybin reflected.

"But, Iza has been keeping me company while I rest," Tybin revealed. "She has helped me to understand Choran's world and his obsession to control everything."

"He is in constant fear and paranoia about everyone who lives there. He trusts no one and kills constantly to make sure those whom do live there stay loyal out of fear. They do not want to die, so they do what he asks to live," Tybin sadly stated.

"Children who are abducted from their families and the children who are born into the Dark Cell are treated like feral animals and live in cages not homes. Many of the older dwellers risk their lives to make sure the young children are nurtured. They have a whole secret network down there to help the children. Fascinating, really," Tybin stated with a hint of anger.

"Iza, Jaeh and Raxton were spared from the cages because of Deiha," Tybin continued. "Because she had the gift of making any food taste good, her master gave her the privilege to raise her children in the cottage."

"Iza said he was a kind man who only pretended to be angry as an enforcer for Choran. From what Iza remembers, he loved Deiha and the children," Tybin softly said.

"Choran found out he was not true to him and killed him. The saddest part of how Choran found out was because of Jaeh and Nahrita," Tybin held back tears as he spoke.

"They were a lot older than Iza and Raxton. Nahrita was jealous of the family bond all of them had and turned Jaeh against them. She convinced Jaeh to tell Choran the enforcer wasn't true to him. Which gave him favor and as a result, Nahrita too gained favor," Tybin's voice cracked as he spoke.

Tybin grabbed Jerin's arm as his eyes watered. "We have got to get all of them out of there, Jerin," he stated with a sense of urgency.

Jerin squeezed Tybin's arm, compassionately saying, "we will, Tybin, we will."

He let go of Tybin and turned to leave. He slightly turned back to see Tybin hold his head in his free hand.

Dread and sadness grasped Jerin's heart as he thought, "Tybin carries a burden, now. Having to act like an enforcer has deeply hurt him."

"I need to talk to someone about his pain," Jerin decided as he left the room.

Deborah was sitting at the workbench when Jerin entered Nadab's shop. "Father, I need you," Jerin stated.

Deborah stood up to leave. Wanting to give the men their privacy.

"No, stay, Deborah," Jerin said. "I guess, I really need both of you right now."

Deborah looked at Jerin with confusion in her eyes. "Are you sure you don't need only your dad," she asked.

"I am not sure what I need," Jerin stated with doubt. "I have just left Tybin and I am very concerned about him."

Jerin sat down next to Deborah. He proceeded to tell them about his conversation with his brother. He turned to Nadab as he finished, stating, "Father you have to help him. His heart has been deeply bruised by being an enforcer when we were in the Dark Cell."

Nadab took his son's hand and carefully looked into his eyes, stating, "I will go to him, Jerin. But you are well aware each of us have to experience our pain in our own way."

"This horror he lived is something he has to walk through. You nor I can take it away from him. We only, can stand with him as he deals with the sorrow," Nadab told him as he intently looked at his son.

"I will let him know we are all here for him," Nadab finished as he patted Jerin's shoulder. He smiled at Deborah and then nodded to her in a manner of silently saying talk to Jerin for me. Deborah smiled her acknowledgement to him as she watched him leave.

Deborah placed her hand on Jerin's, saying, "Jerin, all of us carry bruises on our hearts from this journey. We all need to be aware of each other and like your dad said, 'stand' with each other. Just as you have been there for me, I am here for you."

Jerin's eyes welled with tears as he listened to Deborah. "I have never felt so lost, Deborah," he said.

"My brother is everything to me. And, I do not know how to help him," he said as he heavily gulped to hide his tears.

Deborah stood up and hugged Jerin from the back. Jerin's body lightly heaved as he cried into her hold.

Chapter Eight

The trio slowly traveled upward through miles of pod-like sediment and uneven ground mixed with barren trees and shrubs. Ayden stopped, looked around and said, "Crane said I have to sing all the way. I haven't wanted to sing," she revealed. "It is nothing but ugliness all around us."

Sighing, she sat down and opened her water bladder. Carefully she gave each animal a drink of water.

"How did you survive without food and water for so long, Greysun?" Ayden asked as she took out a bandana to tie around her head.

"Food and water are a luxury. It is not really a necessity for survival here in Hollow," Greysun stated.

"What is dependent on survival is your will. I could not lose hope you would come or I would be no longer," the dog revealed.

"But," Greysun looked away from Ayden before he continued speaking, "when a soul left each person or animal, I foraged for what they hid from the rest. Sometimes, I would find food and water." Greysun laid down near Ayden and covered his face with his paws as he whimpered.

Ayden gently stroked his head as she fought her desire to cry. Slowly she began to hum a soothing melody. Nip climbed onto Ayden's crossed legs and curled up in Ayden's lap. Both animals slept while she rested her head against the side of the debris and continued to hum until she drifted off to sleep.

Loud cracks of thunder roared throughout the sky to wake Ayden and the animals as they jumped with terror. Greysun began to howl while Nip started hissing and jumping. Ayden looked around their surroundings to see where they could take cover. The sounds unsettled her too, but she knew she had to keep calm to stabilize the animals.

Quickly, she dug through her pack to find the shovel. "We've got to dig out a safe shelter," she yelled as she started to dig.

Greysun joined her with his paws rapidly throwing the pod-like dirt away from where Ayden had started the hole. Nip kept hopping and hissing while they frantically worked.

At first, each crash and flash of light across the atmosphere caused Ayden to duck, fearful it would reach them. In her mind, she heard, 'sing in fear.' While she continued to dig, her thoughts raced as she tried to think of a song to sing.

"The wheels on the bus go, round and round. ROUND AND ROUND, round and round," she began to sing as she tried to fight her fear.

"The wheels on the bus go, round and round. All through the town. The wheels, the wheels," Ayden's mind went blank as she felt gripped in numbness with the sky's activity.

"She refocused as she started again, "The shovel in my hand goes dig, dig, dig. The shovel in my hand goes dig, dig, dig deep in the ground," she kept singing.

Finally, there was enough room for all three of them to sit or lay down comfortably in the cave. Ayden made sure each of them had enough food to eat while they tried to relax in their foxhole.

She turned to Greysun, saying, "does this happen all of the time down here, Greysun?"

"No, Ayden. The sky has never been so jumpy before. It started when you entered," he stated.

Ayden contemplated his statement for a long time as she gave each of them a little more to eat. "OK, all of this started when I got here," she said to herself.

"Twice I have been told to sing, even when in fear. Once by Joshua when he gave me the prophecy and then by Ehyah the other day. Just exactly what do they know," she questioned as she listened for more thunder and replayed Joshua's words to her:

Surrounded by dead limbs and bones, deep from the bowels will rise the crane. Sing, child. Sing with joy, sing with fear, sing to hear the stars respond.

"Curious," Ayden thought. "It is less volatile out there while we are in here hidden. Just like when we went into the first hut. There too it became less."

Ayden turned to the animals, saying, "you two, stay inside the cave. I want to test a theory."

Both animals lay at the entrance, watching, as Ayden exited. She lifted her wings out from her sides, allowing them to show their full splendor. Light began to emit brighter from them as she began to hum.

Immediately, the sky showed greater turbulence. It crashed and swirled with lightning flashes everywhere.

She lowered her wings and stopped humming. Silently she watched the sky subside with only the swirling remaining. Again, she repeated the first act with louder humming. And, once again, the sky become harsh and foreboding with thunderous commotion.

"Well, guys," Ayden said as she reentered the cave, "looks like anytime I am out in the open we will have to deal with the crazy thunder. What it all means; I can no way tell you. But we are going to have to accept it and keep moving forward. Or upward as our case seems to be."

"But, for now we rest for the night. And I am really, really, happy we have each other and a safe place to sleep." She settled herself in the middle of her friends as she rubbed their fur. Each animal snuggled into her body where all of them nodded off to sleep.

Ayden woke to crying and sniffling coming from outside the cave. She looked around her where she only saw Nip. She gently put Nip on the floor and moved to the doorway. There was Greysun, a mess in his blubbering state.

"Oh, Greysun what is wrong," Ayden asked.

"I, I, I," is all the dog could say. His body heaved as he tried to regain his speech. Greysun took a deep breath and tried again. "I have never known such love before," he wailed.

"I was born in the Dark Cell," Greysun began to explain as he wiped his face with his paw. "Ayden, it is a horrible, horrible place," he shuddered.

"I was trained to be a herder of people. My master directed me to make sure the workers stayed on task. If they stopped working, or if they tried to escape, then it was my job to alert my master."

"Many, many people died because of me, Ayden. I couldn't take it anymore. Secretly, I helped several of them escape," Greysun disclosed.

"But I got caught and sent to Choran where I ended up here. I was only a pup when I came here. I honestly do not know why I did not become a pod, but was still in my form when I entered. Maybe, the Great Crane saved me to help you," he finished as he started to wail again.

Ayden bent down and hugged him. "Greysun," she said. "Greysun, honey, do not continue to beat yourself up for what you had to do. In the end, you made a very brave choice to fight against evil."

"You have a beautiful soul, Greysun. And, I believe you are right about the Great Crane. He knew you needed to be loved by me and even Nip and all of the rest of my friends when they finally get to meet you," Ayden soothingly told him.

"And, Greysun, we will get all of the prisoners in the Dark Cell out of there and free them. Plus, I believe you are right. Ehyah sent you here to help Nip and I," Ayden hugged him again as he cried in her lap.

Chapter Nine

Nadab found Tybin standing in the sparring hut. "Careful, son," he stated. "You do not want to aggravate your injuries by starting to train too early."

"I know, Father," Tybin agreed. "But I am terribly restless. I feel like I am a caged animal and I need to claw my way out of my prison or die because I can't do the activities I used to do," he stated with pent up frustration.

"Once, when I was a child, I experienced a similar situation as this," Nadab stated. "I crushed my hand by trying to lift a large log by myself. I foolishly thought I could do it alone."

"I had to convalesce away from the shop because my father didn't trust me to not work in other ways with what I loved to do. He was right, I would have done something else and it possibly could have crippled my hand. Still, I was beside myself with pure boredom." Nadab gestured to two chairs, leading Tybin to sit with him.

"It took weeks to heal," Nadab revealed. "I even wasn't allowed to go on any missions because of it. Everyone wanted me to concentrate on other, non-strenuous, things."

"I began to feel uneasy about life and myself. Unexpectedly, anger would rise and consume me. I lashed out at those I loved. It was a very selfish time for me. And, yet it was a deep valuable time of learning, too," his dad stated.

"I found all of us carry anger in our souls. I had to come to terms with how I would use this anger. Would I continue to punish myself and others? Or would I learn acceptance." Nadab continued

"Acceptance because all of us are humans with limitations. Limitations are not setbacks, Tybin. Limitations are events where we are given the great privilege to view ourselves from a different perspective. This is where we reflect on our world we live in," Nadab told his son as he leaned forward in his chair.

"Here is what I found out about my limitations when I was wounded," Nadab continued. "I found I was given a great gift to be there for another."

"You see, your mother was hurting deeper than I. We were friends at the Great Tree, but not romantically involved. Both her parents left to help with a mission against Choran. Gethsemane heard about a group of people who had escaped from the Dark Cell. They were in hiding near the meadow area of Eshra. Her parents went to help bring them to the Great Tree," Nadab revealed.

Tybin interrupted his father, saying, "why have we never heard this story before?"

"Your mother still feels the sting of her loss," Nadab stated. "I chose not to dwell on it or tell it because of her pain. To this day we have no knowledge of what happened to them. They and the Dark Cell people all disappeared."

"Speculation is they were ambushed under a ruse by Choran, saying there were escapees at the meadow," his father revealed.

"Not knowing what happened to them. If they were brutally killed or died in the Dark Cell as slaves has always haunted your mother," Nadab said with deep sorrow in his voice.

"But it was because of my limitations, I am able to tell you how important it is to be there for another. If I had not been hurt, I would not have even looked at your mother's pain twice. I would have been too busy with my desire to create in the shop," Nadab revealed.

"Since I had to find other activities to do until I healed, I stumbled upon Lydia. All alone in her sorrow. She was in the wardrobe room. She was crying as she tried to work with the material in her hands," Nadab told his son.

"For many days, I silently sat with her while she spoke of her life and love for her family. I gave her the freedom to speak and reminisce each day. And, sometimes I held a piece of material for her as she cut it or sewed it," his father smiled at the memories.

Nadab stood, looked at his son, saying, "Because I no longer was consumed with my loss or my untouchable desire, I healed more than my hand. My heart healed because I was there for someone besides myself. Your mother was able to heal, somewhat too, because I was there for her."

"The only way you walk out of pain whether it be physical or emotional is when you help another instead of yourself. This is where true, deep healing happens as it forges your soul into a great man, Tybin. Your mother made me into a great man," his dad smiled at him.

Tybin stood with his father as he grabbed his arm. "I am beyond humbled, father. I have some pain to work through. Which I am sure you already knew if I know my brother. But, still, your words came at the perfect time. Thank you. And, when you get a chance, thank Jerin for me too," he stated as he smiled back at his dad.

Deborah woke before the sunrise and headed towards the lake. There she found Zetia at the end of the dock. "Zetia," she called out.

Zetia turned to see who was calling her name. "Deborah, what are you doing up so early, my girl?"

"Would you let me ride your back when you fly," Deborah timidly asked. "I want to feel what Ayden feels when she flies. Maybe, maybe it will help me not feel so lost with her being gone," she hopefully stated.

"Absolutely, child. It is a wonderful plan," Zetia stated as she lowered her wing for Deborah to climb on her back.

Deborah situated herself, making sure she wouldn't fall off. She looked past Zetia's head as the sun began to appear.

Zetia took off and Deborah caught her breath. She gasped as she realized she was tightly holding on to Zetia's necklace and holding her breath simultaneously.

"Breathe normal, Deborah," Zetia encouraged her. "Even if you were to fall, I can swoop down and catch you. Enjoy this moment, child. Look beyond where you sit. Look at the horizon. And, then look around you at the beautiful land below."

Deborah let go of her fear and the necklace as she fell in love with the freedom of flight. The wind in her hair and the smell of clean air surrounded her in mesmerizing solitude. She couldn't even speak as she didn't want anything to disturb the moment.

Zetia changed elevation where they were closer to the ground. Unexpectedly, off to their left, several crows whisped into view; flying with them. The wind currents created by Zetia's wings allowed them to glide in stunning unison.

"They are absolutely gorgeous, Zetia," Deborah softly spoke. Suddenly, one crow dropped back and whisped on Deborah's shoulder and dug his claws into her skin. Deborah wanted to cry out, but knew better than to scare him.

Zetia began the descent to land, explaining to Deborah the process. "Keep your head down as I come in to land. My back will keep you stable," she told her. As the earth came closer, all of the crows whisped out of sight.

Deborah slid off Zetia's back and pushed her blouse off her shoulder to see the tiny drops of blood from the crow's talons. She giggled, saying, "Look, Marley; at least I am pretty sure it was Marley. He left me scarred. Not really, scarred though, I am just kidding."

"Zetia, I will never forget this moment. I got to fly with you and then I got to fly with the crows. And, and Zetia," Deborah stopped to catch her breath from talking so fast.

"Zetia," she began again, "Marley landed on me and flew with us," she exclaimed.

Zetia looked at Deborah with tender humor. "And, tell me, child, how do you know Marley," she asked?

Deborah explained how he showed himself. She retold Marley's words spoken to her and the gifts she received. She then explained the shooting star. "Do you think he is friends with Two," she asked as she bit her bottom lip to help her not cry.

"Well, first Deborah, what an honor to have Marley as your friend. And, he not only gave you gifts, he gave you one of his feathers. Very powerful, Deborah," Zetia said while she stopped in deep thought.

"Secondly, whether he is referring to Two, I cannot give you a clear answer," Zetia stated. "I am just as intrigued as you about who the friend is. Please keep me apprised if you discover anymore."

She looped her arm into Deborah's arm and began walking back to the home. Both women walked in silence as they contemplated all their new experiences.

Just before they reached the kitchen, Deborah asked, "Hey, I have been meaning to ask, since I am not so wrapped up in anger now. Where is Nekoh?"

"Nekoh decided he was the wisest choice to go with Kit," Zetia cautiously said.

"Everyone agreed Kit could not go by himself. He, well, he is a little flighty in his decision-making skills," Zetia revealed.

"Nekoh presented his case to go by saying he had day and night vision. He could climb out of danger while Kit, being a peacock could easily fly. He understood geography and plant life better than any of the rest of us. And, it would be less conspicuous for two Eshra animals traveling than a human and bird traveling." Zetia explained as they sat to eat breakfast.

"Actually, Nekoh is right," Deborah surprisingly stated. "I don't like that anyone had to go. But since we need answers, he is our best chance at getting them."

Zetia patted Deborah's hand, visibly relieved the young girl had crossed over to healing.

Chapter Ten

Nekoh had never felt so exhausted. With only one day of travel completed, his sense of desperation was getting the best of him. Kit was proving to be a handful to manage.

"The crazy bird. Literally crazy bird," Nekoh thought. "Well, it is mean to say crazy," he reprimanded himself. "But, by the Crane the bird cannot stay on task!"

"If he is not off on one tangent than it's another. Every smell, every new sight of something unfamiliar to him. He haphazardly runs to see what it is without thinking about any danger around him," Nekoh continued, frustrated in thought.

Thankful it was nighttime and they could stop to rest where he didn't have to chase after the bird, Nekoh breathed a sigh of relief as he looked at the peacock.

"Kit, tell me again where we are going," Nekoh asked.

Kit settled himself into the curve of Nekoh's soft lynx stomach; near the back of his legs. He patted Nekoh like one would a pillow to make it more comfortable. Once he decided his resting place was the way he liked it, he let his body go limp.

"Isn't this a wonderful night, Nekoh," Kit began. "It has been a long time since I have gotten to be out in the wilds. Just invigorating," Kit expressed with joy.

"And, I have a great protector in you to join me on this adventure," Kit exclaimed with delight.

"Yes, Kit," Nekoh said as he thought to himself, 'kill me now, please.' "But, Kit, we need to stay focused as to why we are out in the wilds for you to enjoy it in the first place."

"Oh, yes, I totally understand our mission and our destination, Nekoh," Kit said as he yawned. "But," Kit smacked his beak together several times. "But," he yawned again. "I am tired," he stated as he immediately fell asleep.

Nekoh lay dumfounded. He reviewed in his mind all the events which led up to this moment. From his speech to the group saying he was the one who should go. To the whole day of chaos with Kit who was now peacefully sleeping.

All he really knew about the plan from Kit is what was said during the meeting before they left. They had to travel for a day and a half to a cave. Inside the cave would be the answer they were looking for on how to get to the peacock spider.

But, once they exited Zetia's, past the mines, Kit took off like a toddler with what seemed like no exact destination in mind. He would fly one direction and walk in another.

"Thank the Crane," Nekoh thought. "At least tomorrow we have a half day journey to the cave. Or at least this is what Kit has told me. After today I am not really sure he knows how far we have to go," Nekoh forlornly decided as he laid his head down to sleep.

"Nekoh, Nekoh," a tiny voice whispered in the cat's ear. Nekoh batted at the tickle. "N-N-N-e-e-e-e-k-o-o-o-o-o-o-h," the whisper continued from the back of Nekoh's body.

Nekoh stirred while he craned his neck around his back to see what the irritating noise was. He sniffed, looked at the sky and stated, "It is still late night, Kit."

Kit excitedly whispered, "Nekoh we have to leave now."

"What is the immediacy, Kit," he asked as he sat up.

"I was wrong about it taking a day and a half to get to the cave," Kit disclosed.

"Honestly, you can't really blame my miscalculation, though," Kit determined. "I mean it has been years since I have left the sanctuary. And, I have never approached the cave from this side before."

"Did I mention, you have to enter the cave at night and you only have a short window of time to do it?" Kit asked.

"See this mountain next to us? Well, we have to partially climb up it past the trees to reach the entrance. And, you can only see the entrance when the moon shines on its door early, early in the morning," Kit explained.

"The way I figure, we have about a half hour, maybe less to jimmy up that there ol' cliff face. Way-y-y-y-y up there to get to the door. So, we have got to get crackin' if we want to do it tonight," Kit revealed.

Nekoh looked at Kit in disbelief. "Kit wouldn't it have been a lot easier to climb close to the entrance earlier last night. We could have had an easy rest while we waited rather than this strenuous dash to the top we have to do now!" He said loudly with pure impatience.

"Well, yeah we could have climbed last night," Kit reflected. "But then I wouldn't have had such a peaceful sleep like I did. I would have had to struggle to stay in place due to the cliffside."

"You will have to ride my back, Kit," Nekoh ordered with a hint of exasperation. "Exactly what am I looking for as an entrance?" He curtly asked as he helped Kit get secure for the ride.

"It isn't really a matter of look for it," Kit tried to explain. "It is more of a I feel it in my soul kind of thing," he said.

Nekoh bolted through the trees as he maneuvered higher and higher in altitude. He released quick breaths once he started the climb up the rock cliff, saying, "What the Crane, Kit."

Kit wrapped his wings tighter around Nekoh's belly as he said, "Trust me, I will know when."

Shale rock tumbled down the mountain with each leap Nekoh made as he climbed up the face. His paws would slip with the rock where he would have to dig his claws into the next leap to avoid an avalanche descent down the mountain. He couldn't rest to see as he had to continuously do the same act to sidestep an inevitable fall.

Over halfway up the mountain, Kit yelled, "Stop!"

Nekoh repositioned his claw hold one paw at a time as he tried to hang on. His legs slightly shook from the tense strength it took to steady them with his body.

He decided to not look down for fear he would lose his mind and nerve if he saw the shear drop. Out of the corner of his right eye he saw a brilliant bluish green quartz geode twinkling in the moonlight inches above his head.

"Jump into the geode," Kit yelled.

Nekoh hesitated saying, "Kit, it is a small hole. What do you mean jump into it?"

"Now," Kit demanded.

Once again, Nekoh looked at the opening and started to protest. But suddenly he felt his footing slip and he knew they would drop off the side of the mountain to their death.

Without questioning again, he kept his eyes on the center of the rock. He zeroed in on the middle of the stone and quickly leapt into the middle of it.

Their bodies were thrust through a large spacious tunnel which lead down farther in the cave. They tumbled head over heel like a bouncing ball.

Coming to a stop, Nekoh stood up and shook his head to focus. All around were thousands of rock-like pillars. Their base started at the ceiling and grew downward where their pointed ends hung like chandeliers on an expensive lamp.

"The pillars are called stalactites," Kit informed Nekoh. "They are formed from minerals where water drips down them creating this marvelous spectacle before you," he triumphantly explained.

"Now, the geode in the face of the mountain is a well-kept secret from my ancestry. Its color resembles my feathers and is generally hidden because it blends into the mountain terrain. If an unknown soul were to happen upon it, they would see it as a beautiful rock formation," Kit told Nekoh.

"But, as you have experienced, it is not easy to see or get to due to the shale surface. Yet, if you know the lore, you can then take the jump when the moonlight shines to enlarge the opening of the rock. It literally takes a leap of faith to enter this cave," Kit finished with a chuckle.

Once again, Nekoh was dumbfounded. But this time it was in awe at the knowledge and skill Kit had shown.

"Why did you not tell me what would happen before we got to this point," Nekoh asked.

Kit's feathers displayed in full majesty behind him as he looked at Nekoh. "Seriously, Nekoh, would you have followed me if I had told you exactly what you would have to do?"

"Your overwhelming fear at my crazy idea would have caused you to question me. And, as a result I chose to act impish and crazy to keep your mind occupied. Basically, you stayed confused until I needed you to act in faith. Pretty impressive of me, huh," Kit said as his wings slightly moved in a waving motion with his body.

Nekoh had to chuckle at Kit's joy even though he felt manipulated. Relieved they hadn't died, he laid in a resting position on the floor.

"So, what now," Nekoh asked?

"Now we search for the answer. This cave reveals your deepest desires," Kit stated with reverence. "This is how I ended up at Zetia's," Kit humbly stated.

"I was deep in despair from the loss of my friends and family. And the loss of my feathers, too. Choran's enforcers brutally destroyed us when they harvested our feathers." Kit solemnly said.

"Those of us who were not killed scattered throughout Eshra, hoping to survive. To stay together meant sure death. We each had to take a different direction to escape capture," Kit explained as he lowered his head and spluttered back tears.

"My ancestry told of this mountain and its power. As a young chick, I had heard the stories of its mighty ability to help those who believed," Kit stated.

"Aimlessly I traveled in fear and loneliness. Where we slept earlier, is where I ended up one night," Kit said with relief.

"As I sat there in my anguish, I looked up at the face of the mountain. The moonlight was shining on it and I saw what I thought was a twinkling in the mountain stone. For several nights I watched the twinkle, hoping beyond hope it was true."

"Then, one night I tried to reach the stone. I couldn't make it up the shear shale cliff. For months I continued to try to no avail. Finally, on my last try, my wings had grown enough to give me flight. I reached the stone and jumped into it. Just like you and I tonight, I ended up here," Kit expressed with gratitude to the mountain.

"I had no idea what to do next," Kit revealed. "Great I had finally made it to the mountain and had gotten inside. But now what was I supposed to do?"

"I searched the cave for days trying to figure out my next play in life. I came back to this very spot in hopelessness. I started to cry. I cried and cried, falling asleep."

"When I woke, I determined this was not the end of me and stood up. I fanned my feathers out in their full beauty and as I did the cave wall came alive."

"It showed me a vision of a woman with two horses. She was resting in between them and it was night time. She was beautiful with all of her jewelry which looked like my wings and her long dark hair. Her dress was just as beautiful as my feathers."

"The cave guided me to the entrance to leave. As I slide down the mountain, I landed right near the women who was sleeping. It was Zetia, Nekoh." Kit finished as he bowed to the cat.

Nekoh gazed upon Kit with greater meaning than he had before. Humbled by Kit's plight, he realized he had been very privileged growing up at the Great Tree. His heart stirred with anger as he thought of the pain Choran so readily caused everyone he touched.

Nekoh watched as Kit fanned his wings out near the cave wall. Slowly, an image appeared.

A mountain range dotted with strange trees Nekoh had only seen in books, led down to a dark brown sandy beach. The bark on the tightly clustered trees was a smooth light green with notches circling the trunk every four to five inches. The notches wove all the way up to its canopy of long dangling limbs with even longer and thinner leaves extending down.

The other trees which were intermixed in with the bamboo-like trees were shorter. Their bulky trunks were off-white with random patches of shades of brown. They looked like large mushrooms with their green covering. The tree's limbs were full of large fruit pods hanging down, ready to be picked.

Off to the right was a giant grayish boulder with its base covered in ocean water. The waves crashed against its body and the water flew into the air as it hit. As the sun's rays beat down on the rock base, the tiny water droplets which broke from the crashing waves fell like sparkling diamonds in the sun's rays.

Nekoh was mesmerized by the breathtaking view. Even with no sound coming from the image, he felt like he had been transported into the vision and was standing on the beach feeling the sprays of water on his fur.

His eyes followed the massive boulder from the water line to its peak. Its structure was molded like a withered raisin with deep cervices and raised formations. Small pockets randomly held tufts of grass all the way up its surface.

He began to look away when he thought he saw movement on the rock. He froze his stare to see if it was true. He waited for what he thought was an eternity and thought again about looking away.

But his cat instincts had emerged where he knew to dare not move. Like a magnifying glass had been placed in front of his eyes, Nekoh sensed the image zero in on the rock.

Swaying in the breeze on a thread was a spider lowering its body down the rockface. Still mesmerized, Nekoh watched it weave a vast intricate web which glistened in the sun from the mist of water droplets which fell on it.

From one side of the rock to the other the spider meticulously worked its masterpiece. With the web finished, the spider rested at one end. As the pressure from the beating waves blew the air around it, the web fluttered like a sail on a boat.

The spider lifted its back up and fanned it out. The whole area was a geometric wonder of brilliant colors, each outlined in white. Shades of orange, red, yellow, indigo blue, turquoise and purple filled each individual pattern. The spider raised his longest legs to each side of its head which had two big eyes in the center and two small eyes next to each of the big eyes.

The spider stayed in this position for several seconds and then it began to dance. His whole back looked like a tiny peacock with wings. A larger, plain looking spider came from the bottom of the web and stopped.

The spider continued to dance and seemed to gain speed in its performance. The plain one appeared to be paralyzed by the rhythmic dance, which caused the other spider to be able to get closer. As soon as the plain one was close enough, the two of them danced together where the mating ritual was completed. Then the whole vision vanished.

Both Kit and Nekoh continued to stare at the blank cave wall, saying nothing. The overwhelming and stunning show had left them speechless.

Finally, Nekoh sighed as he was about to speak. But before he could, another image lit up the wall with tall flames like a campfire in the wilderness. A loud crack similar to the earth splitting apart reverberated inside the cave.

The picture died down with the glowing fire becoming less and less. At the top, where the flames had peaked was an open crevice with an amber stone protruding out.

Nekoh went over to it, stretched out his body length to the top of the cave wall, where he used his paw to wobble the rock out of its resting place. Once he got it loose, he carefully put it in his mouth and moved away from the wall.

He placed it on the floor where he and Kit intently looked at the fossilized tree resin. It was more than clear amber rock. It had several small seeds encased in its yellowish-brown structure.

Again, before either of them could say anything, the cave wall began swirling with cloud formations and smoke. Once the smoke and clouds cleared, written words could be seen, saying:

Seek the spider to speak
Within the bowels one must go
A web to point the way
When the gift of the Spidersong Lily is paid.

As soon as Nekoh read the words out loud, they disappeared. They quietly waited for anymore wisdom to come from the cave wall. Several minutes passed in silence.

"I know how to leave," Kit finally said. "We slide down the mountain to return to Zetia's."

Nekoh nodded in agreement. He put the amber stone in his pouch, saying, "keep this safe until I need it." He then followed Kit to the bottom of the mountain to begin their journey back to the sanctuary.

Chapter Eleven

Ayden and her two friends continued the grueling climb up several mountains; all void of life. Dead shrubs and trees sporadically stood in their path, but still they were barren.

Whenever she would sing, the atmosphere would make it more and more difficult for them to continue. Several shelters had already been dug and left as they kept their pace upward.

"Let's rest for the day," Ayden decided. She and Greysun dug a new shelter and she prepared their meal. Each day it was the same small portions of food with sips of water.

"I vaguely remember many songs." Ayden stated as the three of them sat and rested. "But, singing partial songs is not want I want. They seem so empty now. I need to come up with my own words. Then, maybe, I won't be so discouraged when I sing."

"Something has got to give here," Ayden forlornly said. "I am just so tired of the same ol', same ol'. The food, the hike, the digging a new shelter each time we stop and the emptiness of life around us."

All of them sat, looking out into the unknown nothingness. Feeling the pain for each other, Greysun put his paw on her leg and whimpered.

Nip nudged Ayden's hand as she jumped into her lap. "Sing, Ayd, sing," Nip pleaded.

Ayden lightly hummed as she caressed the animals. The familiar unrest of the atmosphere could be seen above as she continued.

"Life is here with me, life is here with me," Ayden began singing.

"Because of you and because of me, life is here. Never give up, never forget life is here." Ayden repeated the same words over and over until they all fell asleep.

She woke up many hours later humming the tune she had chosen for the song she made. "Life is here," she quietly sang. She kept repeating the phrase as she prepared for the day's hike.

"Let's get movin' team," Ayden encouraged Nip and Greysun. She put her pack on and begin the trek upwards.

Her friends walked beside her as all three climbed over the uneven ground. Ayden continued to sing, "life is here," as they went. Sometimes, she would aimlessly hum the verses.

Farther and farther they wound up the trail they had to forge. Ayden looked in her pack for the floppy hat Lydia had given her and put it on when they stopped for a second to catch their breath.

"It feels so long ago when Deborah and I wore these hats," Ayden thought.

Her mind drifted as she smiled about her love and memories for all her friends on that journey. She took her bandana from her wrist and wiped her forehead.

"Wow," Ayden thought. "Today I am sweatier than normal."

They continued to walk and hum. Nip grabbed at her pant leg as she hissed lightly. Ayden finally stopped and lifted her up to put her in the sling.

Ayden noticed her fur was a little matted and she took her bandana to wipe her dry. At times, her foot would slip from the semi-wet ground.

On a flat area of the climb they stopped to look around. All of a sudden Greysun began to jump around like a puppy. He would run one direction and jump; then run the opposite way and do the same jump.

His tongue hung outside his mouth where it looked like he was dumbly smiling. Sometimes he would stop and try to catch the air with his tongue.

Ayden and Nip watched him with curious amusement. He kept doing the same behaviors and seemed to become more and more excited.

Finally, Ayden looked up to the sky and gasped. "OH! Holy Crap!" She yelled. "It is misting rain. There is rain coming down."

Nip jumped into her arms and the two of them danced with excitement. Ayden lifted Nip above her head and jumped with pure joy and enthusiasm.

"Life is here," Ayden and Greysun sung as loud as they could while they danced around each other. Nip sang, "life here, life here, life here," over and over again.

All three of them stopped and put their tongues out to catch the rain. They stood there for several minutes basking in the delight of the fresh water hitting their bodies.

Finally, Ayden stated, "We need to build a stronger deeper shelter this time, Greysun. We don't know if this rain will cause mudslides, and we have to be prepared. Going deeper into the ground where the water hasn't penetrated should keep us safe. Plus, we need to dig at an angle to make sure it doesn't flood us out."

The two of them spent hours digging, making sure their latest dwelling was big enough and secure enough to keep them safe. Nip, wanting to feel she was a part of the dirt removal team would jump around the flying dirt and use her paws to swat it away.

Of course, the dirt usually ended up back in an area where the other two had to remove it again. But, luckily, it was such a small portion, Ayden didn't have the heart to tell her she wasn't really helping them.

Pleased with their accomplishment, the three sat to rest inside their new home. Soon, the day's work caught up with them and they fell asleep.

Greysun woke and inched his body forward as he slid on his stomach. He stared out the entrance of their shelter with his snout on his paws.

Ayden opened her eyes, moved in close to him and rubbed him behind his ears. "What are you thinking about, Greysun," she asked?

"I have only seen rain twice before, Ayden," Greysun revealed. "Both times was when I was taken above ground to search for escapees."

"Living in the Dark Cell was, well it was dark. Sure, we had artificial light from the herb growers and dwelling growers. But all those plants still looked sickly in comparison to true light growth," he recalled.

"For example," Greysun explained as he took his paw and pointed, "this plant right here. It is small, but you can see it is healthy because it lives in true light and rain."

Ayden stared at Greysun's paw and exhaled in excitement. "Greysun," she breathed. "Greysun, it's a plant. It's a new plant." She hurriedly walked outside where she saw little sprouts of grass all around her.

Kneeling, she lightly touched the young growth and began to weep. Nip and Greysun joined her where they both howled and meowed in emotional excitement.

"I didn't realize how much I missed seeing green," Ayden expressed as she wiped her tears. She looked to the sky where it was still grey and empty. "How can these little guys break forth in growth when there is no sun from above," she questioned.

"Ayd, you sun," Nip stated confidently.

"Yes, I would have to agree with Nip," Greysun stated. "Your presence in Hollow has caused quite a stirring of life."

Ayden looked at both of them as she said, "Stirring." She repeated the word again, "stirring."

And then, she said, "Listen, child, listen to the stirring. That was what Crane said to me the day we left the huts. Is it the stirring of life coming forth from the ground," Ayden asked? "Just exactly am I supposed to be listening to in this stirring?"

"Not really sure, Ayden," Greysun surmised. "But maybe we should stay a few days in this one spot to see if any answers can be found to your questions."

Ayden looked up at the farthest distant peak. It still would take them several weeks at this pace to get to it. "Maybe you are right, Greysun. I think all of us could use a long break from hiking," Ayden said with relief.

Chapter Twelve

Zetia's dining room was packed with all in attendance to hear what Nekoh and Kit had discovered on their journey. Everyone's anticipation was noticeably high as Deborah searched the room for Nekoh.

She knew the wait to find out what happened had been delayed because Callie and Joshua had not yet arrived from Sunbird Village. Which gave her time to speak to her friend before he was preoccupied with everyone else. She moved between the participants as they ate or talked in a cafeteria style.

Finally, she saw him. He was resting by the front door with his eyes closed. She eased up next to him and knelt down to rub the top of his head.

"Oh, I have missed your touch, Deborah," Nekoh disclosed as he leaned into the rub.

"Nekoh, I should be angry with you for not telling me you were going with Kit," Deborah chastised him.

"I have so much to tell you when we get a chance to talk privately." Deborah said as she leaned down, kissed his head, then wrapped her arms around him.

"Yes, I too have some quirky observations I am excited to share with you," Nekoh stated. "But we will have plenty of time after tonight to talk together," he reassured her as they watched Gethsemane fly into the room followed by Joshua and Callie.

Deborah quickly got up to gather her favorite dishes on a plate. She found Jerin and went to sit by him; excited to hear Nekoh's and Kit's story.

Nekoh moved to the fireplace, jumped up on a small serving table with only a cloth draped over it. He leaned his paw down where he gently helped Kit settle next to him.

The two of them took turns retelling their whole adventure. Then, Nekoh opened his pouch to reveal the precious stone.

Zetia stepped over to it and took it out of the pouch. She gestured to Kalim who brought over a pedestal to put the stone on it for all to see.

"Well, I have to say I was in a trance, visualizing everything by how beautifully the two of you reported your whole encounter," Gethsemane stated.

"Breathtaking," Callie agreed.

"I know the area in your vision; it is in Oshyama. It is called the Groves," Zetia stated. "Kit is right, it will not be an easy journey to reach it."

"The Spidersong Lily has not been seen for many years in Eshra. It would seem this rock carries its seeds. Extracting them will prove to be a challenge. Especially, to make sure we do not destroy them in the process," Kalim stated with concern.

"Before you can leave, then, we need the seeds to be free," Gethsemane stated. "It will take all of your skills to reveal its secrets," he determined as his wings swept the crowd.

"I agree," Joshua stated as he stood and stretched his mountain lion body. "We need to carefully and slowly use all of our abilities for success."

"Deborah and Nekoh," Joshua turned to them and continued, "work with Kalim in his shop over the next few days to come up with a plan. Zetia, Jerin and Tybin you three work on the path for the journey. The rest of us will help where needed," he determined.

The room of spectators nodded in agreement to Joshua's words. With the hour being late, they each retired to their respective rooms.

Nekoh decided he would sleep in Deborah's room on Ayden's bed since neither her nor Nip were with them. He settled into the pillow as he looked at Deborah.

He nodded to her, saying, "tomorrow should prove to be interesting. Even though we only have the amber stone, we may be able to use your knife like you did with the snail fern plant."

"I don't know, Nekoh," Deborah stated. "Seems too convenient for it to work. The cave would not have given you guys the stone if it knew there was another way. There is deep Eshra magic going on here," she worriedly said.

"We will find the answers, Deborah," Nekoh said as he yawned. "But I am beyond excited right now to sleep on this soft," he stopped and patted the pillow, "not forest floor bed. Tomorrow, then. We will succeed, friend," he stated as he lay his head down.

Deborah chuckled at his snoring. She had never heard him snore before. "Boy, he must have been a wreck on the Kit journey," she decided as she, too, lay down to sleep.

The morning found Kalim, Nekoh, Deborah and Nadab sitting in the kitchen discussing what they should do with the stone.

"Nadab, I feel we need your shop more than mine for now," Kalim stated. "Once it is extracted, we can use my skills, but to get it extracted we need your services," he claimed.

"Well, we can put it in the vice to see if we can crack its shell. Or heat it with a torch where it may melt the outer edges," Nadab suggested.

"Kalim," Deborah asked, "didn't I see some old books on your shelves?"

"Yes, Deborah there are many ancient books of Eshra in my shop," Kalim said.

"OK, you and Nadab work your angle while Nekoh and I research the books," Deborah proposed as she and Nekoh stood up to leave.

Once they entered Kalim's, the two of them studiously began reading. Book after book, page after page was perused with hope of finding an answer to their dilemma.

At times, one would stop the other to reveal a new process or truth they found. But by late afternoon, both were perplexed and eye-strained.

"Good ol' Eshra magic," Deborah finally stated. "You get a small piece of magic or word, but it is up to you to wait for the real reveal to be found out. Nothing is ever as it seems. And, you had better learn patience because it will not reveal it until it is ready to show you," she said with frustration.

"True, but it is always worth the wait, Deborah," Nekoh said with insight.

Deborah sat back in her chair as she twirled her pencil. She looked around the shop, hoping some 'wisdom' would come from the room.

"Well, since we have no answers, it is a perfect time to stop so I can tell you about Marley," she excitedly said. Deborah explained every facet about the bird, including his talons in her skin.

"Sounds like you and I both had a sort of an awakening gifted to us by our fowl friends," Nekoh chuckled.

He gave Deborah the unabridged details of his experience with Kit. From his frustration to his humble realization of how beautiful the bird is with grace and intelligence.

"Wow!" Deborah expressed. "Just Wow," she said again.

Elora flew into the shop excited to bring news, "I have been requested to round everyone up for an early dinner," she proclaimed.

After all were seated, Zetia began, "The boys and I have our map laid out to the entrance of Oshyama. To get to the vision we will have to secure a boat from the villagers to reach the island of Lametis."

"The islanders who live off the coast use these boats to harvest the trees and the fruit described in the image. We will have to get their permission to enter the Groves as they consider it to be sacred ground. I am Lametisan by birth. I will speak to the elders on our behalf," Zetia revealed.

"Kalim and I have worked several different methods to break the stone," Nadab stated. "He and I are under the assumption strong old Eshra magic surrounds it. We just have to find the key to open it." He confessed.

"Deborah and I have learned many new traditions and methods from Kalim's books of old," Nekoh stated. "But, as to a clue on how to break the amber we have not found anything."

"Sometimes, one may be too close to the problem to see it clearly," Gethsemane said as he stood up on his perch. "I advise we all take a much-needed break from the current events. Nadab, return the stone to the pedestal near the fire. Let it rest there, where all can admire it at their leisure."

"And, for the next few days I want all of you to rest and enjoy the amenities at Zetia's. From what Tarhana has told me, Tybin's injuries need at least that much time before he can begin his physical training to regain his strength. So, none of you can leave yet, anyways," Gethsemane concluded.

Deborah watched everyone scatter. Deep in thought, she succumbed to Gethsemane's plan. "I think the water fall is what I need," she said to herself. She ran upstairs, changed and came back down to relax in the swirling water of the pool.

"May I join you," Iza quietly asked Deborah.

"Sure," Deborah answered. She watched Iza timidly get into the water. Her eyes could not hide her wonderment of the pool. Deborah lightly smiled at her, realizing this poor girl probably had never experienced this simple joy before due to her life in the Dark Cell.

"How ya doin' Iza," Deborah asked.

Iza's eyes watered as she looked at Deborah. "I, I, I," was all she could get out at first. She lowered her eyes, looked back at Deborah as she breathed deeply and started again. "I have never known this type of luxury."

Her hands played with the water as she intently looked at it as it fell through her fingers. Silence followed for several minutes. Iza lightly touched the beautiful mosaic around the pool.

Finally, she started to speak, "It still feels like a dream. I mean, I wake up in cold sweats, thinking I am dreaming and this is not real. I have to cover my mouth from screaming; afraid I am having a nightmare where I am still a prisoner in the Dark Cell," she said as she looked at Deborah.

"I don't want to scare my mom. Then, as I walk around Zetia's, I feel like I am in a dazed fog, not knowing what I should be doing," Iza expressed with deep frustration.

"In the Cell we had to work constantly and live in fear continuously. I feel useless I am not helping all of you. Not helping the Messenger," Iza confessed.

Deborah's heart bled for Iza as she spoke. The horrible life she lived from birth would always carry a scar on her heart.

She smiled at her, saying, "Iza, none of us but maybe the Ten who Zetia rescued years ago, plus Raxton and your mom know your pain. My heart aches for the life you had to live," Deborah compassionately told her.

"This place of beauty," Deborah exclaimed as she swept her hand around Zetia's home, "will always be your home now. You're safe haven. You never have to leave here. And, it is OK you feel the way you do. What you have lived cannot be forgotten quickly."

"As far as feeling useless, Iza," Deborah said as she leaned into her and took her hand. "You, Iza, saved all of us, including the Messenger from the Dark Cell and Choran. Not to mention from Nahrita and her cruelty. If not for you, we would not be sitting here in this gorgeous pool talking."

Iza let one lone tear drop from her eye. "Deborah," she gulped before she began again. "Deborah, please ask for my permission from Zetia to go with you to save the Messenger," she begged.

Shocked by her request, Deborah found it difficult to form any words. "It is not my call," she finally was able to say. Memories flooded her mind as she thought back to the Great Tree and her worry, she would not get to go with Ayden.

Deborah gazed at Iza knowing she had to help her. "But even though it is not my call. I promise you I will ask Zetia for you,' she said as she nodded her head in agreement.

Iza breathed a sigh of relief, saying, "Thank you, Deborah, thank you."

Chapter Thirteen

Five days had passed since they decided to stay in the same area when it started to rain. Even though it was just a mist, the ground had taken on a rebirth. All around them plant life sprang forth bringing joy to each of their hearts.

Ayden made it a ritual to sing every morning, noon and night. She loved the humorous sound they all made as they sung out of tune together.

Instead of singing the whole song all of the time, she used the 'Life is Here' phrase as a sort of mantra to help Greysun and Nip stay on task to keep singing.

She took her bowl from the Great Tree to catch fresh water and refill her water bladder. Just in case the rain stopped she had decided.

Greysun proved to be an asset on what plants were edible. Since the shoots were small and tender, the sweetness they produced added pleasure to their meals.

"I know we have got to start hiking soon," Ayden stated. "This freedom to rest has been a gift. It has given me a new perspective, too," she revealed.

"Sometimes rest is necessary. It allows your soul to gain strength to continue," Ayden said as she looked towards the distant peak.

She still had no clue what 'listen to the stirring' meant in reference to Joshua and the Crane using the same phrase to her. As usual, she resigned herself to it being Eshra's world of mystery. Which would reveal itself when the time was right.

Ayden watched as Greysun and Nip rolled around in the grass. They would take their hindlegs, push against the ground and slide. The happiness they showed with the freedom to be an animal with no care made her feel at peace. The view all around her, also gave her peace as the whole terrain showed some type of new green growth.

She looked to the sky and said, "Hey, guys, it has stopped misting. I guess it is a sign for tomorrow. We will start the hike again," she decided. She rested her head against the hill outside their cave and continued to watch her friends play.

Off in the distance she thought she heard an unfamiliar disturbance. Ayden lifted her head towards it to see if she could make out what it was.

The eerie silence coupled with the periodic faint sound caused her to be hyper-alert and ready to jump into action. Confused, she couldn't get a grasp on what was making it, she stood, ready to fight.

Greysun began to slowly growl as he moved in closer to Ayden. He sensed her uneasiness which caused him to react to her fear. Nip stood beside Greysun with all four legs apart and ears back. Several minutes passed while they stayed in position.

Suddenly, a raven whisped near them. Startled, Ayden yelped. She looked at the bird and let out a sigh of relief.

"Uri," she breathed. "Uri, you scared me," she stated.

"Forgive me, Ayden," Uri said. "It is not easy to enter Hollow. My friends had to help by cawing in a specifically designed pattern to open a portal. But this portal could not have been made possible if not for you. Your presence here has brought energy to the world," he revealed.

The bird watched as the animals went back to playing on the grass. No longer did they feel the need to protect Ayden.

"Choran is physically deteriorating and the unrest in the Dark Cell is rampant. His plan is to send an army to Hollow to battle you," Uri informed her.

"An army!" Ayden exclaimed with terror.

"Yes, but fear not, Ayden," Uri claimed. "Each day you sing. Each day your wings shine; is a day it makes it more difficult for Choran to succeed. Still, I am here to say you need to continue to move forward, because an army may break through even with his unstable state."

"Before I leave, Ayden, is there a message you would like me to deliver to Zetia? I cannot stay long in Hollow or it will consume me," Uri disclosed.

"A message," Ayden stated with expediency. "Yes, yes there is a message. Tell all of them I love them. Tell them we made a friend in Greysun and Nip is doing great. Tell them all about what you have seen here with how Hollow is changing."

Ayden stopped for a second as her eyes filled, "tell them I will see them soon." Tears rolled down her face as Greysun and Nip moved next to her to comfort her.

"Lastly," Ayden regained her composure and said," tell Deborah how much I love her and Nick too. Tell both of them to use Deborah's and my shake and they need to do it with each other whenever they feel overwhelmed. And, when they use it, they will know I am standing right beside them," she finished.

Uri nodded as he stood. "One final note, Ayden, remember the prophecy. Remember Ehyah has to rise from the bowels. There your friends will be entering at Oshyama and will find you," Uri stated as he bowed to Ayden and whisped.

Ayden stared at the air where Uri disappeared. "Wow, wow, wow," is all she could say. She sat back down where the animals flanked her and she automatically rubbed their fur. Together, they sat in silence.

"An army," she finally said. "Not want I wanted to hear," she revealed. "But, how exciting, guys. We got to send a message to everyone saying we are OK. Strange, though, Uri said 'there your friends will find you,' she confusingly said.

"I thought it would only be me in the bowels, and you guys of course," Ayden continued to process the information she heard from Uri.

"So, we go to the bowels where we release the Great Crane. I guess I just thought I would fly out with the Crane. Now, our friends meet us there? Brother, I will say it again, I am so tired of only knowing part of the story. But it is exciting to look forward to seeing everyone," Ayden concluded as she stood up.

"So, hope rises up, team," Ayden concluded. "We start hiking today instead of tomorrow. The farther we are from the entrance to Hollow the better off we are."

Ayden began to sing as she gathered all of their belongings into her pack. She looked up the mountain, sighed, and stated, "We travel until we get tired. And then we travel some more. We have got to make faster progress than before to stay safe."

Chapter Fourteen

Daily Nahrita watched Choran lose his grip with reality and his ability to maintain control. Still, he was a force and she knew she would have to cautiously maneuver to stay alive.

"Nahrita!" Choran yelled. "Nahrita!" He yelled again.

"Choran, my leader," she said as she entered his domain.

All around the Dark Cell dwelling new growth had sprung forth. No longer was it a barren dark hole where Choran ruled. Even his cave above showed regeneration with the limbs on the trees sprouting small buds of leaves.

As life abounded around him, he was doing the opposite. His body was like a feeble old man where he could only stand on his legs for short spurts. The workers constructed two crutches, one for under each wing, to help him stand.

The more he became disabled, the angrier he became. True to his nature, he blamed everyone around him for his misfortune. Most of the time, he sat in his corner void of any resemblance to a great horned owl. Just a heaping body of nothingness.

Yet, sporadically he could rapidly bring his body upright, where he would devour his prey with lightning speed. The unpredictability of when he would strike caused all around him to approach him with even more fear.

Nahrita kept a good distance away from him as she stopped to hear what he wanted. Silently, she spoke to herself as she disgustedly looked at him, "Fool! He thought he was so smart to devour the girl. Because of her he is diminished in size and ability where he will slowly die."

She chuckled to herself, saying, "little does he know his size is my choice, not the girl's."

Nahrita replayed in her mind the decision to take away his snail fern potion. She had watched closely his every move after the Messenger was eaten. The growth of plants was her first clue something was array.

He thought the Messenger was done and over and was arrogantly planning his rise to the world of Eshra. Workers were already above ground creating a fortress where he planned to rule.

The belief he could now control all of Eshra made him complacent. He refused to listen to her about preparing for future battles as he no longer felt the need for it.

Foolishly, he fantasized all who lived in the realm would bow to him. Especially since hope was gone with the Messenger no longer a threat.

"Yet," she reminded herself, "if it had not been for his pompous conceit, she would not have been able to put her plan into motion so quickly."

For a very long time she had worked her way into being his confidant and lead enforcer. Manipulating him without him knowing took calculated precision. Her loyal deception was her ultimate goal to rule the Dark Cell herself.

She knew by his erratic behaviors she was close to eliminating him as a threat. Then she would be the true ruler of the realm. No longer would she have to take orders, but instead she would give them.

Her decision to slowly reduce his ingestion of snail fern took shape when he acted like a storm was brewing in his innards. He walked around nervous and uncomfortable. Constantly burping where he would grab his side as if his body was reacting negatively to something he ate.

The unrest he felt in his body was a perfect distraction where he would not be cognizant the snail fern was less potent. But she also knew she needed to make sure the Messenger was finally eliminated. Therefore, she had to keep him ingesting small amounts of the snail fern to keep him large enough for her plan to be executed.

"Choran, my leader, time is getting short. You need to devour men and animals to secure your rule in Hollow," she coyly encouraged him.

"Nahrita, if I send them quickly, I will be sicker than I am right now," Choran whined.

"Yes, my leader, but if we send one or two and then wait a day in between it will be less troubling for you," she tried to convince him.

"The Messenger is no more, Nahrita," Choran proclaimed. "Do you think she is the first I have sent there. Thousands have gone before her and I had no problem. She will soon die like the others."

"Yes, my leader. But my concern is you. The terrible bouts of turmoil your body is experiencing could be removed with her dead. An army could help relieve your pain faster," she pushed him.

"Leave, Nahrita," Choran demanded. "You tire me. I need to rest," he stated as he closed his eyes to ignore her.

Nahrita walked out, saying under her breath, "Fool!"

She angrily turned to the potion workers as she walked out, saying, "do not forget to follow my instructions. He is to continue to get less and less snail fern each day."

She had sent Nargaut to live in her old cottage at the entrance to the Dark Cell while she now stayed at the one Jaeh used to own where Deiha and Iza had lived. Her strategy was to stay close to Choran to ensure her plan would not be foiled.

She entered the home and looked at the man who was preparing food for her. Her wolves stayed outside and stood guard. The unrest of the Dark Cell had everyone on high suspicion of each other, causing Nahrita to take extra precautions.

"Choran has become unmanageable, Karth," she stated. "There is only a short window, now, to get him to swallow enforcers to Hollow. I do not know if I can get him to do it. He refuses to listen to reason."

"It is time to inform the selected enforcers to travel to Oshyama, now. If we cannot enter through Hollow, then we will have to kill her near the bowels. Tell Ashel we will join him after he secures the area," Nahrita ordered.

Nahrita waited for Karth to leave before she let her guard down. She took her coat with the leather hood, which covered her body length of almost six feet, off and placed it on the chair.

Her long brunet hair, tightly pulled back from her face in a ponytail merged in the middle at the base of her skull. She moved her neck left and right where each side cracked audibly.

Taking the leather gloves off, where there were openings for each finger except for the completely covered thumb, she looked at her hands for several minutes. Sighing, she slipped her boots off. She released her belt to remove her dark tan cotton pants with leather patches on the knees, and a matching leather pocket on the left thigh.

Next, she undid the tie on her off-white cotton shirt as it wrapped around her thin frame with long straps like a straight jacket. Her sleeveless under shirt, no longer firmly held in place, flowed freely to just above her knees.

She moved to the pantry door and opened it to reveal a long mirror attached to it. Her eyes followed her body from head to toe where she then deliberately closed her eyes and slammed the door shut.

With tears forming, she said, "I will never have Jaeh's child." Anger flared from her eyes as she spoke again, "Because of her I have nothing." Nahrita determinedly stared off into the room and said, "I will kill the Messenger."

Chapter Fifteen

Zetia flew to the top of the first mountain, near the mines, and landed. She lifted her head to sun herself. The morning rays were still warm, but her heart was heavy as she knew winter was coming.

Not that she did not enjoy the season. It was the fear she had with the weather change for Ayden living in it by herself. And for all those who would travel with her to Oshyama.

The journey would become even more treacherous with the changing season. Yet, once they were close to her homeland, the climate would be more bearable with no snow.

"I must talk to Lydia," she determined. "We all will need warm clothes to survive." Her eyes closed while she stayed in deep thought.

The breeze she felt pass her face came from the opposite direction than the wind and she quickly opened her eyes to see what it was. Perched next to her was a raven, patiently waiting for her to see him.

"Uri, my friend, what a pleasant surprise," she exclaimed.

"For me too, Zetia," Uri disclosed. "I come with news from Ayden," he proudly stated.

"Ayden!" Zetia excitedly said.

"Yes, she wishes to tell you she is fine and has a new friend with her and Nip. His name is Greysun and he is a German Shepherd. When I found them, the animals were very playful on the new grass," Uri informed her.

"Life is alive in Hollow, Zetia. Ayden's presence is making its mark in Choran's world," Uri thankfully exclaimed.

Zetia put her hand to her mouth as she listened. Her eyes welled with tears which she let freely fall across her cheeks as Uri spoke.

"She is safe," Zetia softly said.

"She is well, Zetia. But not safe. I warned her she needed to keep her pace up the mountains to get to the bowels where Ehyah needs to be released. Our scouts have confirmed Choran wants to send enforcers to Hollow to reach her and kill her," he revealed.

"Go back, now, Uri," Zetia fearfully said. "Stay with her and help protect her," she begged.

"I, nor any of the rest who are loyal to our cause can go to Hollow and stay. I was afforded a quick entry because of her work there through song and her wings shining. Ehyah came to me and gave me instructions on how to reach her. But he also said if I or another stayed, we would die because we did not enter through Choran," Uri explained.

"Take heart, Zetia," Uri continued. "She will succeed by keeping the prophecy in her heart. She is strong and determined. Plus, she looks very well and happy with her plight. I did tell her she will see all of you at the bowels to encourage her heart. Finally, would you tell the rest she loves them all. And, give them peace in what I have told you today?"

"Yes, Uri, I will deliver her message. Thank you for giving me strength this day. My heart was heavy, and you have eased my worries," Zetia tenderly told him.

Uri nodded to her and lifted his wings. "I have one more promise to keep for her. I am off to find Deborah and Nickalli," he stated and then disappeared.

Nick and Deborah made plans the night before to meet behind the sanctuary where Ayden always sat to write in her journal. The idea was to have a breakfast picnic as they talked about their friend.

Early morning found Deborah hurriedly dressing as she ran down to the kitchen to prepare their feast. The beauty of their meeting caused her to be extremely excited.

Nick was someone, like her, who knew Ayden before Eshra. To spend time with her friend and freely talk about Ayden made her feel as if Ayden was very close to them.

Deborah happily lifted the basket Tarahna helped her prepare and carefully exited the kitchen. Nick came around the corner, took the basket, smiled and handed her a blanket. Together, their steps were markedly light as their anticipation heightened.

"What a great idea," Nick told her as they laid out the blanket and set their makeshift table.

Lazily, they both ate as Deborah sat cross-legged and Nick lay on his side with only his feet crossed. He used his left elbow to hold up his upper torso. Their sense of enjoyment with the food and the peaceful location where the morning sounds caressed their thoughts was visibly noticeable on their faces.

"Ayden loved picnics," Deborah revealed.

"Every summer we would go into the mountains around East Glacier and have them," Deborah softly said.

"Yeah, I knew you guys had them all of the time," Nick disclosed. "I thought about asking if I could join you. But the store was always busy in the summer."

Unexpectedly, Uri whisped onto their blanket. He hopped over to the plate holding the egg sandwiches and helped himself.

Deborah excitedly laughed, saying, "Uri this is an extra special treat, you joining us."

Uri bobbed his head up and down in acknowledgement to Deborah's statement as he continued to eat.

Once he finished, he looked at the two of them and said, "this is a surprising delicacy." Small pieces of egg dotted one side of his beak as he continued. "I never was able to resist egg. It is my most favorite."

He hopped back, fanned his wings, and said, "I have news for the two of you. Ayden wishes you to know she is doing well. She told me to tell you she loves both of you. She has a new friend in a German Shepherd named Greysun. He and Nip are also well."

"You spoke to Ayden," Deborah screamed. "Where is she?"

"She is in Hollow climbing the mountains to reach the bowels," Uri stated with a tinge of frustration.

"Listen, Deborah, she has a message for you and Nickalli," the bird informed them.

Deborah grabbed Nick's hand as she sat on her legs. She nodded to Uri to continue.

"The arm shake you and Ayden have done for years; she wants you and Nickalli to use it whenever you are fearful or are in need of reassurance. You are to strengthen each other with it. And, she wants you to know she is right next to you when you two use it."

"Wait," Deborah quickly said, knowing Uri's propensity to leave once he delivered a message. "Will we see her soon?"

"I gave her the message you would all meet in the bowels," he said and then whisped.

"Great," Deborah cried out. "I am more than thankful for the information. But, really. Couldn't he have stayed a little longer and answered all of our questions," she asked with sadness?

"I am so relieved, Deborah," Nick whispered.

"She turned to him, smiled and grabbed his forearm where he immediately grabbed hers. "Me too, Nick," Deborah gently said.

Elora, who had followed the two of them from the kitchen, landed on Deborah's shoulder. "Deborah, Ayden lov-e-e-e-e-e-s Nick," she excitedly stated.

Nick's face began to flush as he said, "she loves all of us, Elora."

"No, Nickalli, she lov-e-e-e-e-e-e-e-e-e-s you," Elora said enthusiastically as she flew to the leftover egg and started to eat.

Deborah wished she could scold Elora for exposing Nick's heart, but knew Elora was deliberately avoiding eye contact with her.

"You're right Nick, she loves all of us. And, her message to us is to stay strong and lift each other up when we are worried. For one, I am so extremely thankful Uri came to see us today," Deborah exclaimed.

Deborah started to place the plates and other items they had used back in the basket while she spoke. Slyly, she moved closer to Elora and deliberately pushed her, hoping Elora would get the message to keep quiet.

Elora let out an offended chirp as she looked at Deborah. She hopped far enough away from her hand where she couldn't get pushed again.

"I just don't know, Deborah," Elora playfully said. "Seems to me Ayden being all alone in Hollow has given her time to seriously think. And, we know she has always told you she loves you. But, for her to send Uri here to make sure Nick knew he was loved. Well, it just seems to be a little bit more," she gleefully revealed.

Nick busily helped Deborah put everything in the basket, keeping his eyes down. "You know, I think I had better go check on Tybin," he said as he deliberately changed the subject.

"Let me take the basket back for you, Deborah. You two stay here and enjoy the rest of your morning," Nick stated as he quickly got up and left the area.

Deborah waited until he was out of earshot and then said, "Elora! Did we not talk about protecting Nick? How could you expose him like that," she demanded?

"It's true and you know it's true, Deborah. Father always tells me I should tell the truth. And, I didn't lie," Elora stated as she defended her actions.

"Elora," Deborah exasperatedly breathed. "You know that is a lame excuse for what you did."

"Well, I think it is good for him to know. It gives him hope and makes him feel special. Plus, he needed to hear it for his walk to heal. Remember, all of us have to walk past our sorrow to hope." Elora said as she protected her decision to tell Nick Ayden loved him.

"Fine, say what you will," Deborah stated. "But you and I both know we need to walk lightly to not hurt him," she scolded Elora.

"Well, fine then," Elora stated. "I think it is time for me to leave you alone so you can think about how you pushed me. And, you can apologize to me tonight before bed."

Elora flew off when she finished, making sure Deborah couldn't say anything else to her. But, before she left, she turned where she flew high above Deborah, giggled and yelled, "love you Deborah."

Deborah placed her back against the old oak tree, got comfortable and smiled as she thought about Elora. "The little shit," she tenderly said.

Deep in her thoughts about everything Uri told them, she sighed saying, "I miss Ayden."

"As do I," Zetia said as she came up alongside her and sat down. "We, will be leaving soon, though. And, each step we take will be one more step closer to her," she said to encourage Deborah.

"It seems so long ago when we were carefree kids in East Glacier," Deborah sighed. "I wouldn't even know how to act like that child again," she revealed.

"I love what I have learned; and even experienced since then. But, this journey, this enlightenment journey has taken away our childhood. We will never ever again be carefree children," Deborah expressed.

Zetia held Deborah's hand as she continued to let her talk. She knew part of any healing was the freedom to express one's deepest feelings and she didn't want Deborah to stop.

"I am lost in how to help Ayden. But I am not without hope. Uri's message today was like an injection of adrenaline straight to the heart. Just the energy needed to persevere and not forget what we need to do," Deborah expressed.

Deborah told Zetia about Uri's conversation with her and Nick; leaving out the 'love' reveal to protect Nick. Zetia chose to avoid telling Deborah her conversation with Uri to not alarm her.

"I am determined, though," Deborah fiercely stated after she revealed what Uri said. "To be strong and to be there for whatever Ayden needs," Deborah claimed as she squeezed Zetia's hand.

"Speaking of being there, Zetia," Deborah said as she thought about how to ask if Iza could go with them.

"Eshra magic and Eshra," Deborah paused and then said, "how should I say it," where she stopped again to think as she let go of Zetia's hand.

"Ok, Eshra choreography of how everything comes together for the good of our worlds. Such as me entering Eshra, Joshua's prophecy to Ayden, and even you meeting up with us on the journey. All were not expected or planned, but all were integral to our success so far," Deborah stated.

"What it has shown me, about this whole Eshra Plan, is none of us are really fully aware why something happens until it is right in front of our faces," Deborah smiled at Zetia.

"It has helped me to keep an open mind and heart to not judge quickly. Or, to maybe accept more readily and to agree with something where before I would have automatically said no," Deborah continued.

"For example, my first reaction to something I recently heard was to say no way."

"But then my heart pulled up my own memory of when I was at the Great Tree and was learning about Ayden's prophecy. At first everyone was against me going with Ayden, but in the end, it was a wise choice to have me go," Deborah sweetly explained.

"Therefore, Zetia, I present to you a challenge. I want you to consider letting Iza go with us," Deborah declared.

"What!" Zetia said. "She has no real skill or knowledge of this world. She only knows the Dark Cell," she concluded.

"Wait, Zetia," Deborah requested? "She has asked me to talk to you about this very issue. And, before you say no, please think about it and challenge your first reaction," Deborah pleaded.

"True, she has no skill. But she was never given the privilege of an enlightenment journey when she came of age. And, your statement of 'she has no knowledge of Eshra' would seem to be a very good reason to give her a chance to experience it first hand," Deborah debated her reasoning.

Zetia looked at Deborah and smiled. "Well, I can see no matter what I say against it you will counter me with a rebuttal. Therefore, my girl, I promise you I will think on it and not give a definitive answer right away."

"But, realize I am not the only vote here. You may be asked by the rest to present your case, so stay prepared. And, it would benefit Iza for you to tell her to think about what she would say to us if she were to be asked," Zetia said as she stood to leave.

Chapter Sixteen

Raxton stayed close to wherever he found Kalim. Like a shadow, he would silently hover.

Kalim was well aware of Raxton's behaviors and the reasons for them. He too, had come from the Dark Cell and reverently knew the child's fear and, now, sense of lack of purpose.

Slowly Kalim incorporated Raxton into his conversations. He would present a question into the air like he was questioning himself audibly. Then, he would pretend he didn't see Raxton near him and would keep working like he was alone in his shop.

"I am very curious about the amber stone," Kalim stated as he saw Raxton's half-hidden body on the other side of the entryway to his shop. "It makes no sense we cannot break into it. Strange magic certainly covers it," he said as he sat down.

"If only we had greater skills to crack it," Kalim pondered out loud. Silence ensued while he busied himself with organizing the herbs on the shelves.

Slowly Raxton entered past the doorway to see what Kalim was doing. Finally, curiosity got the best of him. "What is in the box, Kalim?"

"This box is another mystery like the stone," Kalim stated. "The exquisite design on its exterior is phenomenal," he said as he picked it up off the top shelf where he had been organizing.

Caressing it, he ran his fingers all around the intricately raised lines made from hard wood. Measuring six inches long, four inches deep and three inches tall the abstract design weaved around the box where it looked like it was covered in roots. The crevasses were all inlaid with gold and merged together underneath the box where a small key hole rested.

"Zetia gave it to me when she returned from one of her art trips," Kalim told Raxton. "She said she found it in an antique store when she was in the other world. No key came with it, though. And, I have tried several different ways to open it to no avail," he explained as he handed it to Raxton.

Raxton carefully took the box where he treated it like it was a fine piece of porcelain which could break if handled too roughly. His fingers felt the keyhole and his brow creased.

"I have seen this design before he said. The opening is familiar to one my master had in the Dark Cell. He too could not open it," Raxton stated.

"My master even tried to melt the gold out of it. Nothing could damage the box. Finally, he threw it in a corner and told me to throw it away. I kept it. I kind of looked at it as a gift from him even though he said to get rid of it," Raxton innocently claimed.

"Interesting," Kalim queried. "It would seem it, well both, must be old Eshra. Since mine came from the other realm, I just assumed it was of that world."

"But now I wonder," Kalim said as he considered the possibility.

"Did your master's have this same root design on it with gold surrounding them," Kalim asked?

"No, his was much smaller with the same type of wood, but smooth," Raxton stated. "And, a single line of gold wrapped around it where the underneath had the same keyhole. He too, had no key for it," Raxton explained with curiosity in his voice.

"Do you want to see it," Raxton asked excitedly.

Kalim lightly chuckled at Raxton's innocence as he said, "Yes, Raxton, I would love to see it."

Raxton reached into his side pouch, produced the small box and handed it to Kalim. "I don't know why I have always kept it with me," Raxton timidly said. "I guess it made me feel like I owned something of value and because of it, I too felt I was of value."

"Hmm," Kalim began, "well, this is a fine piece of workmanship. And, you are right the hole is of the same craft." He handed it back to Raxton, saying "definitely it must be Eshra magic. When the time is right, hopefully, we will be given an answer," he concluded.

Kalim changed the subject, saying, "Raxton have you given any thought to what you would like to train in since you are now free?"

"My master was a potion maker," Raxton started and then picked up speed in his speech. "I am very skilled in herbs and their properties. I was a quick learner in the Dark Cell. I do not tire easily and can work very long hours. When my master gave me instructions, I followed them to his exact specifications. He never had to reprimand me for being lazy," Raxton stopped to take a breath.

Kalim put his hand up as Raxton started to continue his attributes. Raxton immediately stopped and put his head down in submission.

Kalim tenderly lifted the boy's chin, saying, "Raxton would you give me the honor by becoming my apprentice?"

Raxton whispered, "Yes, sir." He quickly lowered his head again.

Kalim could see the young boy was desperately trying to hold back his tears. He went over to him and put his arms around the child. As he hugged him, Raxton put his head in his chest and lightly cried.

Trevin Three found Zetia at the lake sitting on the dock with her feet dangling in the water. He approached, bowed and said, "Zetia, the full moon is in three days."

"The Trevins and I have a request for you. We ask for your help to let us prepare a meal for the special occasion. We want this first full moon since Two is no longer with us to bring joy to everyone and not sorrow," Three proudly expressed.

"Three, what a beautiful idea," Zetia said. "What kind of food," she curiously asked, concerned it may be raw clams?

"Well, it just so happens I have a list of his favorite foods," Three excitedly said. He pulled out a note folded several times in order for it to fit in his pouch and handed it to Zetia.

Zetia took the list and began to read it:

Two's Favorite Foods
1's Gravy (any kind will do)
2's Lemon and raspberry filled birthday cake with candles
3's Butter
4's Potatoes (mashed, cut, fried, baked or whatever)
5's Noodles for the butter
6's All kinds of cheeses
7's Honey bread
8's Coffee
9's Sushi
10's Sugar cubes

Zetia couldn't help herself and snickered. Each number on the list except for 10's and 2's was written in a different style of handwriting.

She looked at Three and said, "OK, Three are we sure this list is Two's favorite foods?"

"OK, then it is all of our favorite foods," Three revealed. "But, Two liked all of them too!" He proclaimed with a little bit of concern.

"We did pick his most favorite, though. I mean, we would be breaking clams open at the lake and all he could talk about were those stupid birthday cakes. Talk, talk, talk about how he couldn't decide which one he liked the best. Talk, talk, talk," Three stated as he gestured with his paw like it was a mouth talking.

"Well, I think it is doable," Zetia stated with a small hint of humor in her voice. "But maybe we should add some main courses to the meal."

"Sure, add what you want, Zetia," Three declared. "But, remember, the Trevins want to help prepare our foods."

Zetia chuckled, saying, "Absolutely Three. Deiha and Tarhana will have so much fun with you guys helping."

Zetia patted his paw, got out of the water and walked to the kitchen. She entered and handed Tarhana Three's list.

Tarhana read it. She handed it off to Deiha and then looked at Zetia confused.

"Our friends would like to honor Two with a dinner at the full moon," Zetia explained. "Not only honor, but they want to help you prepare it. All of them want to help," she said with slight fear in her voice.

"Oh dear," is all Tarhana could say as she sat down. "I am going to need helpers, Zetia. Helpers for each one of them, Zetia," she said with a determined trepidation.

Lydia and Callie were busily talking and designing the journeyers winter clothing when Eleea flew into their shop. He quietly watched them work for several minutes.

As he listened to how each would stay warm, he became increasingly worried. Shelter during a winter storm weighed heavily on his mind. He just couldn't figure out how they could all stay warm if it happened.

Finally, he flew to their table. "Ladies, he began, "I have a pressing concern. How are we to stay safe when a winter storm slows our pace and we have to wait it out to be able to travel again?"

The women stopped to listen to him. "I know Zetia has a small sanctuary, kind of like a cabin retreat three days journey from here," Callie stated. "But, if you are nowhere near it, you will be at the mercy of the elements," she concluded.

"Our clothing will surely have magic attached to them to help you, Eleea," Lydia reassured him. "Yet, even though it will keep you warm and comfortable, a winter storm is nothing to be relaxed about."

"Yes, and even though there are ways to travel with expediency in Eshra, Zetia had to bring us from Sunbird under a secretive night mission. The known portals are heavily being watched by Choran's followers now," Callie revealed. "And, there are too many for her to carry on this journey," she concluded.

Joshua jumped down from his sleeping perch near the back window of the shop where he enjoyed the sun on his back. He came closer to the table and leapt on it to address Eleea.

"Callie is right," he stated. "But what I have learned about obstacles is to not immediately see them as a bad thing. Sometimes, these limitations bring great reward in the end. For whatever reason, the sojourners need to take the path which has been set before them to succeed," Joshua wisely said.

"Interesting," Eleea stated. "Nadab spoke to Tybin about limitations as not a 'bad thing' also. Eleea recalled in his mind the whole conversation at the training hut as he had been resting on the rafters when the two men had their heartfelt conversation.

"Limitations were a gift to view one's world from a different perspective," Eleea said with awe. "Well, this eases a lot of my fears. Not that it won't be dangerous, and maybe even extremely cold. But we were meant to travel this way and we will succeed," he stated with some relief as he flew off.

Gethsemane entered the river behind the sanctuary. He lifted his wings with water to splash his body. Going deeper in, he dove through the waves to clean himself completely. Exiting the water, he stood on a downed branch to preen and dry from the sun's rays.

Oblivious, he first didn't realize all the natural sounds of the outdoors had ceased to exist. He let go of the feather he was cleaning. Confusingly, he looked around and then his eyes slightly filled with tears.

"Gethsemane," the Great Crane, who had been standing in the swirling mist of silence, said.

Gethsemane bowed to him as he jumped from the tree to the grass. "It has been a long time, my friend," he said.

"Yes," the crane agreed. "Gethsemane, I need you," the crane revealed.

"I have always been here for you, Ehyah," Gethsemane humbly stated.

The crane bowed to him and continued, "You must join those who travel to the bowels. Without old Eshra with them, they will suffer greatly. You must go," he said as he disappeared.

Gethsemane was speechless. "Since the beginning we decided not to expose I was old Eshra. Now, I have to travel with them?" He said to himself as he sat down and pondered what would transpire in the near future where he may have to reveal old Eshra.

Chapter Seventeen

Jerin, Tybin, Deborah, Iza, Nick and Nekoh joined Phum and the Trevins at the kitchen table. All were excited to have been called by Tarhana to try her newest pastry.

"I have never made honey bread before," Tarhana stated. "I know it has honey of course, but the Trevins," she turned to them with bit of frustration showing on her face, "were very vague about what other ingredients needed to be in it. So, I have designed three different samples for all of you to try."

Deiha placed three platters on the table filled with small squares of bread. She then placed enough glasses with water, small and large, on the table for each recipient to cleanse their pallet between bites. She finished by passing all of the participants napkins to hold their prizes on.

Tarhana pointed to the first platter, saying, "this one only has honey swirled in the mix of bread batter; the next has honey, sugar, and oats in it; and the third has honey, butter, cinnamon, and sugar in it." She sat down on the edge of her chair next to Deiha and waited with some anxiety for the taste testers reactions.

Each member took from the first plate where mayhem immediately broke out. Every one of the raccoons had placed their bread in the glass of water to wash it. Their bread floated to the top in small pieces and they were frantically trying to save it.

Tarhana immediately jumped up to address the bedlam. "Trevins," she yelled louder than she had planned. Lowering her voice, she started again, "Trevins, you cannot put the bread in the water to clean it before you eat it. Just eat it off of the napkin in front of you. I t is already clean, OK?"

Deborah and the rest hid their grin to not offend Tarhana and continued to chew purposefully to avoid any spotlight on them to be reprimanded. All three platters were quickly devoured, where Deiha then placed more on each plate. Tarhana and Deiha watched all of them while they tried to patiently wait to hear their opinions.

Seven stood up from his chair and jumped onto the table, saying, "I believe the best one is the one with cinnamon. The other two were very good too, but this one had a zing to it. Matter of fact, I have never tasted anything like it or like the other ones before. Cinnamon would have been Two's favorite."

Tarhana's mouth dropped open. Regaining her composure, she said, "Seven this was your list request. Do I still have it wrong," She asked?

"Well, when I wrote honey bread, what I meant was bread that you put honey on," Seven explained. "Today I thought you wanted all of us to try your new recipes," he stated with innocence.

Tarhana slowly stood up and walked outside of the kitchen. Deiha quickly stood up, saying, "Thank all of you for trying our bread. I believe we will keep the one with cinnamon for tomorrow's celebration." She then exited to go comfort Tarhana.

Trevin stood, saying, "Good job men. We have been very helpful today." He grabbed more bread off of each plate, put it in his side bag and scampered outside. The rest of the Trevins followed suit, mimicking his behavior.

Phum nonchalantly picked a piece of bread off of each platter while he said, "Seems it could have gone worse."

Phum smiled at them while he juggled the bread and tried to bow where his treasures almost toppled over. He quickly recovered them and hurriedly followed the Trevins.

The rest of them sat around the table and continued to taste test the goodies where a snicker would sporadically emerge. Tybin, Iza and Nick eventually left leaving Jerin, Deborah and Nekoh.

"I want to go see Kalim," Deborah stated as she cleaned up the table. "Maybe he has come up with a plan to crack the stone," she said.

Both Jerin and Nekoh said at the same time, "I'll go with you."

The three of them walked in silence to Kalim's workshop. As they reached the outer courtyard, Kit came alongside them and continued to walk with them.

Deborah knocked on Kalim's door, asking, "may we all come in, Kalim?"

"Of course," Kalim responded as he moved things around to make room for all of them. "Raxton has given me the great privilege to have him as my apprentice," he stated while he patted the young man on the back.

"What a wonderful plan, Raxton," Deborah excitedly said. "It is the perfect place for your skills and to learn even more from Kalim."

"Yes," Kalim agreed. "But I also believe Raxton is a gift I have received. My intuition tells me I will learn from him too," he tenderly said.

"We were wondering if there has been any progress with the stone, Kalim," Nekoh asked.

"Nadab and I have exhausted all of our resources and skills," Kalim sadly stated.

"Sometimes, patience is not a virtue for me," he chuckled. "Eshra magic and its ways brings all of us to a halt at times. The crux then lies in what will we do in the interim. Sit and brood or move forward with the promise of one day Eshra will reveal its truths," Kalim perceptively stated.

"For example," Kalim continued as he pointed to his shelf, "take this beautiful box I have had for years given to me by Zetia. It too, cannot be cracked open. I have admired its fine craftsmanship and beauty for years. It sits up there as a constant reminder for me to be patient. I have used its presence during those times when I am most frustrated to encourage me to not give up, ever."

"May I see it Kalim," Jerin asked? Kalim smiled and pulled the box off the shelf and handed it to him.

Jerin ran his fingers over the roots and then looked at Kalim. "This box is beyond beautiful,'" he stated. "It looks like something my father would have made."

"Yes, years ago I showed it to Nadab. I thought maybe he would know how to open it. He was very captivated with its beauty and locking mechanism," Kalim agreed.

"Locking mechanism," Deborah questioned?

Kalim gestured to Jerin for permission to take it from him. "Here on the underside is where the gold meets to reveal a keyhole," Kalim said with interest as he turned it over and handed it to Deborah.

Deborah respectfully ran her fingers over the keyhole. Her eyes welled as she whispered, "No way, it can't be."

Jerin moved closer to her for comfort if she needed it. She looked up at him and burst into tears. He put his arm around her and she leaned into him for a second before she spoke.

"I have the key!" Deborah blurted out. Between her tears she explained to the group how she got the key from Marley.

Kalim's excitement overtook him as he said, "By the Crane, Deborah, this is a day I never thought I would really see. I mean, I always had the hope, but it never really seemed possible since I had tried so many different ways to unlock it."

Deborah stood up and unlatched the key from her belt. As she rubbed it, she looked at Jerin and started to cry again.

Jerin clasped his hands over hers, saying, "Deborah, this is a good thing. Eshra brought you here for a purpose and today is only one of those purposes." Deborah nodded her head and handed the key to Kalim.

Everyone in the room watched with great anticipation as Kalim took the key. He looked at them and let out a slow sigh.

He lifted the box above his head to see the keyhole, placed the key in and turned it. The box's top flipped open and its contents seemed to dance with the freedom at being released. Kalim removed the key and set the box on the table. They all peered into it.

An accordion of old papers with writing on them lightly swayed back and forth. Kalim took them out, read the first entry and handed it off to Deborah and Nekoh to read.

"Oh Whoa!" Deborah exclaimed.

"This is old Eshra," Nekoh declared. "Each entry is a lost method on how to mix, design or mine. There must be an answer in these pages on how to release the amber around the seeds," he determined.

"Yes, I agree, Nekoh," Kalim stated with joy. "There is so much here, though, it will take us a few days to find the answer. And, then with whatever instructions are given it may take even longer to extract the seeds."

"Please, may I leave all of you and go to Nadab," Kalim asked? With the groups nodded approval, Kalim hurriedly left his shop with the papers.

Deborah sat back in her chair and breathed a heavy sigh, saying, "how crazy is that?"

Raxton shyly asked as he stayed half hidden against the farthest wall of Kalim's shop, "Deborah can you use the key to open my box?"

"What?" Deborah asked as she sat up in the chair and looked at him.

"I too have a box with the same keyhole," Raxton revealed. He proceeded to tell them the simple version of how he got his box; leaving out the emotional draw he had to it. He explained how he and Kalim had compared their boxes with each other. Then, he took the box out of his pouch to show them.

Deborah took the key from the table, walked over to Raxton and handed him the key. She smiled at him and led him back to the center table where the others were waiting.

Raxton held the key for several seconds before he lifted the box over his head. He breathed like Kalim had done earlier and then set the key and turned it.

The lid popped open and he carefully put the box and key on the table. All of them craned their necks to see what secret the little box had kept for so many years.

Beautiful royal blue velvet material cradled a four-inch forged steel hammer head. The refined steel lines wrapped intricately around its body in perfect polished symmetry.

The right end was rounder than the left where the butt of it was two inches across and flat like a button. Whereas the left tapered to a narrow half inch flat butt.

In the middle where the steel was the same size with no tapering was a hole which could hold a handle. Positioned in the box lid was a forged metal wedge held into place by a loop of leather.

Raxton ran his fingers over the hammer head and then did the same with the wedge. He looked up at Deborah, and with tears in his eyes he said, "I have never seen anything as beautiful as this."

Deborah hugged him as she looked at Jerin, Nekoh and Kit. All three either smiled or nodded to her with approval.

"Well, I think all of us should follow Kalim to Nadab's shop," Deborah said. She took the key, handed it to Raxton, saying, "I believe this belongs to you now."

Nadab and Kalim were deep in conversation as they huddled over the precious papers when the rest entered the room.

Deborah plopped down in front of them and joyfully said, "Do we have exciting news for you two."

The men looked up at her with visible curiosity. Deborah gently motioned for Raxton to come next to her.

Jerin retold the story of how Raxton asked to have his box opened and then had Raxton show them its contents. Nadab's eyes grew big as Kalim slapped his back. Both of them became giddy.

"We were in the middle of reading how to crack the amber," Nadab enthusiastically stated.

"Yes," Kalim joined in. "We had just reached the part where we needed a special hammer," he happily said.

Nadab quickly went to his stored wood on the shelves. He pondered which type would be the perfect handle. "Ash would be the best choice as it is strong and resilient to vibrations," he told the onlookers.

"The hour is late," Nekoh informed everyone. "Zetia will be wondering where all of us are and why we have not arrived for dinner. How about we take our good news to the rest?"

Kalim and Nadab looked at Nekoh. Neither one moved.

Nekoh nodded to them and said, "I will tell Lydia you two would be most appreciative if your meal was brought to the shop. And, it seems It would be wise to include Raxton's meal be delivered here with yours," Nekoh wisely concluded.

The men smiled and turned to the task of making the handle for Raxton's hammer head.

Chapter Eighteen

Miles upon miles had been climbed by the three travelers. Nip had taken it upon herself to ride on the back of Greysun near his neck like she used to do with Nekoh.

Even though the terrain still had early growth on it, they were excited each time they lay on it or talked about it. Their life of no life in Hollow caused them to deeply appreciate any life.

Ayden stayed vigilant in song and spreading her wings for light to shine. Try as she could, she still could not figure out the stirring Joshua and Ehyah spoke of.

The only real fear they all felt was when one would stop and peer down the mountains to see if anyone was following them.

"Ayd, tired. Ayd, Ayd," Nip meowed in a whiny tone while she rode the back of Greysun.

"I know, I know, Nip," Ayden gently said with a hint of frustration. "We will stop in about an hour. I want to get to the top of this ridge before we call it for the night."

"You know my strategy, Nip. Get to the top, build a shelter where we can see down the mountains and rest. But we can never stop watching. If we are always on guard, we won't be surprise attacked," Ayden stated with authority.

Ayden smiled as she climbed and encouraged her friends to do the same. Nip could say full sentences now, and she had developed her r's in speech. But she still referred to Ayden as Ayd.

Generally, she would speak in broken sentences rather than full complete ones. With her muted development, she still was a little girl with some difficulty even though she tried very hard.

Ayden decided to pick her battles with her and let her have her quirky ways; believing when the time was right, she would grow out of it. She even chose to keep calling Greysun, Gaysin which was way too cute to correct.

Finally, the top was reached where she and Greysun could begin the dig for their shelter. This time, Nip lay off to the side on the grass and slept. She kept repeating as she dozed in and out of sleep, "Me too tired!"

The two were entrenched in their dig where they didn't realize the ground had been continuously rumbling. Nip felt one of the rumbles and stood frozen with her four legs apart.

She looked around her, not able to make a sound out of fear. Her eyes darted to Greysun and Ayden. When another rumble struck, like a bolt of lightning she dashed to Ayden. She crawled up Ayden's leg, where she dug her claws in with each step and worked her way around to her sling.

Ayden jerked upright when the first claw met her tender calf and dug into her skin. "Nip, what is wrong," she screamed with partial fright and partial pain. Quickly, she turned around as she adjusted Nip in the sling and looked down the mountain.

Greysun had immediately sensed the need to look down the mountain when Nip had begun her climb. "I don't see anything, Ayden," he stated assuredly as he sniffed the air.

Suddenly, another strong rumble right next to them erupted as it broke the surface of the ground. They jumped closer to the entrance of their shelter and watched with marked anxiety.

Like a fish flying out of the water to grab an insect in the sky, a stem jutted out exceedingly fast and kept growing. All around them the same thing was happening. The ground continued to grumble as it allowed each creation to break forth and grow.

Ayden sat down with her mouth opened in awe. Huge pine trees with their glorious foliage dotted the whole horizon. A light mist began to fall as the three of them sat and watched in wonder.

"Well, I doubt this is what the stirring means," Ayden concluded. "I mean, I guess you could say it is a stirring. But my heart says it's not the one I'm supposed to hear. Wow, wow, wow," she eventually said.

The mist began to strengthen into raindrops and the three hurriedly backed their way into their temporary home. A little chilled, Ayden felt herself and the others slightly shiver.

She took her wings and wrapped them around all of them and huddled up to cover them for protection and warmth. Greysun leaned into her and put his head on her chest while Nip snuggled in the sling. Soon, they were all asleep.

Greysun was sitting at the entrance to the shelter looking out when Ayden woke. She moved closer and sat with him. Both stared in silence, overwhelmed with what they saw.

"It looks like East Glacier or even like Zetia's," Ayden softly said.

She looked at Greysun and put her arm around him. She realized he had no reference to her words. "I promise Greysun you will see other land just like this, but full of life with animals, insects, flowers and my friends," Ayden finished joyously.

Greysun kept his eyes forward and leaned into her hug, saying, "I dream of it, Ayden."

Ayden began to sing where in between her song she would speak. "I'll get breakfast ready for us. Crazy, we were so tired and full of excitement seeing all this happen we forgot to eat last night. More song ensued as she busily made their food. Nip jumped out of the sling and went to sit with Greysun.

"Gaysin, you my buddy," she said as she rubbed her head along his leg. "I teach you when we home. This not home," she said as she bunched her nose with displeasure. "I help you learn all names you don't know. Me a good teacher, Gaysin," she proudly stated.

Greysun chuckled as he leaned down to give Nip a long tongue kiss. "I look forward to becoming your student, Nip," he tenderly said.

The three stayed in the cave to eat as the rain had turned back to mist and they did not want their food to get wet. Eventually, the mist subsided and Ayden started to pack for their next hike.

Song and silence marked their daily treks most of the time. Even though it was exciting to see new life, it still was lonely with no other friends or wildlife around them. Granted, the pine trees were an added plus, but they also made it more difficult to climb with having to maneuver around them and the dead trees and shrubs.

Hours passed as they sustained their pace. Down the winding mountain, up the next one and then repeat. As they reached the top of their fifth mountain, Ayden looked beyond to the tallest peak where no trees dotted its face.

"Well, it makes sense," she said to herself. "Every extremely high peak I have ever seen has little to no trees at its most upper point." Her eyes turned downward below the majestic mountain. "Maybe thirty-some more mountains before we reach it," she silently decided.

"How bout we stop on this mountain and make camp," Ayden asked her friends. "I know it is earlier than usual, but I think we need a good rest," she proclaimed. She didn't want to trouble them with her feelings of hopelessness with several more mountains to climb, so she kept it light-hearted in her request.

With their shelter secure, the three of them ate in silence. Ayden's mind drifted back to Zetia's where everyone was still carefree. No death, no loss and no sorrow. "I actually miss writing in my journal," she thought. "Hmmm, what would I write now with all I have experienced," she silently wondered as she visualized her pencil and journal in front of her.

"If I have learned anything, I have learned to love deeply and freely. What I mean, is to let those whom I love know how I feel rather than hide it. None of us know when it will be the last time we see someone or even be able to talk to them again. That kind of loss cuts deep to the core of my heart.

Sometimes, I have had to stop mid-journey because I was talking like Deborah or Nick or Elora were right next to me hearing what I had to say. I know Greysun and Nip are just as important right now. But, boy do I miss those guys. I am so very thankful I was able to give Uri a message for them. He has given all of us hope we will see each other soon.

There this would have been a good journal entry Ayden thought as she looked at the trees. She stood up, went outside and jumped to the closest limb. She kept climbing higher through the branches, loving the freedom of movement which was so different than their days of hiking.

When she stopped, she realized she was well over fifteen feet above the ground. She looked out across the horizon where trees and grass grew abundantly. Her eyes continued to drift. She looked downhill from where they had come, checking for enforcers. Pleased to see no activity, she looked up and then she suddenly froze.

Squinting, she couldn't determine if her eyes were seeing a mirage or if she actually was seeing a pool of water with a stream running into it on a side of a mountain.

Ayden calculated the distance it would take them to reach the water if it was real. "If we keep on this same course," she privately thought, "we could get to it by midafternoon or early evening tomorrow. One, two, three mountains and we would be there" she determined.

She steadied her gaze to make sure she had her line of sight match their location below. "Yup, we should be good. But maybe I will keep it to myself. I don't want the two of them to get too excited if I am wrong about it being real or wrong about the distance to get to it," she told herself.

"But, if I am right," Ayden breathed, "I so want a bath," she said as she started her climb down the tree to finally reach her bed to sleep.

Chapter Nineteen

Elora flew into her bedroom and landed at the top of Deborah's headboard. "Deborah," she chirped very loudly. "Deb-or-ah-h-h-h-h-h-h," she said again.

Deborah woke and looked at her with squinty eyes. "Elora, it is way too early for you to be making noise," she disgustedly said as she took her blanket, wrapped it around her hand and placed her chin on it to snuggle back into her sheets.

"Deb-or-r-r-r-ah-h-h-h-h-h-h-h," Elora said again. "I have been sent to wake you and to tell you Zetia wishes your presence in the sunroom. Now!" She exclaimed as she flew out of the room.

By the time Deborah reached the sunroom, several of the others were already sitting or standing waiting for Zetia to speak. Curious, she went to sit by Jerin to find out what was so important for all of them to meet together. She noticed Zetia seemed to be very focused and soldier like in her stance with her hands behind her back.

Zetia began her speech by walking up and down the line of listeners. "Today we have a very important mission to accomplish," she began.

"This mission will tire you, frustrate you and make you want to lash out at those around you. What I want for all of you to remember is this is a special request which cannot be taken lightly. Instead of reacting to the moment of chaos you may see around you with short angry words. I ask each of you to take a breath and persevere in silence or with kind words." Zetia said as she stopped to have her message sink in.

Deborah grabbed Jerin's hand as she looked at him. All of a sudden, she felt scared about what they were being asked to do.

Zetia deeply sighed and began again, "Tarhana has requested each Trevin have a helper in preparing all the food they want to have for tonight's full moon celebration. I promised her I would have a worker to corral each Trevin so she would not go crazy with their chaotic ways. Each of you will be given one Trevin as your ward and it will be your responsibility to keep them under control and out of Tarhana's and Deiha's way," she told them

"Seriously, Zetia," Deborah stated with disbelief. "You had me extremely scared and this is all we have to do?"

"Well, you should be scared. You were there for the bread tasting fiasco, Deborah," Zetia retorted back.

Zetia straightened her skirt and pulled out a list as she continued, "Listen carefully for your name and number. Deborah, you have One; Jerin, you have Three; Nickalli, Four; Tybin, Five; Iza, you have Six; Raxton, Seven; and Vexia will have Eight while Lydia will stick close by in case Phum gets into trouble." She sighed again, saying, "we leave for the kitchen and I wish each of you the best of luck."

The group followed Zetia to the kitchen, single file; and with silence. When they entered, they saw Tarahna and Deiha leaning against one counter together with their arms across their chests and stern looks on their faces.

On the opposite counter were all seven Trevins and Phum, sitting, covered in flour. White paw prints from the floor to both counter tops could be seen everywhere.

Deborah tightly pierced her lips together to avoid bursting out in laughter. She grabbed a towel and went to Trevin. "Let me help you Trevin," she said as she started to clean him up.

Looking at the women, she said, "Hi Tarhana and Deiha, so happy we get to help you today." The others took Deborah's lead and began to clean their designated numbered friend while Zetia hurriedly took a broom to the floor.

By late morning a solid routine had been worked out by the helpers. Each put a Trevin on their shoulder, allowing them to keep the workplace free from pandemonium.

Strategically they included their ward by asking them their opinion about how to complete the selected item they were working on. Phum ran around the top rafter watching intently, but staying away from any further trouble.

Gravy was prepared for the roasted chickens and turkeys; butter had been churned; potatoes were mashed; noodles were made and in water boiling; a plate of cheeses was in the refrigerator; plain and cinnamon breads were cooling on the counter; coffee was ready to brew; and sugar cubes, cream and honey were set on a serving tray. Even Two's cakes were made with the required candles on them ordered by Trevin request. Tarhana and Deiha looked very pleased their domain was free from Trevin mishaps as they both sat to rest.

Phum jumped down and stood in front of the two women. "Madame, I have counted off the list and it would appear all is well except for one item. Sushi."

"Phum, have you ever really eaten sushi?" Zetia asked him.

"Well, I really thought I was going to partake of this great delicacy once. I saw its preparation when I was sent to Ayden's world. It was on a big box window in a home where a man showed each step of the different foods being rolled up in a bamboo mat. When he finished, he placed each section on a plate and picked the plate up where he brought it closer so all you could see was the sweet morsels. I thought for sure he would share. But he stopped and jazing it was gone," Phum said with sadness.

Deborah looked at Nick and both of them nodded at each other and smiled. Nick affectionately looked at Phum.

"How about Deborah and I stay in the kitchen and explain exactly how to make sushi since it is from our world, Phum," Nick asked? "And everyone else can be set free from kitchen duty," he claimed.

The sigh of relief was audible by all of them as everyone seemed to instantly relax. Trevin jumped down from Deborah's shoulder onto the table.

"Men you have proven yourselves today," he proudly stated. He scampered over to the sugar cubes, took one and ran out of the room. True to form, the rest of the Trevins did the same.

Three came running back in, looked at all of them and grabbed another sugar cube. "We forgot one for Ten," he stated as he bowed and ran out again.

Everyone quickly left after the Trevins. Except for Deborah and Nick.

Zetia looked at them and said, "You two need not stay. I know we have rice, avocado, fresh salmon, and green onions; we will make it work somehow. Phum will never know the difference since he has never tasted it before. Maybe we will flatten bread or something to look like seaweed. But we will make it work," she reassured them.

Eleea rested on the limb as he looked out at the lake. A flock of geese had just taken off in flight from the water and he was in awe at their grace and beauty. All of nature held a special place in his heart. Each season, each creature and each plant gave him joy as he watched it.

"I still miss Lora," he softly said out loud. "She enjoyed life and its glory too."

From above him he heard, "Her spirit lives on in you and Elora, Eleea."

Gethsemane flew down to Eleea's branch and continued, "to remember our loved ones with memories of happiness is a gift, Eleea."

"No one can take it away from you. And, as you continue to live, their spirit soars with you and strengthens you," the eagle expressed.

Eleea gazed at Gethsemane with deep compassion. "And, what about you Gethsemane," Eleea asked. "How are you fairing with your sorrow after all of these years?"

"To say I know exactly how you feel about losing precious lives to Choran would be accurate," Gethsemane revealed. "It was so, so, many years ago,' he sadly said. "It is the very reason I never felt the need to find another mate. I didn't think I could risk the horrific pain again."

"Orah, if she were here, would scold me right now," he chuckled. "And, she would be right."

"Life must go on and new life must be brought forth," Gethsemane wisely stated.

"Wallowing in self-pity where you shut yourself off is not good. Yet, the way they were all murdered by Choran's deception when she ingested the poisonous fish and then fed it to our newly hatched child. Well, it left me empty for a very long time. The guilt I carried for not being there was insurmountable," Gethsemane said.

"I too went to the Wall of Tears, Eleea," Gethsemane disclosed. "Orah never showed. Lok and Tari's parents did show, though. Which was a tremendous shock."

"Their words to me, have never left my heart," Gethsemane stated as he repeated them:

'It is not your place to stay in the past.
It is ours.
The gift of life is still with you.
Seize each moment and bring joy to the world.
You cannot look to the dead to fulfill you or heal you.'

"Profound words, Eleea," Gethsemane said with reverence as he bowed and took flight.

Eleea pondered Gethsemane's words for a long time. "He is right," he finally said to himself. "But he really should have found another mate. He deserves some happiness and I would have had such fun watching him be a parent. His stoic 'this is the way it is' personality would have been turned upside down with children," Eleea chuckled out loud.

The full moon celebration had finally arrived. Instead of the activities happening in the training hut, the Trevins surprised everyone with one more request. They wanted it outside by the Lake with a bonfire because Two would have liked it that way.

Tables were set for the whole community around a 'controlled' fire which Zetia made sure the Trevins understood what the word 'controlled' meant. Her overriding fear of their antics made her hypervigilant and she gave explicit instructions to Baris and Sahl to guard the fire.

The atmosphere was full of excitement as well as enjoyment by all. The Trevins acted like hosts where they would scurry around to make sure each person partook of their precisely made dishes.

Then they would stand at attention demanding the recipient tell them how delicious the food tasted. Even Ten was in attendance with his own specially made trough where the Trevins would periodically put more food into it.

Phum sat on the ground surrounded by his sushi on three sides. He would pretend he was rolling it, present it on a plate in front of him like he saw in the big box window and then almost squeal as he ate it.

At midnight the fireworks were lit and everyone cheered and hugged. As people and animal began to disband, Gethsemane turned to the table of travelers. "Nadab and Kalim have broken the amber. Tomorrow all of us will meet early in the dining room to discuss plans to move forward."

Chapter Twenty

Ayden hardly slept with her rising anticipation of possibly finding water as they traveled the next day. She quickly fed her friends and got them on the trail while she still tried to stay subtle as to why she was in a hurry.

Good time was made across the first two mountains, but Nip was meowing to take a break. Reluctantly, Ayden gave each of them a snack as she tried to remain patient. To make herself calm down she hummed while she worked.

Noticeably, her mood lightened and she started to think about how it did with song.

"The birds sing all of the time," she thought. "They sing to bring in the beauty of the morning. They sing to learn how to fly. All throughout the day you can hear them sing," she continued her thoughts.

"Seriously, without birdsong our world would be empty and sad," she decided. "Oh, Holy Crap!" She said out loud.

Both animals turned to her concerned. Ready to fight.

"It's Ok, guys," Ayden reassured them. "But I just had an epiphany moment. I now get it why it had to be me. Why I had to come to Hollow. And, why Joshua and Ehyah kept telling me to sing even when I am scared. Birdsong brings life and peace to the world!" She exclaimed.

Ayden's excitement bubbled over as she said, "I wasn't going to tell you guys, but when I climbed the tree, I think I saw water. We have another mountain to climb down and then if I saw it right it will be up the next mountain."

"Water?" Greysun asked. "Water like, in a puddle?"

"No, if I saw it clearly from the distance we were at, it is a pool with a stream trickling into it," Ayden described. "Real water, Greysun. Water we can get clean in and drink," she happily explained.

"So, let's get movin' team," Ayden said as she packed up the remainder of food.

They traversed down the mountain and were a little disappointed to see several smaller rolling hills in front of them. Even though they weren't large, it still took energy to go up and down to get past them.

Once they crossed the last small hill and began the decline, their steps became quicker at the hope the next mountain peak would show them what they hoped for. By the time they reached the top, they were exhausted.

Ayden looked at them, saying, "We will have to go down this mountain and climb partially up the next to see the water. I know we are all very tired, but I doubt I could rest even if I wanted to." Both Nip and Greysun nodded to her in agreement.

Ayden lightly hummed to help all of them stay positive as they hiked. Once they headed up the mountain, she would periodically stop with the hope she could hear the trickling of water.

The trees were thicker than all of the other mountains. It made sense to her she wasn't able to hear anything due to them insulating the land from sound.

Discourage hovered over her where she began to question her eyes. Each time she stopped to listen with no luck, her heart would sink a little more.

"Maybe, I was only really hoping to see water because I wanted to feel clean," she said to herself as they climbed. Swallowed in her self-talk of doubt she didn't realize Greysun had put Nip on the ground.

Suddenly, he took off ahead of them howling. Ayden stopped gripped with fear Greysun had sensed trouble. She reached down, unlatched her knife and picked Nip up to put her in the sling.

She waited to hear if he was in a fight. The seconds seemed like hours as her fear rose.

Abruptly, Greysun came running towards Ayden, still howling. His fur was soaked. "Ayden!" He yelled. "Ayden, it is the most beautiful sight I have ever seen. It's water, Ayden. It's water," he said as he jumped around her.

Ayden bolted in the direction Greysun was leading her. Sure, enough there was a pool of sparkling water with a tall waterfall pouring into it. She dropped to her knees at its bank and cried. Running her hands through it, she brought a handful to her lips and drank the sweet mountain refreshment.

She gazed into the pool which looked like glass and immediately became mesmerized by the beauty of color. Every green imaginable blended into each other as the plants and moss gently moved together with the rhythm of the water's movement. From light chartreuse to deep hunter green the whole pond created a tapestry of green hued designs.

"Nip, it is beautiful," she whispered as she let the kitten out of the sling.

"Can we stay here a few days," Greysun begged.

"Yes, I think it may be a good idea, Greysun, "Ayden said as she smiled at him and filled her water bladder with fresh water.

"But we have to be smart about where we set up camp. We can never let our guard down. If someone has come through Hollow and is on the march now, they will eventually catch up to us," she cautiously stated.

"Near this pool of water is where they would expect us to be. We will have to keep our distance from the pool. And, when we do approach the water, we need to be cautious and not careless," Ayden warned them.

It took several hours of walking around the whole area for them to determine their greatest advantage point to stay hidden. They finally agreed the other side of the pond, farther back and higher up to the left of the waterfall, where it entered the pool was the best spot.

It was difficult to get to and yet, gave them a lookout point to see down the mountain and across to the smaller hills. Plus, they could also see the pond which gave Ayden a sense of relief. Because she knew an intruder would do the same thing they did when they came upon it.

Greysun and Ayden began the familiar dig to build their new home. Once it was complete, Ayden went out of the cave to admire their work.

She unlatched the red vial from her belt. "This will make it easier for all of us to sleep in peace," Ayden said as she spread a small portion of the scent removal she had received from Deborah for her birthday all around their entrance. She climbed up each section of the mound hole to make sure every inch was covered.

"There, now we can eat and sleep," Ayden said triumphantly. She made herself comfortable in their latest dwelling and prepared their food. This time, she decided to cook their meal like a meat stew with the pool water and the greens of the different types of grasses they had gathered throughout their travels.

Greysun had even shown her wild onion growth he found on one of his aimless digging adventures. "That dog," Ayden silently laughed as she cooked. "He loves to dig up dirt for fun."

Ayden pulled out her special bowl she had received from Beynor at the Great Tree. She put all the ingredients in it and ran her finger around the edge to cook them.

Since the food was cooking, Ayden decided to rummage through her pack to see what else she could use to heighten the taste of the meal. Nothing really stood out, but Tarhana's gift of a small utensil of a fork-spoon-knife combo caught her eye.

She picked it up and twirled it in her fingers. The intricate silver design was gorgeously etched with pictures of vines and flowers.

Memories began to flood her heart. From the Great Tree to Zetia's, several moments of eating dinner with her friends engulfed her with sorrow and joy.

Ayden's body heaved with her tears falling freely down her face as she tightly held on to Tarhana's gift. Greysun put his paw on her leg while Nip jumped into her lap and whimpered. She continued to cry as she hugged her friends.

Choking back tears, Ayden said, "I have deliberately avoided thinking about my friends on the other side. My whole plan was to keep us moving where we were exhausted when we stopped. And then to start the whole process over again each day."

"I felt I would be able to keep the pain over all of our loss away from us. And, by the time I could breath and think about them, we would be back with them. So, I wouldn't have to experience the loss at all," Ayden sobbed.

Both animals leaned their bodies against Ayden and cried with her. The three stayed in this position until the food looked fully cooked. She gave each of them a serving in the pods she had kept from the hut. They ate in silence as they looked out the entrance to their home.

Finally, Ayden set her bowl down and pulled out her silver necklace with the wings. "I even avoided looking at this because I wanted to forget my loss," Ayden told the animals.

"There is magic in these wings, and yet, like all Eshra magic no one knows what kind," she solemnly stated. "But they are beautiful and hopefully soon we will know what power they hold."

Ayden looked at Greysun and said, "the man who kissed you on the head, Greysun. I think he was my father. I hope, I mean really hope we will get to meet him in the bowels."

She rubbed the wings as she continued to speak. "Sometimes it is so hard to wait for answers or to wait to see someone that you ache, I mean physically ache, from the pain. It's not an easy thing to do. To wait," Ayden expressed.

Ayden breathed a heavy sigh as she let the necklace lay against her skin. She looked at her ring with the peridot stone, and said, "I wonder?"

Ayden opened the secret compartment and pulled out her peacock feather she got from Kit. She breathed on it as she said, "I want to see Deborah."

The eye of the feather's vibrant blues, greens, yellows and golds began to swirl and separate revealing a window where she saw Deborah sitting at Zetia's dining room table. "Deborah," Ayden yelled. "Deborah! I am here! Look at me Deborah," she cried out. Deborah continued to eat, not hearing Ayden.

Ayden took the feather and put it back in her ring. "What good is the stupid feather if you can't talk to them," she cried out. Greysun and Nip whimpered with her as they stayed close.

"Ayd, Ayd," Nip said. "Ayd, we sleep. All better tomorrow, Ayd."

Ayden picked Nip up, kissed her, and said, "You are right, Nip. It is time for us to sleep right after we eat." The three of them finally curled up together and Ayden put her wing around all of them as they drifted off to sleep.

Chapter Twenty-One

Deborah found Zetia in the kitchen before breakfast. "Zetia, we meet in an hour or so with the rest to plan. Can I tell Iza to join us," she asked.

"I have spoken to Joshua, Callie, Nadab and Deiha but, have not yet talked with Gethsemane and Eleea," Zetia stated.

"Of the four who have heard, only one, Deiha, is leaning towards no. But, before the meeting I will find Gethsemane and Eleea and ask them," Zetia reassured her.

The room was full at the dining table when Deborah came down from her room to join them. The Ten, Deiha, all who traveled with her to Zetia's on the first trip, Callie, Kit and Joshua were already seated. No evidence of Iza nor a chair for her was seen. Deborah felt slightly disappointed the girl was not given the credence she felt she deserved.

Gethsemane flew in from the kitchen followed by Zetia and Nadab. After everyone was seated, Gethsemane began, "It seems before we can discuss our plans to move forward, we have an unusual request."

He looked at Deborah where he ever so slightly nodded to her. Gethsemane turned and said, "Kalim, would you be so kind as to put another chair at the front of the table."

Lydia waited at the top of the stairs for the chair to arrive before she began her descent. Behind her, Iza timidly followed. Lydia gently guided her to the empty chair and then took her own seat next to Nadab.

. Iza kept her head down with her hands folded in her lap and bit her bottom lip. Deborah's heart ached for her as it was obvious the girl was ashen white with fear.

"Iza," Gethsemane started. Iza's head sprang up with her name being called. She determinedly jutted her chin out to keep her head straight and looked at Gethsemane.

"There is one here who believes the rest of us need to agree to her request," Gethsemane stated.

"It seems Deborah has convincingly pled her case to Zetia, to which Zetia has then relayed to the rest of us the importance of letting you go with them. This is all fine, but what I need to know is what makes it relevant from you on why we should approve you going with them," Gethsemane asked.

Iza put her folded hands on the table, she intently looked at Gethsemane as she breathed from deep in her diaphragm. Her eyes looked like golden fire as she intently looked at the eagle.

"First, I wish to give thanks to the Messenger and her friends for freeing Raxton, my mom and I. Even Thunder who you call Ten is thankful he is free," Iza began. "Second, even though I was not an enforcer, I know the ways of the enforcer. I can predict their movements and strategies. Third, my senses are keen from living in the Dark Cell. Fourth, I am skilled at food preparation and,"

Gethsemane raised his wing and said, "Stop!" "I do not want to know a list of skills you may or may not have. I want to hear your heart, child."

Iza, frightened by Gethsemane's loud voice, quickly lowered her eyes. After several long seconds of silence where the whole room seemed to sit on the edge of their seats with fear for her, she began again.

"My mother, Deiha, told me the story of the Messenger and the prophecy since the day I was born. I hear her words in my sleep. I ask to go not out of vengeance to all we have endured while living in the Dark Cell. Yes, horrific assaults have happened to all of us who lived there and still to those who are there. But I ask to go because it is the Messenger who needs us," Iza said with overwhelming compassion.

"She has sacrificed everything to free us. She did not have to take on this burden, but she did. She did because of what she believes. I too, believe her and I am to stand with her and fight. It is all of our jobs to rise with her and conquer Choran," Iza said as she stood and banged her fist on the table. She quickly sat back down realizing she had gotten very emotional in her response.

Tybin tenderly looked at her, stood up and went to her chair. He put his hand on her shoulder, saying, "I can stand for Iza. Since we have arrived back at Zetia's I have secretly been training her with the help of Jerin and Nickalli. She is very sharp and willing to listen and learn. Her skills are, as she mentioned, uncanny on how she can hear differently than us due to living in the Dark Cell. Truly, she will be a great asset for all of us," he finished.

Gethsemane gazed upon Tybin with eyes of deep love, and said, "Tybin, you know the depth of trust I have for you. I have always viewed you as my child." He turned to Nadab and Lydia and regally bowed, saying, "along with Jerin I was given the privilege to help raise the both of you. It was one of the greatest gifts I have ever received in my life. And, even though I have this trust, I am concerned about her infantile exposure to our world. She still has much to learn," Gethsemane warned.

"Yet, I will trust your instincts under the condition you take her as your ward. It will be your responsibility to guide her to make good decisions. Not out of emotion, but out of sound strategical maneuvers which help all of you," Gethsemane instructed.

Gethsemane turned to Deiha who was crying profusely, "Deiha," he said. "Trust the Great Crane to watch over her. You taught her from birth to trust. Now it is time for you to trust."

Iza ran to her mother and put her arms around her. "We will be OK, momma," she soothingly said as she hugged her.

Nadab nodded to Tybin as a proud father would, and then turned to the group. "Kalim with the help of Raxton and I have extracted the seeds from the amber," Nadab proudly stated.

"The precious seeds are currently in an airtight vial as we were not sure if we should grow them here or wait until you are near the stone boulder to nurture their growth," Nadab explained.

"Deborah and Nekoh," Kalim said as he turned to them, "what are your thoughts on this matter?"

"Did the papers give any wisdom," Deborah asked. "I mean, I haven't had a chance to read each page, but maybe there is something in the writings."

"We haven't come across anything yet, but after breakfast it would be helpful if you and Nekoh could spend time with them," Nadab suggested.

"Departure is in two days," Gethsemane revealed. "Whether the plant is potted here or there is of no relevance. Retrieving it from the amber was our goal and it has been accomplished."

"Each of you need to prepare your hearts. As is well known, danger lurks at every turned corner when you are away from Zetia's. Tomorrow night Nadab and Lydia will present their special gifts they have for each of you. Today, rest my friends and enjoy each other. Zetia knows the path to take and will set the pace for travel," Gethsemane stated as he flew away.

Iza grabbed Deborah's hand. "Before you leave, I wanted to thank you for going before me. It is a great honor to have your approval, Deborah," she humbly said.

Deborah squeezed Iza's hand and then hugged her. "Tybin is right, Iza, it will benefit all of us to have you with us. And, look what a badass you are. Secretly training to learn how to fight," she teasingly said as she walked away with Nekoh next to her.

Kit came along side of Nekoh and Deborah and all three walked in silence for a period of time. "You know Deborah," Kit began, "birds have an innate sense of plant life and its properties. Did it ever occur to you, with your love of herbs and mixology, there may be more to your ancestry than you know?" He asked.

Deborah stopped cold. "Zetia said something similar to me before we left to fight Choran," she said with disbelief.

"You have the bird instinct, Deborah," Kit revealed and then walked off.

"Well, blow me away will ya," Deborah said to Nekoh.

Nekoh chuckled, saying, "You have to love Eshra magic. It always surprises."

Nick decided he would spend part of his day of freedom in the pool. He slid into the water and immediately felt all of his tension from the training hut workouts release. His mind drifted to all he had gone through since entering Eshra. "This has been the most rewarding experience of my life," he softly said as he closed his eyes.

An hour passed while he lingered in the pool. Off to his right he saw the water begin to mist as it fell down the scenic rock display. He slowly sat up to see what was causing the haze. He closed his eyes and opened them quickly to focus, not believing what he saw.

"Many more beautiful memories will be rewarding, too, Nickalli," the Great Crane said.

Nick's mouth dropped open in awe at the crane. "You are magnificently beautiful," Nick said.

"Thank you, Nickalli," the Crane responded. "I need for you to listen very carefully to me, my friend," the Crane revealed.

"At the farthest point in the bowels, when all hope seems to be lost, a dim flicker will appear. Follow it," the crane said as he bowed to Nick and disappeared.

"He called me friend," Nick said with wonderment.

Gethsemane flew down from his perch, saying, "Explain Nickalli, I am intrigued by your comment."

"Gethsemane, I was visited by the Great Crane," Nick exhaled with exhilaration. Nick proceeded to tell the eagle his conversation and the Crane's bowing to him.

"Very interesting indeed," Gethsemane announced. He lifted his wing to his beak and thought for several seconds.

"Perhaps, Nickalli, since the Crane mentioned all hope will be almost lost, we should keep this matter between us. You can encourage your friends when the time comes to not give up; but for them to know this, now, will distract them. They may spend waste less energy looking for the light and miss the ever-present opportunity to act appropriately to a situation where timing is important to survive." He looked at Nick for agreement.

"Understood, Gethsemane," Nick responded. "But I would like to tell my uncle," Nick asked the eagle?

"Yes, it would be wise for you to talk to Nadab, Nickalli. Lastly, my son, for the Great Crane to call you friend and to bow to you," Gethsemane stopped as he flung his wings out in full display.

"For him to do this, well, my son, he holds you in high honor," the eagle informed him.

Gethsemane fixed his gaze on Nick. "I too call you friend, Nickalli," he said as he bowed
to the young man and flew off.

Chapter Twenty-Two

Ayden quietly lifted her pack and slipped out of the cave. She relished the thought of having her first moment of privacy to take a bath by herself at the pool.

Entering the water, she swam out to the middle, floated and then dived into it. After she bathed, she washed her clothes the best she could and hung them to dry. Using the light of her wings, she sang while she waited for them to no longer be damp.

"What a beautiful day," she said while she looked around. With her wings in full display, she inspected them to see if she could fly. "Nope, I think they still need a little more growth," she determined.

She turned to look at the pond where they first entered the area. Paw prints and her foot prints could be seen all around it. Quickly she took her knife from her ankle and cut down a large tree bough.

She waded out into the water and walked towards the tracks. She then took the tree branch and slapped its wet limb to the ground to cover up the prints.

Greysun and Nip found her slapping the ground and started to go inspect it. "Stop!" She told them.

"We have to stay away from the pond entrance. If an enforcer arrives here, he can't see our tracks," she explained to them. "We can only enter the water from our cave side to avoid detection. The grass is heavy there and our prints should be hidden," she concluded.

Ayden finished the job and turned to look at Greysun and Nip who were sitting on the far bank watching.

"You two need to take a bath," she demanded. Greysun jumped into the water near Ayden. "Go back, closer to the bank, Greysun," she said.

"The muddy dirt is what you have to use to get clean." Ayden rubbed his whole body down with mud and then washed it off of him.

She looked at Nip and said, "You are next buddy."

"No-o-o-o, Ayd, no," Nip meowed. "Me clean all time. See," Nip said as she licked her paw and cleaned herself.

"Yes, you are clean all of the time, but sometimes you have to get really clean," Ayden told her.

Nip kept meowing as she stood with her four legs apart and began hissing. "Phfft, phfft," came out of her as she hopped straight legged.

Greysun came up on Nip's blind side, took his paw and batted her into the water towards Ayden. Nip meowed and swallowed water at the same time. Gurgling and meowing, she madly pawed the water to try and swim to the bank.

Ayden grabbed her just before she reached it and muddied her down. "Phfft, phfft," mixed with the forlorn meowing is all anyone could hear. Ayden washed her off and placed her on the bank. She let out one final hiss and turned her back to both of them while she took her paw to clean herself.

"Time for food," Ayden told them as she grabbed her dry clothes and folded them into her pack. The whole way back to the cave Nip hissed in disgust as she shook her paws to release the excess water off of her body. Ayden prepared their food and they ate in silence.

Ayden had previously cut boughs to cover the entrance to the cave to make it look like the trees next to them were growing in a pattern around the opening. Numerous times while eating, she readjusted them so they looked as natural as possible. When she was finally pleased with their placement, she sat back down and sighed with relief.

"I have new word for you, Ayd," Nip exclaimed. "irtate," she said.

Ayden looked at her confused. "Irtate, Nip," she quizzed her.

"Yes, as in you irtate me," Nip stated with authority.

"Oh-h-h-h, irritate," Ayden corrected. "Well, yes sometimes we get irritated with our friends," Ayden agreed. "But no matter what I still love you, buddy," she said as she rubbed Nip's head.

"Love too, Ayd," Nip consented as she leaned into the rub.

"I love you guys too," Greysun excitedly stated. "I have never said those words before," he disclosed as he sat down and started to cry. Both Ayden and Nip moved closer to him and hugged him.

"We love you too, Greysun," Ayden said as she put her face into his fur and cried with him.

Suddenly, Greysun jerked away from Ayden. With his ears cocked, he backed Ayden and Nip into the cave with his back legs.

"Unfamiliar sound," Greysun whispered. "Sounds like a man walking heavily and maybe a bird. But not sure about the bird, only heard one possible caw," he said as his body began to tremble.

"As long as we stay inside the cave, they can't smell us," Ayden whispered as a reminder, and then moved to his neck and lightly caressed it. She placed Nip in her sling and waited to see what would happen next.

Ayden could feel her heart beat faster and decided she needed to stay calm for all of them. She sat on her legs, closed her eyes and started to concentrate like she was taught at the Great Tree.

Several minutes passed before the faint sound of boots hitting the ground could be heard. The caw of the bird came closer as it flew around the pond.

"Stay perfectly still," Ayden whispered. "A bird's eye can see even the slightest movement," she reminded them.

The man finally approached the water and said as he kneeled to take a drink, "Flank, we stay here for the night. Both of us can use the rest. We will camp, hidden, on the other side of the pond in case the Messenger is near and comes to get a drink," he determined.

He waded through the water and climbed up the bank. As he headed farther back amongst the trees, Ayden caught a glimpse of him. He was definitely an enforcer with the hooded gear he wore. Extra leather adorned both of his shoulders like a fitted cuff. She saw how the osprey rode his left shoulder with its talons dug into the shoulder pad.

The man made camp and prepared food for his companion and himself. Smoked fish, vegetables and bread spread out on his plate as he sloppily ate. Once in a while he would throw the bird an extra morsel. He settled into his resting spot and became freer in conversation.

"When we get out of this hollow of a hole and get rid of the Messenger, Nahrita had better be thankful we volunteered and reward us handsomely for killing her. I knew it was sketchy to believe others would come with us, Flank. Waiting four days at the entrance was a waste of time. Even though she said she could talk Choran into ingesting more enforcers, I knew in my gut she couldn't," he revealed.

"Now, we are all alone on this forsaken mission. Even after we kill the Messenger, we still have to make it to the bowels. Good thing I was smart about how to get there. Sneaking in the snail fern tied to the underside of your feathers was a brilliant move on my part," he said as he chuckled.

"Nahrita," he said as he yawned. "She better keep her word she will meet us at Oshyama with the rest of the enforcers," he said as he lay his head down to sleep.

Ayden's heart gripped with dread as she heard every word he spoke. His camp was just below their cave and none of them could move for fear they would be heard. She waited until he was snoring, and then slowly inched her friends farther back into the cave.

Her body ached for sleep, but she knew she had to stay vigilant in case the man or the bird heard them. Early in the morning, the man stirred. The osprey took off in flight above as it circled several times and cawed.

Ayden strained to listen as she thought she heard the sound of a different bird. She decided her mind was playing tricks with her because she could have sworn, she heard birds singing to the morning.

"I'm sure it is my lack of sleep causing me to hear strange sounds," she comforted herself.

All of a sudden, she froze as the cawing came closer to the entrance where a small bird flew by trying to get away from the big bird. The bird's talons grabbed the little bird's wing and started to fly upwards. Several other birds came out of the air and attacked the osprey who dropped the bird. He flew to his master loudly cawing.

The man laughed, saying, "you know better than to go out on your own to hunt, Flank. When will you learn you can't beat the odds against so many birds? You, dumb vulture." The man packed up their belongings and waded across the pool with the bird on his shoulder, incessantly screeching.

Ayden could hear his footsteps climbing higher and higher away. But she made her friends stay extra quiet and not move for a very long time. Memories of Nahrita returning when they were hidden in the Dark Cell stable petrified her heart and she did not want the same thing to happen with the man.

After several more minutes a little voice said, "it is safe, Messenger. You can come out."

Ayden slowly crawled to the entrance to see who spoke to her. Sitting on a branch was a flock of sparrows, looking at her.

One sparrow hopped to the branch closest to Ayden, and said, "Your work, Messenger, has brought us from Oshyama where deep in the bowels a small crack gave us passage to Hollow. We bring seed to spread across the land.

"You have to go back through the bowels," Ayden frantically said. "You have to warn the others Nahrita will be at Oshyama," she demanded.

"We have been sent to spread seed, not to return to Oshyama," the bird determinedly said.

"You can do both," Ayden demanded again.

"No, no, we can't. We have been given orders and they are to be followed," the bird said as he flew away with the rest of the flock following behind him.

"Seriously," Ayden screamed after the birds. She sat down, saying, "What a bunch of simple birdbrains!"

She stood, walked outside and continued, "unbelievable! Now we have to worry about the enforcer and his bird ahead of us and about how to get a message to Zetia and the rest of them about Oshyama," Ayden frustratingly said.

Ayden cautiously looked around to make sure the enforcer was still gone. Disgusted, she said, "He was a real piece of work. Look at his camp, he left a mess."

She began to climb down to walk over and clean it up when she almost stepped on the wounded sparrow. She bent down to lift the frail bird up. "They just left you," she said with even more disgust.

She gently nudged the bird to see if it was still alive. No movement came from it. Ayden put her ear to its little chest and thought she could hear a very faint sound. She examined his wounds on its back and noticed his wing was broken.

Greysun and Nip flanked her as she examined the bird. She looked at them and said, "maybe massaging his chest will help."

Gently, she put two fingers to his chest and lightly pushed. She then took the same fingers and slightly opened his beak and put her mouth to it and breathed air into his lungs. Ayden repeated the same procedures, alternating between massage and breathing several times.

Ayden finally stopped, looked at her friends and said, "we need to have a funeral for him, guys." She put the bird down and started to dig a little grave. Greysun, always up for digging, helped her with the hole.

"Ayd, Ayd, Ayde-n-n-n-n-n-n," Nip yelled as she hopped up and down.

Ayden turned to see what was wrong with Nip, now. Nip was frantically hopping around the sparrow. She looked at the bird and bent down near it where she saw his chest moving up and down.

"Yahoo!" Ayden yelled. "He's alive!" She carefully examined him without picking him up. Little specks of blood could be seen on his bill.

Unlatching the blue vial from her belt, she opened it and let a drop fall into his beak. She laid his head back down, put the lid back on the vial and said, "Deborah said this was for sickness. I have no idea if it will work for his wounds. But, better to try than not," she said with hope in her voice.

Ayden walked over to a pine tree and took her knife to peel off some bark. She sat back down near the bird and started to shave the rough edges off of it. She broke the wood in half where she continued to make them smooth.

"Greysun, would you go get my pack," she asked him.

Greysun's back end was in the air above his head as he heaved and pulled with his front feet firmly lower while he dragged the bag out of the cave and then brought to Ayden.

Ayden chuckled, saying, "I do not think the bag is that heavy. Seems we have a little drama there, Greysun?"

She found the dental floss and cut three long strings of it. She placed the bird's wing on top of one of the pieces of wood and put the other piece of wood over the top of the wing. Surgically, she wrapped the strings around all of it and securely tied them off.

"We stay here a few more days," Ayden decided. "Until this little one is safe and, on the mend, we stay."

Ayden yawned, saying, "we all need to rest."

Chapter Twenty-Three

Early morning found Joshua sunning on the bench in the outer courtyard. He watched as Gethsemane landed by the riverbank and decided it would be a good time for the two of them to talk.

He approached the eagle and laid next to him. Gethsemane looked sideways at the mountain lion while he continued to tear the bark from the tree.

"Sharpening your beak?" Joshua asked.

"More like annoyingly tearing up wood," Gethsemane said. "But it does hone the bill," he agreed.

"Troubled, my friend?" Joshua pressed.

"I have not been on a mission in years, Joshua," Gethsemane revealed. "Now, Ehyah desires for me to travel with them instead of meeting them at the bowels?" Gethsemane stated with frustration.

"And, he wishes for me to reveal I am old Eshra. This. This is way beyond my comfort," he nervously said.

"Gethsemane, I am sure others have figured out you are old Eshra," Joshua revealed.

"I mean, they at least assume since you have been around for forever. Granted, no one speaks of it, but deep down they know, friend," Joshua uncovered the truth to the bird.

"Ehyah would not have asked you to do this great exposure if the time wasn't right. And from what you told me after you spoke to him, he believes it is necessary for your success. Trust Eshra magic, Gethsemane," Joshua encouraged him.

Gethsemane nodded in agreement to Joshua's words. "Yes, it is time to trust," he said as he flew away.

The blessing ceremony being held in the evening was highly anticipated. Not only for its glorious presentation and delicacies, but because it meant the next day, they all would be leaving Zetia's.

The whole sanctuary community came together to create the decorations, food and other special effects to make the night most memorable. Tarhana and Deiha were both relieved the Trevins found other ways to entertain themselves.

With all the excitement and activity, the Trevins were in rare form. They scampered through all of the pretties and secretly took what they could until caught and then would have to give it back to the worker.

Still, it didn't detour them from continuously trying to outsmart the situation by using one Trevin to distract while the others pillaged. They strategically placed Phum far away from the training hut to catalog their prizes.

He sat on the ground with seven piles, making sure each heap had the right Trevin treasure in it. To keep Phum happy, they each would periodically bring him a snack since they didn't want the off chance he would leave and another would find their riches.

Deborah sat on her bed, debating if she should take a nap when she finally decided to empty the contents of her backpack to take inventory. The last time she had everything on her bed was when she and Ayden were going through it.

"Even though I made her take most of it, she really needed all of it. I should have had Ayden take it all. She is the one all alone in Hollow and I have everyone else to help me," Deborah sadly lamented.

She took her apothecary kit, placed it inside her laid-out bandanas and wrapped them both tightly together. The twine, paperclips, duct tape and rubber bands were dumped out of the baggie on her bed when Marley whisped next to them.

"Deborah, I see a pretty you have been waiting to give me," he excitedly said.

"Hi, Marley," Deborah said affectionately. "Here let me connect them for you."

She attached one color each of the paperclips, gold, silver, green, turquoise and pink together as she handed it off to Marley.

The string dangled from his beak. He hopped and moved his head side to side as the clips swayed with his movement. He took a couple more hops and whisped.

"Well, I guess I should have held onto them, first. I didn't expect him to just leave," she said with disappointment in her voice.

Suddenly, Marley whisped back. "Thank you, Deborah. I took them immediately to my hiding spot to keep them safe."

As usual, he began picking at her bedspread. Soon he walked up to her knee and cocked his head as he looked at her.

"Uri, told me Ayden looks good," he revealed. "She is a brave Messenger, Deborah," he said.

"Yes, she is very brave Marley," Deborah said with a tinge of sadness.

"Do not be sad Deborah," Marley said as he rubbed his head on her knee. "Here, let me sing and dance for you."

Marley hopped to the end of the bed where he moved his head back and forth and up and down as he began to sing.

"Deep, deep in the bowels yeah mon yeah mon," he bopped to his reggae sound. "Deep, deep in the bowels Ehyah speaks yeah mon yeah mon," he continued.

"Fierce mon is our Messenger yeah mon. She brings Greysun yeah mon she brings Nip yeah mon and she brings Ehyah yeah mon. To the light she brings all of us yeah mon." Marley happily sang as he danced around Deborah's bed bopping his head all around.

Deborah giggled as she watched and listened.

Marley unexpectedly stopped singing and dancing. He stood tall as he said, "Did I get the song and dance wrong, Deborah?"

No, no, it is beautiful," Deborah reassured him. "Where did you learn to sing and dance, Marley? Is this how all crows do it?"

"Well, this is my way," Marley stated. "I spend a lot of time in your world, Deborah. Actually, your world gave me my name. I was named 'Boran' from the egg; but it is too close to boring for me."

"From a very early age I would find the reggae artists down by the wharf and stay with them. They taught me how to dance. Of course, they didn't know I could sing. We crows' are taught to protect our ancestry and its secrets and I keep this lesson close to me," Marley explained.

"Anyways, my friends at the wharf named me Marley. The name fits me, don't you think?" He said as he bobbed around her bed with his head moving up and down and one leg up hopping and then the other leg doing the same.

"Marley, would you like to be my guest tonight for the celebration," Deborah asked.

"We are always at the celebrations, Deborah," Marley disclosed. "We quickly whisp in and out where you do not even see us as we grab our favorite foods to eat. But, thank you for the offer," he said.

Deborah noticed he was preparing to whisp, and quickly said, "Wait. Marley, is Two your friend," she timidly asked. "If he is, would you tell him I love him and miss him," she said as tears filled her eyes.

"I will tell him, Deborah," Marley said and then whisped.

Deborah continued to sit while she put everything back in her pack. Tears flowed down her face as she played memories of Two in her mind. "He must be happy," she thought. "If Marley can talk to him, he must be OK."

Deborah took the yellow little button Marley gave her from whom she assumed was Two and rubbed it. She looked at her scarf with the fringed ends. Carefully she threaded the button through two of the fringe pieces and tied it securely in place.

Next, she took the plant with the purple flowers she had planted from its resting place on her nightstand and smelled them. They were from Two's grave when he died. The plant was known as an Explorer's Gentian. A perfect little six star petaled beauty with a cute yellow center.

Silently her mind wandered, until she finally said, "Wouldn't it be crazy if I had the ability to whisp? I mean Kit said I have the bird instinct." Deborah shook her head and said, "a crazy dream on my part. But it would be awesome to whisp to Two and talk to him like Marley does," she said as she put the plant back and laid down to nap.

Towards evening, Zetia rounded up everyone to walk with her to the celebration. Magical bulbs of light mixed with color lined their path. The training hut was already full with the community where laughter and music surrounded everyone. The travelers were directed to the serving tables and were able to eat and walk around freely.

Deborah noticed Iza at a table by herself. Her eyes were wide with awe and she had barely touched her food.

"Eat up, Iza," Deborah said to her. "Out in the wilds of Eshra there is no food like this," she said as she smiled at her.

"I have never seen anything like this, Deborah," Iza whispered. She looked up to see Tybin standing next to her and she shyly smiled at him.

"You will always see this, Iza. From now on you will be able to enjoy the true Eshra," he tenderly said to her.

Gethsemane flew to the center of the hut where an intricate wooden pedestal had been specifically placed for him to speak from. He raised his wings out to his sides to get the attention of all in attendance. The room fell silent, in anticipation of his speech.

"Tonight, we join in a most prestigious event. Each of you in this room have the privilege to witness Eshra history in the making. This moment will be written about, retold, and will be sacredly remembered by all of you. I turn the floor over to Nadab," Gethsemane said as he flew to the bench near Zetia.

Nadab stood, dressed in ceremonial dress. Dark tan leather pants with fringe up each side of the outer leg had small precious and semi-precious stones and metals attached to the fringe where when he walked it sounded like a musical jingle.

His waist up to the middle of his chest was wrapped in a brilliant turquoise, yellow, and red silk wrap which tied at his side. His off-white shirt tucked into the silk piece and his sleeves reached to the end of his wrists. His signature bandana around his head, to keep his hair out of his face, was deep navy blue with flecks of white and silver.

He bowed to the crowd, and began. "Those who returned from the Dark Cell received a feather from Ayden. I ask each of you to step forward to have your feather returned to you," Nadab instructed them.

"Baris and I have met with you before tonight and you have shown us which feather is yours. Baris and Kalim, would you hand them back to their owners," he asked?

After each recipient held their feather, Nadab continued. "You will see each quill has been tightly wrapped in leather with two free strands of leather for you to use to hang or tie as you desire."

"May these gifts from Ayden bring you clarity and assuredness in your walks. They are a gift to be cherished," he respectfully stated as he gestured for them to return to their seats.

"Now, Zetia, Iza, Kit and Gethsemane please come forward," Nadab requested.

Gasps could be heard throughout the hut as everyone realized Gethsemane would be traveling with the rest. Deborah quickly looked at Jerin and Tybin, who both had their mouths opened in shock.

"Zetia, I have chosen a bracelet as your gift," Nadab told her. He handed her a sterling silver band three and half inches at its longest points. The middle solid stone of lapis, was two and one-half inches in length and one and a half inches in width. It was held in place by a ring of silver around it.

Each side of the band displayed finely designed silver rope and abstract geometric etchings with turquoise, lapis and landscape jasper stone intermixed in it. The same type of silverwork wound its way around the top of the band where it made the stone stand out even more beautifully.

Nadab moved to Iza, and said. "For you I have an enlightenment knife. On it, is a turtle hiding amongst the vines and leaves and his eyes are made out of peridot. Also, I present to you a whip made from the finest leather in Eshra."

"At the end, it is frayed and dyed with a gradation of color to represent the beauty of a feather," he said as he smiled at her. And, one last gift, Iza, is your horse who you will meet tomorrow," Nadab revealed.

"Kit," Nadab said as he stood in front of the peacock. "Your armor of copper rides down your long legs and covers each of your talons. A cloak of emerald green silk designed by Lydia and I wrap around your back and is fastened at your neck with a peridot button."

"Gethsemane, my dear friend," Nadab said with reverence as he stared at him for several seconds.

He put his hand on Gethsemane's shoulder and said, "My friend, I present to you a medallion of copper with a woven chain of seven strands. One side is the moon with the Great Crane standing proud in the middle of it. On the opposite side is silver and brass with the Great Fox in the sun and the hummingbird with flecks of peridot on his wings flying towards it.

Nadab placed the necklace around Gethsemane's neck and stood back. He bowed and gestured for the incense to be lit. A slow melodic sound began to increase as he kept his head down. The same ceremony he had performed for the original travelers at the Great Tree began.

Deborah grabbed Jerin's hand as she whispered, "I have never been a spectator for this. It ought to be glorious to watch." With her eyes transfixed, she felt the butterflies in her stomach as Nadab began to sing.

His voice caused her to lightly sway as she continued to observe. He lifted his head and raised his hands high. In a circular motion, he brought his hands together in a loud clap.

The beneficiaries of the gifts immediately blew on their possessions. The smoke swirled in the middle of their breath and created a funnel cloud. A flash of lightning struck the gifts followed by the crack of thunder where Deborah jumped unexpectedly.

Jerin lightly lifted his hand and peeled Deborah's grip off of him. Deborah looked down, and quietly said, Oh, Jerin, I am sorry." She gently rubbed his hand to get the blood back into it because she had squeezed it so tightly.

Zetia moved to the center of the room and called Deiha, Raxton and Iza to stand in front of her. She performed the ceremony for each of them to receive the hummingbird tattoo in the palm of their hand.

Gethsemane waited until everyone was seated again. He bowed to Nadab and turned around to address everyone.

"Tomorrow we ride. All of us will meet by the Lake to say good-bye. Rest well my fellow travelers and know the Great Crane rides with us."

Chapter Twenty-Four

Ayden had gently laid the bird inside their cave on one of her bandanas with a cushion of tree boughs underneath the scarf. She softly sang to it as she caressed its head. "Stay here, friend. Soon, you will be well enough to join your family," Ayden told the sparrow before all of them fell asleep.

Once awake, Greysun and Nip played their usual tag below the cave as Ayden sat down at the entrance to watch. She continued to softly sing and hum for their newest charge as the bird was still asleep.

Soon, her thoughts filled with anxiety as she became anxious about Oshyama and her friends being ambushed. She stood up, grabbed an overhead limb and climbed the tall tree.

"We have got to plan our next move, you guys," she told the animals.

First, she looked past the pond to the hills to see if there were any others coming from the entrance to Hollow. No movement could be seen. She scaled higher up the tree and looked to where the enforcer had gone. Way up the second mountain she could she a tiny figure moving.

Ayden trapezed down the tree in front of Greysun and Nip. "OK, we can make good progress. It looks like the enforcer is far enough away where he won't see us if we wait until tomorrow to leave," she determined.

"I just don't like it guys," Ayden expressed. "Zetia has no idea trouble lies ahead of them. I know she has scouts and skill. But I have a pit in my stomach. We have wasted way too much time not moving forward."

"Sing, Ayd, sing," Nip tried to comfort her.

Ayden picked her up, saying, "Yes, Nip, I will sing. I know it is part of the whole plan and I have to sing. But my heart is heavy with fear, Nip."

At first Ayden only hummed as the three lay on the grass. Eventually, words began to fill Ayden's mind.

"From the bowels you will rise, Ehyah. Take my wing and ride my back. Together we will soar to the sky," she sang.

"The stars and the sun call your name, Ehyah. Listen to their song to guide you through. Where we will meet to take you home." She finished.

"Where did those words come from," Ayden exclaimed. "Are they prophetic," she asked. "Is that what they meant by sing when I am fearful," she questioned both animals who looked at her confused. Ayden stood up and paced back and forth.

"Ehyah is disabled?" She asked with a raised voice. "What! Is it he can't see or is it he can't fly or is it he is so far down in the bowels he doesn't know which way to go to get out of them?" Ayden stopped as she posed the interrogation to the animals.

"I, I don't know, Ayden," Greysun timidly said. Nip, also fearful, put her back against Greysun's chest and peered her head out past his large paws which held her in place while he sat upright.

"Oh, guys, I know you don't know," Ayden affectionately said to them. "My fear is getting the best of me and I am raising my voice too much. Sorry," she said as she sat back down.

Little chirps could barely be heard from their cave once all of them were quiet. Ayden rose, and said, "the poor little thing. I scared him too."

She climbed up to their cave and lifted him out on his makeshift bed. Gently she caressed his head, saying, "Sorry little guy for scaring you."

"No, no, no, it's, it's OK," the tiny voice said.

Greysun helped Nip climb up on his back. They jumped up to the cave entrance where they both curiously watched the bird and Ayden.

"Let me check your wing," Ayden said as she knelt by him and untied the string and removed the boards. Carefully she felt for damage to its wing.

"No broken bones, it seems," she said while she lifted each feather out. "Looks like your range of motion is good, too. Deborah's medicine must have done the trick," she victoriously said.

"Yep, I am well pleased with your recovery. Now, all you need to do is walk a little and test your wings for flight," she told the bird.

The bird chirped as Ayden set him down. He hopped once and fell. He tried again by standing first before he hopped. Soon he was hopping all around them.

He stopped for a second and fanned his wings out and lifted them up and down where he fell over and chirped like he was in pain. Again, he tried and his left wing drooped like it was broken.

Ayden allowed him the freedom to try each move on his own, knowing he had to do it. But when he let his wing droop, she inspected it.

"OK, my friend, she told him. I don't see any damage to your left wing. Especially since your right wing was the one broken." Immediately the sparrow switched wings and let his rightwing droop.

Greysun and Nip gasped in disbelief. Ayden smiled at them and turned back to the injured party.

"What is your name," she asked while she sat down.

"No, no, no, I am Lyt, and my job is to be the front bird for my fellow journeyers. This is why I was struck by the osprey. I am sent out in advance of my flock to take the hit when predators attack. This way the rest can either defend or escape; whichever is necessary for our survival," he said as he pushed his chest out.

"Well, that sounds gruesome," Ayden stated. "But it looks like you will be able to rejoin them and continue on your mission," she decided.

"No, no, no, I do not feel your decision is a wise choice," Lyt nervously said. "Do you know how scary it is to be attacked by a big bird," he said as he trembled.

"No, no, no, I think it is best I stay with you. I could be your friend. You called me friend. Yes, I believe it is wise, friend to stay right next to you, friend," he determined as he began to walk back and forth in front of Ayden and the animals.

"No, no, no, my name is Lyt, and I am your friend," he anxiously kept saying. "Please do not send me away to my death, friend," he begged.

"If an osprey came after you? You are big enough to bat it out of my way and then I will never get carried in its talons again, friend," Lyt said as he hopped to Ayden's hand and pleaded with his eyes.

"Lyt, we are traveling into danger," Ayden explained to him. "You going with us is more dangerous than you going back to your flock," she tried to console him.

"No, no, no, doesn't matter," Lyt proclaimed. "I don't want to go back to my flock. They left me here to die," he said as tears fell down his eye feathers.

"You saved me and I want to be with you, friend. And, I am a good helper, too. You will see, I can help you, friend," he begged.

Greysun nudged Ayden's back with his nose and quietly let out a whimper. Nip jumped off of the dog and went over to the bird. "Lyt, you stay. Lyt, my friend and Gaysin too," she said as she stomped her paw and determinedly looked at Ayden.

"Fine, I agree," Ayden reluctantly said. "Lyt stays with us."

"No, no, no. Thank you, friend. Thank you, friend. Thank you, friend," Lyt said as he bowed to each of them individually.

"OK, we prepare today for the hike tomorrow. We are not going to stop and take long rests anymore," Ayden instructed them.

"We have a mission to accomplish and we have got to stay focused," Ayden relayed.

"Greysun, she ordered, "you and Nip take the water bladder down to the pond and fill it. Lyt, you practice to get your wings stronger, and I will prepare dinner," she said.

"Ayden, have you thought about using the blue vial on you for your wings. If it helped Lyt, maybe it will help you?" Greysun asked before he helped with the water.

"My wings aren't broken, Greysun," Ayden explained. "Zetia said it is a natural process for them to grow back when you lose them. I doubt it would have made a difference for me," she concluded.

Greysun nodded and picked Nip up to sit on his back. The two of them happily went to get the water.

Chapter Twenty-Five

Lydia entered Deborah's room with her arms full of clothes. She plopped them onto Ayden's bed and looked at Deborah.

"You do not leave until this afternoon," she said as she sat down next to the clothes. "There just never seems to be enough time. I mean, time to be with you, Deborah," she choked out between her tears.

Deborah moved next to her, sat down and took her hand. "There will be years of time, Lydia. Ayden and I will see you many, many times over the years. And, maybe you and Nadab and the boys could visit us in East Glacier, too," she said.

Lydia giggled, "Oh! It would be so much fun to see you two there. Yes, it is a plan, Deborah. We will visit you in East Glacier next year," Lydia said with excitement.

"I look forward to it, Lydia. To be able to show you our world and have you become the student. Well, I am going to enjoy this little adventure," Deborah laughed as she thought about Lydia riding in a car.

"Thank you, Deborah, for making me smile," Lydia sighed. "I have clothes for you and Ayden," she said.

"I am sending Ayden's clothes with you because she too will need warm attire when you find her. An extra pack horse has been assigned to help with all the changes you will experience. Winter is approaching and extra precautions are needed for clothing and shelter," Lydia informed her.

"Both of you have tightly fitted long sleeve pullovers and leggings which hold in heat and repel moisture away from your body. Ayden's are turquoise and brown shades and yours are shades of orange and tan."

"There are contrasting colors in yellow and blue for each of you in sweat pants and sweat shirts too," Lydia told her.

"I have made you a winter scarf like your large scarves which wrap around your waist. These are specifically designed to wrap around your face and head when needed. There is one for Ayden, too. Lastly, leather boots and gloves with wool inside them. Again, Ayden's are navy and yours are light orange. Plus, I almost forgot, four pair of socks for you two to interchange as you desire. They are geometrically multicolored to make it easy to match with what you are wearing," Lydia finished.

"Now, Elora, come down here," Lydia teased her. "I could never forget about you. I have made you a lilac cloak with leggings. When you put your head down to touch it, it will magically cover your body." She explained.

Elora squealed as she hopped around with the cloak on and then sashayed in front of the mirror to watch herself. "How do I take it off, Lydia," she finally asked.

"Lift your head up and say 'remove cloak' and it will fall off," Lydia expressed to her.

"Everything is beautiful, Lydia," Deborah said as she rubbed her cheek against the scarf. "Ayden will love the colors you picked for her. And, I am excited to wear mine."

"Remember, Lydia, Ayden and I grew up in East Glacier. It can get really cold there. We know how to protect ourselves from the elements. So, take heart we will be OK," Deborah reminded her.

"I know you both will be just fine," Lydia agreed. "But I do have one more instruction for you and one request."

"The magic attached is in your new pack I have made for you. See, it is golden tan leather and fits nicely on your horse. It can hold a set of clothes for each of you, including Jerin, Tybin and Nickalli. It will shrink all of these clothes down where you will not even know they are in it," Lydia explained.

"Would you make sure for me they dress appropriately? My boys, I mean. Especially since you and Nickalli are more familiar with the harsh weather than they are," Lydia asked as she grabbed Deborah's hand.

"I will care for them like you would, Lydia," Deborah humbly told her. "And, again, thank you for all you do for Ayden and I. Now, I think I will go see Baris about how I want my feather attached," she said as she gave Lydia one final hug.

"Don't worry, Lydia," Elora yelled as she flew out with Deborah. "We will make sure the boys are kept safe."

Sahl and Baris were in the stables preparing the horses for travel. Deborah nodded to them as she entered. She climbed up on one of the waist high empty stall slats and planted her feet like she was sitting on a stool.

Each animal's coat was shiny and groomed all the way to their hooves. Next to them, each pack and saddle was ready for the travelers with their specially designed gear to keep all of them comfortable.

Deborah noticed Zetia's main horse had her signature bright colors of jewelry and fabric woven into its braided mane. Even his hooves showed inlaid metals and stones of copper, silver, turquoise, lapis and coral.

"Baris, I have been thinking about Ayden's feather and what I want to do with it," Deborah stated. "I was wondering if you could work another smaller feather into it, to keep it safe, for me?"

"Surely, we can come up with a design to keep them safe for you, Deborah," Baris stated as he walked over to her. He put his hand out and Deborah gave him both feathers.

Baris examined them carefully and then looked at her, saying, "follow me to Nadab's shop, I have a plan."

Deborah jumped down and walked with him. Once they reached the shop, Baris said, "Nadab where did you place the glass cylinder with the brass ends?"

Nadab reached up to his shelf and produced the slender foot long tube with smooth brass caps around each end. He handed it to Baris, who then handed it to Deborah.

"This is beautiful," Deborah exclaimed as she looked at the delicate tube.

"I believe Nadab and I can make this work for you to keep your feathers in it," Baris said as he handed the feathers to Nadab.

Nadab examined them and smiled while he said, "Deborah, this was designed for you. I made this unique art piece and had no idea what to do with it. Now, I can see why my heart created it."

He took Ayden's feather and placed Marley's on top of it at the beginning of Ayden's quill "Where did you get the black one from," Nadab asked.

Deborah retold the story to the men of how she received it. She revisited all of the conversations she had with Marley.

When she finished, she said, "Zetia believes there is more to me and Eshra from my ancestry. And, Kit told me I have the bird instinct. It has me very curious; especially when I think about whisping. Do you think I have the gift to do it," she asked both of them?

"Deborah, this is a question you may get the chance to ask Ehyah," Nadab said as he started to manipulate the feathers into the tube.

"Old Eshra would be where your answer can be found and it could definitely come from the Great Crane," Kalim agreed with Nadab. "But I only know of birds being able to whisp," he said.

"Feathers hold deep Eshra magic, Deborah," Nadab revealed. "To be given a feather by a bird is significant. The scapular feather from Ayden and the secondary feather from Marley rest beautifully in the tube," he said as he showed her the cylinder where they laid.

"Both you and Ayden have been given a feather from the raven family. Their lineage of whisping has me very curious, too," Nadab stated.

"What does it mean where both of you have been so highly honored by them? I just don't know, but I know it is not random and it is very significant," Nadab reverently said.

"Nadab, I would like to add one more thing to the bottle," Deborah softly said. She took Two's peridot stone out of her side pouch and rubbed it. She looked up at Nadab with tears in her eyes.

Nadab put his hand over hers and the stone. He smiled and hugged her, tenderly saying, "it is the perfect place to keep them all safe, Deborah."

Nadab gently moved the stone to the bottom of the tube and laid it just above the quills of the feathers. He looked to Deborah for her approval. She smiled and nodded.

"Nadab, I was thinking a brass loop could be forged at the top of one cap to allow Deborah to hang it like a charm," Kalim asked.

"Hold up, guys," Deborah stopped them. "Gorgeous as it stands alone, but a charm? It is way too long to dangle from my belt or around my neck," she nervously explained.

Nadab chuckled, saying, "Yes, it would be terribly cumbersome with it being so long. But there is magic attached to it Deborah. Once we have everything secure, including the caps it will be perfect for you. No integrity of its contents will be compromised and it will fit nicely on your belt or neck," he communicated to Deborah.

Kalim and Nadab worked the brass, making sure the loop would be centered and placed delicately. Metal working tools were all over the workbench as they planned the execution of the new charm loop.

Deborah held the glass tube in her hand while the men worked. Staring at the feathers and the stone, she carefully moved it in all directions to determine if she liked their placement.

Finally, Nadab took the tube from Deborah and nodded. She smiled and nodded back. He secured each section and attached a brass strand through the loop and soldered the ends of the metal.

The men had decided to add a small leather strap to Marley's feather like the ones already on Ayden's. And, then, braided all three leather straps, allowing them to extend out from the end cap as an added effect.

Once all the pieces were in place, Nadab placed the cylinder in a smoldering pit. The flames rose around it and engulfed it and then died down. A puff of smoke released as it lay in the forge. With the smoke still covering it, Nadab instructed Deborah to blow her breath on it to cool it.

Deborah let out a soft cry as it came into view. The tube was only four inches in length and held her precious gifts perfectly. She picked it up and turned to the men. "It is beyond anything I could have ever imagined," she said with tears in her eyes.

"It is beautiful," she breathed. She tightly held it in her hand and hugged both of them. She stepped back and took the brass loop strand and secured it onto another leather loop on the right side of her lower hip pocket.

Happy with how it dangled, she looked at the men who both had their arms crossed with a big smile on their faces.

Nadab stated, "Deborah this vial will only break upon your command. It will forever keep your treasures secure in it."

Elora flew down from the rafter onto the workbench. "Me, next," she excitedly stated.

"Well, what should we do for our friend, Kalim," Nadab lovingly asked.

"I already know what, "Elora claimed. "I want Ayden's feather shrunk too. But I want it to fit right under," Elora lifted her left wing to show them, "here."

"Hmmm," Kalim said as he thought. "The shrinking is the easy part. But to attach it to your body could be challenging," he concluded.

"I think we need Lydia," Nadab nervously decided.

"I'll go get her and send her down here," Deborah said as she walked out of the workshop.

Deborah relayed her message to Lydia and then went to look for Jerin. She found him sitting behind the sanctuary at the river.

"Look," she said as she showed him her new charm with her feathers and stone. "What did you do with yours," she asked?

"I had Father incorporate it into my quiver" Jerin said. "Nicely done on the charm, Deborah. But, more importantly, how are you doing and are you ready for this afternoon?"

"Ready as any of us will ever be, Jerin," Deborah responded. "Am I scared? Yes. Will it stop me from getting Ayden back? NO.!" She emphatically stated.

"But there is one big difference here from when we left the Great Tree," Deborah said as she resolutely looked at him.

"We no longer are children on a ruse of an enlightenment journey, Jerin. All of us are tried warriors united in the same goal to help Ayden accomplish her prophecy. The purpose. The danger. Both are real and need to be faced without doubt. Today we ride, Jerin. We ride to victory," Deborah said as she stood proud.

Jerin listened to her and then stood. He put his hands on her shoulders, steadied his gaze on her and hugged her tightly.

"Deborah," he said while he continued to hold her. "I am very proud of you. It has been one of my greatest privileges to walk with you on this journey."

He pulled back from her and continued, "you have made me a far better person than I ever thought I would be. It is an honor to ride with you and to stand next to you as we conquer evil and rescue Ayden," Jerin humbly stated.

Deborah welled with tears as she listened to him. "Jerin," she started.

"Jerin, I love you. You are everything to me. I too am a better person because of you. Together we will triumph and live long lives to tell our story," Deborah said.

Jerin grabbed her and kissed her with a long tender kiss. He let her go and looked into her eyes and smiled.

Deborah choked in disbelief. She stared back at him and said, "I did not expect that. I mean, it was nice. But I did not know I loved you like that," she surprisingly said.

She turned away from him and continued. "I, I, I never really thought about it before. But, if I were to be really honest with myself, I guess I did. I mean, my whole focus has been on Ayden and protecting her. I surely would have thought if I knew I loved you she would have been the first to know, not you," Deborah forcefully stated.

She turned back to look at him, saying, "yes, I do love you, Jerin. But it is to be kept a secret until I have a chance to tell Ayden, first," Deborah demanded.

Jerin lightly chuckled at her logic, as he said, "agree, we keep it quiet until after the mission is complete and we are all safe." "Now, you better finish what you need to do; it is almost time to leave." He nodded at her and left.

Deborah sat down on the grass, still in shock. "Seriously," she thought.

Fear gripped her heart where she quickly looked all around her to see if Elora was anywhere near. She breathed a sigh of relief.

"I have got to keep a close watch on myself to not alert anyone to this knowledge," Deborah said out loud.

"Close watch on what, Deborah," Elora asked as she flew next to her.

"Shit!" Deborah screamed. "What did you see, I mean hear, Elora," she sweetly asked her.

"I saw you sitting here and saying you have to keep a close watch on yourself," Elora innocently stated.

"Oh, thank the Crane," Deborah stated.

She quickly regained her composure and said, "I didn't want anyone to know how scared I am." Deborah bit her lip really hard until tears formed in her eyes.

She looked at Elora and blinked the tears back, saying, "don't tell anyone, Elora. I would be so very, very embarrassed if anyone found out."

"OH, Deborah, it is OK," Elora tenderly said to her. "I will keep your secret. And, I will always be there to protect you, my friend."

"Thanks, Elora, I knew I could count on you," Deborah sheepishly said.

"Now, that we have this settled, I have been sent by Zetia to tell you we leave in one hour. I have to go tell rest. See you in an hour," Elora said as she flew off.

Chapter Twenty-Six

Ayden smiled as she watched her, now, three friends sleep. Greysun was curled up on his side with his leg lightly around Nip. Nip was snuggled deep into Greysun's hug with her leg lightly around Lyt, who also was asleep.

She decided to let them rest longer so she could enjoy the silence. Knowing very soon their day would become busy with travel.

She rubbed her peridot ring and decided to try its magic again. Quietly, she pulled out the feather, breathed on it and whispered, "show me Deborah."

It swirled and opened its window. Deborah was standing by her tree where Ayden always wrote in her journal at Zetia's. She was talking to someone.

Suddenly, Jerin hugged her. A minute passed and they separated where she was talking again. Then, Jerin kissed her.

Ayden threw the feather in the air and covered her mouth to not scream out loud and scare her friends. Frantically she looked to see where the feather landed. She grabbed it to see what would happen next, but the image had disappeared.

"Show me Deborah," she quietly stated as she breathed on it again. "Crap," she said. Deborah was sitting with no one around her. Ayden put the feather back in her ring and giggled.

"Ha!" She said to herself. "I knew they were meant for each other." Sadness engulfed her as she wished you could have been with them to hear their response to their first kiss.

"Well, it is what it is. And, maybe it wasn't their first kiss," she decided. "Boy, am I going to have fun when we are finally together. If I know Deborah, this is not something she wants everyone else to know."

"And, I may strategically let it slip I saw her by my tree while in Hollow and see how uncomfortable she gets." Ayden giggled again at her newly hatched plan.

The animals began to stir and Ayden hurriedly prepared each of them a bit to eat. She packed their belongings, saying, "we have a long way to go. One foot in front of the other will get us there," she encouraged them. She caressed each of their heads and said, "let's get hiking team."

Life was abundant all over Hollow now. Green grasses, trees, which were mainly Ponderosa pine, mixed with other trees like sage, lodge pole pine and birch were sprouting up throughout the land in front of them. Even the dead shrubs and trees had new growth on them.

Two mountains and several smaller hills had been traversed and Ayden figured once they reached the top of the next mountain, they could take a break. She lightly sang while they traveled.

Her fear was ever present, especially if she sang too loud where she could be heard by the enforcer. Not knowing where he was caused her constant distress. Each time they peaked a mountain, she would have her companions stay extra quiet as she watched for activity.

It was getting late when they reached just below the peak of the mountain where she planned to rest. She whispered, "I will go up farther and look over the top to see if he is close. You guys stay here and remain quiet."

Ayden slowly worked her way up, hoping, by going slow she could stealthy sneak up on the enforcer, if he was there. She noticed as she climbed, the face was less populated with trees and was more shale rock and not pod-like material.

"Interesting," she thought. "My feathers better grow in pretty soon. We won't be able to climb these peaks if they are this dangerous from here on out."

She stopped to determine her next foothold when the loudest shrill of a bird was heard. She looked up where she saw the enforcer, far off to her left, approximately 700 hundred yards away being carried by the snail fern infused osprey with its talons dug into the enforcer's shoulder pads.

Immediately, she let herself slide down the shale rock and ran to the trees where her friends were waiting. She looked to see if the enforcer was following her.

Greysun quietly yelled, "quick get in the cave."

She ran to the cave and felt relief to see he had used precision with his dig. He kept it partially hidden and not easily accessible to possible intruders.

Nip jumped into her sling around Ayden's neck where she continuously trembled. Ayden waited until her breathing slowed and said, "I don't think they saw me. They were flying away from the peak when I heard the bird."

"No, no, no, friend. The bird will take you like he took me," Lyt said as he unceasingly walked back and forth in fear.

"I could ingest the snail fern, Ayden," Greysun said. "We can ambush them and find their vials where I can drink it and fight them."

"Greysun, I have seen the harm drinking snail fern does. When it wears off, you become extremely ill, "Ayden told him.

"No, we have got to think about this and make a well-thought out plan before we act," she determined.

"Each of us will take watch tonight so the others can sleep. I know we are all tired and we need rest. I will quietly sing and be first watch," she told them.

The animals curled up right next to her by the entrance and slept the best they could. Small whimpers, meows and chirps came from them as they would jerk awake and then lay their head back down to try and sleep again.

Ayden exhausted her singing where she was only staring out the cave. She shook her head when she felt herself drifting off. This pattern happened several times until she moved to sit on her legs, hoping it would help her stay awake.

Finally, Greysun nudged her, saying, "my turn, Ayden."

Ayden nodded, curled up next to him where she immediately went to sleep. When she lurched awake, she noticed Nip and Lyt were on guard duty.

Nip turned to her, saying, "we listen and watch, Ayd. Stay quiet. Not talk. No bad bird. No enforcer come."

"Thanks, guys," Ayden said while she rubbed their heads. "I needed the sleep and you did a great job. We eat and then we talk about what to do," she said as she got the food out.

Silence ensued while they ate. Finally, Ayden said, "I know why he had the osprey take the snail fern. The peaks are too dangerous to climb with it being shale and not pod and dirt. We won't be able to climb them either."

"The only real option I see, is to stay hidden until my wings can carry us," Ayden forlornly said. "Since he never came to our cave, I am sure they didn't see me and we are somewhat safe here."

"There is another option, Ayden," Greysun said in a confident tone. "I go and find the snail fern, ingest it and take the threat out. I know you said no. But you have the blue vial for sickness. If it worked on Lyt, it should do the same for me after they are no longer a threat."

"It is dangerous, Greysun," Ayden said as she shook her head no.

"My nose is the only nose able to smell it out, Ayden," Greysun said with determination. "It is my job to protect the Messenger. I made a promise to be here for the Messenger," Greysun revealed.

"I can't lose you, Greysun," Ayden said as her lip trembled and her eyes filled with tears.

"We wait until tonight when they will be asleep," Greysun stated.

"Lyt, the osprey won't even notice you now because he is so big. You will look like an insect to him. It is your job to fly over the peak today and find out their exact camp location. I have faith in you, Lyt. You can do it," Greysun instructed the bird like a sergeant speaking to his troop.

Ayden began to protest when Greysun put his paw on her mouth. "The decision has been made, Ayden. You will not lose me, I promise," Greysun said and then took his tongue and gave her a sloppy kiss.

Ayden hugged his neck and cried. Eventually she dried her eyes and said, "we will follow behind you, at a slower pace. But we will stay hidden in the trees until you give the signal. I won't let you do this by yourself. We will do it as a team," she forcefully told him.

They waited until afternoon to send Lyt on his recognizance mission. Nip put her paw on him, saying, "Lyt, stay low. Stay in trees, K." The other two nodded at him and wished him safe travels.

Lyt stood at the entrance as he prepared to take flight. He turned and said, "no, no, no, friends, I will not fail today. I promise I won't lose you today." He fanned his wings and took off.

The three of them sat silently waiting for his return. Seconds turned to minutes and then turned to a half hour. Nip started to pace. Both Greysun and Ayden tried to console her with nose nudges and hand rubs. But she refused their gestures.

At least forty-five minutes passed before they heard Lyt chirp as he came close to the cave entrance. He landed and excitedly started to talk.

"Camp is down the mountain at the bottom. It is only the two of them. I stayed hidden in the trees and watched them for a long time."

"The man is angry. He says the osprey will have to carry him from now on because the mountains are too difficult to climb with the loose rock," Lyt reported.

"The osprey is very crabby. He pushes the man around and demands more snail fern all of the time. The man fights back, telling him they have to make it last to get to the bowels."

"The man's hair looks like a porcupine the way it sticks out all over his head. The osprey's feathers kind of look like the man's hair, all out of whack and not smooth on his back. They are a mess," Lyt finished as he chuckled.

Everyone laughed with him and at him for how rapidly he told his news. "Nice, work my man," Greysun said. Lyt pushed his chest out with pride when he heard Greysun's words.

Nip sat next to him and bear hugged him. The only part of him visible was his little head poking out. "I so proud, Lyt," she told him.

"Did you see where the man keeps the snail fern," Ayden asked?

"Oh, yes," Lyt said. "He has to keep it in his side pack on his body because the osprey is very demanding. He told the bird he wouldn't get anymore if he kept it up and patted his bag."

"Great, this makes it even more difficult to get it," Ayden said. "Maybe we wait them out and let them kill each other," she suggested.

"No, we defeat them, Ayden," Greysun vehemently said.

"Well, it sounds like they are going farther away to the biggest peak," Ayden continued to argue. "Why do we have to do anything but let them go far ahead of us," she questioned.

"The plan has been set in motion, Ayden," Greysun said as he put his paw down to subtlety tell her the discussion was over. He left the cave and sat outside; signifying he was done talking.

Ayden's heart was heavy as she grabbed Nip and rubbed her fur. Lyt jumped to her knee and lightly sang to her.

"I don't like any of this," Ayden told them. "We are all alone out here and we have to be smart and careful about everything. I am not willing to risk each other when we can clearly avoid conflict," she quietly said.

"What if we have to kill the man," Ayden nervously questioned? "I have never taken someone's life before. Dignity and respect is what I was taught at the Great Tree and what I learned on our enlightenment journey. This is way beyond dignity and respect," she lamented.

"Ayden," Greysun said as he turned to her and continued, "this man you are worried about with dignity and respect has already said he wants to kill you. He looks forward to killing you, Ayden."

"Pull your head out of your heart and act like the warrior you were trained to be. You are the Messenger of Eshra. It is time for you to take the mantle and wear it proudly and fiercely," Greysun implored her.

Ayden stared at Greysun awestruck. The sniveling pup they found at the huts was no more.

"OK, Greysun, if we have to ingest the snail fern, then it should be me," Ayden stated. "Zetia says it does not harm us because of our wings."

"No, Ayden," Greysun emphatically stated. "I have more skill and knowledge by having lived in the Dark Cell with these types of people. It is my job to protect you as well as Nip and Lyt. We go with my plan. Only my plan," he forcefully stated.

Ayden slowly nodded her head at him. "Agree, Greysun, we follow your plan," she unenthusiastically said.

Greysun nodded, saying, "I go now, since we know the snail fern is on his person and he won't take it off."

He began to walk past the cave to the mountain top. The three of them watched him take several steps ahead of them and then followed behind him.

Ayden picked Nip and Lyt up and put both of them in the sling. "You two stay out of the fight," she whispered while she kept walking.

Ayden kept close to the tree line where she would stop occasionally to watch her friend climb alone. Deep in sorrow, she kept her eyes fixed on him.

A rash sound suddenly came from above. The shrill cry of the osprey froze her heart as she watched it fly over Greysun.

The man yelled, "Flank, take me lower, there he is!"

Ayden immediately took her sling off and set it on the ground. She unlatched her knife from her ankle and stood in position to run after Greysun to help him, if need be.

She watched as the osprey circled in closer to Greysun. Abruptly, Greysun jumped in the air at the man. His teeth latched on to the man's side pack and his head jerked back and forth with tremendous force.

The enforcer tried to reach for his knife on his pant leg pocket. But, the talons of the bird kept him too upright from reaching it.

Greysun's forceful jaws finally ripped the bag from the man and it fell to the ground. Greysun fell with it and rapidly tore it open as he smashed the vials with his teeth and drank all of the contents. He started coughing and his body began to contort.

The osprey dropped the enforcer down next to Greysun and the man went for his knife. He took Greysun's head and lifted it up to slice his neck; knowing he had a short window of time before Greysun regained his senses and grew from the snail fern.

Ayden bolted towards the enforcer and screamed in a high pitch battle cry to distract him. The man looked up as she came near him. He threw his knife at her and instinctually she fanned her left wing out to block the blade. Ayden kept running towards the man who stood ready to fight her.

Ayden stopped far enough away to not be harmed by the man and said, "I do not want to kill you, enforcer."

The man laughed with a cold cackle. He kept his grip on Greysun's head, who was still coughing and contorting, and said, "try and stop me from killing you, Messenger." He reached for his other knife to slice Greysun's neck.

Ayden calculated the distance she was at and knew her wings would reach him. She stood tall and took a deep breath as he kept laughing. She spread her wings and used the spine of her right wing to stab his heart.

He looked at her with horror as he choked, dropped Greysun's head and fell to his knees. Ayden twisted the winged knife, pulled it out of his chest, shook the blood off and watched as he fell dead, face down.

The osprey cawed an evil caw and swooped down to attack Ayden. Greysun, who had begun to grow as large as a horse, leapt in front of Ayden and sunk his teeth into the osprey's belly.

The bird screeched as it tried to get away from him. Greysun thrashed his head back and forth while he loudly growled. The osprey fell to the ground and kicked Greysun with his talons. Greysun let go of his hold and ducked the swipes.

The osprey hopped away backwards, took flight and swooped back down where he grabbed Greysun in his claws. He flew higher and higher into the air where he finally let Greysun go. The dog was in a free fall and Ayden knew when he landed, he would be dead.

Without even questioning if she could, she lifted her wings and flew after her friend. She grabbed him as he was rapidly falling and guided him to safety.

The osprey violently and repeatedly screeched in its shrill cry and then did a nose dive towards Ayden as she was putting Greysun on the ground. His claws took her off balance and the bird strategically flew away.

He came back at her from another angle, knowing she was dazed by his first attack. He flapped his wings at her head to deafen her.

Greysun roared like a lion and jumped above Ayden. With teeth bared, he reached the head of the bird, clamped down as it filled his mouth and then bit hard breaking the bird's neck.

All three of them tumbled onto each other. Greysun let go of the osprey and helped Ayden regain her stand. He propped her up by leaning into her body to steady her. Ayden accepted Greysun's body for support and stared in stunned silence.

The battle was fierce and quick, but she was suddenly overwhelmed with emotion. She started to cry as she fell to her knees. Nip and Lyt approached her and stayed beside her while she cried. Greysun, still big as a horse, whimpered for her.

She wiped her eyes and looked around her. The enforcer and the osprey both lay dead. "We have to have a funeral for them," she finally choked out. "Greysun, before I give you the blue vial medicine, would you dig a grave for them," she asked?

Greysun dragged the bodies into the grave after he dug it. All of them helped to fill the dirt over them. Ayden stood to begin her funeral speech.

"Death is never an easy thing to watch. Whether they are friend or foe, someone somewhere cared about them and mourns the loss of their soul. We mourn their choice to follow evil and to not know the joy of freedom from anger and destruction. May the Great Crane receive them and finally set them free," Ayden sadly finished.

She took out the green vial and sprinkled it all around the covered mound. She double checked her friends to make sure they were clear and snapped her fingers where it all disappeared.

Next, she took out the blue vial and said, "Greysun I pray this works. But no matter what we are here for you while you go through your transformation. She dripped several drops into his mouth and smiled at him as she tried to rub his huge head affectionately.

"Greysun," Ayden said as she grabbed his jowls in her hands and gazed into his eyes, "thank you for saving us," she solemnly said.

Chapter Twenty-Seven

The hour had finally arrived to begin the journey to help Ayden. Deborah looked out along the whole lake area where she saw everyone standing to say goodbye.

Baris and Sahl, along with their interns, held the reigns of each horse and guided the animals to their owners. Deborah put her forehead on her horse's head near its eyes and caressed his left ear. She kissed him and jumped onto his back. Elora flew to her leather and wool nest which no longer was on Ayden's horse; but, now, on Deborah's.

Deborah was pleasantly surprised to see a special leather cradle with wool inside it fastened to the back end of her horse where Nekoh jumped up to lay in. She leaned her left arm back and rubbed his coat.

Lok and Tari, both stood proud with Jerin and Tybin. Each had their own osprey wool nest on the boys' horses. Eleea rested in his leather nest which was now on Iza's horse. Nick and Phum mounted their horse and sat at attendance to move forward.

Zetia's horse's pack had a leather strap attached to a horse behind it. Gethsemane and Kit flew to the rider-less horse where they each, also, had a leather nest with wool. Farther up the front of Gethsemane's nest was a leather horned perch where he could ride and look beyond the horse's head to see clearly.

The Trevin's newly designed gear on Ten included a leather wool nest for each of them to ride in comfort all along his back. Iza's horse was dressed similar to Deborah's except for some simpler added ornaments like Zetia's. Behind her were two other horses with leather straps attached to her saddle and loaded with packs and supplies for their journey.

Deborah smiled with hope in her heart when she realized one of the horses was Ayden's. Every single horse had a small peridot stone woven into its leather gear.

There was no longer the need for secrecy in their mission and each member felt the power of strength with the openness of travel. Nadab, Lydia, Joshua, Callie, Kalim, Raxton, Deiha, Vexia and Tarahna stood together near the warriors.

A small platform with three steps to reach its base was next to Nadab. He walked up the steps and turned to the crowd.

"May the Great Crane speak clearly to your hearts and guide you away from danger," Nadab began.

"Each of you carry a part of us with you as you leave to fulfill the prophecy of the Messenger of Eshra. Trust your instincts, listen to your surroundings, and ride with confidence. The winds of Eshra will carry you." Nadab bowed to them and raised his arms with his palms facing them.

He spoke again:

"Cross to the East
Send the seeker to the mighty glaciers
There his search will see the one
Upon the back deliverance comes
At rest the crane stands
Head held high
When the morning sun kisses the day
The messenger enters through
Prepared to take flight
Riding the winds to the mountains
Where the dead tree stands
A fight ensues
The stirring sound rings
Throughout the lands
And, once again the wings of the crane
Bring the light of day."

Nadab lowered his arms and walked down the steps. He went to Jerin and Tybin where they gave each other the handshake of Ayden. "My sons, I will see you soon," he emotionally said to them.

Lydia came beside him where he put his arm around her. She looked up at her boys, saying, "bring her home quickly. My whole heart goes with you, today." Both boys leaned down to kiss her on the cheek. Nadab nodded to them and walked Lydia back to the others.

Deiha, with tears flowing down her cheeks went to Iza. She handed her a small bag of specially prepared food made by her. "My child, the Great Crane knows you. He will be there when you need him," Deiha said.

"Today, I proudly watch you ride as a free woman. I love you," Deiha said as she kissed her on the cheek. Iza tenderly cupped her hand under her mother's chin, smiled and nodded.

Raxton waited until Deiha returned to stand with them and then he went to Iza. "You are a great warrior, Iza," he stated. "They are lucky to have you with them. See you when you come home," he excitedly said as he smiled at her.

Iza smiled back, saying, "Yes, Rax, this is your home. And, I will see you soon," she lovingly told him.

Next, Nadab went to Nick, saying, "Nickalli, hold your vision close to your heart, son. And, do not forget what you were told by Ehyah; it is your key to bringing Ayden home." Nick grabbed Nadab's arm where the two held onto each other for several minutes. Nick nodded and smiled as he let go.

Kalim went to Deborah's horse and presented the precious glass vial with the seeds in it to Nekoh. Nekoh opened his bag and Kalim gently put the bottle in the bag.

Nekoh closed the bag and said, "keep this vial of seeds safe until I need them." Kalim smiled, nodded and rubbed Nekoh's fur.

He then looked at Deborah and said, "the three vials you made for Ayden, I now present you with the same." Kalim bowed to her where he then handed her the bottles. She smiled at him and he walked back to the rest.

Before Zetia mounted her horse, Joshua approached her. "Zetia, I see you standing at a crevasse looking across the horizon. The sky is black and you show concern on your face," Joshua prophesized. "Take the leap and fly, Zetia," the mountain lion told her.

Zetia bent down and kissed Joshua on the crown of his head. "I will heed your words," she said as she stood.

"Deborah," Tarahna said as she grabbed her hand and put a bag in it. "I have packed special treats for you, Elora and Ayden. The smaller bag is Ayden's favorite things. But you need to make sure she does not eat them all at once. It has been well over a month with her only barely eating to stay alive. Her body cannot handle a lot of rich foods. So, you monitor her, OK?" Tarahna smiled and patted Deborah's hand. Deborah acknowledged her and smiled back.

Sahl and Vexia went to the Trevins where Sahl said, "Men, a special pack has been attached to each of your saddles. Vexia worked until late last night to make special treats to put in the pouches. And, I have put an extra special individual shiny in each of them for you," he said as he gave them a big smile.

Havoc broke out as the Trevins started to look for their new packs. Sahl quickly said, "Whoa boys, you are not to look in them until you are far away from the sanctuary."

Zetia turned her horse to face the crowd, she raised her right hand with an open palm. The whole sanctuary of onlookers did the same. Zetia made a fist and brought it her heart. Everyone followed her action in solidarity.

Turning back to look at her fellow travelers, Zetia said, "we turn to leave the sanctuary just before we reach the mines. She heeled her horse and they began their journey to the peacock spider.

With Zetia in the lead, the order established for the rest was as follows Gethsemane and Kit, Tybin and Lok, Deborah, Elora and Nekoh, Nick and Phum, the Trevins, Iza, Eleea and the two pack horses, and Jerin and Tari with another pack horse.

It took almost an hour for them to reach their exit from the sanctuary. Zetia put her hand up to stop the caravan, she jumped down from her horse and raised her hands with palms out. The trees parted to reveal the wilds of Eshra. She guided each member out, followed them and then closed the opening.

Her horse snorted and trotted with excitement as she rode him to the front of the line. She turned to them as she patted her horse on the side of his neck and said, "Lander is excited to travel," she smiled as she kept patting him.

"There is danger in the wilds, but we are not under cloak and dagger this time. Plus," she swept her hand towards the Trevins, Phum and the ospreys, "we have a whole slew of sentries with us to warn if danger is close. Take heart and enjoy this beautiful land as we cross it to our destination." Zetia nodded to everyone, took her place and set the pace for the rest to follow.

The terrain took them higher and higher into the Eshra mountains. Three mountain ranges needed to be traversed to get them to the plains where rolling hills, flat land and deep crevasses would challenge them. Followed next by the swamplands leading to the ocean and Oshyama.

The plan was set to leave Zetia's in the afternoon to get them close to the peak of the first mountain. Here they would make camp and rise early the next day for the long trek across the smallest mountain range. Each step they took after the first range would have the elevation rising higher and higher.

Early evening brought them to the desired camp spot where Zetia and the boys skillfully arranged the site for all to rest comfortably around the fire. Deborah and Iza prepared the dinner while the boys settled the horses.

The Trevins were all over Ten. Causing the others to work around them as they each unlatched their treasure pack and scampered back to the fire.

Once they were all done eating and had cleaned up, Deborah took the time to look around at all of them. "Wow, this is a lot bigger group than our first journey from the Great Tree," she thought. "Extra horses, Iza and Zetia and two more birds. Granted, Ayden isn't here so in reality only one more person, but still, wow."

Deborah diverted her eyes to the Trevins who were lined up in a row with their backs against a long log. They sat with their pack of contents spilled out all over the place. Deborah looked at Nick, they both giggled and grabbed each other's arms in the handshake.

Hard candies of assorted fruit flavors in a jar were strewn out all over each raccoon's area. Packages of different sweet and savory morsels, also emptied, covered their individual domains. Their excitement bubbled to a heightened climax when each of them discovered they had a charm to hang from their belts.

"Trevins," Zetia chastised them. "Do not eat all of it in one sitting. We are not stopping if you become sick and you will have to ride in misery. Plus, it is a long journey and if I have to, I will take all of it away from you and dole out one piece a day. So, you better oversee yourselves and eat lightly."

"Madame," Trevin said indignantly as he stood, "we are only opening everything to see what we have."

Trevin quickly packed all of his goodies away and hid them in his little pack. He bowed to Zetia and ran off to Ten and put it back on his saddle. Of course, the others followed his lead and took off to secure their prizes, too.

"Let's call it a night," Tybin said. He looked up where he saw Gethsemane come in for a landing on his nest.

"I have flown a good distance around us, and have not seen any peculiar activity," Gethsemane advised them.

. "Our rest should be pleasant and peaceful," he finished as he settled himself in his nest and closed his eyes.

Nekoh moved close to Deborah and Kit who hadn't gotten into his nest yet. The cat prepared his sleeping area and laid down.

Kit let out an excited trill. "Oh, my friend I was so hoping I did not have to sleep in the nest."

He put his wing up slightly to cover his mouth and whispered, "I fear Gethsemane's loud snores would have kept me awake." Kit patted Nekoh's side like a pillow and plopped down and fell asleep.

Deborah stared at Nekoh with a humored smile. "This is how we slept in the wilds," Nekoh embarrassedly said. "He feels safe next to me," he finished.

Jerin had joined Deborah and they both nodded at Nekoh as they looked at each other and smiled. Tybin and Iza laid on the other side of Jerin.

Nick was opposite Nekoh and the Trevins placed themselves around everyone. True to Zetia's form, she made her bed with the horses surrounding her. Phum, Eleea and Elora were also comfortably settled in their nests.

The crisp night air and the smell of pine lulled the travelers into a peaceful sleep.

Chapter Twenty-Eight

Greysun immediately began to heave up huge black masses. His whole body wretched in pain as he tried to stay calm. Ayden quickly took her scarf from her wrist, drenched it with her water bladder and wiped his face for him.

"Greysun this what you have to do to get rid of the poison. Go with it," she encouraged him.

Between the heaving and contorted pain, he howled in discomfort. Nip and Lyt nervously walked and flew back and forth close by, watching every move he made. With each expulsion of snail fern, Greysun would shrink a little more.

Ayden was finally able to get him to lay his head on her lap as she caressed him and sang to him. Hours of the same behavior eventually ended in the dark early morning hours where he was finally normal size.

Ayden whispered to him while she gently rubbed his coat, "I know this was horrific for you, but take heart the blue vial worked. You came back to your size quicker than normal. Usually it takes at least ten hours of throwing up and pain to get where you are at right now." She coaxed him to their cave and got all three of the animals settled.

Ayden took Tarhana's gift and filled the spoon with a drop of water and another drop from the blue vial and had Greysun drink it.

Immediately the dog sneezed and sat up. He looked at Ayden with curious eyes and said, "I feel invincible! I feel as if I could run for miles and not tire. Ayden! I feel renewed!" He proclaimed.

Ayden looked at the spoon, fork and knife. "Hmmm," she stated. "I wonder what each of these utensils can do? We will have to try them out later. But now it is time to rest, Greysun."

Ayden sat at the entrance of the cave as the rest were sleeping. Even though the early morning smells of life amongst the trees filled her nostrils and was sweet, her heart was heavy.

Greysun inched his way next to her, and said, "Ayden what is troubling you?"

"I am only fifteen years old, Greysun," she said. "Fifteen and I have killed another human being," she choked out as tears ran down her face.

"I cannot take your pain away for you, Ayden," Greysun sympathetically stated.

"Life and the choices we have to make, at times, can be very real and painful. I ask you to think about this, though," Greysun stopped to make sure Ayden was looking at him.

"One, if you had not killed the man, I would be dead. Two, if I were dead, you too would be dead now. Three, Lyt and Nip would also have died this day if you had not taken action."

"And, lastly, the prophecy would be no more. Ehyah would never be free from the bowels and both our worlds would have died, too, if you had not killed the man," he finished as he put his paw on her hand.

"Wow, when you put it like that, it makes more sense," Ayden expressed. "You are right. All of us and even my friends would have died without the light returning through Ehyah."

"I still don't like it. Life is precious and should not be taken so heartlessly like the enforcer was so willing to do. But it had to be done for our survival. And, I know you can't take my pain, but you have definitely eased my doubts tonight." Ayden curled up next to him and they both fell asleep.

Late in the morning found Ayden in a clearing testing her wings. She could fly to the top of a pine tree, but felt exhausted by the time she returned to the ground.

Greysun, Nip and Lyt sat and watched her try each flight. Several attempts had already ended when she finally turned to her friends.

"I don't get it, guys," she said. "Why am I so tired, especially since I can fly now?"

"No, no. no, friend. Have you eaten any worms lately, Ayden," Lyt asked?

"Worms!" Ayden said disgustingly.

"Yes, worms," Lyt stated with authority. "Ground worms, flower worms, even carcass worms are good for flight," he advised her. "There is a protein and energy in them which helps us fly strong."

"Yuk!" Ayden declared. "Zetia never said I had to eat worms."

"No, no, no, friend," Lyt said again. "No real food in Hollow for you. Just little bits here and there."

"In our world, over there, beyond the bowels is normal and no need for worms after you are an adult. But babies need worms" Lyt advised her.

"Here, you are a baby again because no good food, friend. I will go get you worms, friend." Lyt immediately flew off to find the delicacies.

"Worms!" Ayden said again as she sat down to pout. "I do not want to eat worms," she pushed her chin out defiantly as she spoke.

Greysun began to exuberantly dig around one of the pine trees. He found several worms and lightly put them in his mouth. He came over to Ayden with his mouth full and tightly shut while the squirming prizes hung outside his lips trying to get away.

He placed them in her lap where his mouth looked like he was smiling as he sat in front of her. "Eat, Ayden," he said. "The only way we are getting out of here is when you can fly. And, you can't fly because you have had very little energy and protein."

He pushed the worms with his nose, saying, "I will eat one if you do."

"Oh! That really makes me feel so much better, Greysun." Ayden scowled.

"Boil, Ayd," Nip suggested.

"I don't want to eat the gross things, you guys," Ayden forlornly whimpered.

"Let's wrap them in leaves and you can pretend they are something else," Greysun encouraged her.

Lyt returned with three small worms dangling out of his beak. He dropped them with the other worms and stood back proud.

"No, no, no, friend I would have brought more, but they accidentally went down my throat. Hey! We could pretend you are fresh out of the egg and I could feed them to you like a baby," he excitedly asked?"

Ayden stood up and dumped the worms out of her lap.

"No, no, no, friend you are not going to feed me those damn worms like a baby," she frustratingly said.

She sighed, looked at Greysun and said, "fine get me some leaves you know to be safe and I will pretend it is something else I am eating."

Ayden scooped up the worms in her hand and began to walk. The animals followed her back to the cave where she dug through her backpack. Its contents were dumped out everywhere as she kept digging.

"AH Ha!" she said as she pulled out the chocolate bars. "If I take tiny little bites of the candy bar, and eat them fast maybe I won't taste their grossness," she determined.

"Still, it is going to take days of eating worms to get strong enough to carry us and fly for long distances," Ayden miserably said.

"One foot in front of the other is how we will get it done, Ayden," Greysun reminded her.

"Great now you are twisting my words to help me," she offensively said.

"Fine, all of us have to eat worms, together then," she demanded. "Since we are in this together, we eat together," she smugly said.

No, no, no, friend, this is great news, Lyt happily chirped.

"Ayd, Ayd, me cat, Ayd," Nip meowed nervously.

"Think of it as noodles, Nip. That's what I am going to do," Ayden told her.

Ayden took a worm, washed it and wrapped it in the leaf and choked it down between bites of chocolate and sips of water.

Her eyes teared up as she continued to eat. "You guys don't have to eat this," she finally said. "The more I eat the faster we get out of here," she reluctantly told them.

Each day Ayden had a new supply of worms provided by Greysun and Lyt. She was almost out of chocolate and was regretting the thought of eating them 'raw.' A term she coined when they were freshly brought to her.

By the sixth day, though, she could feel more strength in her wings and in her stamina. She continuously tested her ability by flying to the top of a tree and back down.

Inspired by her progress, she said, "Lyt if it wasn't for you coming with us, we would have never known how to make me strong. I will never like worms, ever. But I am thankful for you knowing their value to a young bird."

"No, no, no, friend, it is a good day I met Nip, you and Greysun. My true family, friend."

Lyt flew to her arm, bobbed his head a little and asked, "may I have one morsel of your worm, Ayden? I have made sure to not eat any and they look so inviting. I know as an adult we don't need them, but they are such a juicy treat for us," he explained.

Ayden took one of the small worms and fed it to Lyt. He chirped excitedly as he swallowed it.

Nip wrinkled her nose, saying, "I think I sick."

Ayden laughed at Nip and deliberately ate one raw. Nip stood up with her legs spread and hissed at Ayden. She then turned her back to all of them.

By the eighth day, Ayden felt she could carry all of them far enough to make it to each mountain. She looked up towards the tallest peak and determined they probably had at least ten to fifteen to cross before the big one.

"Tomorrow, we start the flight to the next mountain," she told everyone. But today we practice with you guys on my back to make sure you will be safe when I fly."

The first attempts were chaotic as Greysun had difficulty holding on. He easily got on her back, but the holding on part was difficult to maneuver.

He only had his teeth to use as leverage. And, his legs sprawled out where he couldn't grip any part of her body.

Ayden sat and thought about possible solutions to keep him stable. She dug through her backpack to see what could help them. She had four bandanas and one on her wrist she could tie together that might work.

Busily she tied them and then helped Greysun climb into the wrap where she tied it in front of her tightly. He immediately slipped out once she gained altitude. She sat again, wondering what to do.

"Hey!" She said enthusiastically. "I have one extra skirt we can use. We will have you put it on over your back legs up to your waist. Then I will put it on and you will fit snuggly against my body. Ayden took the skirt with geometric designs of trees and mountains on it and worked it through Greysun's legs up to his waist.

She looked at him and busted out laughing. He looked so disheartened in the skirt. Even if it didn't make his tail go flat, his tail would have been down because he looked totally dejected.

"That's not nice, Ayden," Greysun whined.

"I'm sorry, Greysun," she tried to sincerely say. "But this is going to work and you only have to wear it when we are flying." She tried to soothe him.

Nip walked past Greysun with a pronounced swishing of her hips. "Gaysin, girl," she giggled.

Greysun took his paw and put it on her back and lightly continued the pressure until she was laid out flat. Nip struggled to get out of his hold.

"Gaysin!" Nip yelled while she tried to wiggle her way out.

Ayden picked her up, saying, "We are sorry, Greysun. Aren't we, Nip?"

"Sorry, Gaysin," Nip meowed.

"Come on, Greysun, sit up so I can get into the skirt too," she instructed him. Ayden faced Greysun and put one leg in at a time. She had to steady herself against Greysun as she squeezed her body into the skirt.

Next, she had to twist her body around so he was on her back. Greysun groaned during the whole process in frustration and embarrassment. Ayden adjusted their skirt and Greysun's body, making sure he was centered.

She opened her wings and took off in flight. They flew around Nip and Lyt several times to make sure he was secure. Lyt flew with them once he saw Greysun wasn't going to fall.

Ayden landed and yelled, "Yahoo, we have a plan for tomorrow." She worked her way out of the skirt by having Greysun sit while she inched her way down with her arms first. Then she finally pushed her head down through the opening.

"There, now it's your turn," she said as she pulled the skirt off of him. Let's get some sleep, team. We fly tomorrow," she eagerly said as she walked back to the cave.

Chapter Twenty-Nine

Deborah rubbed her charm with the two feathers and Two's peridot stone in it while she rode. It gave her comfort to touch it, rub it, or just hold it because she felt like Ayden was with her on their journey. She even felt connected to Two when she held it in her hands.

They had already crossed the small mountain range with no Choran danger and she was feeling pretty comfortable they would make it to Oshyama without incident. Even though the country was gorgeous in its fall foliage, it still had been a very long and monotonous six days of travel.

The last mountain range was proving to be somewhat difficult to climb. The elevation increased with each step they took and Deborah began to notice the air becoming crisper; almost stinging to her face.

Zetia dropped back to talk to everyone, "we camp up ahead to prepare for the storm."

Deborah looked to the sky where concern gripped her heart. East Glacier snow came early in her mountains and stayed late.

"Will we be snowed in for weeks and not be able to move," she silently questioned?

Once they stopped, the boys and Zetia quickly erected poles from cut pine trees. Deborah took her gifted knife from Nadab when she saw them struggling to dig deep to set the poles and sliced the ground. Immediately, they were able to sink the trees into the ground a good four feet.

Jerin smiled at her and continued to work the braces around the poles to form a secure fit. Next, they took huge leather tarps and tied them together tightly to cover the structure. The seams were covered again with more tarps to seal any opening from the elements. But, to be doubly sure, Jerin took his enlightenment knife and ran it down each seam to magically close them.

The finished construction looked like a wood and leather igloo. It was big enough to keep the horses comfortable at one far end with the other end being their sleeping quarters. In the middle, was food preparation with a fire pit and seating.

Tybin took a hollow round copper structure from one of the pack horses and placed it near the right wall of the fire pit. He and Jerin placed rock around its base and Jerin sealed it with his knife.

They had left an opening at the top of the tent structure, during the first build, to pull the pipe through. Tybin went outside and climbed to the roof and he, Jerin and Nick gave each other directions on how to keep it in place.

Then Jerin went outside and climbed up and sealed the outer sides to the tarps. Lastly, Nick and Tybin took rock and logs and strategically placed them all around the outside of the shelter where they made sure the bottom was impenetrable with Jerin's knife.

Cut tree boughs were brought in for each bed and more trees were cut for firewood. The entrance had another huge tarp which could be pulled halfway back for an opening.

A pantry was set up against one wall across from the fire pit. The wall of their sleep area, had blankets and clothing organized for easy access. Past the horses, they even had a makeshift bathroom set up with a hidden trench which led outside and down the mountain.

Deborah sat with Iza. Both were mesmerized watching the efficiency of the boys' work. Zetia walked around the whole inside where she acted like she was decorating her new home.

She would place a short log for a chair or another longer log for a bench. Then move on to the pantry to place the pans nearby and organize all the supplies the way she liked them.

She moved to the bedrooms, where she counted to make sure all were accounted for with each saddle nest nearby and checking to see if everyone had enough blankets and sleeping bags. She even had ornamental containers with candles and potted herbs in mosaic containers.

Zetia walked outside and looked at the sky. Deborah followed her and asked, "How did you know it would be a bad storm, Zetia?"

"I feel it in my bones," Zetia said. "Close your eyes, Deborah. Listen to your body talk to you," she told her.

Deborah stood with her eyes closed. At first, her mind wandered with conversations and images of all the things she saw or experienced. Random, unrelated, scenes crowded her thoughts.

Finally, she took a deep breath and let go and concentrated on her body. Her head slightly jerked to the side as she felt an uneasiness. She rolled her head and her neck snapped. Suddenly, down her spine she felt a shiver.

"Whoa!" She exclaimed. "How did that work!" She shouted.

Zetia lightly laughed and asked, "did you feel your spine respond to the cold?" Deborah nodded to her.

"Well, my girl, it is called a bird's instinct," Zetia revealed. "Birds know to take cover and hunker down to prepare for storms. Not only birds, but most animals have the sense. Feral animals still have the accurate sense; but domesticated and talking ones sometimes miss the cues. Just like you because your mind is too busy and you are not listening to your body to warn you."

"Crazy," Deborah exclaimed. "There it is again, 'bird instinct' as it applies to me."

She looked intently at Zetia and said, "teach me. Teach me to understand. I know we don't know what it means, my ancestry and all, but this is way too deep to ignore," Deborah said with awe in her voice.

"Yes, my girl, it would seem your enlightenment journey is not over. I will teach you what I know," Zetia tenderly told her. "But for now, we need to take cover and prepare dinner."

Deborah turned to the boys when they entered the shelter, and said, "you three relax. It's our turn to work and nice fire, guys."

Iza, Zetia and Deborah thoroughly enjoyed their time together while they made the meal. Light conversation and teasing were abundant.

Deborah caught a side glimpse of Iza's dark brown hair and respectfully lifted it back from her face. Wrapped into a single tight braid was Ayden's feather.

Iza had started the braid close to her head above her right ear. When the braid reached below her ear, she wove in the quill allowing the rest of the feather to hang freely. Her beautiful long natural soft curls easily hid it from view if she kept the braid behind her ear.

"Iza, it is gorgeous," Deborah uttered with astonishment.

"I did not want to show disrespect," Iza quietly said as she kept her eyes down.

"You wear it proudly, Iza," Deborah quickly reassured her. "What you have done with it, is absolutely beautiful."

Deborah smiled, hugged Iza and said, "do not ever feel you have to hide it in your hair, ever again."

It was quite the sizeable group sitting around the campfire as they ate their meal. Even though the conversation stayed lighthearted, the howling wind, at times, would drown them out. The leather tarps would move to the forceful gusts and intermittently a whistling wind would enter from the top of the firepit pipe.

Deborah shuddered, looked at Jerin, who was sitting next to her, and said, "Boy, am I thankful Zetia knew when to stop and build. I would not have wanted to be caught out in this."

"We are lucky to have her with us," Jerin agreed. He looked quizzically at Gethsemane and said, "Gethes, we are very lucky to have you too. But I have to ask, what caused you to make the choice to come with us?"

"Jerin, sometimes one is led to make an unexpected decision like this," Gethsemane explained. "This decision has brought me to this time where it is deeply felt I should ride with all of you," he finished.

Jerin smiled and nodded his head at Gethsemane. He felt an uneasiness with the eagle's answer, but knew better than to probe anymore. Gethsemane was a deep respected member of his childhood and, now, into his adulthood. The bird had knowledge and secrets far beyond Jerin's comprehension where he knew not to question, but observe and wait.

Yet, his heart told him something troubled Gethsemane's heart. Jerin looked at Tybin where their eyes spoke what they both felt. 'Gethsemane was worried.'

Deborah felt the heaviness Tybin and Jerin tried to hide by their eye gesture to each other. She quietly grabbed Jerin's hand and quickly squeezed it and let go.

Jerin patted her leg and stood to get up, but sat back down when he saw the Trevins. They were in a straight line behind each other, waiting for Deborah to notice them.

"Madame, we have come to show you our pretties and to have you bless them with a kiss like you did so long ago for Two," Trevin informed her.

Jerin, Nick, Tybin and Iza each let out a small concealed gasp while they continued to watch. Zetia who was busy cleaning, stopped and stood next to Gethsemane, Phum, Elora, Eleea and Kit to see the ceremony.

Deborah's eyes slightly welled as she took a deep breath to stop from crying. "I would be honored, Trevin, to bless your pretties," she said as she bowed her head to him.

She looked down the row and smiled at their excitement as they each held their charm. Seven raccoons, impatiently waited for their turn.

Trevin handed her a tiny copper fox dangling from a short chain with a clasp. Deborah kissed it, rubbed his head and smiled. Quickly he went to the back of the line and watched. Three handed her his copper charm of an eagle, where she performed the same act as Trevin's.

For each of the copper pretties she did the exact same procedure so none of them would feel one got more attention than the other. Four's was a hummingbird; Five's was a crane; Six's was a lynx; Seven's was a peacock and Eight's was a raven.

Trevin, who was now at the front of the line again, looked at her and handed her his charm.

"Trevin, I already blessed it," Deborah confusingly said.

"Now, we need them pinned on to complete the ceremony, Deborah," Trevin stated with a sense of disbelief she didn't understand the whole process.

"OH! Yes, I almost forgot," Deborah agreed as she remembered doing the same thing for Two so many days ago.

Each Trevin member got their charm clipped to their belt by her and then took off to Ten. They jumped on his back and compared their charms amongst each other while they busily chattered.

Deborah turned to the rest and whispered, "I remember putting the clasp on Two's belt. But I don't remember kissing the charm before I did it," she quietly laughed.

Trevin came running back and yelled, "Nine, we almost forgot you. Sahl put an extra charm in my pack for you," he excitedly said.

All of the Trevins ran back, too, and were standing at attention for the new ceremony. Trevin handed Phum a small copper charm with a bear attached to it.

Phum bowed to Trevin saying, "Thank you." He tried to get away when Trevin grabbed his belt.

"Stand for Deborah to bless you, Nine," Trevin emphatically demanded.

Phum pitifully looked at Deborah with a 'do I have to go through this' look. Trevin pushed him closer to her, not letting go of his belt.

Deborah rubbed Phum on the head, kissed his charm and attached it to his belt. She smiled at him and he took off with the Trevins back to Ten.

"I love those guys," Deborah said while she stood to help Zetia. She looked at the ceiling to their shelter where the storm's bantering was louder than ever. "By the sound of it, I doubt we will be leaving tomorrow to continue our journey."

"Odds are good we are holed up here for a good five to six days, Deborah," Zetia said.

Chapter Thirty

Ayden woke up singing. She got up and walked outside of the cave to the clearing. She bent down to the grass and gently touched the new growth of flowers. "They are beautiful," she softly breathed.

All around her were fields of flowers swaying in a light breeze. Every color imaginable graced the land; yellow, pink, purple, red, blue and white to name a few.

She sat on the grass where she could see a light dew on some of them. Memories flooded her heart of Eleea talking to her in East Glacier about the morning dew. The dew being an elixir with the power to rejuvenate your inner core. He said it 'not only quenched your thirst, it healed your soul.' I wonder," she thought.

She bent down to one of the plant leaves and slurped up the dew. "Well, it didn't quench my thirst," she decided. "And, I guess time will tell if it heals my soul," she silently thought.

Greysun yawned a long yawn as he approached Ayden. He looked around and became overly excited. He laid down in the grass and flowers where he slid across them. Then would get up and do it again.

He continued this odd behavior all around Ayden. Finally, he sat, looked at her and said, "flowers, Ayden. Flowers everywhere," he said as his tongue hung out the side of his mouth. Ayden watched him in stunned amusement.

"I heard stories about real flowers in the Dark Cell," Greysun explained. "I never ever knew they looked like this. Or, smelled so wonderful," he said dreamily.

"Oh, my Greysun," Ayden caringly said. "There is so much more beauty you will see once we are home at Zetia's. I consider it a great privilege to be with you for each new discovery you make."

"Go round up the other two. We need to prepare for flight" She told Greysun as she sang and spread her wings.

Greysun took one final dive in the flowers on his way to the cave. Ayden chuckled at his sweet innocence and continued to sing.

"No, no, no, friend," came from Lyt as he flew towards Ayden. "We do not have to travel far anymore for worms with all these flowers near us," he happily exclaimed.

Ayden smiled as she watched him look for worms where when he found one, he immediately swallowed it. Nip and Greysun had also come out and both of them were sliding all over the flowers. She let them have their enjoyment as she walked back to the cave. She gathered all of their belongings and returned to them.

"Time to put the skirt on, Greysun," she calmly told him; trying very hard to not smile.

She turned to the other two and said, "Nip you will ride in the sling. And, Lyt, I feel it is wise for you to do the same. We don't want to lose you because I can fly faster and higher than you."

Surprisingly, she and Greysun had less difficulty working the skirt this time. Ayden readjusted it one more time to make sure her friend was safe. She planted her feet and spread her wings.

She lifted up and they were in the air. She moved higher and higher into the sky and then circled around. She looked down the mountains they had already traveled to see if there was any movement of other enforcers. Pleased the landscape was empty, she soared higher towards the next mountain.

Ayden figured it took them a good hour to reach below the peak when she began her descent. She landed a little wobbly and quickly had to steady herself.

Putting Nip and Lyt down first, she then reached to help Greysun get out of the skirt. She stumbled once he was out and sat down.

"I think I am weaker than I had planned," she told her friends. "How bout I sit here and you go dig Greysun," she heavily breathed.

"No, no, no, friend, I will go find worms," Lyt worriedly said and took off on his mission.

Nip jumped into her lap and licked her hand. "It OK, Ayd. We stay two day here," Nip comforted her. "I help Gaysin find worms," she decided as she ran off to where he was digging.

A few minutes later she proudly pranced back with a worm wriggling out the side of her mouth and dumped it in Ayden's lap. She licked it to try and clean it for her friend.

Ayden rubbed her fur, saying, "Thanks, Nip. I will just put it the leaf and eat it." She dug through her bag and produced a leaf and wrapped the worm and quickly swallowed each bite.

"Yuk, I will never eat another worm once we are out of Hollow," she declared. She looked down where Nip had found another worm and put it in her lap. She sighed, wrapped it and ate it too.

Lyt flew back and dumped his prizes in her lap. She looked at him, smiled halfheartedly and took them in her hand. Again, she sighed and sucked them in like a spaghetti noodle without chewing them because they were small. She quickly took the water bladder and drank until her throat was clear.

Greysun finished the cave and gently nudged Ayden towards it. She followed his lead and laid down inside. All three animals surrounded her, with Greysun letting her use him as her pillow. She curled up, picked up Nip and put her near her chest. She smiled as Lyt settled next to them. Within minutes, they were all asleep.

Ayden woke to the swirling mist off to her right. She waited for the crane to show himself. He looked at her and she immediately took over the conversation.

"Do you realize what I have had to do for you?" She didn't wait for him to answer as she continued, "you and the other birds may enjoy worms, but I hate them. I am sick and tired of eating them," she yelled.

Ehyah patiently waited for her to finish her rant. She stopped and stared at him defiantly.

"Look at your foot, Ayden."

She glanced down to see a stem with three large leaves, a tiny pinkish white droopy flower and fairly good size blueish purple berries on it laying by her foot.

"Eat these berries, Ayden," the crane told her. "It is a Black Blueberry plant. You will love them. They taste like huckleberries. It is a rare and prized plant that will give you tremendous energy. When you use the fork which Tarahna gave you to eat these berries, it will enhance the properties of them to help you gain strength. And, you won't have to eat worms anymore," he told her as he lightly chuckled.

"Well, thank you, but I do not think any of this is funny," Ayden disgustedly said.

"We are proud of you, Ayden," the crane revealed.

"We? What the hell do you mean by we?" Ayden demanded.

"Remember, listen to the stirring," he said as he vanished.

"Well, that's just great. I could have been eating berries all of this time. You think he would have come to me at the start to tell me about the damn berries," she yelled.

The animals jolted awake from her loud voice and looked at her half-scared and half-confused.

Ayden quickly settled down, saying, "It's OK, guys. I have been visited by Crane and I was mad at him because he told me I could have eaten berries this whole time instead of worms to gain strength.

I'm not yelling at you guys," she reassured them as she rubbed their fur and smiled at Lyt.

No, no, no, friend, these berries are all around Hollow, friend. Why did you not tell me you liked berries," he innocently asked?

Ayden looked at Lyt, dumbfounded. "Innocence sometimes is not a virtue," she said to herself.

She sweetly smiled at Lyt, and said, "well, Lyt, I just wasn't thinking, I guess. But, from now on I will only being eating berries and not worms," she told all three of them with a determined voice.

"I'm going outside to look around," Ayden informed them. She walked outside and looked at the landscape.

"Lyt, it is your job to find us a pond close by. I need a bath," she determined.

"Greysun and Nip, go find me some berries like these right here," she said as she showed them the stem with the flower and berries. "And, then when you guys get back, we will eat breakfast," she said to encourage them to work quickly.

Lyt came back fairly fast and was animated as he lit near Ayden. "Farther up the mountain on the right side is a small pond with plenty of water to take a bath," he proudly stated.

"OK, a couple of things, here," Ayden said to Lyt. "One, is it big enough for me to take a bath or big enough for you to take a bath? Second, can we walk to it or do I have to put Greysun in the skirt to get to it?" Ayden asked.

"OH, no, no, no, friend, yes, big enough for all of us," Lyt declared. "Greysun and Nip can walk with you to it. It is right over there," he said as he pointed his wing to the right.

Ayden walked back to the cave where Black Blueberry leaves, flowers and berries were strewn all over. She looked at Greysun, while she tried to hide her frustration, saying, "did you notice here, Greysun, you dug in a Black Blueberry patch?"

"Hey! Nip and I don't have to go search for them, Ayden. We have plenty right here," Greysun said as he jumped around with excitement and started to gather the berries in his mouth.

Ayden shook her head, went inside the cave and started to prepare breakfast. She looked at the food they had been eating since their entrance to Hollow.

"So, I just don't get it. All of these dried fruits, vegetables, meats and nuts are filled with protein and whatever else. How come they didn't work to keep me healthy and able to fly?"

"No, no, no, friend, fresh is life," Lyt tried to explain. "This food," he pointed with his wing at the dried heap, "is good with plenty of protein, but it is not true, fresh life food."

"Yes, friend it would have helped you. But you hardly eat. I have watched. You make sure everyone else eats and you watch. Not enough food energy to help you fly."

With her hand full of berries, Ayden poked them with the fork to pop them in her mouth as she contemplated Lyt's explanation. "Mmmm, these are delicious. You guys don't even know how excited I am to not have to eat worms anymore," she expressed with relief.

Ayden made three piles of food, each the designated size for each animal. She added berries to their portions and sat back, smiling at their pleasure of gobbling up the food with joy.

Ayden continued to sit with berries in her hand. She stabbed them one at a time to eat them while she thought about the crane.

"Crane said, 'we are proud of you' not 'I am proud of you', but we? The only other person I know to have gone through Hollow and survived is the man you talked to, Greysun. And, that man definitely resembled my dad. It has got to be Zayden who is proud of me," she shouted!

Ayden stood, picked up Nip and swung her around in her arms. "Nip, we get to meet my dad," she said with anticipation.

"Now," Ayden began as she slung Nip under her arm, "we go bathe." Nip started to squirm, trying to get out of Ayden's death hold on her. Ayden kept walking with her, determined all of them needed a bath.

Lyt led the way up the mountain a short distance and then turned to his right around the side of the natural edifice. The pond looked like the one they had seen before, except this one also had flowers all around it. Ayden set Nip down and walked to its edge to soak her feet.

"This is the second-best thing," Ayden revealed. "Not having to eat worms anymore and now I get to take a bath," she gleefully expressed.

Ayden looked at her friends and said," here's the deal, you three, I am taking a bath. Which means I will have my clothes off. You three are to keep your backs to me while I enjoy my bath. No turning to look, no impatience, you sit and look down the mountain until I am done," she demanded.

Ayden waited until all of them were sitting with their backs to her and walked deep into the water. She quickly turned around to see if any of them were watching. She giggled to herself when she saw them. Stone statues, from tall to short staying perfectly still with their heads forward.

Like the last time she bathed, Ayden made sure every part of her body was rubbed down with mud and then cleansed off. She breathed a sigh of triumphant. Once she was dressed appropriately, she told her friends they could look now.

"Your turn, Greysun," Ayden yelled while he jumped to her and she cleaned him. After he was finished, she started to talk to Nip. But Nip was nowhere to be found.

Ayden got out of the water and looked around. "Nip," she yelled with no answer from the kitten. She yelled again as she searched the tall grass.

"No, no, no, friend, Nip is over here," Lyt stated as he flew next to Nip.

Nip hissed at Lyt, saying, "no friend, Lyt," and then continued to hiss at him.

Ayden quickly went to grab her while she was still hissing. Nip tried to bolt when she saw Ayden come close to her. Ayden had to lurch forward to get her back leg, where Nip hissed defiantly.

Every step Ayden took towards the pond, Nip hissed. Ayden held onto her tightly and at the same time tenderly to not hurt her and dunked her in the water.

Nip yelled through her gurgling cries, "Ayd, no give me time to plug nose, mouth," she forlornly meowed.

After she was clean, Ayden set her on the dry grass. Nip shook her paws one at a time as she disgustedly walked farther up the bank, she continued to shake them as she went.

Ayden washed all of her clothes and hung them on a pine limb to dry. She sat near them and gazed at the beautiful scenery in front of her. All around them life was living abundantly.

Peace engulfed her as she lightly sang. She watched as the animals played tag, with Lyt now joining in their fun. She repositioned her body to sit up straight when she realized off to her left, farther up, was a smaller pond with what looked like rock around it. It almost looked like a manmade well to get water out of.

She walked over to it and knelt down to fill her water bladder when suddenly the water began to smoke like a hot spring. She removed her bladder and peered deeper into the pool.

The smoke cleared and showed what appeared to be glass. An image of a reflection appeared and the man seemed to be smiling at her. She saw his long black hair, a pocket with a turquoise button on his loose-fitting smock, and a scarf wrapped around his right wrist. Ayden screamed and then put her hand over her mouth.

"Ayden, you are beautiful," the man said.

Tears rolled down Ayden's cheeks as she stared with a little fear in her heart.

"Don't cry, child," he said.

"Dad?" Ayden questioned.

"Yes, it is me, Zayden, your father," he told her.

"Why now," Ayden asked? "Why not wait until I see you in person. Physically, I mean," Ayden said in a perplexed voice.

She looked at him and continued, "I have so many questions. I, I am, I am so confused right now," she exclaimed. "And, you know what my first question is? Why did you leave me?"

"Ayden, it was a choice I did not want to make," Zayden began. "When you were born, it was the greatest day of my life. I was beyond honored when your mother asked if she could call you Ayden. I loved you and carried you for months and sang to you all of the time."

"We lived in the mountains just outside of East Glacier and were very happy. Your mother did not know about Eshra. I had planned on telling her and taking her there after you got older."

"Then, one night while I was bathing you, I took a closer look at your back. I saw the mark of the crane and knew who you would become," he reverently told her.

"For your safety, I had to disappear. If Choran found you, through me, he would have killed you," Zayden explained.

"I choose to disappear without telling your mother, I made it look like I was in an accident where she thought I had died," he continued to explain.

"I placed a box near her bed with gold, silver, the wing charm you now wear and enough money to make sure both of you were well taken care of. I returned to Eshra and told no one about you. I had to protect you," he desperately said.

"I heard rumors of talk saying Choran was going after the Messenger of Eshra. I traveled to the Dark Cell to gather information on what Choran really knew," he continued.

"Choran only suspected the Messenger was in your world. He really had no clue who he was looking for," Zayden said with relief in his voice.

"I made a decision right there in front of him, to go where he had sent Ehyah in order to make sure you would succeed in the prophecy and in Hollow. The only way for me to go, was for Choran to think it was his idea to swallow me," Zayden disclosed.

"Ayden, I am sorry I could not stay with you and your mother," he sadly stated. "I am sorry for any doubt you have felt because I could not nurture you throughout your life. But we will meet, physically, Ayden. Soon," he promised.

"Don't you leave," Ayden commanded in a raised voice. "I know that tone of deliver a message and disappear. Crane does it to me all of the time. Don't you leave just yet," she begged.

Zayden chuckled, saying, "I wasn't going to leave, Ayden. I still have some information to give you. And, may I say you have a little of Zetia's spunk in you," he chuckled again.

Ayden felt her body relax as she waited to hear what he had to say. She readjusted her position to sit more comfortably while she listened. She looked at him and said, "Shoot."

Zayden chuckled again at her matter-of-fact attitude and began, "Once you reach the tallest peak you will need to look for a passage inside the mountain. This passage will take you far, far down into the bowels. Ehyah and I are in the deep recesses there. It will be difficult for you to find us. Here is where you need to listen for the stirring, it will guide you to us," he explained.

"Zetia and the rest are traveling in a different direction to reach you. It is the only way they can enter the bowels. All of you will reunite, soon," he encouraged her.

"But you must realize they, too, will have difficulty in the bowels. Keep your senses alert for the stirring, Ayden, as it will help all of you," he instructed.

"Those who carry your feather with them hold power they are not aware of," Zayden revealed. "Your feathers are those of the Messenger of Eshra, my child. The feather they hold protects them from Choran's death grip."

"Now, I must go and you must fly to the tallest peak," he reluctantly stated. "I love you, Ayden. And, like 'Crane' said," he smiled teasingly at her; using her term for the Great Crane, "we are so deeply proud of you." Zayden disappeared as the water moved with soft waves across it.

Ayden stood, looked at her friends who she did not know had joined her and sighed. "Well, he answered questions, and as usual he left me with a whole bunch more," she said.

"We stay here until I have enough strength and then we fly," she determinedly stated as she gathered her clothes and began to walk back to the cave.

Chapter Thirty-One

Five full days of wind and snow created whiteout conditions where the travelers barely exited the shelter. Deborah felt like she would go stir crazy as she thought about Ayden.

Zetia helped her understand each feather of a bird and its importance to flight while they were sequestered. From egg to adult she now knew how they learned to fly and how they diverted danger like Elora had done when they fought Nahrita and her followers.

Eleea and Elora were totally thrilled they got to support Deborah in the study of their world. But now she felt exhausted with learning anymore because she wanted to get on the road to Ayden.

Gethsemane walked over to where Deborah was sitting. She hid her smile at his walk; she only remembered him flying into a room, not waddling. Nonetheless even he couldn't fly in such close quarters.

"Time is soon, Deborah," Gethsemane stated to encourage her. "We will be moving forward soon."

"Doesn't seem like it, Gethsemane," Deborah said as she pointed to the ceiling where the wind was strongly whistling through the pipe.

"Would you like to hear how the raven lineage came to whisp," Gethsemane asked Deborah?

Deborah's head snapped back to Gethsemane, as she said, "absolutely!"

Jerin, Tybin, Iza and Nick came to sit next to her to hear what the eagle had to say. Nekoh, who had already been laying by Deborah, made room for Kit to plop down on his belly.

"When the world of Eshra was young," Gethsemane began. "The Great Crane and the Great Fox resided in the day and night sky. A raven approached them, asking for their wisdom. He humbly needed to get a message far away in the other world to his cousin who was a crow. He said:

Dear Crane and Fox, you stand for all of Eshra and the other world. Your trusted wisdom gives those who share these beautiful lands freedom to live freely and abundantly.

To serve you would be a tremendous honor in your endeavors to help keep these worlds in harmony. But, in order to do so, efficiently, would take special skill.

I pondered this very issue when I knew I needed to go to my cousin in the other world to tell him his mother would soon pass across to the World of Souls.

My deepest regret would be to not reach him in time. The distance was far too great to travel and it would take too long to get to him and then for him to return to say goodbye.

How, my great leaders, could this task take less time for my cousin. And, more importantly, take less time for when you, my leaders, need a message to travel immediately to protect our worlds.

The hummingbirds are your communicators to each other. But there are none for those whom reside in our beautiful lands. No expedited communication is available to those who live in our worlds.

I humbly ask you, Great Crane and Great Fox, to consider the ravens and the crows to carry messages quickly as we whisp from one end of Eshra to the other world and back to keep all communication open with those who reside in our lands.

Gethsemane placed his wing on Deborah's shoulder and said, "And this is how, Deborah, the ravens and the crows are able to whisp all over our worlds to this day. Now, granted, they, as you have seen, do not always carry messages from the Great Crane and the Great Fox. The crows are, what should I say, a little short-term minded and a little wild in behavior. Which accounts for their skittish nature. But when they are needed, they immediately rise to the occasion and serve.

"Fascinating," Deborah expressed. "I love old Eshra mythology."

The Trevins came running in from outside, full of excitement. "We should be able to travel tomorrow," Trevin stated with authority. "Past the mountain range, at the start of the meadows it is melting," he revealed.

Gethsemane chuckled, saying, "did I not say it would be soon, Deborah?"

Deborah moved closer to the horses, and flagged down Jerin and Tybin. She stood behind her horse to not be seen by the others and said, "don't you think it odd Gethsemane told me it would be 'soon' for us leaving. Then, we hear the story of whisping and then the Trevins scamper in with news we will be leaving," she questioned them?

Tybin smiled as he lightly laughed and said, "welcome to Gethsemane's world, Deborah. Jerin and I have been in the middle of this type of thing all our lives," he stated as he walked away.

Jerin rubbed the back of her neck with his hand, saying, "to answer your question, yes, it is odd. And, I agree with Tybin, we have seen it many times."

"But," Jerin sat down, "what surprises me is Gethsemane being so free with his speech. Very few know old Eshra and its stories; especially the one on whisping. It is a well-kept secret to protect the birds," Jerin stated in a baffled tone.

Tari flew next to Jerin, looked at both of them and said, "it is a new Eshra, Jerin. The Messenger is bringing light to Hollow and our worlds will change. To learn brings strength. Gethsemane is not speaking randomly. He has a plan." Tari nodded to both and flew away.

"Hold me up before I fall," Deborah told Jerin.

Jerin immediately did as she requested. She looked at him and nervously laughed. "I meant it metaphorically, Jerin. Tari, your osprey, has never said a word to me. And, now he speaks a complete paragraph. And, with such deep wisdom. I am blown away tonight," Deborah said.

Zetia sounded her clangor, just like she did every night to let everyone know it was time to settle in their beds. Otherwise, the Trevins, who love the night, would have kept everyone awake.

Zetia smiled at Deborah and said, "my girl, you have been given a great privilege tonight. Tari never speaks to anyone but his brother and Tybin and Jerin. It would seem your soul runs deep in bird instincts and bird respect."

The next morning had the boys tearing down their camp. The minute Deborah stepped outside she shuddered and grabbed for her warm gear. She quickly ran back in and hid behind the horses to change her clothing to stay warm. She wrapped her scarf around her neck and face, put on the warm socks and boots and slipped on her wool gloves.

She watched as Elora flew around the boys demanding they stop and dress warmer. Deborah giggled at the sight. "Leave it to Elora to take Lydia's words literally," she said to herself.

The boys gently batted Elora away while they tried to keep working. Finally, all was packed and ready. They mounted their horses and trudged through the snow. The wind had stopped and the snow was powdery, but heavy and wet in other areas as they moved.

It was a slower pace than before because Zetia was making sure each footing would hold and no one would slide down the mountain. At times, Deborah felt like they weren't even moving.

Hours passed before the meadows could be seen below the next ridge. Deborah looked at her fellow travelers and noticed all of their eyelashes had what looked like white frozen mascara on them. She blinked her eyes and realized hers did too.

They continued to descend the last high ground and Deborah's heart felt relief they would be out of the mountains soon. She looked to the sky where she noticed night was approaching, but Zetia wasn't stopping to make camp. Fear gripped her with the thought of traveling through the night, not knowing what type of danger could arise from the unstable climate and ground.

It was pitch black by the time Zetia stopped. Deborah was relieved and also frustrated because camp would not be an easy task.

The boys rapidly created a large fire pit and worked the bedding around it. Zetia handed Deborah and Iza the cooking supplies and food as she went to break down the horses.

Instead of the horses staying farther away, Zetia brought each one of them back and had them make a circle around the outside of their camp.

"Smart," Deborah thought. "The horses will stay warm with the fire close and they will block the wind for us while we sleep. No wonder Zetia sleeps with her horses," she quietly said with admiration.

She looked around once the fire allowed her to see. Their camp was on solid flat ground with tall grass all around them. The bedding had pine boughs underneath to keep them dry from the damp ground, which the boys had cut before they left their last camp and tied to one of the pack horses. Back at the last camp, Deborah had been too warm in the down sleeping bag, but tonight she knew she would be thankful for it.

They ate with very little conversation and immediately went to bed when the chores were done. Jerin, Nick and Tybin took turns keeping watch with the fire making sure it had wood. Deborah was sure they also were watching for trouble, but fell asleep before she could ask one of them.

"I never thought I would be so thankful for light," Deborah exclaimed as they packed for the morning ride. "Zetia, promise me we never have to travel so late in the night again," she begged.

"We have a lot of ground to cover, Deborah. I make no promises," Zetia said as she smiled at her. "But, to ease your fear, this next part of the journey would be foolish to traverse at night time. There are deep caverns throughout the plains," she explained.

Deborah was excited as they traveled; no longer did they have to ride single file. The ability to ride next to another rider and talk was exhilarating. Although, it was sporadic due to the deep cavernous holes scattered throughout. Still, she enjoyed it when she could.

Plus, the view wasn't half bad either. Rolling hills upon hills and wildlife galore. Antelope, bison, fox, rabbits and birds followed and watched them as they passed by. Their winter coats shimmered when the sun broke through the clouds and Deborah was beyond excited as she observed the differences from light to dim color variations on the animals.

Zetia wasn't lying about the deep cavernous pits they had to maneuver around to keep safe. She explained the dangers of camping in the bottom of them, especially during spring melting. The water buildup from the snow created forceful rivers and this is what made them so cavernous. Years and years of runoff etched the rock formations like mountains.

On the fourth day of trekking across the plains, Zetia told everyone they would be staying at the next break for two days. They stopped way before nighttime to rest. Camp was made and food was prepared just like every other day of travel.

Deborah went to help Zetia with the horses, and asked, "why two days, Zetia?"

"The swamplands are unpredictable and treacherous," Zetia revealed. "We will be entering them when we leave here. It will take a good three days to cross them. I want us rested before we start through them," she told Deborah.

"I have another question, Zetia," Deborah said. "How come we haven't had to worry about Choran and his followers since we left?"

"Wintertime slows all activity in the mountains and other snow packed areas of Eshra," Zetia began to explain. "Choran does not have the resources in people or amenities to follow after or attack those who are faithful to Ehyah in winter. It actually was a blessing we had to wait to leave until we did."

"The closer we get to Oshyama the more dangerous it will become. The weather is like late summer in the mountains near the ocean during wintertime. It is beautiful and the smells are nothing like the mountains," Zetia dreamily stated.

"The only ocean I have seen was in the Seattle area. And it was really a sound, like Puget Sound," Deborah stated.

"Oh! Deborah," Zetia exclaimed. "You are going to fall in love with the freedom of the ocean and all of its wonders. This makes me very excited I get to show you what I have always loved." Zetia hugged Deborah and gave her the reigns of four of the horses as they headed back to camp.

Kit sat down next to Deborah as they ate. "Five tells me you have a pretty that looks like me," he curiously asked?"

"Well, yes, I do," Deborah stated as she asked Nekoh," can I have your bag." Nekoh came over to her and she took the bag off of his back.

"I need the bottle I got from Finch," Deborah said to the bag. She reached in and pulled it out to show to Kit. She slowly turned it for him to see each part of it.

Gethsemane flew off his perch and came closer to see what Deborah was showing Kit. "Deborah, this piece you possess is old Eshra," he excitedly stated. "Where did Two find it," he asked?"

Deborah relayed the story to everyone as all of them were intrigued by Gethsemane's excitement. At times, she would have to stop to fight back the tears of her memories with Two.

Gethsemane listened intently to each word Deborah spoke and then said, "have you opened it?"

"No, I assumed since it was old there was nothing in it," Deborah explained.

"Before you open it, Deborah," Gethsemane cautiously said, "I want you to think about this question."

'What is your greatest desire.' And, do not open it until you are sure this desire is the most important," he instructed her.

Deborah looked at Gethsemane with worry, as she said, "maybe I shouldn't open it. Especially since it is such a serious question with possible consequences. What if something horrible happens?"

"This bottle will not harm you, child. It cannot kill, maim or put you in any precarious situations," Gethsemane disclosed.

"It will, though, open doors to what is already in your soul and reveal greater knowledge and ability to you," Gethsemane wisely told her.

"This bottle has to be given as a gift for it to work its magic. Just as Kit's feather has to be given as a gift, so does the same magic work on the bottle. With this being said though, it will only work once a year. This is why I posed the question to you to make sure you know your greatest desire," he gravely told her.

"OK, let's say for arguments sake, my biggest desire is to whisp. Will it let me do it?" Deborah asked Gethsemane.

"No, because it is meant to reveal deep meaning. Such as, 'show me what else my knife can do besides grow plants quickly.' This is the type of knowledge I was referring to. The knife is attached to your soul and you could be given, in your soul and mind, the revelation of its other abilities," Gethsemane explained.

Deborah nodded her head to say she understood what he meant. She looked around the campfire. Everyone's eyes were fixed on her. Jerin put his hand on hers, she smiled at him and squeezed his hand. She took a deep sigh, held the bottle in one hand and put her other hand on its lid.

Deborah took the lid off the bottle and said, "my greatest desire is to whisp to Ayden." The opening of the bottle released a small puff of smoke as she spoke.

Everyone around the campfire stared in disbelief. Deborah was gone and the bottle was on the ground with the lid tightly shut.

Chapter Thirty-Two

Ayden checked the cave to make sure she had everything in her pack after she fed the animals. She decided to look for more berries to take with them the next morning. It was early evening when she walked out of the cave and moved towards the pond area to search for them.

She knelt down at a black blueberry patch and was carefully picking the berries, putting them in an open bandana scarf when she felt her hair lift from her face. She quickly stood up to see what caused it.

Ayden screamed and Deborah matched her scream. The two girls stood paralyzed for several seconds, stunned to see each other. Once they realized it was real, they grabbed each other's arm in their handshake and both of them started to cry.

"I have missed you so much," Ayden wailed.

"I never want to be apart from you ever again, Ayden," Deborah wailed back.

Greysun howled to match their wails and Nip hopped around them, yelling, "Deb, Deb," continuously. Lyt flew around both Greysun and Nip, saying, "no, no, no, friend. No, no, no, friend."

The girls continued to cry with joyous tears as they hugged each other and then would stand back to look at each other. They repeated the same act several times, shocked it was real.

Finally, Deborah said, "I hoped beyond hope it would happen. I wasn't sure, nor did I really want to believe it could. I mean, I am a human being not a bird. Yet, I felt this strange draw to it. Whisping I mean. How can I have whisping deep in my soul like a bird's instinct is what I kept thinking. And, then the bottle and on my way here it became so clear. I can't explain it, but in my soul, I know how. I know how, Ayden. And, I know why Marley held whisping in such high regard," she said as she grabbed her arm.

"I have so much to tell you," Ayden expressed. "Have you met Greysun? Of course, you haven't. And, you have to meet Lyt too. I got to talk to my dad, D," Ayden excitedly said.

"OH! WOW!" Deborah exhaled. "I never thought I would hear our signature names for each other ever again, A."

The girls sat down and stared at each other. Nip jumped into Deborah's lap where Deborah hugged and kissed her repeatedly.

Greysun put his paw on Ayden and kept looking at Deborah. Lyt flew around all of them, saying, "no, no, no, friend," like he was a song sound track stuck on repeat.

Deborah looked at Ayden, slightly moved her head as she gestured with her eyes and gave a confused look at Lyt.

Ayden laughed, saying, "meet Lyt, Deborah. We rescued him and healed his wounds with your blue vial," she proudly told her.

Greysun pawed Ayden's leg several times to get her attention. Ayden rubbed his neck, saying, "and, I humbly present to you, Greysun. Without him we would all be dead," she told Deborah.

Deborah acknowledged both animals and turned to Ayden, nervously saying, "seriously, dead?"

Ayden explained how they came to know Lyt because of the enforcer and osprey. She finished her story with the battle and Greysun having to expel the snail fern and his sage words to her.

Deborah listened and took her hand. "I am so sorry, A, you had to make the choice to take a life. But, Greysun is right. The enforcer would have thought nothing about it when he killed you. I am extremely proud of you. And, wait until I tell Zetia. She will beam with pride. She understands death is to be avoided. But she has taught me to not be foolish with my emotions and she totally knows what has to be done has to be done."

"Explain to me, D. How did you get here?" Ayden asked.

Deborah started with Marley and their budding friendship and Kit's belief she had the bird instinct. To Zetia teaching her how to determine the weather through her bones and how she explained to her all about the world of birds. Lastly, she told Ayden about Two's gift of the peacock bottle and what Gethsemane knew about it.

"And, here I am," Deborah exclaimed with joy.

"Are you going to stay," Ayden asked?

"Well, I assumed I would," Deborah stated with doubt in her voice. "Is there something you know about whether I should or not?"

"No, not really," Ayden stated. "I just have an uneasy feeling if you really should stay," she explained. "I mean, I guess I don't have to worry about carrying you since you can whisp. Something is off though and I'm not sure what it is. Uri said he couldn't stay in Hollow long, so, I don't know," Ayden stated with trepidation.

"OK, I get your instinct," Deborah said with a smile and a hug to Ayden. "But, let's give it a couple of days before either of us make a decision," she asked?

"I like that plan," Ayden smiled. She stood up and grabbed Deborah's arm to help her stand. "Let's go to bed," Ayden decided. She guided Deborah to their cave where Deborah looked at her with doubt.

"There's plenty of room," Ayden stated. "Welcome to Hollow and how I have been living while you were in Eshra," Ayden revealed.

Greysun laid against the cave wall to allow the girls to put their heads on his belly for a pillow. Nip curled up tightly next to Deborah and purred, loudly. Lyt burrowed in next to Nip and lightly began to snore to the rhythm of Nip's purring.

"Not so bad," Ayden said while she smiled at Deborah. They both laid with the back of their heads on Greysun.

"I was very thankful Uri came to me to give you guys a message," Ayden stated. "It was a great relief to know you guys were OK. I did try to use the feather from Kit to reach you, before Uri came. But all I could do was watch you and not talk to you," Ayden told her.

"The feather is crazy limited," Ayden slyly explained. "I mean, great I could see you sitting at Zetia's dinner table or standing by my tree where I wrote in my journal. But, to not talk to you and only watch. Well, it was frustrating. Interesting, but frustrating," Ayden hinted at what she saw.

Deborah sat straight up and began to get nervous. Nip meowed irritably at losing her sleeping spot. "What did you see," she demanded.

Ayden laughed as she sat up and grabbed Deborah's hand. "I knew long before you did you had feelings for Jerin," she tenderly told her.

"And, I knew way before I saw your feelings, Jerin had feelings for you. Yup, just a whole lot of feelings flying around Eshra," Ayden teasingly told Deborah.

"I told Jerin we cannot have any more kissing until I got to tell you first that I loved him," Deborah blurted out.

"Well, thanks, D, but I think by what you already said to him, he knew first," Ayden revealed.

"Fine, then," Deborah declared. "I think we all just need to go to sleep now." Deborah grabbed Nip and put her near her chest and laid her head on Greysun and closed her eyes.

Ayden smiled and laid down and proceeded to tell Deborah everything she had gone through since entering Hollow. Deborah grabbed her hand and listened in silence. At an exciting part, she would squeeze Ayden's hand.

When Ayden finished, Deborah told her all about Zetia's and their journey so far. Ayden laughed until tears rolled down her face when the Trevin stories were given. It was late night before they both fell asleep. Neither one of them wanted to, but the overwhelming emotional excitement of being together again finally caught up with them.

The next morning Ayden prepared their breakfast. Deborah looked at the servings and bunched up her nose. "This is no way an appetizing breakfast, Ayden," she said with mild disgust.

"This dried food has kept us alive for many days," Ayden reverently stated. "Once Hollow began to grow trees and grass, we were able to add other ingredients. Thankfully, Greysun knew what was edible and good for us."

"The berries are a newly added delicacy," Ayden stated with deep respect. "But if you do not like them, I could have Lyt go find worms for you. Because, Deborah I had to eat a lot of worms to get enough strength to fly. And, maybe you need the worms too for your whisping," she playfully instructed Deborah.

"No, no, no, friend, I will go get worms for our new friend Deborah," Lyt excitedly said as he flew off.

"Worms!" Deborah yelled. "I am not eating worms. No way, no how," she exclaimed. Deborah picked up her designated portion and started to eat. "You have had it really tough, Ayden," Deborah sadly said.

"It's Ok, D," Ayden said as she patted her hand. "Nip, Greysun and Lyt have made it bearable.

"Come on, I want to show you where I met my dad," Ayden excitedly said as she got up and started to walk towards the pond.

They reached the well and gazed into the water to see if Zayden would appear. No movement came from the water while they watched for several minutes. Both of them sat down and gazed across the land in silence.

"Zayden told me my feathers each of you received hold special magic," Ayden finally said. "He didn't say exactly what kind of magic. He only said they would protect you from Choran's death grip. Whatever that means?" Ayden said in a puzzlingly tone as she pondered his words.

"Both Zayden and Crane say I have to listen for the stirring once I am in the bowels. It is the key to finding them," Ayden continued. "What the stirring is, is anyone's guess," she frustratingly stated.

Ayden sighed, looked at Deborah and said, "this journey has been long and hard, Deborah. Not being able to talk to you, well it has been really long. Even not being able to see Elora or Zetia has been tough." Ayden stopped talking and thought about what she wanted to say next.

"I have had a lot of time to think, here in Hollow," Ayden stated. "It has caused me to examine all my friendships and to see how deeply I love all of you. I seriously miss you guys." Ayden breathed heavily as she let air out of her lips.

"I want you to go back to Eshra, Deborah. I don't want you to stay here. Now, that we know you can whisp, you can send messages back and forth for us. I don't want you to stay here," Ayden emotionally said to her.

"And, Deborah," Ayden intently looked into her eyes.

"Deborah, I have a message for Nick I want you to give him. I heard his pain in Choran's cave when he thought he was going to lose me. I want you to find the right moment, when you guys are alone, to tell him something."

Ayden heavily breathed again, took Deborah's hand and said, "I want you to tell him I love him and to not worry. I will see him soon." Ayden lowered her eyes as her bottom lip trembled and tears formed in her eyes.

Deborah grabbed her hand and cried with her. "I don't know if I can leave you, Ayden. Not, now! I just found you," Deborah said as she continued to cry.

"You must go, Deborah," a voice said.

The girls quickly turned to see the well water swirling with a mist as the Great Crane came into view. He bowed to both of them as he continued to speak.

"Ayden is right in how she feels. You did not come through Choran. Even with him deteriorating with Ayden's presence in Hollow; it still is unsafe for you to stay here for any length of time," the Great Crane stated

"But there is a more pressing reason you must return. You are our key to the other side," Ehyah revealed.

Deborah wiped her eyes and stared at the crane. "You are beautiful," she said to him.

The crane nodded to acknowledge her compliment and continued, "speak privately to Gethsemane. Tell him I have sent you back as you are our key to the other side. He will know what to do."

"Wait," Deborah yelled; sensing the crane would leave. "Can I whisp back here to bring Ayden supplies? Like decent food and bring her messages," she asked?

"To whisp, Deborah, is a privilege. You are like a fledgling who has just learned to fly. Yes, you can whisp where you choose, now. But, because you are so very new at it, I want you to use it only when it is absolutely imperative for you to do so. Bring Ayden food and supplies this one time and then do not use the whisp until your heart says you must," Ehyah authoritatively stated.

"Ayden, the passage you seek is by your foot. Listen to your heart, Messenger, and you will see it," the crane said as he disappeared.

"Great!" Deborah stated. "I am just a little tired of these half-messages in Eshra," she ranted while she walked back and forth. "The prophecy, Marley and now him," she yelled.

Ayden chuckled at her, remembering how many times she had said the same thing. "You get used to it. It makes you have to listen to your heart and instincts," Ayden wisely told her.

"Fine, then," Deborah expressed. "I will return, but I will come back, one time, to you once I gather supplies. What do you need," she frustratingly asked?

"I have to think about it," Ayden stated excitedly. "Maybe, I should have you take Nip with you," she thought out loud.

"No-o-o-o-o-o Ayd," Nip meowed loudly.

"No, no, no, friend! Nip needs me," Lyt screamed frantically as he flew around them.

"OK, OK, Nip can stay," Ayden quickly consoled them.

"Deborah, before you leave, I will show you how Greysun has to ride on my back. Ask the boys to design a harness for him to ride easier and with more respect. I will stay right here until you return," Ayden decided.

"Food, Ayden," Deborah shouted. "It's all fine and good you are concerned about everyone else. You need some real food. What do you want the most," Deborah asked?

Ayden sat down and put her hand to her chin. "What do I want the most," she said out loud and in deep thought. "Fresh fruits and vegetables and I would love some fresh bread with real butter," she yelled.

Ayden walked back to the cave almost skipping as she thought about real food. She called Greysun over as she took the dress and got it ready to put on him.

Deborah failed at hiding her laughter as she watched Greysun and Ayden get into the skirt for flight. "Well, I get it why you want something different," she laughed.

Greysun looked at her with the most down trodden embarrassed look. She rubbed his fur, and said, "Greysun I will have the boys make you something you can be proud of." She bent down and kissed him on his head.

"Ayden," Deborah said as she grabbed her arm, "my friend, I love you so very deeply. I will return as quickly as possible with all you have requested. Soon, we will be together and not have to say goodbyes," she said with tears streaming down her face.

Ayden held onto Deborah's arm and tightly squeezed it while her friend spoke. "It will always be my greatest treasure to have you as my best friend, Deborah," Ayden told her.

"Tell everyone we are well here in Hollow and we fly to the peak and down to the bowels soon. We will meet all of you there and the prophecy will rise in Eshra."

"Tell them I love them," Ayden finished as tears flowed down her cheeks, too.

"She handed Deborah a bandana full of berries and said, "these are black blueberry berries. Make sure everyone gets to try them."

Deborah took the berries, stood back, looked at Ayden and nodded her head. "I love," is all Ayden heard as Deborah whisped out of sight.

Chapter Thirty-Three

"No-o-o-o-o-o," Jerin stood up and screamed. Tybin quickly came to his side and Nick took the other. "Gethsemane, bring her back," Jerin demanded loudly.

Gethsemane was pacing back and forth, speaking to himself out loud. "I, I did not expect her to whisp. How did I miss it? I should have known she had old Eshra blood in her. I missed it. I must be getting weak. Or lazy! It just can't be," he continued to ramble as he paced.

Kit stood in front of Gethsemane, and said, "I knew."

"I just had to convince her she could do it. Pretty, impressive of me to ask about the bottle, don't you agree, Gethsemane?" Kit fanned his feathers in a beautiful display and walked away; totally pleased with himself.

Gethsemane stopped to listen to Kit. His beak fell open while he stood there in a stupor. He looked at Zetia, and asked, "how did he see it and not me?"

"Gethsemane, sometimes we are too close to the answer," Zetia tenderly said to him. "You have seemed troubled since before we left on this journey. You heart was clouded from what your instinct wanted to tell you," she wisely said.

"Gethsemane, bring her back, now," Jerin demanded again.

"Jerin," Gethsemane stated as he nodded at Zetia's sage words to him. "It is not in my power to bring her back. The Great Crane would not have given her the ability if he thought she could not handle it," he consolingly said.

"Then you need to go talk to Ehyah, now," Jerin continued to demand. "You tell him to bring her back, now. She needs to be safe," he said as he sat trying to hide his tears.

Zetia and Iza quickly prepared tea with the sleeping herbs in it for Jerin. Iza handed the drink to Tybin, where he had Jerin drink it. Nick and Tybin led Jerin to his bed where they made sure he was comfortable.

Tybin looked at the rest and said, "we were planning to stay another day. Which is good because we may need to be in the same spot for her to return and not get lost. It is probably best for all of us to retire for the night," he finished.

Jerin sat far away from the rest as he mourned the loss of Deborah. The sleeping tea only partially worked throughout the night. He would wake, sit up and look where Deborah slept. Then the tears would come followed by the groggy sleep. This happened repeatedly until he decided to go sit by himself, outside of the camp area.

Tybin approached him saying, "brother, you have to eat. Breakfast was hours ago. It will do your heart good, Jerin."

"Thanks, Ty, but I don't want anything right now," Jerin stated. Tybin set the food down and walked away.

Tari couldn't resist the egg on Jerin's plate and hopped down to enjoy the feast. Lok, not wanting his brother to be the only one getting the delicacy, hopped down and pushed Tari out of the way to get more food.

The ospreys cleaned the plate, looked at each other and then they both looked at Jerin. "You do know, brother, it takes an intelligent bird, like the raven, to whisp," Lok began the conversation.

"Yes, and good bird instincts, like the crow, to whisp exactly where they want to go," Tari stated. "Ehyah must hold Deborah in very high esteem to give her the gift, brother," he disclosed.

"Yes, I would have to agree, brother. Ehyah will keep her safe and bring her home to us," Lok finished. The birds looked at each other and flew off.

Jerin, watched the birds fly away as he contemplated their words.

Nekoh quietly waited until the ospreys were gone and then said, "Trust Eshra magic, Jerin."

"This is deeper than Eshra magic, Nekoh," Jerin frustratingly stated.

"I understand, son," Nekoh reassured him as he lay next to him to give him silent support.

Suddenly, Deborah whisped right in front of Jerin and Nekoh. "Hey! Hi guys," she said.

Jerin stood up, grabbed her and kissed her. "Don't you ever leave like that again, "he cried while he tried to sound stern.

Eleea flew to Deborah, saying, "how is she?"

"She says she loves you and misses you," Deborah told Eleea.

"Me, me, me," Elora cried out.

"Yes, Elora, she says she misses you the most," Deborah lied to her.

"Let me get some good food, first, and then I will tell all of you what happened," Deborah determinedly stated as she walked towards Zetia.

Iza helped Zetia prepare a heaping breakfast for Deborah as she sat near the campfire to eat. "You guys have no idea how lucky we are," Deborah said as she ate.

"Ayden had to eat worms for energy until she got these berries." Deborah produced the scarf full of berries and the Trevins went wild climbing all over her.

Hold up, guys," Deborah tenderly told them. "I promised Ayden everyone would get to try them." She handed the scarf off to Zetia who meticulously made sure all received a small portion.

"Now, where do I begin," Deborah excitedly said? "I guess, I will begin at the beginning. When Ayden entered Hollow," she decided.

Deborah told her story with great enthusiasm as she included every detail Ayden had told her. She stopped after the fight with the enforcer and osprey to hear everyone's responses.

"My poor girl," Zetia expressed. "And, what a wise friend in Greysun," she admiringly stated. "I could not be prouder than I am right now," she finished with awe in her voice.

"What an awesome battle," Tybin stated with respect. "You kept me on the edge of my seat with that one, Deborah," he respectfully said. He turned to look at Jerin who was nodding his head in agreement. Tybin looked at Nick for the same response, but his head was down.

Next, she relayed the whole story of the worms and how many times she had to eat them. Deborah included the humorous points too where everyone was giggling at Ayden's and her friend's dilemma.

Their laughter heightened when she explained how the Great Crane told her she could have eaten the berries instead. And how Lyt innocently responded to not knowing she liked berries.

From there it was how ridiculous Greysun looked in the skirt, where more laughter ensued. Deborah jumped ahead for a second, and told the boys they had to design gear for Greysun to ride Ayden's back.

Onto the bathing in the pools and how Nip tried very hard, both times, to not be cleaned. Which brought more laughter. Deborah stopped and looked at Zetia, and said, "the next adventure will shock all of you."

Deborah described the pool and the glass reflection. She tenderly said it was Zayden in the reflection talking to Ayden.

Zetia lost it and could not stop crying. Deborah walked over to her and sat next to her. She grabbed her hand and told her how Zayden told Ayden she was spunky like his sister. Zetia giggled through her tears and smiled at Deborah.

Deborah continued to hold onto Zetia's hand as she told the whole conversation Ayden and Zayden had.

Finally, she told them how she whisped to Ayden and what they did while she was there. Certain, private moments, were left out to not embarrass her and Jerin or Nick.

She carefully told what she was allowed to say by the Great Crane. And then she sighed and relaxed.

The boys quickly got up to discuss their ideas for Greysun's new riding attire where Nekoh and Eleea joined them.

Zetia hugged Deborah and pulled Iza into the hug. The Trevins surrounded the girls and hugged their legs and hugged each other.

Deborah suddenly felt exhausted. She went to sit on her bed and watched all of the activity around her.

Nick timidly approached her, saying, "does she look healthy, Deborah?"

Deborah patted her bed for Nick to sit down. "Nickalli, she is as healthy as she can be in that dreadful situation. Her singing and wings have made Hollow come alive with plant life."

"She gave me a private message for you, though," Deborah caringly said.

"She told me to tell you she has had a lot of time to think in Hollow. And, she wanted you to know she loves you and will see you soon. And, you are not to worry about her," Deborah whispered to Nick.

Nick's eyes flared wide open as he looked at Deborah. Stunned, his mouth couldn't move to make a sentence. His eyes watered as he finally said, "I have always loved her, Deborah."

"I know, Nick," Deborah said as they took each other's arm and then she let him cry into her shoulder.

Jerin walked over to them and softly patted Nick's back while he smiled at Deborah. "Did you get a chance to tell her first," he teasingly asked?

"Yes, yes, I did," Deborah lifted her head. She slightly cocked it and looked at Jerin with a stern 'don't mess with me look' and then smiled at him.

"I really need to take a nap," she told the boys as she yawned and moved to lay down and immediately fell asleep. Deborah peacefully slept through the night.

The next morning, she found Gethsemane near the beginning of the marshes which would eventually lead into the swamplands. She approached him and asked, "can I speak with you Gethsemane?"

Gethsemane spread his right wing towards a log farther away from the wet ground. He flew over to it and Deborah sat next to him. They sat in silence for a few minutes before Deborah started to speak.

"You know, I am one to question everything. Not to discount others, but question to learn," Deborah began. "I have listened to you since the Great Tree days and deeply respect you, Gethsemane."

"Before we are finished talking today, I have been given a private message from Ehyah for you. But, before we get to the message, I have questions," Deborah revealed.

"All I know and have learned about Eshra has led me to believe you are more than what you say. You want others to believe you are one thing, but you are deeper Eshra. What I mean is, you hide your truth and do not let others know how truly old you are. Gethsemane, you are old Eshra, aren't you?" Deborah quizzically demanded.

"What is your proof, Deborah," Gethsemane asked?

"One, you knew about Ayden's and my handshake and told us it was old Eshra," Deborah began to prove her points. "Two, you tell the old Eshra stories like you were there and witnessed them first hand. Three, you knew way too much about the peacock bottle and got way too excited when you saw it. Lastly, you intimately know Ehyah," Deborah concluded.

Gethsemane lightly chuckled. He slightly lifted his feathers and shook them and settled them back against his body. "It is a good thing we do not need lawyers in Eshra," he said as he anxiously chuckled again.

"Deborah, all you say is true," Gethsemane revealed. "I am old Eshra. Ehyah has asked me to reveal this knowledge at some point along this journey. I humbly ask you to keep quiet until I do reveal it. Now, what did Ehyah want me to know," he asked?

"Ehyah said to tell you I had to return to here because I was the key to reach him and Zayden in the bowels from this side. Just as Ayden is the key to her side to reach them," Deborah explained.

"Then all he said is you will know what to do. Which is just so Eshra confusing," she frustratingly said.

"Yes, sometimes it can be frustrating to wait for answers," Gethsemane agreed. "What I have learned all of these years is to look to where you presently are."

"What knowledge can you acquire in the present moment to use to help you for the future. For example, you need to learn to whisp better," Gethsemane coached her to see.

"Ehyah was right in saying you are a fledgling. A young bird is not steady in flight until they have practiced," Gethsemane explained.

"Today or tomorrow you will be asked to whisp to Ayden to deliver supplies. Yes, you can reach her, easily. But what happens if obstacles are unseen until you are in the middle of the whisp? How will you handle the unexpected with precision and not fear," Gethsemane asked her?

"What Ehyah did not say to you but knew I would. Is, it is my job to teach you the deep art form of whisping," Gethsemane disclosed. "So, today you and I practice. And your first lesson is to whisp over there and back to me until I tell you to stop," he instructed.

Deborah whisped for a solid two hours before Gethsemane would let her take a break.

Zetia came out with food and drink for them and sat to watch. Gethsemane gave Deborah a short window to eat before he started again.

"The next lesson has to do with battle zones," Gethsemane tutored Deborah. "You will not always have a free environment to whisp to. While you are in the whisp, you must listen to the sounds ahead of you."

"Just as a bird here in Eshra or in your world has to quickly divert their path to avoid danger; so too must you when you whisp. The bird instinct and the hyper-vigilance to sound will keep you alive," Gethsemane sternly advised her.

"There are a couple ways to work this path. One, you enter and sense danger and quickly whisp back out of it. Two, during the whisp, you sense something is not right and you quickly pick a different area to whisp to in the same realm you were going to. Whether it be higher or farther away, do it and stay out of the path of danger," Gethsemane solemnly instructed.

"I want you to go back to where we first started the training. Zetia, you stand where I am. Deborah, when you whisp listen because Zetia is going to move around and will act like there is danger. I will be the danger and you are to divert your whisp. I want you to think of me as a death move. And you have to immediately get away from me," Gethsemane clarified.

Deborah thought she would go crazy. For well over three hours she was doing ridiculous maneuvers to avoid Gethsemane. He was never in the same place twice and her mind and heart felt like they would explode.

Gethsemane had her quickly sidetrack her whisp with each move he made. The longer she did it, the more she realized she was avoiding his danger faster and could reach Zetia quicker.

Finally, Gethsemane said, "nicely done, Deborah. What most ravens and crows have the privilege to learn over several weeks you have learned in just little more than five hours. I know you are tired, but nicely done. Go rest, my friend. You deserve it," he proudly told her.

Deborah nodded and went straight to her bed where she collapsed into a deep sleep.

The boys were exuberantly showing Iza and Zetia their finished harness for Greysun while Deborah slept. They all three agreed Greysun would want to sit and ride rather than lay flat uncomfortably with his legs sprawled out. If he did get tired, though, he could semi-lay down with his paws in front of him and his belly against her back.

The harness fit around his upper body like a breastplate with straps wrapping around it from side to side and around his shoulders. He would have to climb into the breastplate through his head and front legs to make a secure fit where he wouldn't fall off of him.

Ayden would take the several straps and buckle them in front of her. She could make them loose or tight with the several eyelet holes where the prong would fit. There was a pocket on each side of the plate he could untie with his teeth. Once it was untied, a piece of leather tarp fanned out which would allow him to sit rather than lay against her.

Lastly, the boys proudly displayed the goggles they made for him. They had taken a pair of protective shop glasses the Trevins had highjacked on one of their raids from Sahl.

Tybin used bribery and guilt to wrangle them away from Trevin who had been wearing them and walking around bumping into the boys while they worked. The extra black blueberry berries proved to be a good bribe, coupled with what would Deborah say to him if she knew he stole them.

Leather was formed all around the outside of the lenses and fit like a cup around Greysun's eyes to keep them in place and to make sure no bugs would damage his eyes while Ayden flew fast. One strap would wrap around his head and could be tightened by pulling on the leather where it was looped through the brass bracket. Another strap went around the back of his neck and was attached to the outside of each eyepiece like a necklace so he could let them hang in front of him.

Deborah woke and walked over as they were explaining the goggles. She took them from Jerin and said, "Oh! He is going to look so cute with these," She giggled and handed them back.

The boys showed her how to work the harness and all she could do was smile. Deborah noticed dinner was almost ready and walked to Zetia and Iza.

"Can I help you guys," Deborah asked?

"Sure, you can guard the bread with Ayden's berries in it from the Trevins," Zetia said as she gave the Trevins an eye of 'do not touch again.' All seven Trevins were sitting in a row, on their haunches with tiny pieces of bread in their paws, happily eating and chattering.

Deborah sat with her arms loosely cupped around the fresh bread. "Maybe, we could make some to take to Ayden since she needs the berries for energy?"

"Besides the things Ayden asked for, what else do you think we should send, Zetia," Deborah questioned?

"Well, my girl, I have been seriously pondering that very question," Zetia said. "My first thought was a blanket. But her wings seem to be doing the job and I do not want to burden her with carrying too much. From what you described, the weather there seems to be more Oshyama weather and not what we just passed through," Zetia continued to think out loud.

Iza shyly moved to speak and then stopped. The women looked at her, she sighed and started again. "If it was me all alone, I would want something I could look at over and over again to give me strength," Iza said.

"I was thinking we take a piece of the leather tarp and each of us write her a special note. She could easily roll the tarp up and it wouldn't be hard to store," Iza finished and lowered her eyes.

Zetia grabbed Iza in a tight hug, saying, "what a wonderful idea. Oh, it is the perfect gift for her. Very impressive, Iza," Zetia proudly stated as she looked at Deborah who was nodding her head in agreement and smiling at the girl.

"It is your responsibility, Iza, to speak with the boys about it and get everyone's message on it," Zetia said as she patted her on the back. Iza's face lit up with excitement as she nodded and left to talk to the boys.

Everyone sat around the campfire enjoying the food and the fire's warmth. Deborah thought about Iza's idea and how she would cherish the notes if she was all alone. "I really like Iza," Deborah thought.

She looked at all her friends and took time to concentrate on each of their faces. From Jerin to the Trevins, she spent several minutes looking at each of them. "When Ayden reads the messages, I am going to describe for her each note writer so she has a visual of them to pull into her memory when she rereads the notes," Deborah silently determined.

"I have to say," Gethsemane started and stopped to make sure everyone was listening to him.

"It has been a great moment in Eshra history to discover Deborah's lineage. Her bloodline is a sacred one," he revealed.

"When the raven, whose name was Panth, spoke to the Great Crane and Great Fox, there was more said that day then what I have already told you."

The Great Crane said, Panth, this is a humble responsibility you ask to carry.

Forever more you and your cousins will be hunted and persecuted by those who serve evil.

Great glory and honor will also be yours, but the burden cannot be denied.

It will, also, be your responsibility to teach and impress on all future generations the solemn promise you must keep to protect the knowledge of your ability to whisp.

Your home will be in the land of Karabinth, far from the civilizations of Eshra.

But you alone cannot carry this responsibility.

The people of Karabinth will be your link, as they too will carry the power to whisp.

Together, these sacred people, will help you and protect you.

They have this day become your blood relatives.

Gethsemane stopped to watch his friends comprehend what he had told them. Everyone was fascinated as they listened.

"One other important moment came when the Great Crane spoke to Panth," Gethsemane disclosed.

The Great Crane turned to the Great Fox, saying, 'Friend, Panth will need a sage friend he can turn to when he needs support and understanding.

The Great Fox said, I am in total agreement with you friend.

The Great Fox then turned to the golden eagle standing beside him and said,

Gethsemane, will you guide Panth whenever he needs strength and encouragement? And, will you from this day forward be their sage leader?

Great Crane and I ask for you to live in Karabinth where you will have intimate knowledge on how to whisp; but will not have the power to do so yourself. Whenever you are needed, you will help train all future generations the power of whisping.

Every listeners mouth or beak was dropped open except Deborah's, Zetia's, Eleea's and Kit's. "Deborah looked at Kit and Eleea, surprised they both knew.

Gethsemane stood and fanned his wings, saying, "tomorrow Deborah whisps to Ayden with the supplies. The day after we continue our trek to Oshyama. Then he flew away.

Chapter Thirty-Four

Ayden was by the pond where she had just filled her water bladder and was gathering berries to keep her supply full. Greysun and Nip were happily playing near her, and Lyt was busily finding worms amongst the flowers.

Deborah whispered next to her and said, "I told Gethsemane I was staying a full day with you and I would leave tomorrow. He wanted to get on the trail earlier, but I convinced him to wait another day," she excitedly stated.

The girls grabbed each other in their shake and giggled with joy at being together again. Deborah placed all of the food she had brought out on the grass. Ayden walked around the area of treasures several times.

She would pick up a fruit or vegetable and smell it like smelling a flower and then set it back down. When she saw the buttered bread, she grabbed it and devoured it; except for what she gave to the animals.

She looked at Deborah, "you have no idea how good this is," Ayden stated with pure delight. Deborah could not stop smiling as she watched Ayden enjoy everything she had lovingly carried in her pack.

Deborah pulled out the bag from Tarhana. "This bag has special treats from Tarhana," Deborah explained. "She told me to monitor you because if you eat them too fast you will get sick. Especially since your body has not had them for so long in Hollow."

"And, here are three different sized wooden bowls which can fit into each other for the animals. I didn't like seeing them use pods for bowls," Deborah said as she shook her head.

Ayden looked at Deborah, nodded and opened the bag. She let out a gleeful scream when she saw the contents. Tarhana had packed sugar cubes, tea bags filled with real ground coffee in them, fruit licorice of all sorts of flavors, pecan caramel fudge and rice Krispy treats. She looked at every piece several times before she decided on the fudge.

Ayden broke off a small section for each of them, another small section for each animal and they all enjoyed the treat together. She then carefully, packed everything back to keep it all safe.

"I can't wait any longer," Deborah declared. She pulled out the harness for Greysun and showed them how to use it by placing it on the dog. She explained the long straps could stay out of his way when he wasn't flying with Ayden. In the event he wanted to always keep it on.

With a glint of humor in her eyes, Deborah pulled out the goggles. She placed them on Greysun and adjusted them to fit perfectly.

Ayden laughed and said, "Oh, Greysun they make you look like a," she stopped because she wanted to say a cute character from a cartoon, but knew he wouldn't understand the reference. "They make you look like a warrior," she decided to say.

Greysun immediately went over to the well pool to look at himself in the water. He pranced around with his head held high. "Look, Nip, I am a proud warrior now," he exclaimed as he kept prancing around everywhere, testing how to use them.

"Deb, Deb, me?" Nip sadly asked?

"The boys made you an extra special harness, Nip," Deborah tenderly said to her.

She pulled out a tiny little harness with a front pocket made from the tarps. "Nip, this is so you can carry Lyt like Ayden carries you in her sling," Deborah proudly told her as she helped her put it on.

Nip pranced with Greysun as she yelled for Lyt to stop eating and come get in his sling.

Lyt finally flew to her and said, "No, no, no, friend, I can fly."

"Lyt, you ride," Nip demanded as she sat down for him to get in it. Reluctantly, Lyt hopped over to her and jumped into the sling. Nip stood up and walked around with Lyt's head poking out of it.

After several minutes with his head bobbing up and down, Lyt stated, "no, no, no, friend, this is fun."

The girls giggled as they watched their friends while they lay on the grass. Deborah told Ayden all the news about whisp training, the bribery with the goggle making, how she confronted Gethsemane saying she knew who he was, and the great reveal to the rest he was old Eshra; including the story of her ancestry.

"Wow," Ayden breathed. "Just, wow. I agree you and I always suspected he was old Eshra. But, your ancestry, D. Just wow," Ayden breathed again.

"Yeah," Deborah said quietly. "I know there is way more Gethsemane knows about my people. Even though he told us the story, I sense a deep sadness with him as he recanted it. There is something he hasn't said. I will find out, but I have to tread lightly with his sorrow," she explained to Ayden.

Ayden nodded her head in agreement as she thought about all Deborah had told her. "Zetia, Eleea and Kit knew," she questioned?

"I know," Deborah stated. "Do you think Zetia and Zayden are old Eshra, Ayden?"

"Wow, I don't know," Ayden surprisingly said. "I guess it would make sense, really. Since I carry the mark of the prophecy; I guess it could be true. Wow, I just don't know," Ayden stated with confusion.

Deborah pulled out the leather letter and handed it to Ayden. "Everyone wrote you a special note, Ayden," she humbly said. "It was Iza's idea to help you stay strong while you were alone over here," Deborah softly said as she handed it to her and smiled.

Ayden timidly took it and untied the leather straps for it to unroll. Tears filled her eyes as she read each message. "What," she choked and regained her composure. "What a beautiful idea. Make sure you give Iza a hug from me for thinking of it," she told Deborah.

Deborah gave her a description of how each writer looked while Ayden reread their words. She made sure she went slow for Ayden to visualize each of them.

"Nick," Ayden asked Deborah?

Deborah relayed how she told Nick Ayden loved him and what he said in return. "I have always loved her," Deborah repeated his words.

Ayden's eyes welled with tears as she listened. "I think back to East Glacier and how Nick was so very shy," Ayden said after Deborah finished speaking.

"He always seemed to be near to help me where I didn't even realize he was already protecting me," she revealed.

"I mean, now, I see it clearly. Back then I was so wrapped up in my family pain I didn't see it. And, when I think about him and how I used to watch him," Ayden stopped and looked at Deborah and grabbed her hand.

"I realize my admiration for him was deeper than I liked him. Even then my feelings were growing strong for him," Ayden disclosed.

"Back at ya, A," Deborah stated matter-of-factly. "I knew, but I didn't know in East Glacier. It wasn't until I saw him completely lose it, like I did, when you sent us back to Zetia's with the feathers. Then, it all became clear he had always loved you," Deborah agreed.

"OH! Yeah," Deborah shouted. "I almost forgot he made you something special." Deborah reached in her bag and produced a horse's hair bracelet. "The hairs are from his horse and your horse."

"Isn't it cool," Deborah said as she helped Ayden put it on. "He made himself one just like it," she revealed.

"Of course, the idea was too good for me to pass up,"
Deborah continued. "I had him do the same with Jerin's and
my horse," she triumphantly stated as she showed Ayden her
bracelet.

Ayden lightly touched the bracelet with her fingers. It
was a mixture of hues from bright turquoise, off white,
browns, blues, and a hint of red from the horse's natural hair
color. She then looked at Deborah's where the colors were so
Deborah. Yellow, oranges, reds, browns, and off white.

"He even used your berries to create the dark blues,"
Deborah explained. "And, let me tell you, the Trevins were
not too happy about it. They couldn't believe he wasted
berries like that."

"So, to appease them, he made each of them their own
little bracelet," Deborah chuckled as she finished. "Plus, I had
to promise the Trevins I would bring each of them a big
handful of berries back," she said as she chuckled again.

Ayden smiled as she packed everything up to take back
to the cave. She stood up to leave, when Lyt came flying
through and almost knocked her over. He flew around them
like he was darting out of danger.

"No, no, no. No, no, no, friend" he screamed while he
flew erratic. "Big dog, big dog, big dog," he yelled. He dived
in and out around Ayden and Deborah, saying, "danger,
danger, danger. No, no, no, friend. Man, man, man."

Ayden quickly gathered their belongings and quietly
called the animals to follow her. She took Deborah's hand and
led all of them to a patch of heavily packed trees where they
could watch without being seen. All of them crouched down
as they waited to see who would show.

At least twenty minutes passed before they heard the
sound of boots hitting the ground and coming closer. The man
came into view with a wolf beside him. Ayden rapidly took
the scent vial and sprinkled it in front of them.

The wolf stopped, raised his nose to smell the air and said, "they were here. Two humans, a dog, a cat and a bird," the wolf revealed. "I have lost their scent. But they were here," he told the enforcer next to him.

"Then, we stop here to see what shakes out," the enforcer decided. The man and the wolf settled into their camp and seemed to relax more the longer they were there.

Deborah grabbed Ayden's hand. Ayden squeezed it lightly and whispered, "we watch and listen."

"That fool, Sedley and his stupid osprey must have fallen to their deaths," the man said to the wolf. "There has been no sight or smell of them since we entered Hollow."

"The way Choran is looking, I doubt anymore can make it through. Waiting for Nahrita to leave to Oshyama was our only chance to convince him to let us go to Hollow."

"That woman thinks she has all of the answers, but we will rise far above her self-perceived greatness once Choran is gone. Little does she know, there are far more of us who do not want her as our leader than those who whiningly follow her."

The man went to the pond to take a drink. He stood and looked all around him. The wolf followed him and did the same. They both walked back and sat down to eat. They ate in silence while they kept their eyes focused, watching in every direction.

The man stood again and nonchalantly walked closer to where Ayden and her friends were hiding. He acted tired as he came closer and closer near them. The wolf stayed at the camp and laid down not concerned about the man's movements.

Deborah squeezed Ayden's hand harder. Ayden lightly patted Deborah's hand. Greysun started to stand, ready to fight if necessary. Ayden released Deborah's hold on her, put Nip and Lyt in her sling, took the sling off and put the sling behind her.

The man suddenly lunged into their hiding spot and grabbed Ayden by her hair. He started to pull her out.

Greysun jumped, bit down on the man's hold and thrashed his head back and forth. The man screamed and let go of Ayden. Deborah whisped out of the way.

The wolf charged after Greysun, where the two of them circled with their teeth bared and growled at each other. Ayden flew out of the way of the man and landed behind him by the pond; where she knew the distance between them was safe.

"Enforcer," Ayden began, "I do not want to harm you. Leave peacefully. Go back to the entrance of Hollow and you will live," she forcefully told him.

The man laughed, saying, "You have to die, Messenger. Don't you get it?" He taunted her. "With you alive, Ehyah rises and thwarts my plan to rule Eshra."

He started to move in the opposite direction of Ayden as he watched her to see what his next move would be by her response to his movement.

Ayden began the dance with him as they both made a large swath in a circular motion. Their feet slowly walked the circle. Neither one took their eyes off of each other.

The wolf sprang towards Greysun's neck. Deborah whisped in, pushed Greysun out of the way and then quickly whisped out. Greysun backed farther away from the wolf without taking his eyes off the animal.

Deborah whisped back in on a limb far above the fight scene. She watched closely to see how Ayden would handle the enforcer.

She watched as the man coyly put his hand to his forehead and then reached behind his back to produce a knife. He immediately threw the knife at Ayden.

Deborah whisped where she grabbed the knife and threw it back at him. She hit his chest with the blade where he stumbled with shock on his face.

Ayden ran in, took her wing spine and slashed his throat from one end to the other. Both Deborah and Ayden simultaneously turned to run and help Greysun.

Deborah repeatedly whisped in and out around the wolf's head. She would slap one side of his head and then the other side repeatedly. Sometimes she would slap the same side to confuse him. The animal tried to bite each slap and became extremely frustrated.

Deborah waited a few seconds on her last whisp to confuse him even more as he expected to be slapped and was moving his head from side to side trying to predict the next one. She whisped back in with her knife and sliced his neck where he fell with blood pumping out of his throat.

Deborah fell to her knees and cried. Ayden stood behind her and rubbed her back while the animals crowded around them.

Finally, Ayden somberly said, "it is time for another funeral, Greysun."

Greysun found a spot far away from the pond and their cave and began his dig. He came back to them, covered in dirt. He and Ayden dragged the bodies to the grave and Nip and Lyt helped them cover the bodies. Deborah came over as the last bit of dirt was added.

Ayden took her hand and they stood together. Ayden sighed, and said, "It is with a heavy heart we say goodbye to these two comrades. May their souls finally find peace," she finished.

She looked at Deborah, saying, "I don't have it in me for any kinder words. Both enforcers wanted me dead. They choose their path and now they are no more," she resolutely said.

Ayden walked away to grab their belongings. She continued to walk to the cave where she gathered the rest of their things. She packed everything tightly in her pack and stood.

"It is still early enough for me to fly to the next mountain before it gets dark," she told Deborah as she grabbed her arm. "You have to return today and warn them about Nahrita and the other faction."

Ayden called Greysun over and helped him get on her back. She tightened the straps and walked around with him to make sure he felt comfortable.

She decided to put her backpack below Greysun's butt and fasten it around her waist to give him extra support from falling out of the breastplate. Next, she put Nip and Lyt in the sling.

"Deborah, you saved us today," Ayden said as she grabbed her arm. "Today is a very serious reminder none of us are far from danger. Do not let your guard down. Have fun and enjoy those precious moments. But, be on the watch all of the time."

Ayden opened up Deborah's pack and filled it with berries. She handed it to Deborah, who had not stopped crying, and said, "for the Trevins."

"You will be OK, Deborah, you have become a great warrior," Ayden said as she smiled at her and took her hand.

Deborah grabbed Ayden's arm, dried her eyes with her other hand and said, "I love you so deeply, Ayden. I promise to be on the watch. We will meet soon in the bowels," she said as she let go.

Ayden gave Deborah a hug and moved away from her to prepare for flight. She lifted her wings and double checked Greysun. She smiled and nodded at Deborah and took off into the sky.

Chapter Thirty-Five

Deborah whisped to Jerin, who was alone with the horses. She fell into him and cried. Jerin gently set her down on the ground and waited for her to speak. Deborah told him everything in between her sobbing.

The rest of the travelers were eating by the fire and looked up when they saw Jerin. He had his arm around Deborah. Guiding her to them.

Zetia stood up, and nervously asked, "is she OK?"

"She is fine," Jerin stated. "Sit, and I will tell you what Deborah has told me." Jerin recounted all of the events and stopped.

He looked at Gethsemane, saying, "I feel it is imperative we send Lok and Tari ahead to scout our path. All of us have become complacent and have forgotten how serious this mission is," Jerin gravely said.

"Agreed, Jerin," Gethsemane stated. "Send the birds tomorrow and we will prepare to leave early in the morning." He flew off to leave the rest to talk.

Zetia sat next to Deborah, took her hand, saying, "you were brave today, Deborah. I thank the Crane you were there to help Ayden and to save her and her friends. Sounds like they will be the last to trouble her and I am very thankful for that."

"One, last thing, Deborah, remember the words of Greysun, if you did not kill them, they would have killed you." Zetia hugged Deborah and walked away.

"She is right, Deborah," Iza stated. "Enforcers are ruthless. And the ones who command wolves are the cruelest. It is a badge of superiority to have a wolf follow you. Remember, anytime you see a wolf nearby, know an enforcer of extreme power is close," Iza revealed to her.

Deborah nodded to Iza, looked at Jerin, and said, "I think I need to go lay down. This emotional up and down where there is happy followed by sudden death is extremely exhausting." Jerin helped Deborah to her bed, covered her in the blankets and kissed her forehead.

Zetia searched for Gethsemane around the marshes. She found him and said, "Gethsemane, with Choran disabled, I want to fly to Oshyama and secure our passage to the island. What is your view on this," she asked?

"Can Jerin and Tybin safely get us through the swampland," Gethsemane questioned?

"Lok and Tari can guide them. And, I will give all four of them instructions on how to avoid the swamp traps," Zetia informed him.

"Tomorrow, say your goodbyes and we will see you in Oshyama," Gethsemane bowed to her and flew off.

Zetia went back to the camp and sat the boys down with Lok and Tari in attendance. She called Nick and Iza over and said, "you may as well be a part of this." She explained her plan and started to give them information on how to manage the swamplands.

"I have spoken to Uri and he knows you will be traveling without me. He assures me your access will be less difficult due to it being winter. Yet, you must remain vigilant as the swampland solid ground changes all of the time," Zetia told them.

"Look for bubbling in front of you, this is a sure sign the ground is weak with deep water holes," Zetia sternly told them.

"It will take you three days to get through the land. When you stop for the night, each of you will have to sleep under your horse. Again, while resting, listen for gurgling as this is a sign water holes have risen up close by and you may have to quickly move to avoid sinking into them."

"Lastly, each of you are to keep a potted candle lit while you sleep. If you hear gurgling, you can search with your light to see where it is coming from," Zetia said as she nodded to them.

The next morning, Zetia spent a considerable amount of time speaking to her horse, Lander. Next, she went to Deborah and hugged her.

"Deborah, take good care of Lander for me," Zetia said. "He has been through this land with me many times. He can speak, Deborah. But he is one of few words," she chuckled. "He likes neighing better," she said as she smiled at her.

"Elora, you make sure everyone eats while in the swampland. The prepared bags of food for each of you will sustain everyone until they get out of the unstable ground," Zetia tenderly instructed her.

"Eleea, all of the horses know they have to stay in gear for the next three days," Zetia continued her instructions. "There are enough canvas buckets to put on each horse's head with oats for them to eat. Have the boys take the extra canvas buckets and give each horse a long drink of water," she directed.

"Iza, your senses are more in tune to darkness and its sounds. Plus, you can see more clearly in darkness. Stay vigilant to protect the rest," Zetia asked as she hugged her. She turned to the Trevins, saying, "each of you have night vision, help Iza."

Zetia stood back, swept her eyes across to look at each of her friends. "I will see you in Oshyama," she emotionally stated as she lifted her wings and flew off into the horizon.

Lander took the lead, where occasionally one of the Trevins or Gethsemane would ride with him. Tybin was close behind him as they started their three-day trek into the swamplands. Iza went next with the horse for Gethsemane and Kit behind her.

Deborah followed Iza and Nick rode next with the two pack horses behind him. The Trevins were before Jerin, who as usual brought up the rear. The ospreys returned from their first mission and flew above the travelers as they kept watch all around them.

Their first full day was long and tedious due to the added suspense. All of them needed to guardedly watch and listen for bubbles and gurgling. Once everyone was settled under their horse for the night, the Trevins scampered back and forth to make sure everyone was accounted for.

Candles flickered along the side of each horse while the travelers tried to sleep. Gethsemane, Nekoh, Eleea, Elora and Kit opted to sleep in their designated wool nests since the saddles couldn't be removed from the horses.

The next day, Deborah looked out across the vast swamp while they ate their breakfast. "It would actually be pretty if it wasn't so treacherous," she thought.

Tall thin trees with long moss hung from the tiny upper branches. The majority of the tree trunks were limbless, except for near the top. The trees were numerous with them being only a few feet apart from each other.

The sound of toads and crickets rang throughout the swamp area. High grass in bunched clusters at their base swayed in the soft breeze. Deborah decided the grass would be green in the summer, but now it was golden tan.

Everyone mounted and their 'Day of Silence' was in progress. The ground they had to travel across was semi-dry except when they saw bubbling where they would have to stop, back up and redirect their path.

Finally, the Trevins and Phum took over. Because of their size, they could easily see the route everyone needed to take. They strategically scampered ahead of the horses where each of them stayed about five feet apart and directed the rider to follow them.

Deborah breathed a sigh of relief at their skill. Her anxiety lessoned since they no longer had to carefully back the horses up to take another direction.

When they settled for the night, Deborah called the Trevins and Phum over to her. "I forgot to give you guys Ayden's gift. I want all of you to know I am extremely proud of you. The intelligent way you have maneuvered this land to keep all of us safe has been amazing," she said as she opened her backpack to reveal the berries.

Chaos ensued with fourteen little raccoon paws and two squirrel paws grabbing as quick as they could for the most berries. Deborah laughed and let them go wild while she tried to avoid an accidental slap to her head. Soon, the night slowed and they all tried to rest.

Iza jolted awake. The early morning dawn produced fog all around them causing her to strain to see and hear. She crawled to Tybin's horse to ask if he heard the feared gurgling like she was hearing. He wasn't there and her heart began to pump harder. She deliberately calmed herself as she kept inching forward, past Tybin's horse.

Suddenly, she heard Lander struggling and Tybin yelling. She stood up to see the horse up to its back in water with Tybin trying to pull the animal out.

She took another step and realized she was ankle deep in water. Backing up, she yelled to the others for help. She unlatched her whip from her side and yelled to Tybin to take the end of it. He tried but he was too far out and couldn't grab it.

Tybin moved to the front of Lander and held the horse's head out of the water. Deborah yelled to Jerin to get a rope as she ran to Iza. Jerin tried the same move Iza had done earlier with no luck.

Deborah looked around her and whisped to the trees off to the side of the caravan. She held on tightly to one thin tree by bracing her back against it and putting her feet on another to steady herself. She reached to the next tree and took her knife to cut a six-foot length, making sure when it fell no one would be crushed by it.

She whisped back down to Jerin telling him to get the logs to Tybin. Deborah continued to whisp to other trees using the same technique to cut them down.

Jerin and Nick swiftly moved each log to the edge of the water. They placed the logs long ways to create a ramp. The Trevins took the moss end of the logs and wrapped it the best they could around the structure to keep it together and to help soak up some of the water.

Tybin gently, yet forcefully turned the horse around in the watery muck. Iza gingerly walked out onto the logs and snapped her whip. The whip's end sailed like a light feather and then dug into the horse's saddle with deep barbs. The whole time, Tybin spoke encouraging calm words to keep Lander from fearfully over reacting.

Jerin held onto Iza in a bear hug and started to move backwards. Nick swiftly wrapped a rope around both of them and secured the end to Tybin's horse. He gently backed the horse up to help Jerin and Iza.

Slowly Tybin and Lander moved closer to the ramp. Finally, Lander felt the log structure and bolted up it. Tybin tightly held onto Lander as he flew in the air when the horse swiftly got out of the watery grave.

The Trevins and Phum surveyed the whole area to make sure no more swamp traps were nearby. Deborah dug through her bag to get Tybin dry clothes while Iza, Nick and Jerin wiped Lander down to get him dry.

Gethsemane flew to Tybin's horse and said, "the weather is warmer the closer we get to the coast. There will be more swamp traps now. We ride and eat on the go to get past the swampland before the next nightfall."

Everyone quickly secured their belongings and mounted their horses. Each step their horses took, they looked around in a hyper-cautious way after the near fatal scare.

The Trevins and Phum guided their path. Their method was to have the Trevin closest to the rider wait until they reached the next Trevin. Then they would run to the front of the line and move ahead another five feet. In this way the riders were never alone because the closest Trevin helped guide them.

Deborah wanted to cry, but knew it would do no good while riding. "If it's not enforcers and wolves, it's the unpredictable environment," she silently lamented.

Gethsemane flew to her horse and rode with her in silence for a while. "Deborah," he finally began, "these last few days have seen you experience a whirlwind of emotions. I want you to know, I could not be any prouder of you than I am right now."

"You quickly learned to use whisping to save many lives. Ayden, her friends, you and now Tybin and Lander. The true art of the whisp is to know where it will benefit others. And, you, my friend, have perfected the whisp." Gethsemane nodded to her.

Deborah's mouth slightly dropped open. "Wow, would never have expected that from him," she said to herself. "Definitely makes me feel better. But I will feel completely better when we see no more swampland," she silently determined.

Deborah quizzically looked at Gethsemane, saying, "Gethsemane, what happened to Panth? What happened to other people like me?"

"Deborah, not all stories of Eshra have a positive outcome," Gethsemane began. He lowered his head and breathed deep from his chest as he lifted his eyes to look at her.

"Panth foolishly trusted an ally who secretly had been following Choran. This person was highly charismatic and weaved his way into being a cunning confidant with a strong level of importance on Karabinth. He convinced the settlers to whisp to your world to set up new communities and to live amongst those people in your world. His plan was to create a network for communication where they could whisp between the worlds to build a stronger alliance for Choran. The people of Karabinth were unaware of his true reasoning and were only pawns in his game of deception. Panth discovered the imposter's treacherous intent and tried desperately to stop the migration of people to no avail," the eagle explained.

"Karabinth was barren with only the birds left to live there. The traitor strategically poisoned the fish to kill all of the crows and ravens. My wife and newborn child ate the meat and died with the other birds," Gethsemane stated with deep sorrow.

"Once the birds realized they were dying, they summoned Panth. He attacked the traitor and killed him. The birds who had whisped to other realms returned to see the carnage. They found Panth in despair where he explained what had taken place. They then called for me to return from my mission," Gethsemane disclosed.

"The people who left Karabinth were considered by the ravens and crows to be less than worthy and all communication ceased with them from Eshra. Panth placed a barrier around Karabinth where no person from either world could enter. Over the course of hundreds of years, the people of Karabinth lost their knowledge of how to whisp." Gethsemane gravely stated.

"This, Deborah, is why you see very few ravens and crows speak to humans or animals. The sting of being used in such a manner has never been forgotten by them. The loss they felt for their loved ones has been etched into their souls for generations," Gethsemane looked past Deborah as if he was reliving the whole memory of pain.

"Panth never forgave himself for being deceived. He resides on Karabinth; he feels he has to serve his punishment alone on the land," Gethsemane finished.

"You and Ayden have been given a high honor from the raven family, Deborah. Both of you have received a feather and you alone have been given the gift to whisp. It is of utmost importance for you to know their plight and for you to take extreme caution in whom you trust," Gethsemane respectfully stated as he bowed and then flew back to his horse.

Deborah's heart ached for Gethsemane and even for Panth who was betrayed. "All of us make mistakes," Deborah said to herself. "To live in solitude for a mistake is devastating. I would go crazy not talking to anyone," she thought as she looked at the sky.

Dusk had rolled in and they were still moving. Fear began to grip Deborah's heart as she worried, they would be in danger again like earlier. She watched as Trevin jumped to each rider and spoke to them. Finally, he reached her.

"We have approximately three more complete Trevin lengths and we will be out of the swampland" he explained and jumped to the next rider.

Deborah giggled at his measuring technique and calculated the Trevin length. "Each of them seems to be about five feet apart. There are seven Trevins and one Phum. So, forty feet times three is one hundred and twenty feet which is forty yards. Not bad, we can make it before it gets completely dark," she exhaled.

They reached the edge of the trees as the sky came alive with the night stars. Ahead was a bonfire with a hut like structure on the far end of it. Deborah could see a figure standing in the doorway, she squinted her eyes to try and make out who the person was.

"Welcome to Oshyama," Zetia said as she walked closer to the travelers.

Chapter Thirty-Six

Ayden circled back to see Deborah whisp. She flew farther down the mountain to watch for movement, in case any other enforcers made it through to Hollow. Relieved she saw no activity; she took off for the next mountain.

Greysun's tongue was hanging out of the side of his mouth as he sat with the goggles on and the strap to tighten them flapping in the wind. At one point he began to howl with excitement. "Ayden, this is the best way to travel," he told her.

They reached the mountain with still some light left. Greysun jumped down once Ayden unlatched him. He searched for the best place to dig their cave. Ayden let Nip and Lyt out of the sling and went to help Greysun.

They settled in for the night while Ayden prepared their dinner. She sang to them while she cooked. Cut vegetables, dried meats, fresh herbs from the land they were living in and water went into her bowl. She ran her finger around the lid of it and watched it steam.

We are in for a treat tonight," she told the three of them. Ayden carefully dished each of them some of the broth and food, being careful to not waste any of it.

After dinner she cut an apple in small slices, added the black blueberries and cut one of the fruit licorices for dessert. "I forgot what it was like to eat a dessert," she dreamily said as she thought about her time at Zetia's and the Great Tree.

Next, she brewed the coffee with sugar in it. "Guys, this is an extra special treat," she told them as she gave each of them a small amount of coffee in their bowls.

Ayden smelled the coffee for several minutes before she took her first sip. "I love coffee," she told her friends.

"I like Deborah," Greysun stated as he chewed his apple. He cocked his head at Ayden, and said, "Who is this Nick?"

Ayden almost choked on her berry, not expecting the question. She looked at Greysun while she finished eating what was in her mouth. "He is," was all she got out when Nip overtook the conversation.

"Nick-a-lee is Ayd's," Nip said as she smacked her lips together several times like she was kissing and purred in a long sweet purr.

"Nip!" Ayden scolded her with an embarrassed voice.

Nip jumped at Ayden's scolding. She sat back down and indignantly said, "it true!"

Greysun chuckled at their bantering, and said, "he must be a very strong, special man to hold your heart, Ayden."

"Yes, yes, he is, Greysun," Ayden quietly revealed.

She thought for a moment and said, "maybe, Greysun, I should give you and Lyt a description of everyone we love back in Eshra. This way if Nip or I are not with you two, you guys will know they are safe for you to talk to them. I know you heard Deborah's description already, but I will give you more to help you remember."

Ayden spent the next couple of hours explaining every detail and behavior for each of her friends in Eshra. When she finished, she heavily sighed, saying, "well, that was a mouth full of information. I think it is time to go to bed." All four of them curled up next to each other and soundly slept.

The next morning, Ayden surveyed their surroundings. She flew to a high branch on a pine tree to see how far the highest peak was away. "Still at least six or seven mountain ranges," she forlornly thought. "Maybe we can cover two in a day if we get going early and take a small break in-between," she decided.

Ayden quickly fed the animals and secured them for flight. While she was in the air, she started to sing and felt herself dance with the air currents. It was exhilarating feeling the wind beneath her wings as she lifted up higher in the atmosphere.

Ayden looked to her left wing and then her right, while in flight, and was shocked to see they were glowing brighter than ever. "Hmmm," she thought, "flying must be good for Hollow."

They reached the end of the first mountain range in plenty of time to take off for the next. She landed, pulled out her pack and fed the animals. Greysun nudged Nip into chasing him while Lyt flew around both of them. Ayden laid on the grass letting the sun warm her face.

Suddenly, she jumped up and cried out, "it is getting brighter in Hollow. Every time we are in the air, we bring light," she joyously yelled.

"We've got to get moving," she told at the animals. "The end is in sight and I want out of here. And, the only way out is to free Ehyah," Ayden stated while she packed and gestured for everyone to take their places for flight.

It seemed to Ayden it took less time to reach the end of the next mountain range. She wasn't sure, but her heart was soaring when she landed for the night.

Greysun, we won't need a cave," she advised him. "I doubt there will be any more enforcers. And, my wings can keep us warm."

Greysun looked at her and with concern in his voice, saying, "Ayden, it is not wise to be so careless. Yes, you may be right about enforcers. But, what about lone wolves or other animals?"

"Well, you do have a very good point, there," Ayden responded. "Fine, make a cave," she agreed.

The friends settled into their latest cave and tried to relax. Ayden prepared their food, as usual, as she became somewhat agitated.

"I am just going to tell you guys right now," Ayden stated with frustration. "It is no fun to be chased like a criminal, having to look over your shoulder all of the time!" She said with a raised voice.

"And, now we have to worry not only about Nahrita, but, about the other faction too," she stated.

"Your friends are well aware of this by now, Ayden," Greysun tried to console her. "Deborah reached them and told them everything the enforcer spoke about." Greysun put his paw on Ayden's leg to support her emotionally.

Ayden sighed, rubbed her face with her hands, and said, "I know. But I have seen how vicious Nahrita can be. She is scarier than Choran and he is almost no more if we are to believe what the enforcer said. What happens if she is allowed to roam Eshra after we release Ehyah?" Ayden questioned.

"I mean, will there ever be peace, here," Ayden rhetorically asked? "Seriously, this beautiful land will be no different than our land where there are always groups of people fighting each other," Ayden sadly stated.

"Since the beginning of time there has always been good and evil, Ayden," Greysun told her. "The good will prevail."

"And, you need to see it more clearly," he implored her. "If there were not good like you, Ehyah, Nick, Deborah, Nip, Lyt, me; what would the world look like," Greysun asked her?

"Good is the constant which keeps evil on the run. Not evil keeps good on the run," Greysun continued to explain.

"You stood tall and strong with Deborah to fight off evil and won. Evil is afraid of good, Ayden," Greysun exposed his truth.

"Evil is chasing you because it is afraid of you," Greysun finished.

Ayden stared at Greysun in awe of his wisdom. She thought back to the fight with Choran.

She had told him, "what do you consider power? Fear? Pain? Death? All you ever wanted in this world was to be respected and honored. But, because you were lazy, you took what you considered your entitled right for your perceived power by force rather than earn it by work and honor."

"Choran was scared of me," Ayden said as she realized why he was so angry and willing to follow evil.

"He decided to compromise his core values of good in his soul, and turn to a path of evil and jealousy. He took what wasn't his by force and stayed angry so he wouldn't lose what he wrongfully took," Ayden realized as she spoke.

"He made a choice to stay stuck in anger rather than look to remorse to right his wrongs," she whispered.

"Every single follower I have seen of Choran's is full of anger," Ayden stated. "Every one of them is afraid they will lose what they have or want. Whether it be material things, power, or magic, they are afraid they will lose it. And, they stay in anger to avoid seeing the truth that it never was theirs in the first place," she said as her mouth dropped open in disbelief.

"Greysun, thank you," Ayden said. "You are so perfectly right. Evil is afraid of us and I will no longer fear facing it. Which means, I won't be foolish like not digging a cave. I will be cautious and watch always."

"But, no longer will I feel troubled by its presence in this world or mine. We will let the good in us shine through the wrong," Ayden triumphantly stated.

"Now, let's get some sleep," Ayden requested. "These heady talks are exhausting," she said as she laid down.

Ayden held her crew to a tight schedule for the next four days. They had crossed six mountain ranges and were now at the base to the prized mountain. The upper most peak in Hollow.

As they continued to fly higher in altitude each day, she noticed fewer and fewer trees and more shale rock. Thus, the reason she made the decision to camp at the base of the mountain.

She planned to explore the peak each day to determine how to enter the bowels. Knowing the entrance would not be an easy find, camp at the bottom was the safest choice.

Ayden and Greysun scouted the area for the best encampment. Nip sprawled out on the grass, complaining she was tired and refused to fly anymore. Lyt flew off to find fresh worms.

"What do you think, Greysun," Ayden asked as she pointed to a spot near the mountain base.

"Well, I was thinking farther away on this hill would be better," Greysun said. "We may be here several days, and this spot has a better ability to see up the mountain and down too. We can see all around three sides in case someone unexpectedly shows up," he determined. "Plus, there is a nice grove of tall grass on top of it. We could easily sneak into the grass and watch from all angles in case of danger."

"Sounds like a solid plan, then," Ayden said.

They quickly went to work to make their new home. This one they made bigger since they knew they had to stay in it longer. Ayden prepared dinner and they sat around afterwards not wanting to move. All of them seemed to sense the relief of not having to travel anymore mountain ranges.

"I wish I would have taken sticks, rocks or something for each day we have been here. Then we would know exactly the number of days we have been in Hollow," Ayden sighed. "It's got to be like two months," she decided.

"Hollow, it is a weird world, ya know," Ayden stated as she continued to elaborate. "Once I started to sing, it seemed to accelerate in growth; not like a normal growth. I even think my feathers grew faster than normal," she told her friends.

"Speaking of feathers, Zayden said they have special magic in them," Ayden stated.

"So, while we were in the air, it occurred to me I better protect you guys with a feather each. Nip did you keep the feather you were supposed to go back to Zetia's with," Ayden asked?

"Ayd, no fead come wiff me," Nip nervously said.

"It's OK, Nip," Ayden soothed her fear. "Maybe you were too close to me to have the feather reach you and this is why you got stuck with me here. It probably just dropped in Choran's cave."

Ayden looked at all of her feathers and decided the ones closest to her body would be the best as they were the smallest. She plucked three and set them in front of her.

"Lyt, you get the fuzzy one as it is definitely a new growth and the smallest," Ayden decided as she placed it in front of him. "Nip, you get the next smallest one. And Greysun you get the biggest one. Now all I have to do is figure out how to keep them on your bodies so you guys don't lose them," Ayden told them.

"No, no, no, friend, birds can take the quill and work it back into their feathers. I will do it with mine," he joyously said as he grabbed his feather and started to work it into his feathers.

Ayden smiled at him, while she said, "only two left to figure out."

"Got it!" Ayden exclaimed excitedly. She pulled out the leather note Deborah brought and cut off the leather ties. She took one of her bandanas and retied the letter and put it back in her pack.

Carefully she sliced the first one into three pieces; leaving one end intact. She put the untouched part in her mouth and began braiding it part of the way down. She took Nip's feather and weaved it into the rest of the braid and measured the complete strand around Nip's neck and cut off what she needed to make it fit fairly snug, but loose enough to not choke her.

The feather lay flat against the braid and cradled her neck like a choker necklace. Ayden finished it by poking a hole in the end she had in her mouth and tied it off securely.

Pleased with the finished look, she told Nip, "now you have a beautiful necklace to wear all of the time. Tomorrow, Lyt can find us a pond for you to see yourself. You look beautiful, Nip," Ayden told her.

Nip pranced around the cave, saying, "I full of beauty."

Ayden turned to Greysun, saying, "what about you? What do you want?"

"I want a necklace too," Greysun howled with excitement. "I want to look beautiful too," he continued to howl.

Ayden tried to hide her giggle from him as she said, "well, the strap from my letter will be too short. But I can use it to put the feather in it and then take your long strap from your goggles and work all of the pieces to fit around your neck," she said victoriously.

Ayden weaved everything together and measured Greysun's neck to have it fit like Nip's. "There, now all of you will be safe from whatever you need to be safe from," she said with relief.

Lyt hopped over with Ayden's feather in his mouth. "Oh, Lyt, are you having trouble getting it to stay in your feathers,' she asked?"

Lyt dropped the feather and said, "no, no, no, friend, I want to be beautiful too, please, friend,"

Ayden smiled; desperately trying to stay stoic and not laugh. "Great idea, Lyt," she finally was able to say. "Let me see what pieces of leather I have left and we will make it work." She found enough scraps to weave together and made Lyt his own necklace.

All three animals bumped into each other as they pranced back and forth in the cave, extremely proud of their new treasure.

"Well, I have to thankfully say everyone who holds a feather from me will now be protected from Choran's death grip," Ayden stated with relief.

Ayden finally said, "bedtime, guys. Looks like we will have a busy day looking in the water at your reflections before we fly to the top of the peak."

Chapter Thirty-Seven

Deborah jumped off her horse and ran to Zetia, giving her a huge hug. "I never want to go through the swamplands again," Deborah cried out.

Zetia hugged her back, saying, "you're safe, now. Go in and eat." Zetia ushered everyone into the building and then left to go tend to the horses. When they were settled with their coats rubbed down and fed, she returned to the hut.

"Tybin, thank you for saving Lander," she said as she sat near him with her plate of food.

"Iza and Deborah are the true saviors of Lander, Zetia," Tybin stated.

Zetia patted his hand, smiled and stood up to address the travelers. "Lander said he foolishly was eating the tender sweet grass and did not pay attention to his surroundings. Before he realized it, he had walked too far and began to sink. He has asked me to tell you his thoughts."

Zetia turned to Tybin, "he said your bravery to immediately jump in and to keep talking to him will forever be etched on his soul."

"Iza, your ability to hear the night sounds and see without light proved to be their salvation to get them out of the water before they both drowned," Zetia told her.

"Deborah, Lander bows to you. Your warrior instincts with the logs was a brilliant tactical move," Zetia smiled at her.

"Trevins and Phum, Lander believes all would have perished if not for you. From securing the logs to guiding all of them through the swamplands. He says even I wouldn't have done it as well as all of you did," Zetia stated as she bowed to them.

"Jerin and Nickalli, your quick thinking to hold onto Iza and wrap the rope and tie it to Tybin's horse was the hope he needed they would survive," Zetia humbly stated.

"The swamplands were not the path I would have chosen if not for Nahrita. I did not tell you when we left the sanctuary the seriousness of getting to Oshyama. The easier path was blocked by Nahrita and her followers. Uri has been tracking their movements since all of you arrived back with Ayden's feathers," Zetia revealed.

"By entering Oshyama the way we did, we were off her scent. She expected us to follow her path and she placed enforcers at several strategic points along the way, hidden, to ambush us. We had to come this way to succeed," Zetia explained.

"We will stay here at least two days to plan the best move to go forward," Zetia informed them. She swept her hand across the room, saying, "my friends you see amongst us are here to help you and teach you about this land. Rest and relax freely, you are safe, now. Take this time to refresh and prepare your hearts for what lies ahead," she stated as she went to hug each of her friends who survived the swamplands.

Deborah sighed as she finally felt safe and could afford the luxury to look around without the fear of bubbling and gurgling. She looked at Nick and both grabbed each other's arms, silently saying, 'we made it out of the scary swamp traps.'

The hut looked like a summer home or cabin on the inside. Rustic stained wood in grays, blues and corals graced the furniture and walls. One whole side of the building was covered in slated shades from the floor to almost the ceiling. The opposite side had several windows and benches to sit at to look out towards the swamps.

The new faces of people brought Deborah back to memories of when they first entered Zetia's sanctuary months earlier. Besides new people, she saw animals too. Her heart jumped with excitement at meeting new, friendly, souls.

Five men, six women, a fox, a goat, a woodpecker and a small bear walked around, freely, obviously very familiar with Zetia and her ways. Most of the men and women had different shades of beautiful olive skin like Iza's. Their dark brown hair flowed in the same manner as Iza's too.

Deborah sadly thought, "Iza's mom said she was stolen from this region."

She noticed everyone was retiring to their designated sleeping areas, and she was excited it was beds they got to sleep in. Her bed was the farthest away from the activity and it was barracks type sleeping.

Iza's bed was next to hers and she was already sitting on it. Just staring. Deborah sat down next to her and said, "Iza, are you OK?"

"The women look like my mom when she was young," Iza whispered. "I mean before my mom's hair turned gray." Iza looked at Deborah and slightly smiled. "Do you think any of them know my mom? Her relatives, I mean," Iza asked Deborah?

Deborah grabbed Iza's hand, and said, "I don't know. I am sure you will get some kind of answers from them while we are here." She gestured for Iza to lay down and she did the same.

The next morning, Deborah quickly ate and excitedly told Nick and Jerin, "let's go exploring." The three of them got up and walked outside.

Deborah hadn't realized the night before they were walking on sandy ground. She immediately stopped and said, "listen! The ocean is close to us!"

Deborah ran to the farthest side of the hut and squealed with joy. "No wonder I felt like I was lulled to sleep last night," she proclaimed.

"The sounds and the smells of the ocean wrapped me in peace," she dreamily said as she walked towards the water.

"Take off your boots, Deborah," Jerin encouraged her. All three of them sat and removed their shoes. The sand squeezed between their toes while they walked. The ocean lazily flowed to the shore with bubbles staying as it ebbed back out.

Deborah waded up to her ankles and stopped. "What a wonderful sensation to have it continuously flow in and out over your body," she blissfully expressed.

Zetia walked up beside her and laughed. "I knew you would love Oshyama. It fills me with joy I get to see your first experience to the wonders of my land," she proudly said.

Deborah grabbed her hand, and said, "thank you, Zetia. There is no other I would have wanted this first moment to happen with." Zetia hugged her and walked back to the hut.

Deborah looked to her right side and saw Jerin and Nick standing like her. "Have either of you been here before," she asked?

Both of them shook their heads no, not able to speak as they were enthralled by the scenery and sensations all around them. The three of them stood in silence for several minutes, not saying a word as they watched everything.

Finally, Deborah giggled when she noticed the Trevins farther down the beach. All of them had their arms full of clams and were trying to walk without dropping them in the unlevel sand. Phum was sitting even farther up the beach with a pile of rocks. She laughed when she realized they needed the rocks to break the clams open.

Jerin and Nick decided to leave and go off in another direction. Deborah sat on the dry beach, playing with the sand as she continued to watch the landscape, ocean and wildlife.

"Absolutely beautiful," she quietly said.

"I am pleased you like my land," a brownish furred fox with red and white highlights at the tips of the brown stated. Deborah turned to the animal, smiled and nodded.

"My name is Suna," the fox said.

Elora, who had had joined Deborah earlier, said, "what a pretty name, Suna. It reminds me of the sun and Sunbird Village."

"My name comes from the Sunflower starfish because my coat looks like the sea creature. Not from the village name. But, oh! I have wanted to visit Sunbird Village for a very long time," the fox said. "Zetia has promised me she will take me one day," she gleefully stated.

"How do you know Zetia," Deborah asked?

"My mother was pregnant with my brothers and I when she was beaten to near death by Choran's enforcers. They were on a search for young children to steal for the Dark Cell," Suna began to explain.

"My mother fought bravely to hide three four-year-old girls under a shed after it was burned down by the evil men," Suna proudly claimed.

"They killed everything in the village which is way on the other side of Oshyama. It was my mother's home. It is close to the mountains, just before the elevation starts to go flat and then goes to the ocean," Suna stated.

"Zetia came upon the massacre after the men left with the girls. She walked around to see if there were any survivors," the fox continued her story.

"She found my mother and another girl my mother was able to push farther down in the rubble to not be seen. My mother distracted the men from finding the girl by getting up after the men thought she was dead. She ran the best she could with her injuries away from where she had hidden the girl. They beat her again and she lay on the ground, feigning death," the fox said with deep sadness in her voice.

"She was able to tell Zetia the men only got two of the girls and then stopped talking."

"Zetia flew my mom and the girl to the Great Tree. Zetia, herself, cared for my mom and helped her deliver her babies."

"My brothers were dead in the womb, but I survived and my mother died too after she gave birth," the fox whimpered as she relived the story.

"Zetia brought me here to be raised near the ocean and named me Suna," the fox humbly finished.

Deborah thought, "Choran, Nahrita and the other faction are nothing but pure evil. It disgusts me how they spread sorrow wherever they go."

Deborah quickly returned to the present and asked, "what exactly is this place we are at?"

"This is a sanctuary of Zetia's," Suna stated. "Not like the one you came from with magic, but a sanctuary because it is difficult to get to it. It is called Black Grove Outpost. "It is a remote coastal inlet surrounded by high craggy rock and the black mangrove trees," the fox explained.

Deborah looked to where the fox was gesturing and saw huge trees with their massive roots weaving around each other. Their beautiful canopy of leaves lightly swayed in the breeze while their trunks and roots were gnarled and withered from the ocean air.

It seemed like the roots deliberately stayed above ground to soak up any salt-free water and light they could find. The black mangrove trees with their exposed roots looked gorgeously regal in their ability to survive in even the most difficult environment.

"To arrive here you have to come on boat; unless you dare come through the dangerous swamplands. But, not too many are foolish to do that." Suna quickly flashed her eyes in horror and said, "not to say all of you are foolish. You are all brave, of course."

Deborah chuckled at the fox's fear she had offended them. "Well, we had Zetia as a guide sort of, anyways. She gave good instructions to help us stay safe. But, I agree, it is foolish to come through the land. It was really, really scary," Deborah stated.

"How many live here," Deborah continued to question?

"Well, this is an outpost where only a few of us live," the fox answered. "The main village is farther away, around the largest rock formation over there," she said as she pointed to the left with her paw.

"This camp was set up by Zetia as a lookout for intruders who were senseless enough to try and cross the swamp. I have been here for eight years and have only seen five make it through."

"The minute they reach solid ground they are so relieved they didn't die. But, no one can be sure if they are evil. So, their first drink is a potion to keep them dazed and docile," she explained.

"Our villagers take the weary soul to the mainland, but before they let him on dry ground, they slyly give him tea with the potion Kalim from the sanctuary made. The powder is to erase their memory of the outpost stay. They keep all their other memories because it is only a twenty-four-hour memory potion. In this way, the traveler can never return, nor tell others about us," Suna revealed.

"Here, at camp, there are usually ten to fifteen people and plenty of animals which come and go as they please. The village has over a couple of hundred or so humans. There are certain villagers who have chosen to take three month shifts to live here and then go to their homes at the village for a new group to come and watch for intruders," Suna told them.

"Zetia set up the needed watches as a vacation destination for the villagers. While they are here, all food is what they request beforehand and is brought with them. Whatever amenities they want, she makes sure they have it. Plus, while they are gone from their home, they can make a list of repairs or new things they want built and Zetia guarantees it will get done." Suna enlightened Deborah and Elora.

"Most of the outpost watchers come from the island while others come from a Zetia sanctuary. Some came directly from the Dark Cells. First, though, she took them, the Dark Cell dweller I mean, to a sanctuary to make sure they would be allowed to enter. If there was darkness in their soul the sanctuary would refuse to open its portal. She would then take them wherever they wanted to go in Eshra; but not a sanctuary or here," Suna knowledgably told the girls.

"To leave here, you will have to take a boat to get to our village and then another boat to get to the mainland," she continued her report.

"Before Zetia, this whole area, the outpost and our village, was uninhabited land," Suna finished with a sigh. "Lots of information, huh?" She said to the girls.

"Yes, I would definitely agree with you. Lots of information," Deborah stated. She jumped when she unexpectedly heard a new voice.

"I may want to stay here when this is all over," Kit stated. "I think I would like living here," he concluded.

"I didn't see you come and join us, Kit," Deborah declared.

"Yes, I am stealthy like that," Kit agreed and walked away.

The bell rang and one of the men yelled it was lunchtime. Deborah was surprised they had been on the beach for so long.

Zetia waited until everyone was seated and eating before she stood to address them. "I have already gone to the island of Lametis to secure passage to the area in the vision. The elders have given me specific instructions on who will be allowed to go with me."

"Deborah and Nekoh," Zetia turned to them to say, "the elders are extremely excited to see if you will be able to restore the Spidersong Lilly to the Groves since it hasn't been seen in hundreds of years."

"You two will go, along with one male. Jerin will help me man the boat and, of course, Kit will be with us. It took some convincing, but I was also able to ask for three more to go. Trevin, Phum and Eleea will join us," Zetia stated

"I will fly the ones allowed to go to Lametis tomorrow. The rest of you will stay here until we return. Our next move will be determined by what the peacock spider tells us," Zetia concluded.

"What is the purpose of staying here rather than your island, Zetia," Gethsemane asked?

"Gethsemane, this outpost is a well-kept secret, but not beyond knowledge. Yet, it is fairly impenetrable to outsiders," Zetia stated.

"There are those who do not hold the same value as we do to Ehyah. Choran has, over the years, placed spies in Oshyama. They blend in and work amongst the islanders," she grimly stated.

"None the less, it is difficult to get to this outpost," Zetia explained.

"But, Lametis has changed. The elders still make the decisions, but I sense an unrest. My fear is Choran's spies have become deeply infiltrated in the island. All of you are safer here than Lametis," Zetia gravely stated.

"We stay here until your return," Gethsemane agreed as he nodded to Zetia.

Chapter Thirty-Eight

Lyt came flying back into the cave overly excited. "No, no, no, friend, I am beautiful," he declared. "I have found water to see my beautiful necklace," he exclaimed.

Greysun and Nip immediately jumped up. "Show us, now, Lyt," Greysun demanded.

Lyt happily guided his friends to a stream with a pocket of still water off to the right of it. Greysun and Nip stared in the water and Ayden knelt next to them to turn their necklaces around their neck to show the feather to them.

Lyt jumped and flew at the same time saying, "no.no.no, friend, turn mine, too!"

Ayden helped Lyt see his feather and then stood up, saying, "do you guys want to stay here while I go to the top and search?"

"I go where you go," Greysun loyally stated.

Lyt immediately jumped into Nip's sling and Nip said, "team, Ayd."

Ayden giggled saying, "OK, team let's get going."

The peak was ominous in size with very few trees on its face. The last tree was at least twenty-five feet below its uppermost point. Ayden flew around it several times to try and determine the best place to start their search.

Finally, Ayden found a spot where she could land which was close to the top. One where she could safely stand without falling off the rock.

She looked around, touched different sections of the pillar, and decided no secret doorway could be opened. Each act she performed, she explained to her friends what she was doing, hoping they may accidentally run across what she was trying to find. She did not let them leave the security of the sling or her back, worried they could fall and hurt themselves.

"No, no, no, friend, let me fly around the rock," Lyt begged. "I know what you seek, now. I can help," he continued to beg.

"Fine," Ayden stated. "But, Lyt, you be careful and do not do anything rash," she advised him.

For two days they did the same procedure down the face of the rock until they got to the trees. All four of them felt the other's frustration each day they stopped and went back to the cave to eat dinner and sleep.

"I am totally baffled," Ayden stated as they ate. "Tomorrow we take a break and relax. I need to take a bath and have clean clothes," she told her friends.

"I mean, seriously, Ehyah wants me to rescue him, but he only gives half-messages to do it. What is up with that," she disappointingly asked as they all laid down to sleep?

Living in Hollow, since the enforcer invasions, caused Ayden to always be on guard duty. Her normal was to make sure she was prepared no matter what. Lazily leaving things around in the cave or wherever she worked or played was not an option.

Each time she finished something she packed everything back in her pack in case she had to bolt to safety. Or, in case they had to quickly flee and not return; she wanted all of her belongings always with her.

This vigilant take on her normal followed her to the water the next morning to get all of them clean, including her clothes. As usual, Nip was a mess, believing she knew how to clean her own body best. Ayden succumbed to Nip's cries and let her clean herself.

Ayden packed everything back in the pack after they bathed and ate. She sat to watch the animals play for a while and then decided to lay down on the grass. She propped her back and head up on the little hill near the stream and closed her eyes.

Dreamily she hummed to the sound coming from what she thought were her memories. Her mind wandered, questioning her as to what memories she was remembering. "Birds," she decided.

"Hummingbirds to be exact," she confirmed. "When did we hear them," she asked herself? "Well, on the way to Sunbird Village when they wouldn't leave me alone. Constantly fluttering around me, stirring up my hair and clothes," she told herself. Suddenly, she shot up and placed her ear to the ground.

Greysun tried to place his ear to the ground too. "What ya hearing, footsteps," he nervously asked?

Ayden looked at him and shook her head no. She tried to hear the sound more clearly.

"No," she whispered. "I hear the stirring," she told him. "It's the sound of the hummingbirds' wings," she explained.

Nip and Lyt came over to try and hear the sound too. Both of them put their head to the ground like Ayden.

"It's close," Ayden said. "Somewhere near here is the opening. Not the top of the peak. Doesn't surprise me, really. Eshra riddles and half-messages all of the time. I know I am right this time. We are close to the entrance," she said with relief in her voice.

She put her backpack on, turned to her friends and said, "you guys stay close to me."

Ayden continued to walk, stop and listen all around the area. "OK, I walk this way and the sound disappears." she explained.

"I walk closer to where I first was resting and the sound is a little more," she stated with a tinge of frustration.

"But, if I go any farther than right here where I first heard it, I don't hear it," she said as she sat down.

"And, once again, I am baffled," she told the animals. "So, does it move around and not stay in one place," she questioned?

She stood back up to fill her water bladder. The animals, followed her first order and kept right next to her. They almost tripped her when she finished filling the container.

She began to fall back and caught her balance, saying, "Oops, sorry guys. I forgot I told you to stay close."

Ayden looked down at her feet to make sure she was on steady ground. Next to her left foot was a strange looking vine; unlike any they had seen in Hollow before.

In her heart she heard the Great Crane, *'the passage you seek is by your foot. Listen to your heart, Messenger, and you will see it.'*

Ayden bent down, picked it up and tugged on it. It was taunt, like it was anchored to something. She lifted it up farther, where she saw it led up the stream to the base of the mountain.

Hand over hand, she kept ahold of it as she followed it to where it seemed to end in the face of the mountain. Not wanting to lose it, she kept one hand on it and used her other hand to see if the rock had an entrance.

She moved the leaves back away from the end of the vine and gasped. Molded into the rock face was an indentation for her to place her two halves of her necklace.

Impulsively, she grabbed and held on to her silver wings for several seconds. Ayden pulled the chain out from under her shirt, looked at the design made by Nadab at the Great Tree and then at the depression in the rock.

Greysun sniffed the formed stone, looked at Ayden and said, "Try them, Ayden."

Ayden nodded to Greysun and took the chain off of her neck. She placed the wings to fit in the rock and stood back to look at them.

The ground began to rumble. Nip jumped halfway up her leg where Ayden caught her and put her in the sling. Lyt flew close to her and she opened the sling for him to jump in also.

She held onto Greysun's necklace and waited to see what would happen next as the two of them helped keep each other keep steady. The rock face began to tremble.

Like an old door creaking open in a horror movie, the rock slowly separated to reveal an entrance into a cave. Not letting go of Greysun, Ayden and he walked into it.

They got a couple feet past the opening when it slammed shut with a loud sound of thunder. Both of them jumped and checked each other to make sure they were not hurt.

Pure blackness surrounded them once the door was shut. Ayden lifted her wings for light to emit from them.

"Well, guys," she whispered. "I guess we are in the bowels of Hollow, now. Greysun, I am taking a couple of my bandanas, tying them together and tying one end to you and the other end to me. This place is way too creepy to lose one of us in it," she determined.

Ayden decided three scarves were a better rope than two and quickly secured them to her and Greysun. She spread her wings to look around with light, trying to decide what their next move should be.

A smooth marble path with rock walls on each side looked to lead farther down into the mountain. She took a step and almost slipped. Ayden sat down and inched onto the smooth surface.

Suddenly, she and Greysun were sliding down the path like they were on a sled swiftly traveling down a snow packed hill. Greysun's body hugged Ayden's back as they slid to the bottom and stopped.

Ayden stood up and fanned her wings. A huge room with a flat granite surface led to several different passageways which looked like the one they first entered.

"Great!" Ayden said in frustration. "Which one do we take?"

"Listen for the stirring, Ayden," Greysun reminded her.

"Right. But I am a little too frazzled right now to hear," Ayden told him. "How about we sit and eat. We need to gather our senses and be wise about what we do next," she decided.

Ayden pulled out the food, using her wings for light she cut up vegetables and greens to add to her bowl of dried meats and ran her finger around the edge of it. "We need to eat as hearty as possible to maintain our strength," she told them while she cooked.

Nip and Lyt huddled together for moral support near Ayden while Greysun sniffed around the ground to make sure no unsuspected traps were close by for any of them to accidentally fall into. All of them ate in silence, trying to listen for unfamiliar sounds.

Ayden and the animals finished eating and she put everything away. She put her ear to the ground to see if she could hear the stirring. There was nothing.

She stood up and began to go to each entrance, putting her head to the opening to listen. The animals followed her lead and did the same act. Her eye caught a shimmer off to her right.

She snapped her head towards it hoping to see it again. Slowly she moved closer to the one entrance they had not listened to yet.

Hanging in the middle of the opening, on a jutted-out rock was her necklace. Carefully she held it, not wanting to pick it up fast in case something happened.

With her free hand she gestured for Nip and Lyt to get into the sling. She reached down her leg, not taking her eyes off of the necklace and made sure she and Greysun were still tied together.

Ayden gradually took the necklace off the rock and put it around her neck. Abruptly, the four of them were in the air whirling down farther into the core of the mountain.

Ayden grabbed Greysun and held onto him tightly as she put her chest to him to make sure Nip and Lyt didn't fall out. The speed they were traveling, caused Ayden to catch her breath to try and breathe normally.

With a thud, they hit the ground and Ayden quickly checked her friends to make sure they were OK. She stood and spread her wings for light.

They were on flat ground. But not ten feet away, all around them, was a gigantic crevasse which led farther and farther into blackness.

"No way," Ayden expelled. "We have to fly. We have no choice but to go down," she solemnly stated.

Chapter Thirty-Nine

Zetia double checked to make sure Jerin, Deborah, Trevin, Phum, Kit, Nekoh and Eleea were snug and secure on her back. She nodded to Gethsemane and lifted her wings for flight.

Deborah who was in the front, became extremely uncomfortable when Jerin's grip became tighter and tighter around her waist. She moved her head to her shoulder and said, "Jerin, relax you won't fall. Look around you and enjoy the beauty of flight," Deborah advised him.

She felt Jerin's body loosen as he gasped. "Beautiful, isn't it," she asked him?

"Unbelievable," Jerin softly breathed.

They flew for approximately thirty minutes before land could be seen ahead of them. A large island with an offshoot of a smaller section barely connected to the larger one appeared.

Zetia set down at the outer tip of the smaller one. Two men with five horses met them as she helped her passengers off of her back.

"Raiah and Tayden, thank you for meeting us," Zetia said as she bowed to them. "I would like you to meet," she gestured to her traveling companions to move closer and introduced them to the men. Everyone bowed to each other in acknowledgement.

"We landed here," Zetia swept her hand around their surroundings, "to avoid detection from spies," she soberly stated.

"To reach the elders, we will have to travel to the main island. Raiah and Tayden will be our guides for the next two hours," she explained.

Everyone mounted their horse with Trevin and Phum riding on Jerin's, Kit on Zetia's and Nekoh and Eleea on Deborah's horse. Raiah took the lead while Tayden brought up the rear.

The land was mainly sandy beach mixed with rock formations which they had to carefully climb over to reach more sand. Finally, the ground became more dirt-like and less rocky and sandy.

Deborah saw palm and coconut trees everywhere. Tall grasses of all sorts, still green, flowed with the breeze of the wind and dotted the horizon. Small hills soon emerged, covered in lush green grass which almost looked like moss.

Huge flowers with shades of pinks yellows, reds and blues began to show amongst the moss hills and her heart was full of wonder as they passed by all of it.

Still mesmerized by the sights, Deborah felt the familiar fight or flight sensation crawl up her neck. She quietly looked around her as fear rose in her throat.

She felt like darting out of danger, but only saw a wolf laying on a hill farther away from them. She turned her eyes away and then she snapped them back.

"Wolf," she yelled. "Enforcers," she yelled again.

The caravan immediately stopped to take cover and search for where Deborah saw the wolf. Raiah and Tayden quickly took the horses and made a circle. Everyone's weapons came out to defend their friends as five enforcers with five wolves and another man approached them.

"Zetia," the man said. "How good to see you again," he smirked.

"Your elders are dead," he continued to taunt her. "Well, all of them but one who didn't show when I requested their advice to a problem I was having with my children," he continued to smirk with an eerie laugh.

"Arnden, this is a path your father will weep over," Zetia sadly stated.

"Nahrita has promised me greater reward than anything my father could have given," Arnden angrily stated.

"He can weep all he wants in the soul world," Arnden haughtily declared.

"He, too, chose to die this day as an elder by my hand when he denied me this land to do as I desired," Arnden revealed.

"My reward comes when I kill you, the last one who can fly. And those who go to help the Messenger," he yelled as he charged.

Zetia immediately flew up away from him where she landed behind the enforcers and swiftly killed two of them with her wings.

The closest wolf to her, jumped up to grab her arm where Nekoh jumped on the animal's back and Jerin's arrow downed it with blue smoke pouring out of its chest as the sharp point hit its heart.

Jerin quickly turned with an arrow in his hand and released it where it hit another wolf with flames. The wolf let out a blood curdling scream as it withered in pain from the fire which surrounded and engulfed him.

Deborah whisped out of the way and perched on a small tree higher up from the fight. She waited for her chance to join in.

Another wolf lunged at Raiah. Raiah jumped back and showed his wings which looked like Zetia's where he sliced the throat of the wolf.

Tayden flew to his friend and circled another wolf and enforcer. Strategically watching for a chance to engage in combat.

Eleea attacked the fourth enforcer around the man's face with his winged blades. Phum and Trevin climbed up the man's legs to his neck where both of them sliced his throat.

Deborah watched the wolf dive at Tayden and saw her chance to act. She whisped in when the wolf jumped up to expose his chest. She dug her knife into the animal's belly and kept slicing upwards where the wolf's guts sprawled out of its cavity.

Tayden kept his watch on his enforcer as Deborah killed the wolf. The enforcer jumped out of the way of Deborah's fight and Tayden moved in for the kill. His winged spine struck the man's chest where he twisted the blade and the man fell to his death.

The fifth wolf didn't know what hit him when Jerin's arrow froze the animal as it died in midair. Jerin looked at Deborah and nodded. Her mouth was dropped open as she had not seen the wolf jump at her.

Nekoh jumped on the back of the fifth enforcer where he dug his teeth into the man's exposed neck. Raiah took his winged spine and struck the man in the chest and sliced him open. The man fell to his death with Nekoh still holding on.

Zetia and Arnden began the dance to see who would attack first as they made a wide walk around the other fighters.

"Arnden, Nahrita will kill you the minute she is through with you," Zetia informed him. "What of your family? How will they feel to see you turn on your father and your land," Zetia sadly asked?

Arnden maliciously laughed, saying, "I sent my wife and children to the Dark Cell. They do not fit into my plan to rule Lametis. And," he gestured towards Raiah and Tayden, "it would seem my father is nothing but a liar who never told me there were others like you!" He jealously yelled.

"My heart aches for your family, Arnden," Zetia stated. "Today, they not only lost a legacy with your father, but they have also lost all hope because of your act to send them there."

Arnden snickered an evil laugh as he said, "you don't get it, Zetia. They are of no value to me. None of them," is all he said as Jerin loosed three arrows into his chest where he fell to his knees. He looked at Zetia with shock and died.

Zetia, stunned, looked at Jerin. She put her hand on his arm.

Jerin put his bow back in his quiver and resolutely said, "he did not deserve to say anymore." Jerin turned and went to the horses to make sure they were not harmed.

Deborah came up beside Jerin and rubbed his arm, saying, "we will get his family out of the Dark Cell, Jerin." Jerin looked at Deborah with tears in his eyes and nodded.

"How many more are there of you, Raiah and Tayden," Zetia asked with guarded excitement.

"There are ten more, Zetia," Tayden stated. "We were told to stay hidden and tell no one we had wings by the elders," he sadly stated as he wiped tears from his eyes.

Raiah came next to him and put his hand on his shoulder to comfort him. "Our parents were all killed by Choran," Raiah revealed.

"Arnden's father kept us hidden and protected. He silently raised us amongst the people of Lametis. He chose families he knew he could trust to protect us. Arnden knew nothing of our existence until today," Raiah revealed.

"When it was time for our wings to show forth, his father sent us far away on a remote island for our enlightenment journey to learn how to use them properly," Tayden stated.

"We were told the stories of you and Zayden. As well as all of the stories of old Eshra.," Raiah proudly said.

"Arnden was always jealous of us because he never got to go on the same type of journey. He blamed his father, as he felt he was slighted by the elder," Raiah disclosed.

"Our journey included training in how to use our wings in battle," Tayden continued. "Uri was one of our teachers along with Joshua and Callie from Sunbird," he stated.

Everyone listened intently to the two men. Zetia moved towards them and put a hand on each of their shoulders. "I mourn with you for the loss of your friends at the hand of Arnden today," she humbly told them.

"Our plans have changed. The village is no longer safe and we set up camp here. Take Arnden's body and one of the enforcers and one wolf back to the village. Explain he attacked both of you while you were out searching for a lost lamb. Tell them what he told us about killing the elders and his desire to follow Nahrita and where he sent his family," Zetia told Raiah and Tayden.

"It is imperative for both of you to watch the reactions of those you tell," Zetia instructed them. "See who is shocked and who is disappointed in the news."

"Phum and Eleea will ride with you until you are close to the village. They will stay out of sight, but will watch too. They will be your extra eyes to see who is a spy."

"Speak to those who are trusted and have them help you determine who is a mole and then sequester the followers of Nahrita. Bring Eleea and Phum back to us when all is done," Zetia instructed them.

The men nodded and went to get Arnden's and the enforcer's bodies. They laid them and one of the wolves over a horse's back. Raiah turned to Zetia and said, "It will take us less than an hour to reach the village. We will leave two horses with you in case more trouble is near." Eleea and Phum jumped and flew up to his horse and they rode off.

Zetia turned to the rest, saying, "My heart is heavy and full at the same time. To lose the elders like this is devastating. But, to know there are more with wings is exciting. Two extreme opposite emotions and I am overwhelmed," she said.

Deborah went to her and they hugged each other for a long time. Trevin grabbed their legs and cried. Jerin came in next and put his arms around both of them. Kit fanned his feathers out and sang the sweetest birdsong Deborah had ever heard.

Nekoh began the sad job of gathering the bodies for burial. Once everyone saw him, they all helped.

"There are few words I can speak tonight," Zetia started to say over the fallen. "Yet, each soul came into this world innocent without blemish. Possibly, each of these souls, at one time, hoped to not have to follow the path they ended up on."

"Maybe, they were so deeply wounded they gave up all hope and turned to the convenient path of hate and jealousy. Still, it was a choice they made which is still very wrong to harm another because of what they have experienced. May they find peace this day," Zetia lowered her head and wiped a tear as she finished.

Deborah took her green powder and spread it all around the mound of bodies. She checked to make sure all her friends were clear and snapped her fingers.

Zetia gave all of them one final hug. "We move farther back where there are plenty of trees to set up camp," she told them.

Jerin and Deborah rode the horses with Kit, Nekoh and Trevin while Zetia flew to the spot she felt was best to stay for the night.

Raiah and Tayden reached the village where it was already evident a mourning bonfire was in place with the bodies of the elders on display. Four slatted beds for the bodies to be carried out to the ocean were covered in flowers and leaves of the island.

Arnden's mother fell to her knees when she saw her son on the horse. Cries and gasps could be heard throughout the village.

Raiah jumped down from his horse and lifted her to stand. Tayden came up on her other side as they guided her to the village main hall. The dwellers who lived there, followed the three of them into the building.

Tayden watched everyone assemble as they waited for him to speak. He deliberately kept his gaze away from Raiah to not alert anyone to their strategy.

Raiah quietly backed away from the center. He quickly spoke to a trusted few to explain the plan Zetia had set forth.

One man each stood at the back of the crowd in four different corners to watch who would rapidly leave when Tayden spoke. Eleea and Phum took two other spots away from the men to cover more area.

Once Tayden was sure Raiah was ready, he explained how Arnden had attacked them with a wolf and an enforcer. In great detail he told Arnden's words on who he killed and what he did to his family and why. Tayden emphasized Arnden's desire to follow Nahrita with the hopes of ruling the island.

Shock and gasps could be heard throughout the people. Three men, separated by several others in between them listened. And, then, coyly backed away from the crowd while they still faced forward. One step at a time they slowly moved until they were the last ones in the rows of those who were looking at Tayden as he spoke.

Quickly they each turned to leave and were immediately stopped by the men who were trusted. A potion was blown in their faces, they went limp and were carried away without the other villagers seeing what happened.

Eleea flew to Phum and whispered, "watch the girl next to Arnden's mother. Does she seem more agitated then sorrowful?"

Phum nodded to him and took off to Raiah. He told Raiah their suspicions and Raiah nodded he understood.

A new slatted bed was brought out for Arnden's body. He was laid on it and placed next to the elders. Some protested him being honored with those he killed while others simply cried.

Raiah raised his hand to stop the clamor and waited for silence before he spoke. "Lena has lost two of her family members this day to death. And, she has lost her daughter-in-law and grandchildren to the Dark Cell," he began.

"None of us can fathom the pain she and her ward, Bari, are feeling this moment. Yet, all of us feel the depth of loss for our elders and we need to respect their spirits as they lay here to prepare to leave for the water tomorrow," he reminded the crowd.

"It was terribly wrong of Arnden to do what he did today. But his soul also belongs to the Great Crane and he can do no more harm. Let the Great Crane mete out his penance in the World of Souls and let us put to rest our discord," Raiah wisely asked the villagers.

The crowd quietly began to disperse as they realized Raiah was right. Some stayed behind to comfort Lena and Bari while others placed wreaths on Arnden's body.

Raiah walked over to Tayden and told him what Phum and Eleea suspected. Their other friends who helped also heard his words. All of them kept watch on Bari without her knowing they were doing it.

Lena was surrounded by her friends who were helping her get home when Bari slipped away from the group. She turned to run and Tayden stopped her and lightly grabbed her arm, not letting her go.

Tayden acted like he was consoling her. He kept a tight grip on her once he was out of sight of the villagers as he led her to a hut where the others were waiting to talk to her.

"Please don't hurt me," the girl cried out. "He told me he would kill my family in the Dark Cell if I did not help him," she whimpered.

"Who told you this," Tayden asked?

"Arnden," the girl said.

"Very convenient, Bari," Raiah replied. "He is dead and we have no proof if you speak the truth."

"There are others," Bari defiantly lashed out at Raiah.

"Arnden always said you were weak Raiah. Following after his father acting like he was the Great Crane himself. Looking for a father because you never had one," Bari vehemently stated.

"Aw, true colors, Bari," Tayden responded.

"Nahrita will rule," she said as she tried to break Tayden's grip on her by thrashing her arm back and forth.

From the shadows a voice spoke out, "send her and the others to the remote island where they can live in peace and not harm others. If they choose to kill each other there, rather than learn to live harmoniously, so be it."

Raiah and the rest turned to acknowledge the voice. "As you wish Elder Kadrich," Tayden responded.

Chapter Forty

"OK, guys," Ayden nervously said. "Before we take the leap, I am going to shine my wings as bright as possible to see if we can find a place to land down there."

Ayden gingerly moved to the ledge and even more carefully opened her wings to shine. All of them looked into the cavern and all of them saw blackness past her wings with no ledges anywhere. Ayden moved back to the center of the solid ground and sat down.

"This is way scarier than I had planned," Ayden told her friends. Maybe we should sleep first?" She timidly stated. "If we are rested, and we have to fly for a long time, then we won't be as tired," she tried to convince herself and her friends.

"Ayden, the Great Crane wouldn't dump you into this predicament and then leave you," Greysun advised her.

"He believes in you. I believe in you. Nip believes in you. Lyt believes in you. Take the leap, Ayden," the dog encouraged her.

"Right, take the leap," Ayden heavily breathed out. She stood, double checked everyone to make sure they wouldn't fall and breathed heavily again. As she walked to the ledge, she continued to worryingly breath.

She lifted her wings and let them become brighter. Ayden decided to sing as she took off. "Life is here with you and me," she sang as she jumped.

She let herself go into a free fall for several minutes before she started to flap her wings to slow her descent. The light from her movement allowed them to see deep caverns which continued to lead farther down.

Ayden kept flying lower. Soon, she began to realize there was plenty of room for her to not worry about her wings bumping into the sides of the rock.

As she soared along the rock, she became familiar with the strange sensation of flying down rather than up. They traveled in this manner for several hours when Ayden noticed a different sound.

"Listen, guys," she said. "Is that water I am hearing," she questioned? Ayden flew towards the sound where she found a ledge she could land on. She easily planted her feet on solid ground and breathed a sigh of relief. "Look," she excitedly said.

Moss and green vines covered the wall of rock and each time her wing shined on it, it sparkled with the gentle water trickling down the growth. She moved her hand across the greenery as she walked along the ledge.

Unexpectedly, her hand fell through the moss and leaves to reveal a cave opening. Ayden deeply breathed and prepared herself as she walked into the entrance.

Once inside, they saw as far as they could see other cave entrances with the same foliage around their openings. Tiny little hills and flowers led up to each one and they noticed the one they were in had a plethora of flowers, vines, moss and other green growth all around a peaceful waterfall.

At the bottom of the waterfall was a small pond with the clearest water Ayden had ever seen. The rock veins along the outer edges of the pool were a rainbow of colors from pink, yellow, red, crystal, blue and turquoise where they looked like waves as they layered each other.

"We are staying here tonight," Ayden excitedly informed her friends.

She let Nip and Lyt out and unbuckled Greysun. Ayden put her hand near the water where her peridot ring glowed the closer she got to it.

She looked at it and decided it was because of the beautiful rock in the pool. She felt a tug on her hand and looked around her, and saw it was no one pulling on her.

She repositioned herself and used her other hand to make a cup. Ayden drank from the pool and said, "Mmmmm, guys it is delicious." The animals followed her lead and drank until they were full.

Ayden woke and for the first time in a long time she didn't care to look around her surroundings for danger. All she wanted to do was sit and soak up the delicious water and freedom of no fear.

She went to the pool and became engulfed in the wavy rock colors. Greysun nudged her as she must have fallen asleep again by the pool.

"Hey, Greysun," she said.

"Ayden, Nip is hungry," Greysun nervously stated.

"OH, sure. I'll get you guys food," she said. Ayden strew out their belongings all over the moss floor by the water and found the food.

She dumped the food out and said, "here you go." Ayden gazed back into the water. She took another drink and stared into the beauty of its formations.

Greysun nudged her again and she dreamily looked at him.

"Ayden, you have been sleeping for almost two days," Greysun worriedly said.

"It's OK, Grey," she managed to say. "Just let me rest," she asked as she fell asleep again.

Since they entered and slept the first night, Greysun had asked Ayden if she was ready to go and she would give another excuse to stay. He became overly sensitive to her behavior of how she didn't care if things were repacked or if the animals felt safe.

Even when he asked if she could hear the stirring, she would tell him it was no big deal. It was almost like she was in a trance with pleasure and sleep being her only comfort.

Ayden was by the pool when Greysun quietly gestured to Nip and Lyt to follow him. He walked as far as he could to avoid Ayden hearing him.

"Something is terribly wrong," Greysun whispered to them. "It is like a spell has overtaken her and she no longer cares about the prophecy and why we are here in the first place."

"Ayd sick," Nip stated matter-of-factly.

"Yes, Nip, she is very sick," Greysun agreed.

"No, no, no, friend, we have to save her," Lyt proclaimed. "Give her the blue drink, friend," he suggested.

"Great idea, Lyt, "Greysun stated. "But how do any of us get the bottle away from her or even get the lid off," he asked?

"No, no, no, friend, Nip and I hold it tight and you use your very large teeth to pull it off," Lyt explained.

"OK, how do we get her to drink it," Greysun asked?

"On candy," Nip proposed.

"Alright, we will work together, as a team to save her," Greysun thankfully decided.

Nip hopped over to Ayden's bag and began to rummage through it. Greysun lazily laid on Ayden's waist as he tried to claw the bottle loose while Lyt flew around her head.

"No, no, no, friend, tell me about your friends on the other side," he coaxed her. "I want to hear more about Nick," he continued to bug her.

Ayden laid back on the little hill and rubbed Greysun's fur. "Nick," she said as she closed her eyes. "Nick is a friend, Lyt." Ayden yawned and tried to stay awake to say more, but soon she was snoring.

Greysun gently pulled the bottle away from Ayden's belt to not wake her. The three of them went back to where they first hatched their plan.

Lyt and Nip hugged the blue vial as tight as they could. Nip had her front legs wrapped around it as Lyt put his wings around her legs.

Greysun took his front teeth and moved them back and forth while he held on to the stopper. It slightly moved and then it popped off.

Carefully he clenched his teeth to the glass and moved the bottle to his paws and held on to it, making sure it wouldn't spill. Nip tugged at the candy bag and used all her teeth strength to untie the knot Ayden had in it. She found the pecan caramel fudge, knowing it was Ayden's favorite and nudged it towards Greysun.

Greysun cautiously tipped the bottle to pour a few drops of the medicine on the fudge. Lyt flew with the topper in his claws and set it on top of the bottle where Greysun pushed it down tight with his teeth.

Nip carefully carried the candy back to Ayden in her teeth. "Ayd, Ayd," Nip yelled.

Ayden rubbed her eyes and looked at Nip. "What do you need, Nip," she lazily asked.

"Ayden, remember, you asked me to get the candy for you," Nip told her.

Greysun looked at Nip. Shocked she said a full sentence.

Ayden smiled and said, "Well, thanks Nip," she took it and devoured the whole piece.

Her three friends sat in anticipation to see what would happen. Excruciating minutes passed where it was obvious all of them were becoming more and more panicky.

Ayden shook her head and looked at them, saying, "where are we? Am I back at Zetia's? All I remember is dreaming of Zetia's. I felt for sure I was there and safe," she said in dazed voice.

She stood, looked at everyone and sat back down. "I feel funny," she said to them.

"It feels like I have been in a dream." Ayden steadied herself against the little hill and said, "maybe we need to go back to sleep."

All three of her friends yelled, "no. no, no, Ayden."

Startled, Ayden, said, "what is wrong with you guys."

Nip jumped in her lap and put her paw on Ayden's chin, saying "Ayd, you been sick, Ayd."

"What? What do you mean sick," Ayden questioned?

"We have been here for almost three days, Ayden," Greysun revealed.

"No, way," Ayden exclaimed. "We just got here, like maybe an hour ago or we just woke up from sleeping through the night, or maybe it is morning. Wow, I am totally confused," she cried out.

Greysun gently explained to her all the events leading up to her asking where they were.

"How come it didn't affect you like it did me," she asked? "I mean if it was the water, you guys drank it too," she confusingly said.

"Ayd, member when you come for me and I sick," Nip asked her?

"Yes, when we met at Sunbird Village. Choran's poison worked on humans but not animals," Ayden slowly said out loud as she remembered the event.

"This is scary," Ayden expressed. "I thought I was done with Choran and his evil ways."

"Why didn't my wings protect me from Choran's death grip? Zayden said my wings carry magic against Choran," Ayden angrily asked as she stood up?

"I don't know, Ayden," Greysun confessed as he whimpered because he couldn't help her find the answer.

Ayden felt remorse for her selfish rant and smiled at him, saying, "I know you don't. It's OK," she sympathetically said to him.

She stood up and looked around. "Wow! What a mess. I must have really been out of it to not pack everything back up each day." She sat back down and carefully gathered all of their belongings.

"Where would I be if not for you guys," Ayden humbly stated. "Thank you, again, for saving me." she said through her weeping. She took one more look at the beautiful water and sighed.

With tears streaming down her face, she said "I really hate Choran's evil ways."

Ayden gestured for her friends to get in place on her back and in the sling. She stepped outside the cave and breathed heavily. She looked over the cavern as she readied herself to take another leap to reach Ehyah.

Chapter Forty-One

Raiah flew back with Phum and Eleea to Zetia. He told her what happened when they arrived at the village. He explained the responses of everyone and how many of the spies they caught. He finished with Elder Kadrich's decision to send the defectors away.

Zetia listened closely and then said, "Raiah, it is too risky to put the village in danger. We cannot take the boats to the Groves. Go back and speak to Elder Kadrich. Tell him I request for you to fly with us to plant the seeds and talk to the peacock spider. We will wait here for his response."

Raiah nodded and flew off to talk to Elder Kadrich. Zetia looked at her friends and smiled.

"It is late, I will take first watch," Zetia told them. "Get some sleep, tomorrow will be a busy day."

Jerin was on watch when Raiah and Tayden returned. They landed and Raiah said, "Elder Kadrich agrees with you, Zetia. You have his blessing to do what you need to do. And I will fly with you," he finished.

Tayden gathered the horses, saying, "we wait for your return. May the Great Crane guide your path." He then strapped two horses to his saddle and rode off on the other one.

Zetia acknowledged both of them and asked everyone to prepare for flight. Deborah, Jerin and Kit rode with Zetia while the rest flew with Raiah.

They chose to take a longer route behind the village. Being, it would be farther away from the coast where the villagers would be saying their last goodbyes to their elders.

They flew for miles along the coast after the village was out of sight and then headed out to the open water. Dolphins jumped through the air and followed them as they glided above the water's surface.

Finally, the shoreline became visible with bamboo trees looking like they were touching the sky and smaller trees mixed in between them. The closer they got; Deborah could see the fruit pods Zetia talked about when they first met.

Off to the left was the rock fortress Nekoh described in the cave vision. It stood magnificently strong, surrounded by the ocean.

Zetia landed near the trees, helped everyone touch solid ground and walked over to the fruit pods. She plucked one and cracked it open. Smiling, she smelled the sweet nectar and cut off a piece for everyone to try.

Deborah couldn't decide if it was lemon or orange she tasted. She kept trying little bites to see if she could decipher what it was.

She looked at Zetia, saying, "this is amazing. I have never. Well, I don't know what to say it is so very different."

Zetia laughed, saying, "did I not tell you it was nothing like you have ever known before."

Nekoh kept turning around to see everything. "It is just like the vision," he kept repeating.

"Tomorrow we plant and see what happens," Zetia stated. "Tonight, we enjoy the sound of the ocean and the beautiful smells it creates while we sleep."

Raiah guided everyone to the hut deeper in the forest of trees. It looked like the one they left near the swamplands, except no other humans or animals were around.

Raiah explained only a select few from the village travel to harvest the fruit. Even though the fruit is ripe for picking, the unrest around the islands and the deaths of the elders had delayed its harvest. Everyone settled in for the night and slept peacefully, like Zetia promised.

Morning lulled the sleepy travelers awake with gulls on the beach screeching as they found bugs in the air or tiny sea creatures in the moist sand. Deborah walked out of the hut and watched them.

Her eyes followed the seashore where she saw three brown birds with fat bodies and fairly long legs and beaks all in a row. They were walking slowly up the beach with their heads down and their beaks in the wet sand, grabbing food. She knew the birds to be sandpipers, but had never seen them in real life before.

Zetia, Raiah and Nekoh stood outside the hut and looked towards the trees. "What do you think, Nekoh," Zetia asked?

"Well, if Deborah and I read the old books at Kalim's right, this type of plant likes to grow amongst the green grass," Nekoh told her.

Deborah walked up with Jerin, to join the conversation. "It is a peculiar plant, in that it seems to thrive in difficult terrain," she added.

"OK, over there is green grass and rock," Zetia stated.

All of them walked to the area Zetia pointed to. It was farther away from the trees and tufts of grass grew out of the rock where they gracefully flowed in the wind.

Deborah kneeled down, lightly touched the grass and then played with the soil around it. She looked at the rest of them, and said, "let's give it a try."

Nekoh asked his bag to give him the vial with the seeds. Deborah carefully removed one seed, took her knife and struck the rocky dirt, and removed the blade.

She looked at all of them and then placed the seed in the ground. They all stood back to watch. Nothing happened.

Deborah struck the ground in another spot, saying, "I really would like a Spidersong Lilly to grow." Still nothing happened. "Maybe, the seed has to germinate longer," she asked the others?

Silently, they stood still and waited. Kit walked up to them and asked, "what are you guys doing?"

"Trying to grow the Spidersong Lilly," Deborah stated, trying very hard to not show her frustration. She looked at Nekoh and Jerin with a look of, 'Really? He asks us what we are doing when this is the whole reason we are here?'

Nekoh lightly put his paw on Deborah's arm to show her support and turned to Kit. "What do you think Kit? Are we doing something wrong," he asked the bird?

"What have you already done," Kit asked? Nekoh explained everything they had already tried.

"Well, it is the Spidersong Lilly," Kit stated. "And, it is prized by the peacock spider, obviously. And, I am a peacock cousin of sorts to the spider," he continued to explain.

"And, the vision did mention 'when the gift of the Spidersong Lily is paid,' so maybe-e-e-e-e," Kit stopped and thought for a second.

"Maybe-e-e-e you need a feather from me to plant with it as a gift." Kit concluded.

"Absolutely, Kit," Nekoh appeased him. "Let's try your idea."

Deborah looked at Nekoh like he had lost his mind. Nekoh put his paw on her again and nodded to her. She shook her head and struck the dirt, again, with her knife in a different spot.

Again, she carefully extracted a seed from the vial and waited for Kit to give her a feather. Kit pulled a small feather from his chest with his beak and dropped it in Deborah's hand, saying, "this is a gift for the Spidersong Lily."

Deborah removed her knife, put the feather in first and then put the seed on top of it and covered it up with dirt. Everyone stood back, again, to watch.

Almost instantaneously, a green shoot could be seen breaking through the dirt. It continued to grow where large leaves folded out like a star. In the middle of the star a flower bud emerged with the most beautiful hues of purple which laid on top of the green leaves. More buds rose out of the center where the deepest blues mixed with streaks of white and yellow formed and rested on the flower petals in layers.

All of them gasped at its beauty. Unable to speak, they were stunned the feather worked.

All were stunned except, Kit of course, who said, "Yup, I think I am going to stay in this land." He plucked several smaller feathers, gave them to Deborah and said, "these are gifts for the Spidersong Lilly. He walked away, totally pleased with himself.

"The rock where the peacock spider lives in the vision has tufts of grass on it," Nekoh stated. "I say we save at least five feathers and seeds for the rock. The rest we should plant around this same area."

All were in agreement and Deborah, with the help of Zetia, planted the seeds. They quickly were surrounded by beautiful flowers which looked like a peacock's tail as they swayed with the soft breeze from the ocean. Shades of purples, greens, golds, blues, reds, oranges, yellows and teals graced the landscape when they were finished.

Jerin called all of them to lunch and everyone sat around the table. They looked out the door and stared in awe at the flowers while they ate.

Zetia turned to Eleea, and said, "I have an uneasy feeling about the others. Not that they are in danger. Yet, my heart says we all need to go the peacock spider together."

"Raiah and I will fly back to Black Grove Outpost and bring the rest here," Zetia decided.

"Elder Kadrich told Raiah I have his blessing to do what I believe is best. And, I believe it is best for all of us to stay together," Zetia determined.

"Especially with what has happened at Lametis, we need all of our skills to reach Ayden quickly," Zetia feverishly finished.

Eleea watched as Zetia and Raiah immediately took to the skies to bring their friends to the Groves. He looked at the rest, saying, "relax. This may be the last bit of respite we get."

Deborah heard a familiar sound and arched her neck up to the sky where she saw Tari flying around them. She smiled, at his subtle gesture to his best friend, letting Jerin know he was close. Jerin looked at Deborah and smiled back.

Deborah and Jerin walked to the beach and sat. "I don't like death, Jerin," Deborah said with sorrow in her voice. "So many lives have been lost due to senseless anger and greed."

Jerin took her hand and held it in both of his. "All of us have seen too much, Deborah," he said. "The pure ugliness of what we have had to do and see is because of one source, Choran."

"His twisted desire to rule what is not his has created disorder everywhere," Jerin remorsefully stated.

"But, if we chose to walk away and do nothing because of how we feel when we have to confront it," Jerin stopped, took his hand and lightly touched Deborah's chin and turned her face to look at him.

"If we chose to walk away, we are no better than Choran. To do nothing is to still do something. It is a deliberate act to allow others to suffer because we didn't want to see the suffering anymore," he resolutely finished.

Deborah studied each word Jerin spoke to her and silently let them soak into her heart. Finally, she said, "Jerin, I really do love you. Your words hit me deeply. I have been wrapped up in the pain of seeing and taking lives; forgetting the reason we have had to do it."

"There are still so many people in danger around Eshra and oppressed in the Dark Cell. We are not foolishly on a journey. We are on a mission of mercy to repair the harm Choran has created," she agreed.

"Thank you for always being there for me and helping me to see truth," she said as she hugged him and whispered in his ear, "no more tears it is time to fight for what is right."

Jerin hugged her back, saying, "Deborah, this fight is vicious. I have been concerned since the battle you and Ayden had with the enforcer and the wolf. You whisped and grabbed his knife. You were lucky to not be cut by it. I would like to help you train with a non-sharp knife while you whisp to hone your skill a little better."

Deborah stood up and excitedly said, "Awesome idea, let's get started."

Jerin produced a wooden replica of a blade with a handle. Deborah laughed, saying, "so, you just happen to have a non-sharp blade on you?"

"Yes," Jerin sternly said. "I made it when we were still in the marshland area. Right after you returned," he stated in a protective tone.

The two of them practiced the whisp and the skill to read a knife's trajectory by the sound it made when in the air for several hours on the beach. The better Deborah got at catching it the more they would laugh and play with the sound of the ocean behind them and sand between their toes.

The friends stopped to catch their breath from whisping and throwing. They looked out to the ocean where they saw Zetia and Raiah off in the distance.

Deborah grabbed Jerin's arm, and said "They're here. I am so happy to get see everyone." Both of them kept their eyes on the gorgeous view of Zetia and Raiah riding the Eshra winds.

Nick and Iza were still wide-eyed when they landed. Deborah laughed, saying, "unbelievable experience, huh, guys?" She tightly hugged both of them, telling them how much she missed them. Everyone walked back to the hut for dinner and conversation.

Chapter Forty-Two

The four traveled farther and farther into the bowels with only the walls of rock on each side for a view. Even though the descent was easy to traverse as she flew, Ayden was feeling weary of the hours without any place to land for a break.

"I don't know how much more I can take of this," she told her friends. "It is endless with no sight of relief," she forlornly said.

"Maybe, instead of thinking about flying down to nothingness you could listen for the stirring," Greysun suggested.

"Fair enough," Ayden agreed.

"Ayd, Ayd, sing," Nip piped in for her suggestion.

"Another good idea, Nip," Ayden stated.

"Life is here with me. Life is here with me. Because of you and me, life is here. Never give up, never forget, life is here," Ayden continued to sing as they flew. Soon, they were swaying with the beat of the song as they looked at the sides of the cavernous void on the way down.

They descended for another forty minutes when it finally dawned on Ayden the structures on each side were less rock and more dirt with some plant life on them. She kept singing as she slowed their pace and looked more closely at them.

Ayden also realized her wings were brighter with her singing as she kept her stride. She tried to fly closer to the walls to see if the plant life was growing while she was singing. Her heart told her it was, just like when they were in Hollow. But she couldn't be absolutely sure.

Abruptly, their downward trek leveled off where they were flying perpendicular into a smaller walled rock formation. Ayden barely was able to keep her wings from hitting the sides as she passed through it. On the other side of the narrow hallway was a floor of granite and dirt to match the walls.

Ayden landed and kept her wings out to allow them to continue to shine brightly. She moved to the barrier closest to her and felt its surface. Sure enough, there was grass growing on its face.

Her hand stayed on it as she kept walking to see how far the floor would go. She wondered if they would have to leave the sweet feel of ground under her to fly even farther down into the bowels.

The rock wall curved around to another larger area of stone and dirt floor. Ayden stopped to access for possible danger. Greysun nudged her to let him down and she unlatched him from her back, not taking her eyes off of her surroundings.

Once completely inside the floored area, she saw several entrances to tunnels. Her fear got the best of her and she went back to the middle of the floor.

She sat and listened while she watched for any dangerous activity. "Greysun, I am going to go to each entrance and try to look farther in them. But I am not going to enter any of them in case there is magic attached to them," she said.

Ayden slowly walked towards the first cave entrance where when she reached it, she placed her hand on the side of the opening and peered in. It was black darkness. Her peridot ring lightly glowed and seemed to pull her where she quickly lowered her hand. She tried every opening and received the same reaction.

She retuned back to where she first sat down. Lifting her wings to let the light shine, she saw all seven entrances. Each had new growth all around them like vines up a wall.

"No idea what cave we should take," Ayden told her friends as she let Nip and Lyt out of the sling.

"Even though no idea, I am thankful we are no longer flying down and down and down," she said with relief. "We stay right here tonight. At least I think it is night. Honestly, I have no idea what time of day it is. Doesn't matter, I am calling it our night," she decided.

Ayden pulled out the bag of food and they all ate. Greysun sat against her back while Nip sat on one side and Lyt sat on the other side of Ayden. Each of them watched for any foreign movement in their area of sight.

Ayden yawned, saying, "enough is enough. We all need to sleep. We explore our options tomorrow." She gently guided all of her friends with her right wing and they curled up next to her and slept.

"Life is here," Ayden hummed and sang while they ate the next morning. She stood to look at her options again.

She went to the first cave entrance and put her whole ringed hand in. The peridot glowed brighter and shocked her. She jumped and quickly pulled her hand out. Down the line she tried each opening with the exact same reaction. Ayden went back to the center and sat.

"Crazy," she said. "When we were at the beautiful pool of wavy water my hand did the same thing. So, I changed hands to drink the water, not thinking it was anything important."

Ayden looked at Greysun, saying, "do you think my ring is warning us," she questioned?

"I would heed its warning," Greysun said as he remembered the fear of almost losing Ayden at the pool.

"Since we can't enter any of these caves," Ayden wondered. "What do we do? Go back out and look for another path," she pondered out loud.

All four of them sat together in silence. Despair gripped them as they began to feel hopeless with no solution in front of them. They couldn't fly deeper as there was no more cavern leading down.

When they looked up, there was a ceiling of rock. And each cave possibly meant death. It seemed like the only option was to go back out the way they came in.

Ayden lowered her head and shut her eyes, hoping her heart could lead her. She quieted her mind and lyrics of an old, familiar Kansas song drifted into her thoughts. *"I close my eyes, only for a moment and the moment is gone. All my dreams pass before my eyes in curiosity. Dust in the wind. All they are is dust in the wind."*

Slowly, she opened her eyes and observed everything around here. She quietly lifted her wings to make it brighter in the room. A swirling of dirt, like a dust cloud, led up the rock wall where they first entered the big room with caves.

"Dust in the wind," Ayden screamed. "The dust is going somewhere above us. There has to be a way up there," she excitedly told her friends. She lifted her feet and flew to where the dust disappeared.

She hovered as she tried to see where it was going. It seemed to vanish into the plant growth on the wall. She flew back down to the floor to regain her balance.

When she thought she had enough strength to try again, she flew and hovered in the same spot. She looked at her ring, placed her hand where the dust seemed to go. It wasn't rock, but heavy growth which could be separated. And, her ring didn't give her any dangerous warning.

The dust particles swirled bigger when she made more room for them to pass through. She pushed with the front of her body and almost fell through the opening. Her heart was pounding extremely fast from the exerted energy to stay in one spot. She flew to the floor and waited until she felt she could hover again.

She turned to the animals, gestured for them to get in position to fly and then she made sure they hadn't left anything behind. Ayden flew up and hovered for a second near the opening.

She took a deep breath and dived in after the dust swirls. They broke through the vines and leaves from the force she used and tumbled onto a small grassy knoll. When they looked around, they saw what looked like another realm of the bowels.

Ayden gently turned a full circle around her as her eyes became bigger and bigger. Quickly she looked at her peridot ring to see if it was giving her any cautionary sign. It sat on her finger as it always had with no glow or pull. She sighed in relief and released the animals from her body.

The four friends kept turning in circles as they soaked in the view. Spacious blue sky with whimsical clouds playing across it seemed to be welcoming them. Hill upon rolling hill with lush green and floral growth danced in the wind.

To their right were water falls lazily flowing into a pond with water lilies and tall grass. It even had cattails and frogs. Animals! There were animals peacefully walking and flying all around them; acting like they knew them.

Ayden fell to her knees and wept. She choked out, "life is here," and continued to cry. Off to her left she heard a voice.

"Don't cry child, you have found us."

Next to Ayden stood her father and Ehyah. She slowly stood up and stared. Finally, she said, "I thought I would find you in a dark cell or something. Not a beautiful paradise."

"The bowels possess many realms, as you have already seen," Ehyah told her.

"So, why would you want to leave here," Ayden asked? "It is absolutely gorgeous and peaceful."

"This is the World of Souls. It is for the dead. Not the living," Ehyah stated.

"Ehyah and I are prisoners here, Ayden," Zayden revealed. "Choran could not kill Ehyah because of Eshra magic. Just like Eshra protected us where he could not kill you or I. But what he could do was close any access for Ehyah and I to return to the world of the living," he continued to explain.

"The prophecy was set before Choran first turned to evil," Ehyah stated. "Great Fox and I knew we needed to secure the worlds for what would eventually happen if Choran choose to follow evil and stop at nothing to rule all of Eshra."

"With me being the force, as the moon, to bring light to the worlds, we knew it would be me who he would attack. Yet, we still tried many times to show him his errors and to remind him of his role he had asked to have," the crane continued to explain.

"When the hummingbirds were chosen to be our communication, Choran became very manipulative to hide his displeasure with us," Ehyah began to tell the story of Choran's request and his role in old Eshra.

"He came to us and gave an excellent argument on why he should manage the World of Souls. He knew the skies of day and night with his vision and because it allowed him to travel through both with ease. Well, he suggested he would be the best choice to be the Keeper of Souls." Ehyah stopped to let Ayden process all she was being told.

"We gave him limited power in which he could be the Keeper of Souls, but he could not use his power of ruling these souls in Eshra or your world. He would have to let the natural course of life take its path and not manipulate it to his own desire."

"Great Fox and I felt the unrest very early on after he was granted the privilege for the World of Souls. But the decision had been made and old Eshra magic would not allow for it to be revoked. All magic has limitations and rules, Ayden," Ehyah disclosed.

"Once a word is spoken, it takes on a life of its own. It has been released into the universe to perform what was said," Ehyah instructed her.

"It is not any different than free will, Ayden. The path to choose good or the path to choose evil is up to the individual and it goes into the world with good or bad consequences."

"Choran felt slighted by us because he didn't have free will to do what he wanted. He had rules and boundaries. His anger boiled to where he decided he could create the Dark Cell where there, no one would tell him what he could or couldn't do."

"He chooses to live there, away from our seeing eyes. He found ways to use magic for his own selfish benefit," Ehyah said as he revealed Choran's anger to Ayden.

"I went to him to reason with him, again," Ehyah sadly stated. "I had hoped he would see he had been given a special and reverent part of old Eshra which would carry him forever with importance in our worlds."

"He was warned the snail fern would destroy his body over time. He had honor in his position as he was trusted to make sure the souls were at rest. He didn't want only honor; he wanted the glory to be worshiped."

"I explained to him the snail fern would not give him glory. He asked me to show him how I was right with the words I spoke."

"I went with him to the bowels and showed him the humble importance these souls felt for having a home of peace and rest. He waited until my back was turned and closed the portals to exit this realm."

"He set magic all around it and professed in his drunken hunger for power, 'it will take your mighty hummingbirds to carry you out of here.' He laughed at his humor, knowing the birds were too tiny to rescue me." Ehyah stopped, lowered his head and then looked at Ayden with a tear rolling down his face.

"Any hummingbird who dies is sent farther down in the bowels by him. None have enjoyed the freedom in the World of Souls. He was too fearful they would find a way to carry me out," Ehyah stated as he continued to cry.

Ayden sat down and cried with him. She looked at him, asking, "so, I have to go farther down and release the hummingbirds?"

"Yes, this is why you can hear the stirring, even though it is faint. They are calling to you," Ehyah joyously stated.

"Your friends are entering the bowels close to where they are kept. And, you will meet them there where a portal is weakening from Choran's hold. He is deteriorating rapidly because you entered Hollow to sing and fly."

'Life is here,' is more than just simple words to a song you made up, Ayden. Those words spoken, went into the universe and performed," he proudly told her.

"Why did it have to be me," Ayden changed direction, wanting more truth from Ehyah. "Why did I have to carry a birthmark all over my back," she quizzed the crane.

"The whole prophecy revolved around you finding me. We had to bring hope into Eshra, knowing it would take several hundreds of years to come to fruition. These were the words spoken at the same time the first part of the prophecy was set. Only a few knew of these words:

From the seven winds let Eshra choose the one
A child born with the mark of the crane
Hidden on the back deliverance comes
Mineral and spirit fuse when the chosen one
With Lametis blood rides
The Winds of Eshra
And, again the light shines in the land

"The most elusive way we could find to protect you was to give you a birthmark and to put you far away from Eshra. Great Fox and I hoped Choran would never figure it out. At least, not until you showed him who you were. We separated the two prophecies to protect you from Choran," he explained.

"We had to bring hope into Eshra. But fundamentally, it was Eshra magic which made the decision it would be you," Ehyah humbly stated.

"If you wish, Ayden," Ehyah began to ask. "Your mark can be removed by me, now that you have found us."

Ayden looked at the crane and then at Zayden. Her mind drifted to all the times she had been shamed for the mark. How she had to cover it up for so many years to avoid ridicule. And, then her mind drifted to what it meant to her now.

"When I was young, I would have easily told you to take it," Ayden told them. "What I have learned since, is it doesn't define me. Yes, it is a part of who I am. But I am more than a mark on my back."

"What I hold in my heart. How I choose to live my life with integrity, decency, respect and compassion is stronger than anything my body outwardly carries," Ayden passionately said.

"No, I will keep it. I have earned it. It belongs to me. And, I stand strong with it on my back," Ayden determinedly told the crane.

Ehyah regally bowed to her, while Zayden stood proudly smiling at her. Both sat on the hill next to them as they looked at Ayden.

"Since we are telling all," Ayden expressed. "I have a few more questions I want answers to. Why all the riddles instead of just telling me what I needed to know to get to you. And, why didn't my wings protect me from the water I drank," she asked defensively?"

"The short messages you received honed your skills to listen to your surroundings," Ehyah began to explain. "Plus, by giving you only partial explanations, we were able to keep Choran confused too. In this way, if he were told by another or overheard himself; he would not have been able to decipher the information."

"Yes, it is very frustrating for you and for others who also receive messages from me," Ehyah agreed. "But, ultimately, Choran could not know the true plan," he explained.

"Now, the water you drank, Ayden. This is Choran's world. He placed many such spells throughout these realms to thwart any chance of success by you. His fear caused him to be very thorough with evil magic," Ehyah continued to explain.

"All magic good or bad has limitations and expectations. The water was one of Choran's greatest feats as it almost destroyed you. Yet, even with its power it did not kill you. It only caused you to sleep. It was meant to kill any human who drank it. Your friends saved you and realistically your wings also saved you because you are not dead," the crane disclosed.

"So, since I have to leave here," Ayden returned to the original conversation. "Are you guys coming with us," she nervously asked?

"This brings us back to the hummingbirds," Ehyah illuminated. "The magic Choran put around this realm stated I could leave but the hummingbirds in the Soul of Worlds would perish with no rest. But, if I stayed, the birds would exist even though they would still be in blackness."

"He knew I would not leave unless the hummingbirds were free. He knew I would refuse to sacrifice my moral values to trade their souls for my own freedom. Pretty clever of him, really," the Great Crane revealed.

"When Zayden came; he came with a scar," Ehyah told Ayden. "Choran told him, 'if you try to leave Hollow or the bowels, I will know. You then forfeit the hummingbirds as I will never let them rest.' Choran marked Zayden with his claws, telling him the mark would warn him if Zayden left."

Ayden nodded, saying, "Zetia has the same mark, Zayden. She went to the Dark Cell to find you. She battled Choran and he did the same by tricking her."

Zayden acknowledged Ayden's remarks with pain in his eyes for his sister. Ehyah sadly shook his head and continued.

"Once you release the hummingbirds Choran's distorted magic will crack and become less," Ehyah educated her.

"But, in order for his magic to be completely removed, I must be in the skies of Eshra. You will have to return with the hummingbirds to us and fly us out of here," the crane explained.

"Your wings of silver, forged from the depths of Eshra rock and mineral have tremendous power to break through all of the bowels to reach the open skies. The lockets which lay against your chest hold the very essence of Eshra." The Great Crane proclaimed.

"It is only on your wings we will be able to ride the winds of Eshra, Ayden," Ehyah said as he bowed to her.

Ayden nodded at the crane and turned to Zayden, stating, "I am thankful I have found you. But I am angry you left my mom with no knowledge of who you were or who I am. You left us with no hope," Ayden hurtfully expressed.

"I was wrong, Ayden," Zayden remorsefully stated. "I did not trust Eshra to protect you. Ultimately, I did not trust your mom to keep you safe and I am sorry. I ruined her chance for happiness and for this I feel very remorseful. She was a beautiful woman and I destroyed her by leaving so abruptly. And, as a result, I damaged your childhood. All I can ask is for you to allow me to make it up to you when this is all over?"

"Well, it is going to take a lot of talking and trust for me to see you as a father. But I am willing to give you a chance," Ayden finally decided.

Ayden was relieved to have many of her questions about who she was and why her wings were silver answered. Yet, she sat stunned over the amount of information she was given from Crane. Filled with every emotion possible, her heart and mind seemed to be flooded with reactions.

Although, one emotion stood out amongst the others as the most important. The one of what needed to be done: to finish Choran's reign of evil. She nodded to Ehyah and Zayden, stood up and looked at her friends.

"You guys know how much I love you. My world became full and complete when you came into my life," Ayden passionately said to them.

"I am not choosing out of favoritism here, OK." She picked up Nip, hugged her, kissed her and set her back down. Next, she let Lyt fly to her hand where she kissed his head and let him fly down to sit with Nip.

"Nip and Lyt you are to stay with Ehyah and Zayden. Both of you are too little for this part of our journey. I promise I will return for you," she affectionately told them.

"Greysun," she said, "it is time for you and I to finish this prophecy and go home."

Chapter Forty-Three

"Suna, I am surprised and pleased to see you," Deborah stated while they walked to the hut.

"Yes, Zetia asked me to come and join the quest with all of you," Suna stated. "I am very good at burrowing. And, Elora has been a wonderful teacher and explainer about all we have to do and why," she said with admiration.

"We leave tomorrow," Zetia started to explain the plan while they ate. "We will be able to walk to the rock, but Raiah will also man one of the boats from the Groves."

"Uri tells me Nahrita has found a type of new magic to blast into the core of Eshra, in hopes to reach Ayden before we do. Her and the enforcers are two islands away from us."

"We will be deep in the bowels once the peacock spider tells us how to enter. It will be dark, void of life and probably full of caves. Suna is adept with this type of environment. Hopefully, she and the Trevins will succeed at being our eyes." Zetia sat back down as she finished saying what she wanted everyone to know.

Deborah turned to Iza, saying, "and, again, I have to thank you. If not for your kind words to me when Ayden and I had to kill the enforcer and the wolf, we may not be here right now."

Deborah and Jerin told all of those who stayed at the Black Grove Outpost about the battle with Arnden and the elder's decision. Tybin stood up after listening to all of the events of the fight. Obviously very emotional.

"We will not leave one soul in the Dark Cell, Jerin. Do you hear me, Jerin," Tybin proclaimed with tears in his eyes?

Jerin stood next to him and grabbed his arm in Ayden's handshake. "Tybin, brother, we will watch each soul leave to freedom." He locked his gaze on Tybin where Tybin nodded to him and sat back down, still emotional.

Deborah looked at Iza who was noticeably showing the same emotions as Tybin. She took Iza's hand in moral support.

Iza turned to her, whispering, "I understand his pain. For that man to send his family there is nothing but pure evil. My heart aches for them."

"Tybin, timing is everything, son," Gethsemane tenderly told him. "You will see your desire come to fruition. But, until the day is at hand, stay in the present with us. We need you here, not emotionally there."

"Gethsemane, I will not let you nor them down," Tybin fervently said and walked away.

Deborah caught Jerin's eye where they both read each other's thoughts, 'we need to keep an eye on Tybin.'

Iza looked at both of them and said, "I will keep a watch over him and help him settle down." They acknowledged Iza's words where she quickly left to follow Tybin.

Deborah and Jerin looked at each other, again, with semi-shocked eyes. Deborah lightly smiled at Jerin and arched her left eyebrow, silently saying, 'something is happening with those two.' Jerin smiled and nodded his head in agreement.

Deborah patiently waited on her bed for Iza to retire. She watched as the girl carefully tried to not wake those who were already sleep.

"Iza," Deborah whispered. "Did you find any answers about your mom," she asked?

"Yes," Iza whispered back. "Well, kind of, yes. One of the women was very familiar with Choran and his ways," Iza stated.

"Her name is, Maran. And, she said the people of this region are a prized possession of the Dark Cell," Iza revealed. "It seems our skin color and our skill with food is highly sought after down there. It didn't surprise her my mom was talented."

"She couldn't tell me exactly where my mom came from, but by looking at me she knew my mom was from Oshyama. I told her my mom knew she came from this region but didn't know any more. So, I got some answers, but mostly I got more questions," Iza sadly smiled.

The girls retired to their beds, but sleep was difficult with concern and thoughts of what the dawn would bring.

An unusually large breakfast was served when the day broke. Iza smiled at Deborah and said, "Zetia wants all of us filled with protein and fruit with some breads in case we need energy. We have only dried food to take with us from here on out."

After the meal, Zetia handed each traveler a large bag of dried food to put in their magical pack they had received before their journey. Each knew the pack would not burden them and would show itself when they needed it. Zetia triple checked to make sure all were prepared and they began the trek to the rock fortress.

Raiah took Kit, Tybin, Iza, Phum, Nick and all of the Trevins except for Trevin One in the boat with him. The water was choppier than normal and they had difficulty getting past the incoming tide.

Raiah finally, stood on the bow of the boat, and spread his wings. He took the attached rope and flew it past the tide.

The rest walked along the beach until they reached the craggy terrain where they had to climb up and down to move closer to the desired massive rock. It took both teams a good thirty minutes to reach its foundation. Water splashed all around it as the ocean water moved in and out.

Zetia looked at her team and said, "Gethsemane and I will fly around it to determine if there is any flat landing for us to all fit on."

Raiah threw the anchor in the water and said, "this won't hold against the ocean unrest. I have to find a stronger way to anchor us."

Raiah flew off to search the rock stronghold to see if he could use a rope around it. He met Zetia and Gethsemane in flight and explained his dilemma. Zetia flew back with him to the boat.

"We have found a ledge deep and long enough to hold all of us close to the top. Tybin and Iza get on Raiah's back and Nickalli and Kit get on mine. We will fly to the ledge and come back for the rest of you after I get the others secure."

Nekoh and Deborah assessed the rock face from the ground where tufts of grass were already growing. They had decided earlier to bring seven seeds and feathers with them instead of five.

The first tuft of grass was only inches above them. Deborah moved the plant to see if the dirt could be dug up. Very little soil was available as the grass was embedded deep in the rock.

"Thank the Crane my knife can cut anything like butter," she told Nekoh. She carefully pushed her knife into the rock next to the grass and moved the blade to one side. She put the precious treasures in the hole and moved the blade back to close the opening.

Within seconds the flower emerged, gracing the rugged surface with glorious color. Deborah let out a gleeful sigh as she smiled at Nekoh.

Zetia returned and Deborah asked her, "Zetia, can you fly and hover for me to plant a few more on the roughest part up there.?" Zetia nodded and Deborah got on her back with the seeds.

The first and second planting went as planned with the flowers blowing in the wind. The third one, Deborah lost her balance trying to reach too far. The vial went into a free fall down the side of the rock while all of them watched in horror.

Zetia yelled, "Deborah hold onto me or you will fall with it!"

Raiah flew in below them and grabbed the bottle before it crashed against the base of the rock. He then placed the vial in Nekoh's bag and flew both Nekoh and the bag to the upper ledge to wait for Zetia.

Sighs of relief could be heard by all of them. Zetia flew Deborah to the others who were waiting above them.

The wind was brutal as they all tried to keep their balance against the rock. The sounds from the heavy gusts muffled their speech, causing them to have to look directly at the person to be heard and understood. Yet, their speech needed to be short in order to be able to brace their backs to the rock wall and not fall.

Above them, were three more areas Deborah could plant the seeds. She could reach them without climbing, but would need support to not drop off of the ledge.

Tybin took his staff and placed it front of him Nick and Jerin. The weapon curved around them and dug into the rock to anchor them. They linked their arms together and stood in front of Deborah. She slowly turned her body to face the rock while Zetia held the vial. She would cut the opening and hold her breath until the seed was secure with the feather.

Each time one was finished, everyone breathed with her. All three flowers danced in the wind. Tybin released his staff and the boys moved back against the wall.

Nekoh could see Kit was having difficulty with each flurry of wind. He quickly pressed his body into the bird to keep him stable. Jerin reached down and picked up Trevin as his small stature was also becoming unsteady with the wind forces.

Suna jumped into Deborah's arms and they held onto each other tightly. Nick unlatched one button on his shirt where Eleea and Elora flew into it and he buttoned it back up to protect them.

Raiah flew up to them and tried to hover to talk. He rapidly said, "I cannot bring the rest of the Trevins or Phum here. It is too dangerous for all of us with this much air turbulence."

Zetia nodded to him and heard Trevin say, "tell my men to go with you to the Groves. And tell Nine he is their leader until I return." Raiah bowed his head to Trevin and took off for the boat.

The Trevins and Phum were told the new plan and Raiah safely got them to the beach. He secured the boat, looked at Phum and said, "I will return. I am going to the base of the rock to see if they need me."

Gethsemane dug his claws into the side of the rock and said, "the spider is weaving a web above the three flowers." Everyone looked to where he was watching.

The peacock spider was rapidly weaving a geometric wonder in front of their eyes. The web laid flat against the rock like a stencil on a piece of paper.

Over half of the rockface was covered when he stopped and flared his back to show his colors. He took a silk thread of web where his body descended on it to where Kit was.

"Cousin, I thank you for your beautiful gifts," he said. "Where these travelers are going is too dangerous for you."

He then attached a silk web string to Kit's chest and said, "take the fall and go with Raiah back to the Groves." He looked at Nekoh saying, "Let him go."

The spider jumped onto Kit and pushed him off the cliff and climbed back, retracting his line to look at the rest of them. Kit free fell down the rock with his silk emerald green cloak waving in the wind to slow him. Raiah caught him as he reached the bottom and put Kit on his back.

"One by one you will enter the web," the spider told them.

For each, he attached a web string and guided them into the center of the beautiful silk creation where he then individually pushed them into a huge cavern. The spider weaved another web inside the structure where light emitted from it.

"The Messenger's work has opened portals. This one you entered has been named the Cavern of the Crane," the spider told them.

He looked at Deborah and said, "hold your glass cylinder for me."

Deborah did as she was asked. He hopped onto it and weaved another web around the glass vial containing the feathers and peridot stone.

"Because of your heart and your ability to bring the gifts to life, I give to you a guide of light to help you on this journey." He bowed to Deborah, fanned his tail out and danced for her on top of the bottle.

Deborah and the rest were transfixed with the grace and beauty of the spider's movement. His whole backend flared in his dance, showing his gorgeous geometric marvel. He stopped and looked at all of them and said:

"What you seek to mend must first be severed. Only then will the web of life return to its rightful place. Follow the path set before you."

"Along the way, when you see the light of the web, your steps will be sure. But, if you wander off the given path, you will be lost. The light will last until it is needed no more. The deeper you go, the less it will be. He bowed again and left the cavern.

Everyone stood silent; almost as if they had no idea what to do next. The spider's agile skill to get them out of the dangerous squalls of the ocean, to opening a door to enter the cavern, to where they were given a riddle to solve left them speechless.

"What I do know," Gethsemane finally spoke, "is we must first release the hummingbirds from where Choran has sent them."

"Choran was enraged the hummingbirds were given honor over him by Great Crane and Great Fox. It was not enough for Choran to trick Ehyah to enter the bowels and subsequently capture him with magic where he could not leave," the eagle explained.

"He wanted to continuously hurt both the Great Crane and the Great Fox," Gethsemane sadly stated.

"Because he ruled the World of Souls, he felt he could do whatever he wanted with those whom entered his domain. Therefore, he refused to let any hummingbird's soul enter paradise and rest. He sent all of them to exist in a dark part of the bowels."

"Choran knew this act would be the most ultimate cruelty for Ehyah and the Great Fox to feel every moment they breathed." Gethsemane stopped to ponder their next move.

"Thus, we must follow the light to release the hummingbirds," Gethsemane determined.

Deborah walked around their surroundings, using the vial to see if it would glow stronger one way or another.

From what she could surmise, it glowed stronger as the trail led deeper into the cavern. She looked at the rest of them, and said, "well, the only way out is to go down."

Chapter Forty-Four

"OK," Ayden asked, "how do I reach the hummingbirds?"

"Choran moves them around deep in the bowels constantly, to keep them confused and unable to break free to fly," Zayden revealed. "But, with him being disabled, he has not moved them as much."

"Which brings me to another question," Ayden stated. "Where am I supposed to start looking for them?"

"Below us, where you first entered, are seven caves which lead to the seven corners of Eshra," Ehyah explained. "Listen to the stirring and it will guide you to which entrance to take."

"I can't enter them," Ayden stated with exasperation. "My ring won't let me."

"Then your ring stays with me," Ehyah told her.

Ayden studied Ehyah for a few seconds before she responded. "Fine, the ring stays."

Greysun jumped to her back and Ayden helped secure him in place. She looked at her ring for a long time as she caressed it, took it off and handed it to Crane.

"Here is a message for you, Crane," Ayden said with a hint of pleasure. "One day in Hollow, these words crossed my lips. When I spoke them, I was confused by what they meant. Now, I know their meaning." Ayden lifted her head higher, closed her eyes, and recalled the words:

From the bowels you will rise Ehyah
Take my wing and ride my back
Together we will soar to the sky
The stars and the sun call your name, Ehyah
Listen to their song to guide you through
Where we will meet to take you home.

She looked at Crane and smiled. "We will be back soon," she told him. He bowed to her. She looked at Zayden, who smiled at her and bowed, also. With one final kiss to Nip and Lyt, she and Greysun exited paradise.

Ayden went to each of the openings of the seven corners of Eshra and listened. She went back to each cave entrance several times to make sure the loudest one was the one she needed to take. Double checking, she had the right doorway, she went to all of them two more times.

The fifth doorway had loud booms coming out of it. But her heart told her it didn't matter as she knew it was the seventh opening she needed to take.

Once inside, Ayden could see it was like a long hallway leading farther down into the bowels. She kneeled and took Greysun off of her back. One side of the wall was gray rock while the other seemed to look like semi-clear crystal quartz.

The two of them walked for miles, going further and further down. Their only solace was they could hear the stirring become stronger. At times, she thought she could see reflections come from the quartz side with movement and she would abruptly stop to watch to see if it was the hummingbirds.

They entered a large open space with vast cavernous voids all along the gray rock side. The quartz side was still intact with the path going along its wall.

Ayden looked down into the caverns, wondering if she should stay and walk or fly down. "What do you think, Greysun," she asked?

"The stirring is the key," Greysun stated. He then said to Ayden while she was looking down the cavern, "Thank you for choosing me."

"There was no real other choice, there, Greysun," Ayden stated. "Nip and Lyt would have been too little and very little help."

"Zayden. Well, I don't know him. Sure, he is my dad. And, sure he made an incredibly difficult choice to leave me for the bigger picture of our worlds. But I still don't know him," Ayden truthfully stated.

"And, even though Choran is weakened, he still would have known we were on the move and where we were at if Zayden was with me."

"You I know and trust," she explained. "Besides," Ayden said as she gave him a smile, "you give great dog kisses, Zayden can't do that."

Greysun jumped on her and toppled her over and dog kissed her repeatedly. Ayden laughed and hugged him.

Suddenly, she saw a flash across the quartz. She stood and put her hand to the rock. There were people walking on the other side of it. She tried to determine if they were alive or maybe souls who had arrived in the World of Souls. Then she saw a bird with huge wings fly ahead of them.

Ayden screamed, "Gethsemane, I'm over here!"

The whole procession on the other side stopped and looked around. Ayden kept yelling at them to look at her. She saw Deborah who had her hand on the rock wall while they were walking, start to scream. The girls screamed together.

"Uri said we would find each other in the bowels," Ayden cried.

She dropped her hand to wipe her eyes. "Deborah, I am looking for the hummingbirds. Their wings beating is the stirring," she said.

Deborah shook her head and lifted her hands up to motion she couldn't hear Ayden. Ayden put her hand to the wall and gestured for Deborah to do the same. She repeated what she said. Deborah nodded her head she understood.

Zetia came next to Deborah and put her hand on the wall. Ayden screamed again. "Zetia, I love you," she yelled. All Zetia could do was cry and shake her head up and down.

Nick came around Zetia's side, Zetia looked at him and smiled as she lowered her hand. Nick put his hand where Ayden had her hand.

"Nick," Ayden screamed. Tears rolled steadily down her face as she said, "Nick, I love you, Nick."

Nick matched her tears as he choked out, "I love you, too, Ayden."

Each member on Deborah's side put their hand, wing, or paw to Ayden's hand and cried with her.

Deborah whisped to go to Ayden's side. She hit the quartz wall and fell down. She looked at Gethsemane, confused.

"Only a few have the gift to whisp in the World of Souls," Gethsemane stated. "Marley is one of the few," he gently said to her.

"We will walk together on each side," Ayden explained through Nick who hadn't removed his hand since they found Ayden.

Nick nodded and all of them slowly began to walk the same direction. Ayden and Nick ran their fingers across the rock as they traveled to make sure communication would stay open. Their rock path descended at the same rate on both sides as they strode further down.

Approximately an hour after they started together, Ayden stopped. She listened for the stirring and realized she would have to leave her friends.

Ayden put both of her hands on the rock and Nick did the same. Deborah and Zetia also put their hands on it.

"I have to follow the stirring," Ayden sadly stated. "I have to fly down farther into the cavern to find them," she cried out as she put her head to the wall.

"We will find you," Zetia encouraged her. "Our paths are meant to come together at some point down below," she softly spoke to Ayden.

Ayden nodded to Zetia, looked at Deborah and Nick and raised her right hand. With the palm out, she made a fist and brought it to her heart. All of her friends did the same to her.

Ayden bent down to let Greysun jump on her back, she secured him and took one last look at her friends. She smiled and jumped into the cavern to fly lower to the hummingbirds.

"So, what do we do," Deborah asked?

"We stay the course," Zetia stated. "Down below is our answer. And, our path still leads us that way. Ayden will get there faster than us, but we will see her there if we keep up the pace and not stop."

Mile after mile they wound their way into the dark and deep crevices of the cavern. Deborah led the way, making sure her light was still glowing. Finally, they entered a room where several caves converged in a long row on one side.

"These are the caves to the seven corners of Eshra," Gethsemane told them. "Souls enter through these portals and travel up to different parts of the bowels. Within this underground universe are many points for a soul to stop. Each soul is allowed to stay or move on as they wish. And, they can return and go again as they desire."

"The World of Souls was meant to be a place of ultimate and continuous rest," Gethsemane explained. "You see, a vessel may die, but the soul never does. Those who died in anger and hate are sent to a special area to be cleansed from their pain. In this way, they can finally have the rest they sought when they were above ground," Gethsemane finished and bowed his head.

"Can we stay here and rest," Zetia asked?

"Yes, the natural passage of their journey is not hindered by our presence," Gethsemane proclaimed. "You do not see them as they pass. And, they choose to not see you," He explained.

Everyone sat down to eat as they tried to not feel uncomfortable with the knowledge of souls passing by them. Deborah grabbed Nick's arm in the handshake and they both slightly smiled to reassure each other. Soon all were asleep.

Choran, who knew every dead soul activity as well as every soul's entrance and exit in Hollow and the bowels, had felt Zetia enter his realm. He kept track of her progress and was pleased to see her stop for the night.

Even though he had been greatly stripped of his ability by the Messenger, he slowly worked his way deeper into the bowels. He owned the whole world of the underground and could walk freely anywhere he wanted in them.

His disfigured body struggled to keep going, but his anger seemed to fuel him. He brought wolves with him to help him walk. They stayed by his side and slowly marched to help him stay upright.

His desire to reach the Messenger near the hummingbirds and kill her, kept him pushing his body. He stopped at the pool of wave rock to drink its water and rest.

After he drank, he sat farther back on one of the small hills. He closed his eyes and then opened them again quickly. Next to his right wing was a vial with a blue lid. He worked the top off with his beak and sniffed its contents.

He eerily cackled with joy and drank the whole bottle. Choran waited to feel the medicine work on his joints and organs.

Once he began to feel its effects, he stood and spread his wings. His rejuvenated body stood well over four feet tall. No longer were his talons curled under where he could hardly walk. And, once again, his beautiful plumage took on the natural shape and color of a great horned owl.

He exited the pool realm to reach Nahrita. He was well aware of Nahrita's foolish attempt to enter the bowels without real magic. He flew to a side entrance from where she was tirelessly directing her minions to blow holes in Eshra's core.

He quietly flew to a tree and watched for a while as she angrily forced them to work harder. He quickly tired of her rants and flew to a rock behind her.

Nahrita's wolves cowered when they saw Choran. They tried to warn her with low howls.

Nahrita turned to them and furiously said, "shut up you fools." Her eyes slowly moved up from the animals and she gasped, but quickly recovered.

"Choran, my leader, with you disabled we looked for another way to defeat the Messenger," she tried to humbly say.

"Nahrita, the only fool in this world is you," Choran began. "Do you not realize after all this time of being in the Dark Cell, you can't destroy me?"

"I knew from the beginning, when you coerced Jaeh, you were only serving yourself." He exposed.

"Jaeh so proudly told me Haran was not a true enforcer. He was so smitten with you. He had to look to you for approval instead of keeping his eyes on me," Choran revealed.

"I watched you for months on end groom him to make sure his reality was yours. You twisted what he knew to be true and replaced it with lies. When he begged me not to kill his family, I was actually surprised he had any of himself left," Choran taunted Nahrita.

"I knew you were playing a long game of deception to get what you wanted. One you wanted to rule the Dark Cell. And, two you wanted to be cherished. Your jealousy of Jaeh's family's love for each other enraged you," Choran scolded her.

"To humor you, I let you believe you had manipulated me. Decreasing the snail fern was part of my plan. I needed to be smaller to move more freely through my realm. By telling the potion makers to give me less and less was the perfect way to make sure my body would not go into convulsions. You only helped my cause, you fool," Choran angrily said to her.

Nahrita, full of fear, yelled at her wolves, "attack and kill!" Then she turned and rapidly began to run.

Choran swooped down, swept his wings towards the wolves who tried to protect her and deliberately clawed each until their entrails were strung throughout the work area of the enforcers. He then, methodically followed each enforcer as they ran and killed them in the same manner as the wolves.

Choran stood after the last man was dead and lifted his body to the tallest tree. He watched the horizon for any small movement. Off in the distance, he saw Nahrita still running. He allowed her to get another thousand feet before he glided into flight.

To cause her fear to rise he began to screech like an owl would as it approached its prey. Choran swooped down and grabbed her by her shoulders in his talons and flew higher with her. He dangled her for several minutes before he flew lower and dropped her.

He took his wings and slapped her repeatedly. Each time she tried to stand he would slap her down again. When she no longer could get up, he stood off to the side of her and deliberately waited to make her terror rise higher.

Finally, he tired of his play and picked her back up in his claws and carried her for many miles. He dumped her far out into the immense ocean and then flew back to the bowels.

Chapter Forty-Five

Ayden had traveled miles upon miles into the bowels where she found the source of the stirring. But she could not reach them.

She put her ear against the rock bastion which served as a solid door she was unable to open. The flapping of the hummingbirds' wings was almost deafening. As she put her hand against the wall, she could feel their wings beating to get out.

Tenderly, she said, "I will get you out. I don't know how, yet. Believe me, I will set you free so you can rest." Ayden sat down and released Greysun from his harness.

"Don't know how, Greysun," Ayden said. "Somehow we will free them." She pulled out her pack and the two of them ate. They both laid down and fell asleep.

Zetia woke, confused. Her mind seemed foggy to her and she thought she heard Zayden calling to her. Suna touched her leg and asked, "you hear it too, Zetia?"

"What do you hear, Suna," Zetia asked?

"I hear my mother asking me to find her and help her," Suna stated.

Zetia picked Suna up in her arms, and sleepily said, "I will help you and Zayden."

Zetia walked to the first cave and listened in the doorway. She went to each entrance and did the same thing. When she reached the seventh one, she entered it.

Deborah screamed, "Zetia don't go in there. Not without all of us together. The light, Zetia!"

Everyone, startled by Deborah's words. Stood to fight. They watched as Zetia's body disappeared into the cave. Tybin began to run after her. Gethsemane put his wing in front of him and stopped him.

"It is too late, Tybin. She has entered where she should not have gone," Gethsemane formidably stated.

"Bring her back, Gethsemane," Deborah cried out.

"It is not in my power, Deborah," Gethsemane stated as he continued. "Choran's magic is at play here. She and Suna are hearing voices call to them," he stated.

Deborah quickly checked each of her friends, asking, "do you hear voices?" Everyone nodded their head no. She turned to Gethsemane bewildered.

"So, why her and Suna and not the rest of us," Deborah questioned?

"Think back to what Ayden told you when you were in Hollow, Deborah," Eleea encouraged her.

"Zayden stated her feathers held powerful magic against Choran's attempts to use magic. They would protect us from his death grip. All of us, except Gethsemane who is old Eshra, have a feather from Ayden. Zetia and Suna do not," Eleea concluded.

"Great, how could I have been so blind to not get a feather for Zetia when I was there with Ayden," Deborah frustratingly exclaimed. "Now, what!" She asked?

"Choran is steadily diminishing. We need to trust it will be enough to break the enchantment over them," Gethsemane reassured her. "All is not lost. She still could find Ayden in her walk."

"Well, this has taken an ugly turn," Deborah called out. "Now, not only do we have to worry about helping Ayden. We have to worry about helping Zetia, too."

Deborah reluctantly nodded at Gethsemane as she looked at her bottle with the feathers. She stood up and watched to see where the glow was the brightest and guided her friends to follow her.

They continued to travel farther down in blackness. The hours of very little talk and lack of scenery except for the grey dank walls caused everyone to silently dread each step they took. Deborah started to relentlessly talk.

"We should have picked who came with us," she stated. "I thought we would have to do some epic enforcer battles or something," she continued as they walked.

"Just walking into blackness doesn't require all of us to be here. Elora, Eleea, Suna, Trevin, Zetia, Iza, Nekoh and even the boys didn't need to come. Gethsemane and I could have handled this dreary trek into nothingness," she forlornly decided.

"Deborah, the Great Crane did not put up one warning sign to say 'do not come.' Gethsemane authoritatively stated.

"The only road blocks given were for Phum, Kit and the rest of the Trevins," he reminded her.

"What you do not see or understand does not make it any less important. Each soul with us is here for a reason," he cautiously demanded of her.

Finally, he said, "trust Eshra magic, Deborah."

Deborah fell silent, realizing she may have really angered Gethsemane. Their walk continued and continued.

Thankfully, she saw a larger opening ahead where they could stop and rest. The room they entered showed the same seven corners of Eshra caves, several feet apart as they partially circled the room. The other end of the room led to deep caverns of the bowels. Nonetheless, all of them breathed a sigh of relief.

Extra light shone in the room which seemed a little odd to Deborah. Her feather bottle went dim and she felt a sudden fear of losing their power source.

In one corner of the room there was a shadowy darkness which caused her senses to run or fight. She unlatched her knife and grabbed Jerin's hand.

He looked at her and she motioned her head to the corner. Tybin and Iza noticed her reaction, and also prepared their weapons.

From the shadows, an extremely large bird walked out with six wolves at his side.

"Welcome, Gethsemane, to your end," Choran maliciously laughed.

Gethsemane turned to face Choran and spread his wings to get everyone behind him.

"It has been a long time, Choran," Gethsemane stated.

"I see you are still unwise in your decisions, Gethsemane," Choran snickered. "Following exactly what Ehyah and Fox tell you to do. Never thinking for yourself."

"Seems you only know how to act for yourself. Look where it has gotten you, Choran. What honor you were graciously given has been destroyed by your selfish pride and jealousy," Gethsemane schooled the owl.

"At least I have honor. I still rule Hollow and the bowels, Gethsemane. What do you rule? Nothing! You only take orders and follow," Choran bellowed at him.

"Choran you were given the World of Souls under the command to do what was right and just. The words spoken to you the day you received this valuable position from the Great Crane and the Great Fox were:

This honor to be the Keeper of Souls, Choran, is one to be reverently accepted. Only when they pass from the worlds will they reside in your domain. No manipulation or secret agenda will hold their souls above or below. They are to be free to rest for their journey has ended.

Before you accept this great responsibility consider what you ask of us. If you agree to our terms, then so be it, your reign shall be true without void of life.

"You accepted the terms freely, Choran," Gethsemane stated. "In your twisted selfish desire to destroy the hummingbirds and to one day trap Ehyah, you did not listen to the terms you agreed to."

"The key phrase is, 'void of life,' Choran. By not letting the hummingbirds rest at the end of their journey. By manipulating the dead souls to be Bones for you to kill others. By sending others to Hollow to perish. You made a conscious choice to manipulate souls for your evil purposes. These actions were your secret agenda to selfishly use souls and it forfeited your right to live forever in Eshra or anywhere else," Gethsemane revealed Choran's mistake.

Gethsemane released his wings from his sides and flew at Choran. His claws grasped Choran's neck where blood spewed out.

Choran broke away and flew as high as he could in the room. Gethsemane flew after him. They grabbed each other's talons and began a freefall where their wings continued to gain speed as they twirled out of control.

Choran broke free again and darted out and down into the caverns. Gethsemane dove after him. Constant screeching from both echoed in the room as the fight continued in the dark crevices of the bowels.

Then, there was silence and everyone wanted to move to look in the cavern, but the wolves were still nearby with teeth bared. Yet it was obvious, the wolves, too, were distressed by the silence and didn't know what to do.

Suddenly, Choran reappeared in the room and tried to enter one of the caves. He hoped he could exit the bowels and lose Gethsemane in the tunnels.

Gethsemane's talon latched onto Choran's wing and he thrust the owl back into the middle of the room. Gethsemane pounced on Choran's chest with both feet and ripped his chest open with his beak and spit out part of his heart.

Choran choked as his heart spewed blood out, saying, "I cannot die. I am old Eshra."

Gethsemane flew back away from him and said, "you were old Eshra."

The wolves howled at the loss of their leader and separated as they went to attack.

Tybin pushed Iza back as he took his staff and impaled the first wolf. Jerin did the same to Deborah and shot an arrow into one of the wolves where it froze in place. He shot another arrow of green into a third wolf where it fell, paralyzed.

Nick turned into a bear with his gift and jumped on the fourth wolf, tearing into the animal's neck where blood rapidly pumped out.

Eleea and Elora, in their winged armor, attacked the fifth wolf around his head and disoriented him. Trevin climbed up the animal's tail and dug his knife into its hind quarters. Nekoh came next to them and said, "I've got him," where he tore open the wolf's neck.

The sixth wolf fell back around the fight and quietly waited for its chance. He saw Deborah and Iza holding each other's hands. They were focused on Choran and Gethsemane, as well as the others fighting and did not see the wolf sneak up on them until it lunged at Iza.

The wolf screamed, "Iza, you made the wrong choice." Iza increased her grip on Deborah's hand and Deborah used the tight hand grip to throw Iza out of the way of the wolf.

Iza fell to the ground and Deborah went to drive her knife into the wolf's neck when an arrow reached it first with blue smoke causing the wolf to be disoriented. The wolf ripped the arrow out its chest and leapt at Deborah.

Deborah stood steady and thrust her knife into the wolf's head and sliced it in half with her gifted knife.

Iza turned to Deborah when it was all finished, her eyes were wide with shock. Deborah smiled at her, realizing she finally saw a battle where the animals who had always controlled her in the Dark Cell were defeated. And, for her to see Choran, who had spread fear in her heart for so many years, finally meet his end.

Tybin tenderly put his arm around Iza. She looked up at him and burst into tears.

Deborah watched, stunned, as she thought to herself, "I have never seen Iza cry. A little tear here and there, but not break down emotionally." She then looked for Gethsemane to assess his wounds.

"Gethsemane, sit," Deborah demanded. She took one of her bandanas, wetted it from her water bladder and began to wipe away the blood areas. Only one was a deep gash on his upper left leg, close to his stomach. Deborah applied honey salve to it and smiled at the eagle.

"You do realize, I am old Eshra, Deborah," Gethsemane informed her.

"I know," Deborah agreed. "But, even if you can't die, you still need my loving touch," she smiled at him. She intently looked at him and asked, "with Choran no longer is everyone safe and can we go home?"

"He can do no more harm," Gethsemane stated. "Yet, his magic is still in play. The scars he has left behind will take time to heal. And, to remove all of the magic Ehyah must reach the skies," Gethsemane dauntingly told her.

"We still have to help Ayden fulfill her prophecy and Choran's danger is still real until she releases Ehyah," Gethsemane instructed everyone.

"What about Zetia? Will she be free to return to us, now," Nick asked?

"Nickalli, with Choran void of life, she will have a stronger chance to return. It will have to be her strength of will to do so. Trust Eshra magic she will find her way," Gethsemane told him.

Gethsemane sympathetically looked at Iza as Tybin held her while she continued to sob. He was rocking her back and forth as he soothingly talked to her.

Gethsemane looked at Deborah, saying, "Deborah, would you have denied her this moment by telling her she wasn't needed on this journey?"

Deborah's eyes teared up as she said, "I get it, now. Eshra magic is wiser than I will ever be. I will remember to trust it, G."

Chapter Forty-Six

Zetia woke from her slumber by Suna pushing her to wake up. "Zetia, we are lost," Suna's voice whimpered. "I am scared," she cried out.

Zetia rubbed the fox's fur and tried to focus her eyes. They were sitting against a rock wall, huddled together on a ledge to avoid falling. Carefully, she assessed their stability. "How did we get here," Zetia asked herself?

"Suna, do you remember anything," she asked?

"I remember I was following my mother's voice and then I woke to now," Suna stated.

Zetia looked beyond, across from where they were sitting, to see if she could find a way off of the ledge. Blackness filled her eyes with no hope of walking out to secure ground. She pondered the whole mess the two of them were in.

Deep in her soul, she heard Joshua's words to her:

'I see you standing at a crevasse. Looking across the horizon. The sky is black. Take the leap and fly.'

Zetia held tightly onto Suna in her arm as she took her other arm and kept it touching the wall behind her. She slid her body up slowly until they were standing.

"Suna, I am going to slowly let go of you. I want you to crawl onto my back," Zetia instructed her.

"Then, I want you to burrow into the top of my legging where you will turn around so only your head is sticking out. When I start to fly, you will be safe there," Zetia explained.

Zetia took a deep breath once Suna was settled. "Sun," Zetia affectionately said to the fox, "hold on."

The initial shock of flying downward rather than up was unnerving for Zetia. To add to the increased shock, was the silence and darkness where she could see or hear nothing.

She determinedly forced herself to trust the mountain lion's words to her and Eshra magic.

The two of them flew for hours. Zetia didn't deviate from where she first entered the abyss in that she stayed in the middle, hoping to avoid hitting any walls or jutted rock. Suna would periodically encourage her by telling her she was doing a good job.

Approximately three or four hundred feet in front of them, Zetia's heart jumped to see a small flash of light.

She kept her pace to not accidentally spiral out of control from hitting any rock formations. The closer she got, she was able to see more and more light and realized where the light was coming from.

Zetia landed next to Ayden and Greysun, asleep on the floor of the cave. Ayden slightly stirred while Greysun rose to fight.

He looked at the woman and said, "you must be Zetia, but I do not know the animal with you. Ayden never gave me a description for a fox?"

Zetia quietly giggled as she helped Suna get down. She tousled Greysun's fur and watched Ayden sleep.

"My girl has been in very good hands with you, Greysun," Zetia whispered to the dog as she bowed to him.

Ayden lifted her head to see who Greysun was talking to and screamed. Then she cried matched by another scream and more crying.

Zetia knelt beside her and cried with her as they hugged. "Zetia," Ayden choked out. "Zetia, I have dreamed and dreamed of this day. I am so tired, Zetia," she weepily told her aunt.

"I know, my girl," Zetia said as she hugged and rocked Ayden in her arms. "I am so, so proud of you, Ayden," she soothingly spoke to her. "It is almost over and we can go home. But, now, you are no longer alone. I am here to help you."

"The hummingbirds are in the rock fortress," Ayden revealed. "I can't find a way to break through to release them," she confusingly stated and began to cry again.

Zetia brushed Ayden's hair away from her eyes as she continued to rock her. "Think, Ayden," Zetia encouraged her. "Why did Ehyah send Deborah back to be on our side and not Hollow," she asked?

Ayden sat up, excitedly saying, "he needed her on one side and me on the other side to break the hummingbirds free. Where is she? Where is Deborah and how come you are on this side and not on her side," Ayden nervously asked.

Zetia explained to Ayden what she could remember about her and Suna's ordeal. She then said, "Ayden, trust Eshra magic. Deborah is on her way down to her side to help you. We will wait and talk until the rest arrive."

Ayden nodded her head as her bottom lip trembled. Zetia pulled Ayden to her chest and continued to rock her and let her cry as she told her about how they entered through the Groves.

"Well, Two would never forgive me if we didn't have a funeral for Choran and the wolves," Deborah stated. "Not a good idea to have a fire, though. There are unknown gases down here and we all could go up in flames," she educated them.

The boys piled the wolves on top of Choran and stood with the rest to see who would speak. Everyone silently waited.

Iza timidly looked at Gethsemane, saying, "may I speak for them?" Gethsemane bowed to her and spread his wing out to give her the honor.

Iza lowered her eyes for several seconds. She then looked up and began, "I speak for all those who have died because of Choran. I speak for all those who are still living in fear in the Dark Cell because of Choran. This needless death we see in front of us could have been avoided if not for greed, anger and jealousy."

"Lives have been permanently altered because of what Choran chose to do with his honor. Let none of us forget the tragedy of losing sight to do good and to be righteous in all we pursue. May their souls find peace and may those who will soon be freed find the same peace." Iza looked to Gethsemane where he nodded to her in approval.

Deborah put her hand on her side to release the vial she got from Kalim. "The green topped bottle will make anything disappear," she stated.

Gethsemane stopped her saying, "it is not necessary, Deborah."

He stood in front of the bodies and lifted his wings out towards them. In one quick arch he fanned his wings. Instantaneously, their bodies turned to ash and Gethsemane blew their dust into the seven corners of the Eshra caves.

Everyone was dumbfounded, realizing Gethsemane was way more enmeshed in old Eshra than any of them had ever known. Curious, but respectful no one dared ask him anymore.

Deborah took her feathers to see what the web around the bottle told them on the way they should go. It barely held a light since they entered the room and she became concerned.

She looked at Gethsemane, saying, "what are we going to do?"

"We need to go down farther. We follow the light until no more and then put Trevin and Iza in front to use their sight," Gethsemane responded.

It was less than an hour of travel when they had to turn the reigns over to Trevin and Iza. Trevin jumped on Iza's shoulder as they worked together to guide their friends.

The path was slow with the darkness and the unsureness of where they should take the next step. They continued to wind farther and farther into the bowels of Eshra.

Iza stopped after hours of the same route and sadly said, "my eyes are overly strained. I am starting to see halos and feel I need to rest. My fear is I will take us down the wrong path."

Trevin took her hand, saying, "Iza, you have been a strong and brave leader. You are right we need to rest to gain a better understanding to our surroundings."

One by one everyone slowly sat in the spot they were in when they stopped. Deborah began to nervously tap her finger against her feather bottle. The sound echoed in the darkness like a gong of doom.

Jerin put his hand over hers and the bottle. She tightly grabbed his hand and stopped.

"Maybe, if we inch forward on our butts, we can keep moving," Deborah asked in the darkness; not able to see any faces for a reaction?"

Silence followed her suggestion. All hope seemed to drain from them as they all sensed each other's despair.

Nick quietly stated, "at the farthest point in the bowels, when all hope seems to be lost. A dim flicker will appear. Follow it."

"We wait until I see the light," Nick boldly told them. "Ehyah came to me at Zetia's and told me this moment would come. We wait," he said with fierce determination.

Silence engulfed everyone as Nick's words wrapped their hearts with anticipation and courage. No one wanted to break the quiet in case it disturbed Nick and his ability to see the flicker.

Ayden and Zetia talked for hours. Tears and laughter filled their hearts as they sat. Greysun laid the front of his body on Zetia, totally happy to have a new friend and because she gave such deep hand rubs. Suna laid curled up in Ayden's lap, totally content to be safe.

After a while, Ayden laid her head against Zetia's shoulder and they both hummed to each other. Ayden's wings lightly glowed in and out of brightness as they peacefully matched each other's pitch.

Nick methodically crawled around all of his friends to be in the front. He squinted while he was on his knees. "We follow Deborah's suggestion and slide as we continue to go down," he told them.

"Deborah, your large scarf. Can it reach all of us to be used as an anchor for us to stay connected," Nick asked?"

Deborah quickly untied it from around her waist and handed Nick the tip of it. The last person in line was Tybin and she gave him the other end.

Nick tied his end to his belt and said, "each of you drape your arm over it, so you can feel it. Tybin you tie your end to your belt. And, Trevin, Eleea and Elora ride someone's shoulder."

Once all were secure, Nick began to inch forward. At times, a gasp could be heard from one of them as they slid too fast down the decline of the mountainous rock.

Steadily, they moved forward, even if it was slow. Nick had to use his hands to check for solid ground in front of them or they would have plummeted into the chasm.

As they progressed, Nick would intermittently stop to cautiously look farther down the cavernous descent. He knew the light was there, but it would sporadically disappear and he would have to wait for it to show again. Deep in his heart, he knew it was Ayden's wings showing them the way.

What seemed like days, was in actuality a few hours of threading their way down. Abruptly, their path ended with a huge rock wall in front of them.

Deborah whispered, "listen. It's the stirring. I hear the hummingbirds" she excitedly said.

Nick yelled, "Ayden."

All of them saw a shot of light rise partially up the wall. Then the light began to jump up and down.

"Nick", Ayden yelled back. Her wings began to glow exceedingly bright the more excited she became.

Nick stood up and practically pulled everyone to a standing position with him as he continued to yell. They were at the bottom and on stable ground and everyone shouted with him.

Both sides danced, cried and cheered for several minutes. They easily could see each other as it was a clear quartz wall separating them and Ayden's wings provided the light.

They were all relieved they could hear each other without having to put their hand on the rock. Their excitement increased when they realized Zetia and Suna were with Ayden.

Ayden looked at Deborah. "Deborah, it is you and I," Ayden tried to clarify. "Crane said we both needed to be here on each side to break the wall for the hummingbirds to be released. I have no idea how we are supposed to do it," she reluctantly explained.

"Well, let's think about it, A," Deborah said as she cocked her head to the right. "What is it about you and I which is totally different than all of the others?"

"We're both from East Glacier," Ayden stated. "But so is Nick," she concluded.

"OK, East Glacier isn't it," Deborah continued to ponder. "We're both girls and the same age," she proposed.

"So, what," Ayden exclaimed. "I do not think that is the great key, D."

"Key, hmmm," Deborah thought out loud. "Is there any place on your side for a type of key. And being Eshra magic don't just look for a normal keyhole," Deborah instructed her.

Ayden nodded her head. She and Zetia began to feel the rock for an indentation. The others did the same on their side.

As Deborah was looking, she continued to evaluate what made it so different where it had to be them and no one else to break the wall. She stood with her hand on the wall and thought out loud.

"Could be our deep friendship," Deborah began her reasoning speech. "Could be we started the handshake up again in new Eshra. Could be we were both in Hollow."

"Or it could be," Deborah stopped and thought for a long time. "Or, it could be we both have a feather from a crow and a raven," she screamed.

"Yes," Ayden screamed back. "But, what kind of keyhole will work for feathers," she asked?

Deborah looked at her beautiful bottle with the feathers and Two's peridot stone. She sighed, kneeled down, lifted her hand to break the bottle against the quartz but was stopped by a little hand.

"No, need, Deborah," the little voice said.

Deborah looked away from the hand to see who it belonged to and immediately broke down sobbing. It was a paw hand and it was Two's.

Jerin quickly came to her back and kneeled next to her. Everyone was crying. Ayden knelt on her side with Zetia, crying and watching to see how Deborah would handle everything.

Two jumped into Deborah's lap and waited for her tears to slow. "I have missed you so much, Two," Deborah wept. Two hugged her neck and Deborah cried even harder.

Slowly the tears ebbed and Deborah cupped Two's head in her hands and stared at him, smiling.

"I am happy, Deborah," Two said. "I have pretties all over. Hidden, of course," he giggled. "I knew you would like the key I gave Marley to give to you. There are shinies everywhere down here," he proudly stated.

He jumped off Deborah and handed Trevin an old gold coin with a raccoon embossed on it. He hugged Trevin who was a blubbering mess.

"Trevin, Two started, "I get to play with my family. They told me you are the greatest warrior they have ever known. And, they would like to thank you for taking care of me until I could be with them.," Two said as he hugged Trevin.

Trevin took Two's hand and looked into his eyes. Tears rolled down his cheeks as he choked, "Finch I am so sorry I did not protect you from Dariat."

"Trevin, you are not to take this burden to your heart," Two stated. "Eshra knew I needed to be here for Deborah, Ayden and the rest of you. Without me and the key and Marley none of you would have been able to succeed."

Each member on Deborah's side cried when Two went to them and gave them a hug. He left Jerin for last who had kept his head down the whole time, trying to hide his tears.

Two gently lifted Jerin's chin in his paw so Jerin had to look into his eyes, saying, "Jerin, stop blaming yourself. Each of us must come to the seven corners of Eshra at some point in our life. I am happy and Marley visits me all of the time to tell me how all of you are doing," he explained.

Jerin nodded to Two and continued to cry. Deborah gently held Jerin's hand and cried with him.

"Come back with us," Deborah finally cried out.

"Deborah, it is not possible," Two gently told her. "Even though I can come to you in my old form, I am spirit now. My soul moves freely here where I can take on the shape I desire whether it be my raccoon self or my soul self. I am where I am supposed to be. When I need to talk to old friends, I use this form," he informed Deborah.

"But," Two excitedly said. "One day, when I meet you as you enter through the seven corners of Eshra. I will show you everything and we will never be apart again. And, we can everyday say I love you," he happily told her.

Deborah welled with tears. She took Two's charm, 'My Friend, My Hero' off of her belt. She kissed it and put it in his paw. She kissed his head and said, "yes, Two, that will be a joyous day."

Chapter Forty-Seven

Two nodded to Deborah and disappeared. He reappeared on Ayden's side where Ayden broke down in tears. He waited for her to stop crying and hugged her neck. "I love you, Ayden," Two said.

Ayden sat on her knees and cried again. She choked out, "I love you too, Two." Ayden looked up and saw her mom standing next to Zetia.

"It is time for you to leave, Ayden," her mom said.

"Mom?" Ayden questioned.

"I was given the great privilege to arrive through the seven corners of Eshra because of you, Messenger of Eshra," her mom revealed.

"Would you please tell Zayden, thank you for me. Choran kept the doors to Ehyah locked. Your dad doesn't know I am here and he will be gone before he will be told."

"On your wings you will carry them out, Ayden." Her mom explained. "Go, I will see you again one day. But, for now I must go to continue to heal," she said as she disappeared.

Everyone on Deborah's side watched Ayden and her mom. Tears and sniffing could be heard all around.

Quietly, a voice said, "Eleea, I am so proud of how you have raised Elora. She is a beautiful reflection of our love, Eleea."

Eleea turned to look behind him. He saw Lora resting on a limb jutting out of the rock across from the quartz wall.

"Lora," he cried out. "I have missed you. So deeply I have missed you," he softly said.

Lora flew down to him where they took their heads and placed their foreheads against each other.

"Momma. I have not forgotten," Elora said. "Everywhere I go, you go," she cried.

"Elora," Lora said as she touched her head to Elora's forehead. "This moment to be able to touch you is a memory I will always carry with me. I love you, Elora."

"I must go, now. Two came to me and brought me here. He knew I would want to see you both. It is time for you and one day it will be time for us," Lora told both of them as she disappeared.

Eleea went to Elora and touched his head to hers and they cried together.

Ayden looked at Zetia who had Two in her arms. "How are we supposed to break the wall," she questioned?

"Easy, Ayden," Two stated. "Marley told me what you and Deborah needed to do. Take Uri's feather and place it on the quartz wall."

Ayden did as Two requested. The feather's individual tips created a design like an ink blot leaking onto paper. The spidery mark kept spreading across the whole quartz wall.

Two jumped down from Zetia's arms and said. "Deborah, take your bottle and lightly tap the rock on your side."

Deborah did as he told her. The whole wall shattered as thousands and thousands of flying hummingbirds emerged from the rock and began to fly upwards.

Ayden instantly knew she had to get ahead of them to break through to the upper realms of the bowels.

She quickly looked at Gethsemane and nodded. He nodded back to her. Ayden released feathers from her wings for Zetia, Gethsemane and Suna.

"Back all of you go to the Groves," she stated as she took off after the hummingbirds.

Ayden rapidly flew above the stars of Eshra and began to spin in a circle as she gained speed. She lifted her wings up above her to drill the bowels as they all climbed higher and higher. The hummingbirds' wings lifted her body as she kept her wings above her head.

"Ehyah," she yelled. "Listen to their song and follow it. I will meet you there,' she commanded.

The birds simultaneously began to sing the most melodic chorus which sent chills down Ayden's spine. Their song was one of freedom and it actually strengthened Ayden's ascent as she drilled with her wings. Thousands upon thousands of hummingbird wings carried her body higher and higher.

All of them landed in the room of the seven corners of Eshra, where Ayden had arrived earlier. The birds flew through all the openings and disappeared. Ehyah walked out of the shadows with Zayden who had Nip and Lyt inside his shirt.

Ayden nodded to them and said, "hurry, get on my back." She helped both of them on and took to the skies of Eshra through the seventh cave door.

Ayden's strength in flight even surprised her as she flew like the wind. Once she saw the light of the sky, she increased her wing velocity and dove through the opening.

Ayden went higher and higher into the skies of Eshra and leveled out to a glide. It was nighttime and the moon and stars lighted her path.

Shooting stars danced across the sky as she flew on the winds of Eshra to take them to the Groves.

Everyone Ayden had sent out of the bowels before she went after the hummingbirds were on the beach looking around, dumfounded.

"Not again," Deborah cried out nervously.

Jerin placed his hand on her arm and pointed up. Deborah looked at where he was pointing and cried. She knew Ayden had made it out by the hundreds of shooting stars dancing in the sky.

The Trevins, Kit, Phum and Raiah joined them on the beach and they all continued to watch the glorious display the stars were performing. Tears flowed freely amongst all of them.

Iza caught her breath, put one hand over her mouth and took Deborah's hand with her other hand. Deborah searched to where Iza was looking. Bright silver wings could be seen off in the distance descending closer to them.

Ayden gracefully landed and stooped down to let her passengers off her back. Zetia ran to Zayden and almost crushed Nip and Lyt in her hug.

Nick ran to Ayden and grabbed both her arms in his hands and just stared at her with tears running down his face. Ayden put her hands on his arms and cried with him. The Trevins were a mess. They hugged everyone's legs over and over again.

Ayden smiled at Nick and they both let go of their arms. She walked over to Deborah and they took each other in their familiar handshake. Both of them stared at each other for several seconds.

Finally, Ayden said, "D, I could not have done any of this without you."

Deborah squeezed their hold, and replied, "A, I am at a loss for words."

Ayden laughed as she said, "never would I have believed to see you without words."

Everyone turned to watch Gethsemane walk up to Ehyah and bow. The crane bowed back and his long graceful neck almost touched the ground as he did it.

"Gethsemane," Ehyah said. "My friend, you choose wisely when you gave Great Fox and I the words to give to Choran on the day he became the Keeper of Souls."

"We will be forever grateful for your wisdom. I bow to your grace and your decision."

He then turned to Ayden and bowed. "Messenger, a decision is required from you as well," he proclaimed.

"It does not have to be made this moment. But you will need to make it. You are offered life everlasting. If you choose, yours is a new Eshra life for eternity. Think on it and one day you will be asked to give an answer," the Crane told her.

Ehyah looked at the rest of Ayden's friends and said, "Great Fox and I are enduringly grateful to each of you, also."

"You carried our Messenger when she needed it most. Your souls will forever be forged together from this day forth. Great Fox and I will never forget you."

The magnificent bird spread his wings, bowed to all of them and lifted off the ground. He flew around them once, dipped his wing and then took off towards the ocean's horizon.

The stars danced with him as he flew out of sight. It seemed as everyone watched, they could hear them singing a joyous melody of welcome home.

Deborah looked at Gethsemane and said, "OK, G, what did he mean you made a decision?"

Gethsemane chuckled, saying, "leave it to you, Deborah, to catch the nuance."

"When the decision was made to give Choran his position for the souls, another decision had to ride with it. One Choran knew nothing about."

"My heart said he would turn to evil and this is why we put a hidden message in his acceptance to rule the World of Souls."

"If he chose to not heed its warning, he would no longer be allowed to be old Eshra. He would be void of life. His anger and jealousy clouded his judgement and we all know what happened because of it."

Gethsemane stopped and thought about how he should proceed. "I made the decision to be the Keeper of Souls when Choran finally was void of life."

"I will not be a prisoner in this world as I can freely go wherever I want in Eshra and your world, Deborah."

"I explained to Great Fox and Great Crane when I gave them the words to speak to Choran we would need an immediate resolution on the day it happened. I will not return to the Great Tree nor to Zetia's at this time. I have a world which needs to be cleansed and nurtured," the eagle explained.

Ayden started to cry where Gethsemane went to her and lifted her chin with his wing. "Do not be sad, child. I will always be close to you. Watching you. And, I promise to come and visit you in East Glacier one day," he told her. Then he wrapped his wings around her and hugged her.

"Zayden, my dear true friend," Gethsemane turned to him and began. "Without you, none of this would have been possible. Your sacrifice to leave Ayden to protect her and to travel through Hollow to the bowels to stay with Ehyah," Gethsemane stopped and put his wing on Zayden's shoulder.

"The depth of my love for you, friend, is without measure. You and Zetia will, too, one day need to make the same decision as Ayden," Gethsemane revealed.

"But, until the day is at hand, I give you the gift of my medallion. This work of art was specifically commissioned by Ehyah, himself," Gethsemane disclosed.

"He tasked Nadab to design a piece to keep the Great Fox, the Great Crane and I connected. For you see, the peacock spider knew what needed to be mended."

"To mend, it first had to be severed. All three of us needed to be in the same room to break Choran's honor to rule the World of Souls," Gethsemane revealed.

"What other secrets it holds, now remains to be seen. It has served its purpose for us. And it is free to be in your hands. The pleasures it will reveal to you only Eshra knows." Gethsemane then bowed to have Zayden take it off his neck.

Zayden placed the necklace over his head and put his hand on Gethsemane's shoulder. The two of them stared for a lengthy time at each other. Both of their eyes filled with tears. "Until we meet again, friend. And, I accept the decision, now, to be old Eshra, Gethsemane," Zayden said as he took his hand off of the eagle.

Gethsemane nodded to Zayden. He stood back, spread his wings and bowed to everyone.

Before he took to the skies, he said, "Tayden and the others who fly will arrive tomorrow to return all of you to Zetia's. The Great Crane will guide your path and bring you safely home. To each of you I say, 'I love you.' Until we meet again, my friends," Gethsemane said as his wings took flight.

Zayden walked to Ayden, took her hands in his and said, "I ask your forgiveness for leaving you. One day I hope you will give me the privilege to make it up to you." He kissed her on the cheek and handed her the peridot ring she had given Ehyah to hold.

Ayden looked at Zayden and smiled as she put the ring back on her finger. "It will be a wonderful day when we sit to learn about each other. I look forward to it. You will always be my dad, Zayden. I will always be forever grateful for you sacrifice to save all of us," she said.

Ayden kissed him on the cheek and then took his forearm in her hand where he then took her forearm. They stared at each other for several moments and then Zayden hugged her and cried.

Kit looked at Zetia, and said, "if it is OK with you, Zetia, I want to stay here. Raiah and I have become quite good friends and he said he would take care of me when I need it."

Zetia bent down to Kit, saying, I believe this is a perfect plan for you, Kit." She kissed him on the head and smiled at him. He spread his wings in full display to show his love for her and walked away.

Suna came up to her next and said, "I think I will help keep an eye on Kit at the Groves." Zetia hugged her saying, "Sun, I will see you soon."

Chapter Forty-Eight

The whole sanctuary rejoiced when they saw the travelers return. All of their horses had already arrived with a note from the Great Crane reading, 'Great Fox sent friends to gather your horses and bring them home when you entered the bowels. Always, Ehyah.'

Ayden turned to her friends, saying, "I am taking a real bath. Then I am sleeping for two days and I do not want to be disturbed."

Everyone agreed with Ayden on the bath and separated to their rooms. Before Ayden went to bed, she made Greysun take a real bath, telling him he could not get on her bed until he did. Nip shot out of the room when Ayden spoke to Greysun.

It actually was one full day when Ayden finally made her way down to eat dinner with the rest of them. She looked at Two's pedestal and then looked at Deborah. They both smiled, knowing the pain was less severe now with him gone.

Eleea turned to Ayden and asked her, "when would you like to return to East Glacier?"

"I was thinking in a couple of days I would fly Deborah, Nick, Greysun and I back," Ayden revealed. "But I need to make sure I do it right to pass through to our world," she asked?

"Elora and I will fly with you and we can show you then," Eleea stated.

Nip stood up and indignantly asked, "Ayd me too, Ayd. Me and Lyt, too, Ayd."

"Oh! Yes of course, Nip," Ayden stated. "But you are going to have to be really careful because people in my world can't talk to animals. You can't let them know you can talk," she told her as she looked at Deborah with fear in her eyes.

"We will make it work somehow," Deborah apprehensively stated.

Ayden looked around the table and asked, "where are Jerin and Tybin? And Iza is not here either," she questioned?

"Jerin promised Tybin he would be there with him when they set the Dark Cell free," Zetia explained.

"Iza went to help them coordinate and to show them who were prisoners and who were there to further the cause of Nahrita and the other faction," Zetia told her.

"Uri told us Choran went above ground and attacked Nahrita where he took her body and dropped her into the ocean."

Ayden anxiously asked, "are they safe doing it on their own?"

"Raiah, Tayden and the other ten with wings are in charge," Zetia comforted Ayden. "They have a whole network set up to make sure the boys and Iza are safe. It will take a lot of help to bring the Dark Cell dwellers to a sense of peace."

"The huge fortress Choran was building above ground is where they will live. The Ten who were rescued by me years ago, along with Raxton and Zayden, have also gone to help acclimate them. But, before you leave, Tybin and Jerin will return," Zetia reassured her.

Ayden breathed a sigh of relief. With everyone done eating, she decided time at the pool with her friends was next. She and Deborah ran upstairs to change with Greysun close behind them.

She looked at Greysun and said, "I am making it your responsibility to help Nip in our world. No talking or we will all be in big trouble," Ayden sternly told him. They ran back downstairs and slipped into the pool.

"A, we can't just go home with the animals.," Deborah revealed. "We will have to make it look like we found them or maybe say Nick gave them to us. I don't know, but they can't immediately be with us," Deborah proclaimed.

"Yeah, I was thinking the same," Ayden thoughtfully said. "Plus, we have to figure out how to change our dress, too. I don't want to wear my old clothes, even though we will have to when we leave here. But I like my new look."

Nick joined them, saying, "I have thought about this while you were sleeping. I say we have Zetia bring the clothes to our shop. You guys pretend to buy them and then presto, you have your clothes," he proudly stated.

Ayden nodded her head as she listened to him. "Sounds like a fair plan," she agreed.

Deborah looked at the both of them, got out of the pool and said, "sounds like a fair plan for you two to finally have a talk, too."

She called Greysun who the whole time had been jumping from one end of the pool to the other. Between his jumps and his excited speech, no one really stayed dry or got a chance to really talk.

"Greysun, how about you join me for a treat in the kitchen," Deborah coyly coerced him.

Once they were both gone, Ayden looked at Nick and began, "Here's the deal, Nickalli, this whole love thing is way too new for me. I mean, I like it. But I have some rules to set down. One, no kissing, at least yet. Two, let's take our time to enjoy each other as friends, first. And lastly, we do it without all the lovey huggy stuff," she informed him.

Nick chuckled, as he responded, "totally acceptable. I like our friendship and I do not want it spoiled. We go slow and have fun. I am very pleased with where we are at right now. Both of us safe and happy," he concluded.

A day later, Jerin and Tybin found the girls in the sunroom talking with Nick and Zetia. Jerin wrapped his arms around the back of Deborah and kissed her on the head.

"The amount of people freed was more than we realized," Tybin stated. "We had to do it in stages in order for Iza and Raxton and others they knew who were true to separate the good from the bad."

"Raiah and Tayden set men at the end of the cottages to guard and make sure none broke through to the other dwellings past them. The powdery agent used for people to become dazed and docile proved to be very beneficial in making the whole process go quietly," Tybin explained.

"It was overwhelming," Jerin continued. "Most walked out and cried, but some had to be carried they were so devastated and thankful."

"Iza was a powerhouse, though," Jerin said as he smiled at Tybin. "She and Raxton had Zayden by their side the whole time. The three of them determined truth from fiction. Iza set up a separate barracks for the enforcers and their animals."

"At the end, she spoke to all of them, offering them freedom in Eshra. But only if they turned from their old ways. If they said they would abide by her wishes, they were taken to another building. Magic was set around it and they were told they had to prove themselves to be true," Tybin continued to explain.

"They were given a select staff of people and animals to help them and to watch them for their true colors. Any deviance and Raiah's men sent them to the island where Elder Kadrich sent the others." Jerin finished.

"It's not the most perfect plan," Tybin informed them. "Most have gone where they are supposed to be. Yet, many of the animals and some men escaped through the Forest of Roots. Time will tell what they will do with their freedom," he cautiously stated.

"All in all, it was a very rewarding experience to see them free," Jerin continued. "Especially when Raiah and Tayden rescued Arnden's wife and children," he quietly revealed.

"So, what is the plan with you three," Tybin asked Ayden?

"We say our goodbyes today and tomorrow we head for home. A quick stop at the Great Tree to say goodbye and then East Glacier," Ayden told him.

"You guys are aware all of us are following you to the East Glacier portal to say goodbye," Jerin advised Ayden.

"Yes, I figured it would be an entourage there," Ayden said as she smiled.

The next day, with all the well wishes from Zetia's to the Great Tree, Ayden, Deborah, the animals and Nick stood for their last goodbyes. Because it was winter, Nadab had workers erect a large tent for the event.

Zetia stood in front of them and began, "this is not goodbye, really. Many of us have found this strange desire to visit East Glacier in the near future," she exclaimed.

"I know Nadab and Lydia have already begun their vacation plans for next spring. I even heard rumors Nick's parents are in need of an extra helper at their shop," Zetia smiled as she looked at Jerin.

Marley whisped onto Zetia's arm and she continued, "Marley has decided it will be his job to keep all of us apprised of the other. He will whisp in and out of East Glacier and Eshra to keep everyone updated." She smiled at him and he bowed to everyone. Then, he whisped.

"Eleea and Elora have also decided to live in East Glacier," Zetia continued to reveal. "Phum and Nekoh have been asked to replace Gethsemane at the Great Tree as sage advisors. Of course, they will have unlimited access to Gethsemane and Joshua.

"And, to no one's surprise, except maybe Tarhana's, the Trevins have decided to make the sanctuary their home base."

"Lastly, Greysun, Nip and Lyt will stay with me until you two are settled back in your home. Then, I have the great privilege to arrive with them in East Glacier," Zetia revealed.

"Plans have already been put in motion to explain my position as your aunt, Ayden. More will be revealed once things are back to normal for you two." Zetia went to the girls and Nick and gave them a long hug each.

Nadab, Lydia, the Trevins, Phum, Nekoh and Tybin said their last words to the travelers. Each one found it difficult to let go and tears flowed freely all around.

Jerin took Deborah's hands in his, and said, "you are my greatest gift. I will see you very soon." He lightly kissed her and stood back to watch her leave.

Zetia looked at Ayden, saying, "my girl, we feel it best to not let the towns people know about Zayden. At least not yet. He will visit you next spring. Right now, he and Iza have a whole lot of work at Greysun Village to finish."

Ayden flashed a look at Zetia. "Greysun Village," she asked?

"Yes, the new establishment has been named Greysun Village" Zetia said with a big smile.

"Everyone sat around a table to decide what they should call the new fort. If not for Greysun's perseverance when he was left in Hollow to help you, none of us would be here today. Greysun was the obvious choice depicting hope, life, truth and just plain good ol' fashioned love only a dog can freely give," Zetia tenderly laughed.

Eleea perched on Ayden's shoulder, Elora flew to Deborah's and Nick stood beside them. They looked at their friends they were leaving and smiled.

Each of them turned to watch the horizon in front of them. As a group they placed their hands in each other's. Ayden sang with Eleea and Elora as they took a step and disappeared from Eshra and entered East Glacier.

Epilogue

Deborah quietly said, "we have to be careful on how we get the shape shifters out and us in." She let her body rest against her window to her room as she spoke.

"Nick," Deborah said, "we will see you tomorrow, go. Eleea, you and Elora stay hidden in my flower box."

Ayden and Deborah nodded to Nick as he left. They looked at each other and climbed into Deborah's room. The girls separated to their individual beds.

The shape shifters were sleeping and both girls gently woke them and searched for their medallion in the pillow. The girls breathed on them where they received all of the memories from the shape shifter while they were gone from East Glacier.

Soft muffled screams came from both rooms as the girls slowly walked towards each other. Their eyes were wide with fear as they came together.

Graycie stood in the doorway of Deborah's room and said, "hello girls. Did you enjoy your adventure?"

"Mom. I can explain," Deborah tried to cajole her.

"OH, I don't think I need an explanation," Graycie told her. "You two do realize I am a doctor of biology. What should this title tell you," she asked?

"It should reveal to you I study life forms from the beginning to the end," Graycie's voice raised as she spoke.

"Sure, a shape shifter is very adept at shifting one's perception,' she continued to school the girls.

Graycie walked over and took the medallions out of the hands of the girls. "These little gems are really handy, don't you think," she taunted them.

"Too bad a critical eye can deduce their ongoing inconsistencies. I will have to say, though, when I sat both of them down to tell them I knew something was up; they tried extremely hard to convince me I was wrong. But, unfortunately for them, I refused to let them move until they told the truth."

"Mom," Deborah tried to say again.

"No, mom is not an available answer here, Deborah," Graycie chastised her.

"And, as far as your dad is concerned, Deborah. He is not to know anything. If he knew what you two have been up to? It would send him into a fortress building frenzy to keep you two sequestered from ever being out of our sight," Graycie revealed.

"No, mom will not excuse either of you from what you did all summer right into the winter where now it is Thanksgiving," she quietly screamed.

"Get some sleep, we will talk tomorrow." Graycie turned to walk out of the room, stopped and turned back. "I am so relieved both of you are safe," she said as she went to the girls and tightly hugged them.

The fishing boat captain looked at his deckhand, bewildered. "What do you mean you have a woman on board," he asked?

"Captain, the woman must have been floating on the other side of the net where we couldn't see her when we hauled in the catch," the worker tried to explain. "She fell into the salmon when we released the net."

The captain set his coffee cup down and quickly walked to starboard. His crewman hurriedly followed him, still trying to explain the situation.

"Cap, be careful," he warned the man. "She is worse than having a shark on board. And, she refuses help."

"She is yelling at the crew. Plus, she has a strange silver feather. When Pete tried to help her up and took her hand with the feather, she almost bit his head off. She keeps saying, 'this is my feather, don't touch it,' the deckhand said.

The captain cautiously approached the woman who slid on the fish when she tried to stand. She quickly regained her composure and defiantly looked at him.

She stood at almost six feet tall. Her long brunet hair was matted against her sleeveless shirt which hung to just above her knees.

"I demand to be released immediately," the woman commanded. "I am an enforcer and you will listen to me. Take me to the shores of Oshyama," she demanded of the captain.

"Lady, I don't know where you think you are," the captain started. "This is America and I have no idea where this Oshy whatever is you are talking about."

The woman looked at the captain as her mind tried to comprehend what he was saying. She straightened her stance and put her hair behind her ears as she changed her demeanor.

She sweetly smiled at him and said, "fine, then, take me to shore and provide me with directions to East Glacier."

****

Author Bio

Born September 10, 1957 in Great Falls, Montanan. Raised in a world where my Native side was only touched upon when I visited Trenton, North Dakota to see relatives live the simple life with outhouses and no running water.

I come from the Turtle Mountain Band of Chippewa Indians. Falcon is the namesake of my family. I am Metis.

Deep in my spirit the call of the indigenous people would rise in my soul and ground me as I created. From abstract jewelry known as Found Art to writing fiction, I found my voice in a world where lines are blurred and the soul cries out to be found.

My childhood was not one of dignity and respect...but one of survival. The survival anthem to stand tall and rejoice in who you are and in who you have become. It rang loud throughout my years of growth as I stumbled with mistakes and doubt. Each misstep was a stone I firmly placed to climb higher to make my stand.

Instilled into my two beautiful children, Joshua and Trevor, was the determination to be better...to be stronger...to show we can survive with dignity and respect as our testimony.

We live in Great Falls and teach kids through video game design camps with our business Add-A-Tudez Entertainment Company. We teach what we live: How to overcome and shine as a light of encouragement to others. (check out our story by SONY Playstation on Youtube: My Road to Greatness: Josh Hughes.)

Truly, I stand tall because of what I experienced and witnessed as a child. It is the Native spirit of perseverance and of remembering we belong to the Earth. Deeply rooted in this is the belief of a God who carries us as we trek across this land to make our mark in a world of diversity and beauty.

358